THE CITY OF SPLENDORS

A WATERDEEP NOVEL

ED GREENWOOD
AND
ELAINE CUNNINGHAM

THE CITY OF SPLENDORS
THE CITIES

Distributed in the United States by Holtzbrinck Publishing. Distributed in Canada by Fenn Ltd.

Distributed to the hobby, toy, and comic trade in the United States and Canada by regional distributors.

Distributed worldwide by Wizards of the Coast, Inc. and regional distributors.

FORGOTTEN REALMS, WIZARDS OF THE COAST, and their respective logos are trademarks of Wizards of the Coast, Inc., in the U.S.A. and other countries.

All Wizards of the Coast characters, character names, and the distinctive likenesses thereof are property of Wizards of the Coast, Inc.

Printed in the U.S.A.

Cover art by J.P. Targete
First Printing: August 2005
Library of Congress Catalog Card Number: 2004116877

9 8 7 6 5 4 3 2 1

US ISBN: 0-7869-3766-1
ISBN-13: 978-0-7869-3766-0
620-88776000-001-EN

U.S., CANADA,
ASIA, PACIFIC, & LATIN AMERICA
Wizards of the Coast, Inc.
P.O. Box 707
Renton, WA 98057-0707
+1-800-324-6496

EUROPEAN HEADQUARTERS
Hasbro UK Ltd
Caswell Way
Newport, Gwent NP9 0YH
GREAT BRITAIN
Please keep this address for your records

Visit our web site at www.wizards.com

THE CITIES

The City of Ravens
Richard Baker

Temple Hill
Drew Karpyshyn

The Jewel of Turmish
Mel Odom

The City of Splendors: A Waterdeep Novel
Ed Greenwood & Elaine Cunningham

DEDICATION

*To the sages and scribes of Candlekeep, and to
The Hooded One for gracing the loreseekers of
cyberspace with her tireless efforts
and effortless charm.*

PROLOGUE

30 Ches, the Year of the Tankard (1370 DR)

Sharp gusts of wind buffeted Laeral Silverhand as she strode along the ramparts of Waterdeep's Westgate, dodging among archers and the wizards and sorcerers hurling fire at the besieging host below. Her beautiful face was grim, and her lithe body glowed slightly through her well-worn battle leathers. That glow was the only outward sign of the great power being drawn steadily out of her by the man she loved.

All about her, wizards were dropping with exhaustion. Two mages, their minds scorched by overuse of Mystra's fire, cowered behind merlons, gibbering like the madmen they might forevermore be. Laeral passed by without breaking stride. Later she'd weep, but nothing could be done for them now. Waterdeep was very far from being saved.

The wind off the sea blew cold and strong, too capricious and cruel even for early spring. Fell magic was at work. Sudden gusts snuffed the archers' flaming arrows and made small fire-spells to guttering like empty lamps. The Weave around her was aboil, stinging her skin like thousands of ceaseless needle-piercings. Laeral had not expected such magic from the seas.

Alas for Waterdeep, none of its defenders had, not even the mighty wizard who commanded the guard over the Westgate.

Khelben "Blackstaff" Arunsun, Archmage of Waterdeep, stood atop the gigantic stone gate-lintel. In the throes of spellcasting, he let slip the face and form he'd worn for many a year. Briefly, all eyes could see him as Laeral did: tall, ageless, elf-blooded, feral as a rampant dragon, barely recognizable as a mortal being. The building power of a mighty spell sent his somber robes and raven-black hair swirling, and motes of silvery light coursed around him like moths drawn to flame. In both hands he held his long black staff high overhead, and in an awful voice like a chorus of all his mortal lives combined, declaimed a ringing chant.

The tiny lights began to multiply and grow, each swiftly taking the shape of an enormous silvery fish. A vast school of these flying creations spun briefly above Khelben and then swept out to sea, drawing the winds in their wake. Laeral's windblown tresses settled around her shoulders as the invaders' wizard-wind faded.

As he lowered the Blackstaff, Khelben seemed to sink back into himself, becoming once more a pepper-and-salt-bearded man in his later middle years, cloaked in black robes and imperious dignity, strongly built but no taller than Laeral's own slender height.

She slid a steadying arm around his waist. "And now, love?"

For a moment Khelben was silent, glaring along the city walls. Laeral followed his gaze.

Magic burst into the twilit sky beyond Mount Waterdeep like fireworks celebrating a festival of death. To the south, the harbor flamed. A strong stench of burning pitch was drifting from the docks, where the oily smoke of burning spars and sails was billowing up into the sky. Low tide was approaching—but if the sea was retreating, its minions were not.

The sands below the Westgate were littered with blackened, smoking sahuagin bodies, yet fish-men beyond number were still storming the gate furiously, undeterred by the carnage. To Laeral it looked like all the devils of the Nine Hells had come to host a fish-fry.

Their strivings had taken a heavy toll of the city's defenders. Many mages slumped in utter exhaustion, and several hung out over the walls, retching helplessly in the foul smoke. A few stood muttering together, casting dark glances at the Archmage of Waterdeep.

It was widely—and correctly—rumored that enough magic blazed in Khelben's staff to melt all the rock and sand along Waterdeep's shores into glass and turn the entire harbor into a simmering saltwater cauldron in which the sahuagin would boil alive.

Therein lay the problem, Laeral knew well: The Art always had its price. The more powerful a magic, the greater its cost. She didn't need to glance at her beloved's face to feel his anguish and frustration. Waterdeep was his city, his home, and—perhaps even more than Laeral herself—his deepest love. The Lord Mage of Waterdeep had power enough to protect the City of Splendors . . . but only at the risk of destroying it.

Khelben turned his head as sharply as a hunting hawk. "I dare not call down the ward-wall, not with the Weave so strained. 'Tis small magics and force-of-arms we need now."

With a snarl he gestured at the nearest merlon. It exploded outward like a great tumbling fist, to topple down onto the crowded sands below.

They watched its fragments roll, raking red crushed ruin through the sahuagin. Before the great stones stopped, fresh sahuagin were surging forward, rising out of the blood-dark waves where so many bodies of their brethren already bobbed, filling the beach once more with unbroken fish-men.

"Ahghairon's enchantments weigh on me like yon mountain," Khelben growled. "I'm holding them from crashing down on all our heads right now. If I wasn't calling so much power out of you, I'd be crawling-helpless."

Guardsmen were trudging along the walls toward the Lord and Lady Mage of Waterdeep, faces grim and eyes full of questions.

Khelben watched their approach and sighed. "I need you to return to Blackstaff Tower and summon all aid-of-Art you can, right down to the last tremble-fingered novice. Use the Tower magics to send your plea afar."

Laeral looked down at the roiling sea, where sahuagin were still rising out of the blood-red waves to splash ashore, crowding against their fellows. "You're saying we can't hold them?"

The Lord Mage shook his head. "A few might scale the walls and fight through, but the gate will hold."

She shrugged, not seeing his reasoning.

"They've got that far." Khelben waved grimly at the harbor and then back at countless staring eyes and wet scales below. "You know the merfolk would die before they let these sea-scum into the inner harbor."

Sorrow thinned Laeral's lips. In the fury of the fray she'd forgotten what the bold advance of the fish-men must mean. Some of the harbor merfolk were dear friends.

Had been dear friends.

"Without them," she murmured, "the storm drains are undefended. Each is well warded, but whoever sends the sahuagin against us is no stranger to the Art."

"Aye," Khelben agreed, clasping her shoulders briefly as she turned to go. "For all we know, there could already be sahuagin in every sewer in Waterdeep—and once they're down there, there's no place in the city they can't go."

Laeral nodded grimly. "I'll send for everyone who can hurl a spell or swing a sword."

"We've not much time," the Blackstaff warned, "and many of our friends may be busy elsewhere. This strike from the sea isn't limited to Waterdeep."

"I'll contact Candlekeep first." Laeral, never much of a scholar, gave her lord a swift, ironic smile. "Surely the monks have nothing more pressing to attend to."

⚓ ⚓ ⚓ ⚓ ⚓

A small snake, a bright garden slitherer banded in tropical turquoise and green, wound a soundless way through room after dim room full of books. With sure instinct it made its way to a certain dusty alcove deep in Candlekeep and spiraled gracefully up one leg of a study table.

The young man seated there greeted his familiar with an absent-minded nod and returned his full attention to the book open before him: a thick history of fabled Waterdeep. Mrelder had always been fascinated by the City of Splendors, his hunger for its lore almost stronger than his ache to master sorcery. Almost.

The sorcerer seemed an ill match for the bright little snake. Lean, fit, and intense, he was pale from many hours spent with books. His once-dark hair had already gone gray, and his narrow face was seamed with thin, pale scars and dominated by fierce dark brows over mismatched eyes. One was a muddy gray, and the other (an old glass eye he'd bought in a manygoods shop) an odd pale green hue. Mrelder wasn't vain, but hoped to have coin enough someday to have a glass orb made to exactly match his surviving eye. It would be one less constant reminder of the horror known as Golskyn.

Light footfalls whispered on stone, approaching his corner. Mrelder paid little heed. Candlekeep was a quietly busy place, where many came to learn or, like him, to hide. The little snake, however, took alarm, darting into its master's sleeve and coiling about his forearm.

Thus alerted, Mrelder swept up his books and rose—just as a red-bearded giant of a man rounded the nearest shelf. Though one of Candlekeep's Great Readers, Belloch looked more like a warcaptain than a scholar. Just now, his face wore a dark expression better suited to a battlefield than a library.

"Come," Belloch rumbled, dropping a massive hand onto Mrelder's shoulder. Without pause he wheeled, jerking the young sorcerer along so sharply that books tumbled. Mrelder stooped to retrieve them, but Belloch's grip tightened. "Leave them."

Mrelder stiffened. To treat precious tomes so was unprecedented in Candlekeep! In a sudden flood of wild speculations, he fetched up chillingly against a dire prospect: perhaps a certain priest by the name of Golskyn had recovered from his latest "improvement," somehow found Mrelder's trail, and come here.

No escape, even here . . .

Striding hard, Belloch marched the young sorcerer out of the chamber and down hall after hall Mrelder had never walked before. Some short time after he'd become thoroughly lost, they descended a winding stair and crossed several darkened rooms to emerge in a large circular chamber.

Mrelder's heart sank. Several senior Readers were gathered, and with them his favorite lore-guide, the visiting monk Arkhaedun. Six of his fellow scholars were also in attendance, looking frightened and confused. Armored guards—and where had *they* come from?—ringed the walls, faces impassive and long spears held ready.

It looked as if a court had convened to condemn Mrelder for his part in Golskyn's crimes—*or perhaps*, a small voice whispered deep in his mind, *for his own inability to duplicate them.*

"Arkhaedun informed us of your training," Belloch said curtly, stepping away from Mrelder only to turn back and glare. "He says you possess considerable fighting skills—not just small, untutored magics."

The Reader's dismissive tone wasn't lost on Mrelder. Belloch had been a battle mage; many wizards scorned the inborn—and to their minds, *unearned*—powers of sorcery. Long used to far worse treatment, Mrelder was years beyond taking offense.

"I've learned much in my time here, lords," he replied, trying to sound calm. "May I ask what this meeting concerns?"

"We've received an urgent summons for every willing warrior and magic-wielder we can spare. A great battle rages, spawning small fires that can best be stamped out by such as you." Belloch grew a mirthless grin. "Your fascination with the city of Waterdeep has been noted; it should serve you well."

"Waterdeep? You want me to go to *Waterdeep?*"

Something in Belloch's face changed at Mrelder's awed tone. "I'll not lie to you, lad: this task may be your last. Monks' sparring is poor preparation for bloody war—and Binder forgive me, even all our books and scrolls leave many of that city's secrets untold."

"I'll go," Mrelder said eagerly. "Of course I'll go."

The Master Reader nodded and turned to the other scholars. "Choice made? Well, then: When 'tis time to return, say *'arranath'* aloud, and so hear the way."

As he silently mouthed that word to fix it in memory, Mrelder's thoughts were of Waterdeep. To see the City of Splendors with his own eyes!

How often he'd dreamed this dream without really expecting it to become truth! Yet what crisis could threaten mighty Waterdeep that his small skills were needed? Had the great wizards of the city somehow ... fallen?

Wilder thoughts whirled through Mrelder as he watched Arkhaedun step onto a circular mosaic in the middle of the chamber floor, an intricate rune outlined in flecks of colored crystal. A fractured rainbow of light shot up from the crystal shards—and the monk disappeared.

When the soft shafts of light faded, a sturdy, fair-haired lass Mrelder had seen frowning over high-piled tomes of battle magic stepped onto the rune. She was followed by a tall, silent scholar from the Inner Sea lands. When the soft glow of his journeying faded, a scholar of Tethyr was waved forward.

Then Belloch nodded, and it was Mrelder's turn. The young sorcerer hastened into the circle.

A searing flash of white light was his prompt greeting, as painful as falling into a hearthfire. Groaning, Mrelder fell to his knees, hands clapped to his burning eye.

When his mistily swimming vision returned, he saw spearpoints. The circle of guards had closed around him with deadly intent.

Belloch pushed through them and dragged Mrelder roughly to his feet. "Are you a traitor or a fool?" he thundered. "Only one living thing at a time may pass the gate! What secret are you hiding?"

Belatedly, Mrelder remembered what he bore coiled about his arm. "My familiar," he gasped, plucking back his sleeve. What had been his snake fell limply to the floor like a bit of severed rope.

Chagrin twisted the Great Reader's face. "I—it did not occur to me you might have a familiar. It appears your sorcery hasn't been ... sufficiently regarded."

"I seldom speak of my Art," Mrelder murmured. "If there's fault, it's my own."

He should have anticipated something like this. Of course any magical portal in this most precious of strongholds would be carefully warded. Allowing but one living thing to pass at a time was a wise safeguard, given the worth-beyond-price of Candlekeep's irreplaceable treasures.

He gazed down at the little snake, the latest of many creatures to die in his service, and allowed himself a sigh. Then he looked at Belloch. "I'm ready to go."

The Great Reader shook his head. "No. You'll be a staggering weak-wits until morn, no use in battle."

Mrelder held out rock-steady hands. "I've ... learned to withstand worse pain. I'm ready, and I am needed. Send me."

After a moment's hesitation, the burly monk nodded and thrust Mrelder into the circle.

The crystal mosaic blazed up and seemed to give way at the same time, and Mrelder found himself falling through a void of soft colors and eerie silence. In the utter absence of sound, the faint but constant ringing in his ears—another reminder of Golskyn—seemed deafening. It was almost a relief when he jolted to a stop on solid cobblestones amid the clanging cacophony of battle.

Mrelder glanced quickly around. He stood in a reeking, rat-scurrying alley between two old, large, rather crumbling stone buildings—warehouses by their look. Over the stench of rotting refuse and a heavy smell of smoke, the stink of fish was strong in the air. Mount Waterdeep loomed up behind him, its first rising rocks only paces beyond an alley-blocking mound of rotting crates, barrels, and garbage. The other end of the alley opened into a larger cross-street filled with a hurrying crowd.

They were all fleeing to Mrelder's left, shrieking and jostling as they ran. The crackle of fire and the clang of hard-wielded weapons sounded very near, off to the right.

Beyond the warehouse to his left stood a taller, finer building. Wisps of steam coiled from a door left ajar, bearing the soft tang of seawater. This must be one of the heated saltwater baths said to be popular in Waterdeep. Mrelder stepped closer.

A soft plash of disturbed water came through the steam.

Mrelder frowned. It was unlikely even the notoriously jaded citizens of Waterdeep would be idly soaking in the public baths as their city burned around them.

Then he heard something more from inside the bathhouse. Faint converse. The tongue was strange, liquid-sounding and guttural: Clicks, grunts, and deep thrumming croaks that plumbed depths no human voice could reach.

Mrelder looked around for a likely weapon. One nearby crate looked sturdier and less rotten than most strewn about the alley. He pried loose one of its boards, noting with approval two long iron nails protruding from one end. Sidling up to the bathhouse door, he peered in cautiously.

Three large, wet, green-scaled creatures were padding softly through the steam of the lofty, many-pillared bathing hall, finned tails lashing. Barbed-headed spears were clutched in their webbed claws, and their staring black eyes were intent on the panicked crowd visible through the multi-paned windows along the streetfront.

Vaguely human, they resembled enormous upright frogs with tails that brought to mind merfolk or gigantic tadpoles. Their fish-like heads bristled with spikes, and were split by gaping jaws filled with lethal-looking fangs.

Sahuagin.

Mrelder swallowed hard, slipped inside, and followed them, flitting from pillar to pillar as silent as a shadow.

Dripping, the fish-men stalked to the ornate front doors of the bathhouse. They glanced at each other—and then kicked the doors open, leveled their spears, and charged into the street. A chorus of screams and desperate shouts rose above the battle-din.

Mrelder hurled himself into a run. Bursting from the building, he slammed his board into the head of the central, largest sahuagin, driving the nails deep into the glistening scales at the base of the creature's skull—

—and breaking the board into splinters.

The sahuagin was thrusting its spear viciously over the shoulder of its comrade to the left at a tall armored warrior beyond. As

Mrelder's strike slammed home, the creature shuddered. Before it could turn, he leaped onto its back and rode it down to the cobbles.

The sahuagin writhed and bucked, trying to free itself of both imbedded weapon and stubborn attacker. The broken board swung wildly, slamming into Mrelder's clenched jaw.

He struggled atop the fish-monster, avoiding its spines as best he could. Around him was confusion, swords swinging on all sides, scaly limbs waving, bubbling screams rising wetly from beneath him. Angry shouts were laced with squalls of rage and pain that didn't sound human.

Finally Mrelder managed to tear the broken board-end free. Tossing it aside, he seized the finned head by two of its spines, and threw all his strength into a quick, brutal twist.

Something broke sickeningly under those wet scales. The sahuagin shuddered again and went limp.

Seeking the ruins of his board again, Mrelder sprang off it, afraid the other fish-things would—

And found himself staring up into the open visor of a fine, burnished war-helm, into a face lined by well-spent years—and a calm swordpoint of a gaze, leveled at him by eyes that were kind and wise.

This, marveled the awed sorcerer, *is what a king looks like.*

The regal man looked right through Mrelder, as if able to see everything the young sorcerer was and his every last guilty secret. Sudden dread rose in Mrelder and was as swiftly gone; the man was giving him an approving smile.

"Ably done," he said, in the rich voice of one cultured yet commanding. "Without your aid, that spear would have found me."

Mrelder tried to return the smile, but his mind was awhirl. He'd never seen such splendid, silver-blue battle armor. Knights in warsteel just as fine were gathering beyond the tall warrior's broad shoulders, but Mrelder's attention was on the bright silver crescent of metal covering the tall warrior's throat, a device that bore an elaborately wrought stylized torch—the arms of the Lords of Waterdeep.

Mrelder had seen its unmistakable likeness that very morning, on a page of an obscure book of Waterdhavian lore. He was looking at the Guardian's Gorget, a magical device of great power, fashioned for and worn by only one man.

"My Lord Piergeiron," Mrelder breathed, awed to find himself in the presence of the Open Lord of Waterdeep.

Piergeiron clapped him on the shoulder in a soldier's thanks to a battle-comrade. Drawing a long dagger, he pressed it into Mrelder's hand.

"Well met, lad. That board of yours is not good for much more fighting; take this." The lord grinned. "If you're so minded, there's work yet for us all."

If? At that moment, Mrelder would cheerfully have followed Waterdeep's Lord into a volcano!

A deep rumbling shook the cobbles under their boots then, and everyone turned to peer at Mount Waterdeep. Another thunderous impact followed, and then another.

The young sorcerer followed their gazes and found himself whispering "Mystra's sacred shadow!" in fresh wonderment.

A man-shaped colossus of weathered stone, ninety feet tall or more, was striding down the mountain, finding—and sometimes making—a sure path to the harbor. Mrelder had never expected to set eyes on one of the fabled Walking Statues, much less watch it walking!

"*That* should hold our foes," Piergeiron said in satisfaction, watching the great construct lumber along.

He turned his head. "Are you with me, lad?"

"I'd not want to be anywhere else, just now," Mrelder said firmly, and they traded heartfelt smiles.

⚔ ⚔ ⚔ ⚔ ⚔

Time passed in a bright haze of blood and fire. Never far from Lord Piergeiron's side, Mrelder fought errant flames, vicious fish-men, and men who swarmed the shadows of Dock Ward like rats to loot and steal and stab.

It seemed as if the lord's band was a running, tireless whirlwind. When at last Piergeiron barked a halt in the courtyard of

Greenwood and Cunningham · 11

some grand mansion, Mrelder's shoulders sang with pain, and his eyes swam with smoke and stinging sweat.

Around him, the grandly armored knights of Piergeiron's guard sprawled wearily on smooth stone benches or leaned against statues, tending small wounds and seeing to their weapons.

One handed Mrelder a water flask. "Whence do you hail, monk?"

The sorcerer drank deep before murmuring, "I'm no monk. Trained to fight as one, yes, but I've not taken orders in the service of any god or temple."

The knight smiled. "Smart lad. Gods are like women: When there are so many fine choices, why should a man limit himself to but one?"

This philosophy was greeted with a few tired chuckles from around the courtyard.

Piergeiron turned to give Mrelder that commanding gaze. "Listen but lightly to Karmear. 'Tis a fine path you've chosen. My father was a paladin, and I've always held the deepest respect for all who choose the way of the altar."

"My father's a priest," Mrelder blurted. Surprised by his own outburst, he stammered hastily, "Or was. I'm not sure . . ."

The Open Lord's brow furrowed. "You know not if your father lives?"

"No, Lord. We parted badly, some time ago." Mrelder hesitated, not sure what to say. "I was . . . I could not be the son he wished me to be."

"When you leave Waterdeep, you must find him," Piergeiron said firmly. "From what I've seen this day, I'm certain any father would rejoice in such a son."

The words, spoken with such assurance, kindled hope in Mrelder. Could it be that he, who'd proved capable in a fray and was at least comfortable as both sorcerer and monk, might be weighed in Golskyn's grim measure and finally found worthy?

Suddenly, Mrelder could imagine nothing more important than learning the answer to that. He looked at the Lord of Waterdeep. "As you say, I will do. This I *swear.*"

Piergeiron nodded. Eyes never leaving Mrelder's, he reached into a belt-pouch and drew out something small, black, and gleaming. "This is a Black Helm. I'd like to hear how matters fall between you and your father. If you return to the city, present this at the palace, and the guards there will know you as a friend to Waterdeep and to me."

Mrelder stared down at the charm. It was a tiny replica of Piergeiron's own war-helm, rendered in fine obsidian and pierced to be hung on a neck-thong.

"My lord!" was all he could find to say.

The tall paladin waved away his stammerings and turned to address his knights. "The city's quiet. There'll be much to do come morning, but our night's work is done."

At this dismissal, the men rose slowly and stiffly, taking up swords and helms. Mrelder politely refused an offer of lodging for the night in their barracks and waved farewell. Candlekeep was expecting his return and report. The last he saw of that shining-armored band was Piergeiron's answering wave and smile.

🏰 🏰 🏰 🏰 🏰

Twilight slid into night as Mrelder made his way deeper into Dock Ward. Dazed citizens stumbled past, wandering like sooty ghosts amid the ruins of homes and businesses.

As the weary sorcerer trudged along, he murmured, "Arranath." Belloch's gruff voice promptly announced in his mind: *To find Candlekeep, seek the same circular symbol that adorns our floor, and say aloud 'Arranath' when touching it. The symbol is in the wellhouse behind the shop called Candiera's Fine Shoes and Sandals, on the west side of Redcloak Lane three shopfronts south of Belnimbra's Street, in Dock Ward.*

Mrelder's destination looked humble indeed. Timber-framed buildings leaned dark and close over narrow streets. Ramshackle balconies and catwalks meandered from one to the next, many crossing overhead and casting the streets below into deep shadow. Belnimbra's Street, however, was long, broad, and well-known, and Mrelder soon found Redcloak Lane.

He turned into it, shouldering past merchants morosely trying to salvage wares from a tangle of wrecked and charred carts—and stopped in dismay.

The corner shop stood intact, but most of the west side of Redcloak Lane beyond it was gone. Candiera's Fine Shoes and Sandals was just a few plumes of smoke drifting from blackened ruins.

Mrelder stared at the mess, sighed, and strode forward. The soot might make things look worse than they really were, and along Redcloak two or three buildings rose undamaged out of the swirling smoke like surviving teeth in a crone's grin. Perhaps . . .

Perhaps not. The second building, a shop offering stools, benches, and chairs, seemed largely untouched under a thick veil of soot, but the third was a tumbled pile of blackened timbers, fronted by a crazily leaning doorframe that now led nowhere but still sported a blackened signboard proclaiming to all Waterdeep that this was Candiera's Fine Shoes and Sandals.

Mrelder sighed again and started to pick his way through the still-warm embers, dodging drifting cinders as he went.

His boots grew warm as he trudged through tumbled, blackened spars and over a heap of stones that had recently been a chimney into an open area beyond: a stretch of back alley that hadn't disappeared under the rubble of fallen buildings.

Right in front of him, like a gift from the gods, stood what he'd been told to seek: a communal wellhouse, a small stone hut that had escaped the flames.

Opening its peg-latch door, Mrelder felt his way down the stone steps inside. The wellhouse was damp and dark, but dim light beckoned ahead. A single stroke of crumbling glowpaint had long ago been splashed across the ceiling. In its glow he made out an uneven stone floor, a few scattered pebbles, and the well, a simple circle-wall of stone covered with a cross-braced wooden disk like a barrel-end. Mrelder lifted this lid by its rope handle and held it up to the glowpaint.

There on its underside was a crudely carved rune, the echo of the mosaic in Candlekeep that had brought him here. He smiled—which was when the faintest of grating sounds came from beyond the well, hinting of unseen places and stealthy lurkings. Mrelder ducked down, easing the well-cover to the floor. Leaving it there, he crept around one side of the well, drawing the dagger Piergeiron had given him ... had it really been just half a day ago?

He could make out things in the gloom now. He'd thought the cellar drew down to an end just beyond the well, but now he saw its deepest shadows hid the mouth of a stone-lined passage.

Wet feet slapped stone in its darkness, pounding quickly toward him!

A huge sahuagin lurched into the well-cellar, its dark-eyed, spiny head nosing this way and that as it sought to see all perils. It was larger than any sea devil Mrelder had seen before, and its hulking torso sprouted two—*two!*—pairs of long, heavily muscled arms. One limb hung limp and useless, shattered ends of bone protruding from a deep sword-gash, but the other three all held bloodstained blades of various sizes. Seized in battle, no doubt, from men this fish-beast had slain.

It hissed at Mrelder and leaned forward, seeking to reach over the well with its swords.

At full stretch, its trio of blades could just span the stone circle, but it could not seriously menace Mrelder so long as he could move freely.

He moved now, backing to the steps with his lone dagger raised. He mounted the first step by feel alone, keeping his eyes on the sahuagin.

The fish-beast hissed again, the gills on its neck flaring convulsively, like a hooked fish gasping on a riverbank. It occurred to Mrelder that the sahuagin was dying, *drowning* in the thin air.

The creature tried again to lunge across the well, but the act of reaching made it shudder in pain and draw back, swaying. In a moment, it would choose one side of the well or the other and come around the stones in another charge.

Mrelder readied his dagger for a throw. It was well-balanced, the finest war-steel he'd ever wielded, and would fly straight and true. At this range he couldn't miss, and if he feinted first to make the sahuagin commit its arms and blades in an attempt to block his strike and *then* flung his steel, it would have no time to dodge or deflect. A quick toss would win Mrelder time enough to race back up the steps and flee into the ashes and drifting smoke.

From what I've seen these past hours, I'm certain any father would rejoice in such a son.

Piergeiron's remembered words stilled Mrelder's arm.

He stretched forth his other hand, palm down and fingers splayed, and worked almost the simplest of spells.

The wooden lid rose into the air and spun toward the sahuagin. Three blades batted at the spinning disk, but the force of Mrelder's magic kept it on course. The lid caught the fish-beast just below its ribs and sent it staggering back.

The sahuagin slammed solidly into the stone wall and slid down it, too winded to draw breath.

Mrelder advanced, chanting another spell, this one of his own devising and used on his last familiar: the bright Chultan snake that had once been large enough to swallow two of Golskyn's servants.

The sahuagin began to shrink. It dwindled, spasming and clawing the air in a violent,—and vain—struggle against the magic.

When the fish-man was no taller than the length of Mrelder's hand, the sorcerer ended the spell. The moment the sahuagin was released, it hissed and darted toward the tunnel.

Mrelder snatched up the tiny creature in one hand and tugged a vial from his belt-pouch with the other. Ignoring the sahuagin's fierce struggles—an easy matter, as its fangs and webbed talons were now no more vexing than a kitten's claws—the sorcerer pulled the vial's cork with his teeth and tapped a single drop of fluid onto the sahuagin's head.

Gills flared, instinctively grasping the proffered moisture—and the tiny creature went stiff and still.

Mrelder tucked vial and immobilized sahuagin into his pouch. Then he moved the inverted wooden lid to an open stretch of floor and stepped onto the rune-design. With but a word, he and his prize would be in Candlekeep. "Arr—"

Just in time, he remembered his familiar's fate. The sahuagin was no good to him dead.

Hissing one of his father's viler oaths, Mrelder drew it from his pouch and scowled at it. A dead sahuagin wasn't hard for a man like Golskyn to acquire. Capturing one alive, now, was another matter, but how could he keep it living until he was ready to face his father . . . and endure the grim transformation that must follow?

Mrelder stepped off the gate to think.

He could see only one path: hide the creature here and return for it at some later time. If he couldn't take this prize to Golskyn, he'd bring his father to Waterdeep. Surely even the great Golskyn wouldn't scorn such an offering as a four-armed sahuagin, nor the son who'd brought it to him!

He caught up a handful of pebbles in case he needed to toss or drop them to judge unseen distances, then strode into the dark tunnel. Unpleasant wet and rotting smells assailed him as he felt his way into deepening chill and damp, groping at the rough walls in search of hiding-places.

Eventually he found one: a small niche in the uneven stones to his left, well above his head and near what felt like an empty but sturdy iron torch bracket. Mrelder hid the tiny monster there behind most of his handful of stones and then cut free one of the leather thongs that criss-crossed his soft boots to ensure a snug fit. He tied the thong to the bracket, letting it dangle there to mark the hiding-place for his return.

Mrelder stood listening for a breath or two, afraid the small noises he'd made thus far might have lured other sahuagin—or worse—hither.

He heard nothing, not even the plink of dripping water, and with a relieved sigh returned to the wellhouse, took his place on the gate, and murmured, "Arranath."

Once again, the floor seemed to give way under his boots, plunging him into a silent, dreamlike freefall.

He emerged into warm lamplight in the circular chamber in Candlekeep where an anxious Belloch was pacing.

The monk's scowl fell away as he rushed forward to clasp Mrelder by the shoulders. "You're the first to return! What news?"

"Waterdeep's secure," Mrelder mumbled, suddenly weak with weariness. "Our work's done, the Open Lord told me."

The Great Reader smote the young sorcerer's shoulder, in a painful reminder of Piergeiron's salute. "Victory, lad—glorious victory!"

"Yes," Mrelder agreed, managing a smile.

He was not seeing battles in the streets of Waterdeep, however, but a confrontation to come, one where he'd not stand shoulder-to-shoulder with the Open Lord of Waterdeep and a score of veteran bodyguard knights.

When he faced Golskyn again, he and the sahuagin *would* prevail.

Even as he made that silent vow, Mrelder seemed to hear the mocking echo of his father's taunting voice, saying this bid would fail him as so many had before.

⚓ ⚓ ⚓ ⚓ ⚓

Monsters, observed Beldar Roaringhorn glumly, were damnably unreliable fellows. According to everything Beldar knew of swordplay and monsters—and he prided himself on his knowledge of both—the ugly green bastard should have won that fight. Handily.

He counted out the ten dragons he'd lost betting on the scarred half-ogre, and with a casual flourish that told the world he tossed away gold at least a dozen times a day, slid the coins across the table. The peg-legged sailor who stood waiting for it grew a nastily delighted leer.

Beldar studied him. The strange, dirty, spidery-looking fellow appeared to be held together largely by years' worth of accumulated grime. His arms were long, thin, and ropy with sagging remnants of muscles. He wore no shirt, but his faded red breeches were belted high over a tightly rounded belly that seemed at odds with his emaciated limbs. His remaining foot was bare, and gold toe-rings gleamed down there through layers of dirt.

The old man grinned at Beldar, displaying three blackened teeth, and flipped one of the coins to the half-ogre. The brute caught the gold deftly and gave Beldar a mocking, almost courtly bow.

"Son of a sahuagin," muttered the young noble.

"My friend Gorkin's not what you'd call sea-devil spawn," the old sailor said smugly, "but you'll be seeing plenty of *those* soon enough. Word is Waterdeep's under attack right now! Wouldn't put it past yer perfumed pretty-women to drag the scalies into those public baths fer a quick ... swim."

The look on Beldar's face sent the wretch into gales of laughter that promptly turned into a coughing fit. It lasted, relatively speaking, a tenday or so, ere the salt spat a thick gobbet of pipeweed onto the floor, wheezed, and gave Beldar that grin again.

"You'd like that, would you?" he taunted. "Comin' home to Waterdeep to find yer women's got a taste for seafood, so to speak? Might be they'd find the sea-devils a closer thing to a real man than yer fancy-pants, soft-handed, white-livered, sorry sons of—"

The old sailor's words ended abruptly with a sharp *urp!* as Beldar sprang lightning-swift from his chair to drive a fist deep into that capacious gut.

The salt went to his knees, wheezing, coins bouncing and rolling in all directions. In an instant, the makeshift sparring floor emptied as the trio of mixed-blood outlaws currently fighting for the entertainment of Luskan's lowlives hurled themselves at a richer prize, not to mention the young nobleman who'd provided it.

Beldar's eyes lit up at the prospect of battle. With a widening smile he clapped his hand to the hilt of his sword.

Suddenly a larger hand took hold of his collar, and he was jerked up and back so sharply his feet left the floor.

Green muscles rippled as that arm twisted, turning the momentarily strangling Beldar to almost touch noses with ... Gorkin. The half-ogre's other hand clamped over Beldar's sword-hand, holding the noble's magnificent weapon firmly sheathed.

"Easy, lad. I'm just takin' you out of harm's way."

Beldar blinked. There was no menace in the brute's face. Avarice, yes, but what face in Waterdeep didn't bear the same stamp?

"Very kind of you, I'm sure," he replied, "but hardly necessary."

The half-ogre held Beldar off the floor a moment longer, because he could, then lowered him, stepped back, and jerked his bald, green-skinned head at the widening brawl where knives were out, and men were dying over a few spilled coins.

"More needed'n'you might think. Yonder's Boz." A stubby green finger indicated a furry mongrelman not much larger than a halfling. "Might as well thrust your arm into a dragon's maw as draw steel on him. Mean little bastard."

"Really." Beldar watched the small fighter kick, bite, and stab for a moment, and saw Boz's teeth take out a second throat as thoroughly as his wickedly hooked knife had served the first one. "Gods! He looks as if his mother had carnal knowledge of a badger."

Gorkin grinned. "Fights like it, too."

"So I see," the nobleman murmured.

The little mongrelman pinned an orcblood foe tusks-down to the ground and wrenched one thickly muscled arm back so sharply that Beldar imagined the thick, wet sound of rending bone and sinew. Not that he could have heard it over the shrieking. Boz was calmly biting off fingers, one at a time, to get at the coins clenched in the orc-blood's fist.

Beldar rubbed his chin thoughtfully. Yonder mongrelman might prove to be a creature he'd long sought. It was certainly worth the price of an introduction to find out.

He met the half-ogre's speculative gaze. "You know who I am?"

The brute nodded. "I know who, but I don't know *why.*"

Beldar smiled thinly. In certain circles he was known for his fascination with monsters. Of course, he wasn't the first wealthy well-born with a taste for exotic creatures, but Beldar's interest was less easily explained than most. He slew not for bounty, nor entertainment. He did not line the walls of Roaringhorn mansions with mounted trophies, nor did he collect living specimens. Occasionally he purchased some of the more interesting bits of slain monsters for magical uses, but what man with his resources did not?

The truth was something Beldar pondered daily but had never spoken aloud. It sounded too vainglorious, even for a noble of Waterdeep, to announce an important destiny awaiting him. Stranger still to claim his path to greatness would begin when he mingled with monsters. So he'd been told years ago by a seer of Rashemen, and so he believed, with every breath he drew.

It wasn't Beldar Roaringhorn's way to wait for destiny to find him. He seized every chance to seek out the company of monstrous creatures. Fortunately, the travels expected of an idle younger son of a noble house of Waterdeep afforded opportunities aplenty to do so, far from the ever-watchful eyes of kin and the expectations of Waterdhavian society.

Boldy, he clapped the half-ogre on the shoulder. "Gorkin, is it? Let me buy you a drink! Perhaps we'll find business interests in common."

"*Perhaps*?" the brute scoffed. "You think I kept you from yon tangle out of the softly dawning love in my heart?"

"That possibility never occurred to me," Beldar replied with a wry smile. "How's the ale in this establishment?"

"Wouldn't know. I'm not allowed to drink here. They say it makes me mean and ugly." Gorkin bared his fangs in an ironic smile.

"Hmmm. Had I known," Beldar responded dryly, "I'd have offered to buy you a drink before I wagered on the outcome of your fight."

The half-ogre's bark of laughter sounded like a file rasping on a rusted blade, and he gave the noble a friendly swat on the shoulder. "A place down on the docks'll let me in—or used to, before I bought me one of their girls."

His small, piggish red eyes studied the young nobleman, turning thoughtful.

They beheld dark chestnut hair falling in waves to shoulders, a fine-featured face with skin that evidently—remarkably—held its sun-browned hue year-round, dark eyes rimmed with sooty lashes that must be the envy of many a woman. Wiser than most idle young wastrels out of Waterdeep, by the looks of him, with a swordsman's lean and fit build. Small, dapper mustache, and that air of style all wealthy young Waterdhavians wore like a golden cloak.

"Could be I'd get me another girl, if *you* was doing the asking," the half-ogre wheedled.

Beldar fought to keep revulsion off his face. "Let's start with a drink. If the wenches offer you their favors, what befalls is your choice."

"But you'll pay?"

The nobleman gritted his teeth. This sort of "mingling with monsters" hadn't featured in his dreams and speculations.

"I'll pay," he said shortly.

Gorkin grinned wickedly. Turning, he pushed through the crowd, out into the deepening night, and led Beldar down a steeply sloping street to the docks.

The Icecutter stood hard by Luskan's longest wharf, a first port of call for sailors just off the cold waters. It was a tavern only slightly less rundown than the fighting-den they'd left and full of patrons only slightly less disreputable. Oddly enough, its taproom was scrupulously clean. They took the nearest empty table.

A small, slim serving lass came over to them at once, a tray of battered tankards in her work-reddened hands. She placed two foaming drinks before them and swayed deftly back beyond the half-ogre's hopeful reach.

"The ale comes with Vornyk's compliments," she said flatly. "He doesn't want any trouble. Drink it and leave, Gorkin."

The half-ogre emptied one tankard without coming up for air, thunked it down on the table, and belched mightily.

"Another," he demanded, tossing his head toward Beldar. "He's paying."

The wench glanced at the Waterdhavian, fire rising in her brown eyes. "You'll pay for all damage, too? And a healer, if need be?"

"I hardly think such will be necessary," Beldar replied coolly.

"Tell that to Quinta," she snapped. "Enjoy your ale. 'Tis all you'll get this night."

Beldar watched the wench's quick retreat to the kitchens. She wasn't conventionally pretty; too thin for beauty, and not gifted with the lush charms Beldar usually sought in women of negotiable virtue. Yet unlike many dockside wenches, she was clean and neat, her long, thick brown hair carefully pulled back into a single braid. Those brown eyes were large and very bright, and something about her light step and swift, efficient movements appealed. A little brown bird, come to roost in an unlikely nest . . .

"That's the one I want," Gorkin announced.

The nobleman chuckled mirthlessly. "I'd not wager a copper on your chances. Who's this Quinta?"

Gorkin plucked up and drained Beldar's tankard. "My last girl. Haven't seen her since."

Before Beldar could inquire more closely as to just what *that* meant, a huge man was bustling up to them, a large, well-laden food tray nestled against his food-splattered apron.

He gave Beldar an oily smile and with swift skill served more ale and set surprisingly appetizing fare before them: a thick seafood stew in hollowed-out roundloaves, a small wheel of cheese, and a bowl of pickled vegetables. "Two gold, the lot."

An outrageous price, but as the half-ogre was already devouring cheese and stew as if starvation loomed large, Beldar dropped two gold dragons into the man's outstretched hand and threw in a sigh for good measure. One coin was promptly bitten, whereupon the man grunted approvingly, gave the half-ogre a curt nod, and left.

Watching him go, Beldar murmured, "Your peg-legged partner is surprisingly good at games of chance, considering how poorly he bluffs."

"Poorly? Got the better of you, didn't he?"

"I refer to his comments about Waterdeep."

The half-ogre raked his stew with a finger and caught a plump mussel. Tossing it between his fangs, he swallowed without chewing.

"'Twas no bluff. Kypur heard it from an old mate what has an ear out for wizard-talk. There'll be lively times a-plenty hereabouts, once most folk hear. 'Course, some Luskan ships'll run afoul of the sea-devils, but most jacks'll quaff to their own misfortune so long as Waterdeep's harder hit."

Beldar nodded absently, but his thoughts were not of the long-standing rivalry between the two northern ports.

So 'twas true. Waterdeep was under attack by sahuagin, in numbers sufficient to be a serious threat. His family and friends were in danger, his home threatened. The rising bloodlust of a warrior bred and trained sang through his blood, but not loud enough to silence a single, devastating truth:

Waterdeep was under attack, by *monsters*, and Beldar Roaring-horn wasn't there to seize his destiny!

He wanted to dash out and find a fast coach or ship about to sail and ask Gorkin a thousand questions, too . . . but the half-ogre waved away his first few to empty the pickles into his mouth. Making a face, he followed them with the soggy remnants of his loaf—and then reached for Beldar's. The noble waved at him to eat it all and waited impatiently until the last crumb disappeared.

Gorkin leaned back, patted his belly in satisfaction, and growled, "I've one more need to settle, then we'll talk."

He rose and stalked to the back of the tavern, most likely to seek relief in an alley out back. In Beldar's opinion, the quality of the ale was such that Gorkin might as well return his portion directly to the cask and call it a loan. No one would notice the difference.

A woman's scream tore through the tavern clamor. Chairs scraped on the bare board floor as drinkers turned to see why, but not a single patron rose to help.

Gorkin was backing out of the kitchen, dragging the serving

wench under one arm. He strode toward a stair leading up to what Beldar assumed were coins-for-the-night rooms. The lass shrieked and struggled, but the half-ogre merely grinned.

The girl gave the apron-clad tavernmaster a terrified look of appeal. "Vornyk, *please!* He beat Quinta almost to death!"

The man shrugged, unmoved. "If he's buying, I'm selling."

Rage tempered fear on the wench's face. "So I've heard, from this one and a hundred like him!" she spat. "The sooner he turns me loose, the sooner the two of you can go about your business!"

Gorkin released the girl long enough to backhand her savagely across the face. "Watch your tongue, wench, or I'll cut it out and eat it," he growled, watching her drag herself dazedly up from the floor. "'Tis women for me, and none'll say otherwise."

"*This* woman isn't for you," she hissed. "I'll die first!"

The half-ogre sneered. "Makes little difference to me one way or 'tother."

The wench seized a heavy tankard from the nearest table and threw it at him, contents and all. Gorkin batted it aside, snatched her up and over his shoulder, and headed for the stairs.

Amid some cheers from around the taproom, the lass kicked, swore, and screamed, but never cried to patrons for help. Beldar decided she knew better.

Gorkin grinned and struck a pose, his prize struggling vainly in the curl of his arm. He made a show of starting to unlace the cods of his breeches, as men laughed and shouted lewd suggestions.

For a moment—just one—the young Roaringhorn noble weighed his life-long quest for an unknown monstrous ally against the sullying of a tavern wench's virtue. And then, with a disgusted growl, Beldar rose to his feet, reaching for his sword.

Another sword sang out faster. The taproom turned in almost perfect unison at the sound to behold an aging warrior in full armor, with the hammer and scales of Tyr bright upon the chest of his surcoat and his eyes shining with terrible wrath.

Holy wrath. A paladin of Tyr drawn by the screams, the doors of the tavern still swinging behind him. Beldar peered at the man. He seemed familiar, as if Beldar had seen him before. In Waterdeep, most likely, but . . .

The paladin strode forward, and the patrons of the Icecutter sprang to sudden life. Leaping from their chairs, they pulled tables aside in a trice to clear a battlefield of sorts. Bets were shouted, and coins slapped down on a dozen tables.

The paladin paid no heed. Crossing the room in a few long strides, he plucked the girl from the half-ogre's grasp as if she weighed nothing.

Gorkin whirled with a roar and found himself facing a raised and ready sword, the wench safely behind the man wielding it.

Without hesitation the half-ogre sprang back, drew steel, and then plunged at his foe. Steel clanged on steel, sparks flew, the old paladin's blade circled arrow-swift up and under Gorkin's guard, and the half-ogre spat blood in astonishment, stared at the ceiling . . . and fell, eyes wide in disbelief.

Beldar was tempted to applaud. Four quick, precise movements, done in less time than it took to count them aloud, and Gorkin lay dying. It was a marvel of efficient swordsmanship, if lacking the showy flourishes Beldar favored.

The holy knight wiped his weapon on the sprawled half-ogre, sheathed it, and swept the taproom with a slow, measuring glance. Beldar got the uneasy notion the paladin was judging each man there. His grim expression suggested he saw little difference between those who committed evil deeds and those who merely sat and watched.

Then the paladin looked at the tavernmaster. "The girl leaves with me."

Avarice battled fear in Vornyk's eyes and won. "Aye, as long as you pay her price."

The paladin's cold expression deepened into a killing frost. "Is slavery legal now in Luskan?"

"She has debts," Vornyk growled. "An indenture. Not the same thing."

"I'd sooner challenge a skunk to a pissing contest than argue ethics with the likes of you. Name your price."

That amount was ridiculously high, but the paladin paid it without comment and left the tavern, gently leading the girl by one hand. As she passed Beldar her expression was wary, even cynical, but she probably preferred her chances with a grim stranger than a drunken, violent half-ogre.

Her chances were almost certainly better, the noble thought bitterly, with a champion of Tyr than with Beldar Roaringhorn of Waterdeep, the hero who might have been.

CHAPTER ONE

Midsummer, The Year of the Unstrung Harp (1371 DR)

Taeros Hawkwinter strode quickly through Dock Ward, one hand on the comforting hilt of his sword and the other keeping an open vial of scented oil under his nose. Above the sagging rooftops of this lowest-lying, dirtiest part of Waterdeep, the summer sun shone high overhead, and its baking heat brought out an incredible mingling of stinks in the narrow streets. Even more incredibly, no one around Taeros seemed to mind.

On all sides, sweating dockworkers and fishmongers with unspeakable slime smeared on their bellies and boots were breaking off work to seek their midday meal, jostling under the cries of street-sellers hawking highsunfeast: thick-crusted handpies, wooden skewers of still-sizzling roast meat of dubious origin, handwheels of strong cheese, and plump twists of saltbread.

Taeros elbowed his way through them all until he found a particular building—no easy task, given the frenzy of dockside rebuilding after last year's fish-men war.

He tossed a coin to the sour-faced doorguard. The burly warrior gave the noble's black hair and storm-gray Hawkwinter eyes a slow, hard look ere nodding, waving a "fire not" signal to the crossbowman in a window across the street, and stepping aside.

Taeros sprinted up a long, narrow flight of stairs, eager to leave the scents and sounds of the Dock Ward behind. His ascent ended on a small landing before a massive door.

Black with age but richly carved from a single plank of oak, it was obviously a relic of some vanished, far grander building. Taeros took a large black key from a belt-pouch and tried its massive lock. It swung silently open on well-oiled hinges, and he stepped into the room that, he fondly hoped, would become a second home to him and his five closest friends.

This new lair was a far cry from the luxury of the Hawkwinter estates, but Taeros was well pleased with it. The room was spacious and lofty, open to the building's bare rafters and lit by rows of tall windows. Comfortable chairs were scattered about, flanked by small tables ready for tankards or friendly games of dice or cards. Polished wooden cabinets held a suitably lavish assortment of bottles, goblets, and tankards, and a keg of ale sat ready on a metal rack. White wisps of steam, like breath on a wintry morn, curled up from a pottery dish situated just beneath its oak staves.

Taeros nodded approvingly. They'd done well to entrust the furnishing of their new haven to Korvaun Helmfast. True to their family name, Helmfasts were steady and practical folk, and Korvaun bred truer than most. He'd forgotten nothing—including the perpetual ice-smoke, a common but very handy little enchantment that kept ale pleasantly cool and local alchemists in ready coin.

Leaving the door ajar, Taeros strolled to one of the west-side windows. The casements had been thrown open to catch the ocean breeze, and the room was pleasantly cool despite the midsummer heat. The sun had just begun its descent, which meant he'd arrived at precisely the agree-upon meeting time. Even so, he didn't expect his friends any time soon. They had many virtues, but promptness was not among them. Taeros didn't mind; in fact, he'd been counting on their tardiness.

Between his family's mercantile affairs and jollity with his tardy friends, the young Lord Hawkwinter found few quiet opportunities to indulge his private passion. Taking ink, parchment, and quills from his thigh-satchel, he chose the table in the best light and settled down to write.

The title page was done, brought by the scribe's runner this very morning. "*Deep Waters*," it proclaimed, in large script embellished with colored inks and surrounded by an elaborate border.

It was a fine thing, certain to capture the eye of any child—even that of Cormyr's young king.

Taeros dipped his quill in black ink and began to write: *Humbly offered to King Azoun, fifth of that name to rule Cormyr, a gift from one who is a loyal subject in his heart, if not by his birth.*

He considered this phrase, and decided to let it stand. The wording was awkward and the sentiment would infuriate his family and puzzle his friends, but it was truth nonetheless.

In the courts of Cormyr, a young man of noble birth could rise as high as talents and ambition would take him. There, as a counselor, envoy, or even a royal officer, Taeros could have had a hand in the important work of governance.

What awaited him here in Waterdeep but the endless gathering and flaunting of wealth? No one knew who ruled here, and few cared, so long as trade was strong and coffers full.

Taeros swallowed old bitterness and bent to the task at hand. If he was to complete this book by the time young Azoun the Fifth was able to read, he'd scant time to waste on self-pity.

No shortage of heroes plagues your land, he wrote, *but it is said that a king must know the ways of many lands if he is to rule his own wisely and well. Waterdeep cannot match Cormyr's thousand-year dynasty and proud and noble traditions, yet our history is not without tales worth telling.*

He dipped the quill again and pondered. Where to start? Ancient times when dragons ruled all, or when elves founded the haven of Evermeet? Or perhaps with the first barbarian settlements? Something heroic, certainly, from the days before true heroism in the shadow of Mount Waterdeep was drowned in the endless clinking of coins.

A battle, perhaps. By the gods, Waterdeep had survived enough of those!

Recalling his childhood fascination for glorious sword-swinging tales brought to mind less pleasant memories: the frowns of nursemaids when they found him bent over forbidden books.

No, too stirring a tale would prompt the young king's minders to snatch this book from small royal hands and put it on a high

Greenwood and Cunningham · 31

shelf and thence, perhaps, into a waiting hearthfire.

Perhaps a humorous tale? Surely the Obarskyrs shared a strong sense of humor; how else could they have endured the counsel of the wizard Vangerdahast all these years?

No, that wasn't quite the thing, either. The wit of Taeros Hawkwinter was too often a kettle that seethed and scalded. Heated words from afar were even more likely to be swiftly introduced to devouring flames.

Better to start with a nursery tale, one Taeros had favored as a child. Yes, safe enough to pass the judgments of nursemaids. Something they might enjoy reading aloud to a boy king.

Eagerly he began to write, the familiar story flowing swiftly onto the page. This had always been one of his favorite tales. For once, the hero wasn't the strong young chieftain *or* the beautiful golden maiden. From such sprang worthy heroes, of course, but why not the occasional quick-witted lass?

Or for that matter, an ink-stained nobleman?

Swiftly ascending boots thundered on the stairs: Two pairs, at least, of expensive heels.

Hastily Taeros powdered his page, blotted his quill, capped the ink, and shuffled pages out in a concealing fan over all, leaving a satirical poem—something suitably frivolous he'd dashed off over morning ale, to explain away ink-stained fingers—atop the pile.

Familiar grumbling echoed on the stair, too low-pitched to make out words, but from an unmistakable source: *Starragar.*

Taeros grinned. Ho, then, Faerûn, salute you Starragar Jardeth, tireless voice of dissent! Every circle of friends seemed to have a Starragar. His constant nay-saying annoyed as often as it amused, but that didn't mean the man wasn't occasionally correct. Even a water clock run dry told the right time twice a day.

On cue, Starragar poked his head into the room, surveying it with distaste already riding his pale face. His hard gaze fell upon the portrait over the hearth, and he sighed loudly.

A Hawkwinter grin widened. Last winter, they'd all sat together for a portrait. As a joke, they'd had the painter render Starragar entirely in black and white. In this, art fell not far short of life.

With his lank black hair, customary somber garb, and skin no blaze of sun could brown, Starragar seemed strangely colorless.

The young man just behind Jardeth was his opposite: Korvaun Helmfast was tall and fair-haired, with serious blue eyes and a quiet, thoughtful manner.

"Dock Ward," Starragar said flatly and dismissively, as if that alone was sufficient condemnation.

Korvaun slipped past Starragar. Catching the grin Taeros wore, he greeted his friend with an easy nod.

"Nicely done," Taeros offered, sweeping his hand to indicate the entire room. Starragar's predictable response was a disdainful sniff.

A belly-shaking burst of laughter rolled up the stairwell from below. The friends exchanged delighted smiles, and even Starragar's face lit up. As one the three nobles rushed to the door.

Malark Kothont was mounting the stairs two at a time, despite the large wooden crate in his massive arms. Keeping pace with him was Beldar Roaringhorn, their unofficial leader, darkly handsome face smiling but arms empty.

As usual, an inner annoyance rose in Taeros. Unlike the rest of them—young blades of Waterdeep born to wealth, whose proud merchant families had claimed nobility generations ago—Malark had royal blood. His mother was from the Moonshaes, distant kin to High Queen Alicia. Malark was, quite simply, better than the rest of them. His blindness to this grated on Taeros.

Malark tossed the crate onto a chair and threw his powerful arms wide. "I'm back, lads, and thirsty as a Ruathymaar sailor! I see ale in plenty, but *where* are the wenches?"

"There're no women in the Moonshaes?" Starragar asked dryly.

Malark winked. "Aye, but I've been there a year and more, haven't I?"

Long enough to acquire considerable bulk, it was evident, not to mention considerable facial hair. Though Malark was only two-and-twenty, he was muscled like a dock worker, and the curly red beard spilling down his tunic would be the envy of many a dwarf.

Beldar clapped him on the shoulder. "Run through all the women, did you? No wonder you've come home. We've business to attend to, but tonight we'll drink the taverns dry."

"Speaking of which—" Taeros untied a small bag from his belt and tossed it to Korvaun. "That's for covering me the night I was coin-short for ale and breakage."

Beldar's face darkened. "Time was—not long gone, either—when a noble's word was coin enough until his steward came to settle up."

"You said something about gifts?" Malark asked with smooth eagerness, eyes wide and bearded face innocent. The others grinned. Beldar lifted an eyebrow to show he'd recognized the ruse, but let his temper drop. Prying up the lid of the crate with his silver-mounted belt knife, the Roaringhorn folded back linen wrappings within and lifted a length of shimmering cloth into view, its rich amber hue as bright as a copper-backed candle. Not bothering to shake it out, he tossed it carelessly to Taeros.

"A cloak. I'm told flame-kindle is a good color for a man with black hair and gray eyes."

Taeros momentarily struck the taunting pose of a coquettish high lady, making a show of smoothing his hair, then shook out the garment. He abandoned playacting to hold it up and raised his eyebrows, impressed. It was very fine, woven with threads that sparkled brightly. He moved it, watching them wink and catch the light.

"What's this?"

"Amber and topaz. I found a weaver who can work gemstone into cloth," Beldar replied. "For a suitably lofty stack of coin, she agreed not to sell her wares to anyone but us for the rest of the season. By then, we'll have set the fashion, and anyone who takes up wearing gemweave will be seen as a come-lately."

Turning, the Roaringhorn tossed a black cloak to Starragar. It started to unfold in the air, tumbling into a shimmering cloud of darkness.

"Hematite," Beldar said with a grin. "A stone said to absorb negative energies."

"Let us hope its capacity rivals Malark's thirst, or it'll shatter in a tenday," Taeros said dryly, drawing a ripple of laughter—even from Starragar.

"For Korvaun, what else but true blue?" Beldar continued, handing the fair-haired blade a cloak that displayed a spectrum of jewel shades from pale blue to darkest sapphire. Korvaun nodded and smiled silent thanks.

Malark snatched the next cloak from his friend's hands the moment its emerald hue gleamed forth. "You needn't be saying it. With this hair and beard, I'll look like an overfed leprechaun, but you haven't the imagination to be picking any other color. Jade, is it?"

"Emerald, you ingrate," Beldar told him, scowling with feigned wrath, "and worth far more than you are. As for me, it's rubies and garnet." He swept a glimmering red cloak about his own shoulders and struck a pose.

Taeros did not share Beldar's preoccupation with fashion, but had to admit his friend looked dashing. A fine horseman and keen hunter, Beldar had the sun-browned skin of an outdoorsman and the lean physique of a swordmaster. His dark chestnut hair swept his shoulders, and his small, elegant mustache gave him a raffish air.

Taeros crooked a critical eyebrow. "All you need is an oversized pirate's hat to complete your garb."

"Why d'you think we were late?" Malark whispered, loudly enough to be heard clear down the stairs. "We had to stop in every hattery 'tween here and the Northgate to try on great wagon-wheel things, but no one had a hat quite big enough to suit him."

Beldar shrugged off the resulting laughter. "Well, we have our club," he began, nodding approvingly to Korvaun, "and our name."

"Gemcloaks?" ventured Taeros.

"Of course. The question remains: What shall we Gemcloaks do?"

"Gossip, gamble, drink, wager, and plot little schemes to pry money out of rich and title-hungry merchants—all of which we'll promptly loose in various bad investments," Malark replied promptly. "In short: The usual."

"Add to that list a haven for younger sons," Taeros said glumly. "'Tis my misfortune to have a paragon for an older brother. When Waterdeep was attacked, I was away on a 'pleasure trip,' but Thirayar slew ten sahuagin with a salad fork—or so our proud parents tell the world."

"At least you still have a brother," Starragar said sharply. "Roldo wasn't so fortunate."

An uncomfortable silence fell. Roldo Thongolir was still on his wedding trip. His older brothers had both died in the defense of Waterdeep, leaving him heir. Roldo was a fine companion, the first to lift tankard in tribute and a stout lad at your back in a tavern brawl, but he was fashioned to follow, not to lead, command, or administer. Thongolir elders had swiftly chosen a bride for him, a brisk and competent young woman who would manage the family fortune capably and, no doubt, Roldo as well. Never was a man less suited to the duties of a noble of Waterdeep, but Roldo did as his family bade without a word of complaint.

Beldar cleared his throat sharply and nodded at the crate. "Roldo's is of rose quartz, as he honors the Morninglord."

"A thoughtful gift," Malark said with a grin, "and practical. With one of us sporting pink, we're sure to be invited to a brawl early on. Get the fighting over and done first, and we can devote the better part of the night to the ladies."

"As to fighting," Beldar said firmly, "if Roldo had been here, he'd have acquitted himself better than either of his brothers. 'Tis Waterdeep's misfortune that none of us were here when the attack came."

"And ours," Taeros added under his breath.

Though none of them liked to admit it, they all wore the weight of unintended absence from the battles. Who'd have expected the sea to erupt with scaly beasts bent on destroying Waterdeep?

One and all, they were younger sons of proud Waterdhavian noble houses. Come every spring, until circumstances or family decrees thrust them into posts of responsibility, they were expected to wander and learn the ways of rivals, buyers, and would-be clients in the family trades all across Faerûn. If much of their time was spent in festhalls and taverns, did that make them wastrels any idler than their sires had been? Didn't every traveling merchant of Waterdeep do as much, insofar as coins allowed?

A shared sigh of relief arose in the room when Beldar's eyes lit with new mischief. He pointed out the nearest window. Across crowded and ramshackle rooftops, one structure stood out, bright with new timbers and scaffolding—one of many Dock Ward buildings damaged in the sahuagin fighting. Fire had all but gutted it, but restoration was well underway.

"See yon scaffolding? All those ropes?" Beldar smiled. "An excellent place for some fun, I'm thinking ..."

"A battle!" Malark said gleefully. Slapping his knees, he bounded to his feet. "Beldar and I against you three."

"Beldar's the best sword among us, and you're the biggest and strongest," Starragar complained.

"Two against three," Beldar pointed out, "and you've got Korvaun. He's nearly as good as I am."

This teasing boast brought a bow from Korvaun and a groan from the others. It occurred to Taeros that—Beldar's claim notwithstanding—if one set aside flamboyance and showmanship, it just might be that Korvaun could best them all. Moreover, Korvaun probably knew as much, but considered it unworthy of mention.

Not that it *mattered*. The day was fair, and the glorious game unfolding once more! Amid general laughter and swirling of new finery, Taeros tucked his things into his satchel and became the rearguard of the general rush downstairs.

🏰 🏰 🏰 🏰 🏰

"I *cannot* believe," Beldar Roaringhorn announced in aggrieved tones, whirling his drawn sword in a gleaming flourish to underscore his pique, "that some fool-head of a shopkeeper needs a building of this size to sell a few *sandals*."

"And I," Starragar added, "find myself mired in similar disbelief that a shop on Redcloak Lane in *Dock* Ward can truly sell 'Fine' anything."

"Well, then," Malark roared, drawing a frown from a worker

peering down over a fire-scorched sign proclaiming this no mere half-rebuilt shop, but the one and only Candiera's Fine Shoes and Sandals, "we are collectively affronted. Does this establishment deserve a continued existence? I say *no!*"

"Whereas I," Taeros responded with a grin, entering into the spirit of the thing, "stand against you, sir, and say that it should and must! For humble shops like this, howe'er overblown and spurious their claims, have been the backbone, lifeblood, and ever-rising *greatness* of the City of Splendors these passing centuries, and bid fair to remain so! To strike at Candiera's Fine Shoes and Sandals is to threaten true Waterdhavians all!"

"Well shoveled," Korvaun chuckled, as hammerings and clatterings fell silent above them, and the faces of workers—younger ones grinning, but older ones frowning apprehensively—began to gather to gaze down at the Gemcloaks.

"Moreover," Starragar added hastily, recalling which side he was supposed to be on, "I can only view any attack upon this establishment's claims, however embellished they might be, to be an assault on the essential character of what it is to be Waterdhavian! Endless mercantile disputation and strife is the very lifeblood of our city! In short, to demand the destruction of this shop is to decry the very soul and core of Waterdeep!"

"What, by all the watching *gods*...?" a grizzle-bearded carpenter demanded in bewilderment, shouldering between his suddenly idle trustyhands to gaze down and try to discover why they'd all stopped work.

"Foolblades," an older worker spat scornfully, hefting his mallet. In response to his employer's sharp, inquiring frown, he added in explanation, "Young wastrel nobles. At play, as usual."

"And when foolblades play," another worker grunted, "things always get broken."

The carpenter leaned forward and bellowed down at the Gemcloaks, "*Ho!* Be off with you! Yes, *you!*"

Malark seemed not to hear. "Well, then," he said grandly, continuing the game, "only one solution remains to men of honor!"

"Indeed," Taeros replied politely. Four blades sang out of scabbards to join Beldar's already-bared steel, and the Gemcloaks drew themselves smoothly into two lines, facing each other in mock menace.

Someone hummed a mock fanfare, and one man from each line glided forward to stand blade-to-blade. With matching grins, Beldar and Taeros indulged in a mocking, finger-crooking parody of the elaborate lace-wristed courtesies of old nobles. Grand flourishes were made, bows performed, and blades crossed delicately, steel kissing steel.

"Insomuch as thy tragic and injurious delusions must fall, have at you, miscreant," Beldar intoned, stepping back to strike a dramatic pose made resplendent by his ruby cloak.

"And to rescue all Faerûn against thy grievous and ever-burgeoning errors, have at *you*," Taeros replied, his fierce grin belying the haughty styling of his words.

With a whoop, Beldar lunged and charged, hacking hard twice at Hawkwinter steel as he came, the drive and direction of his assault seeking to back Taeros over a handy bucket.

Taeros, who'd marked that hazard before crossing steel, sprang over it without looking down. In a swirl of amber finery he retreated nimbly into the litter of boards, chopping-blocks, dangling ropes, and sawhorses that crowded the building's ground floor.

Beldar advanced, kicking the bucket at his Hawkwinter foe. If the bucket chanced to contain fresh and very sticky mulehoof glue, and if Taeros happened to be adept at sliding aside and letting such missiles hurtle past him to strike and topple a leaning sheaf of boards, and thence ricochet hard into the face of the first charging worker to come thundering down a rickety temporary stair, well, that was merely the will of the gods, was it not?

And if the Gemcloaks burst into the wood shavings and barrel-littered worksite with enthusiastic roars, wild slashes, and kicks that upset most of the barrels and toppled an entire run of thankfully unoccupied scaffolding with a deafening crash into the stout stone wall of the shop next door, well, that too was as the gods willed and merely to be expected when the future champions of Waterdeep's honor took the field with blades bared and battle in their eyes.

"*Ho!*" Malark boomed cheerfully. With wondrous economy of movement he parried two blades as he landed a kick to Starragar's ornately filigreed codpiece.

The midnight-cloaked Voice of Dissent went staggering back, but his yelp of pain was not quite the sob it might have been. The freshest flower of House Jardeth had experienced this particular favorite Kothont attack a time or two before and protected himself accordingly.

As it was, Starragar's helpless retreat took him crashing through and over the low, stout brazier kept alight to warm and soften the carpenter's peg and wedge glues, sending it and an array of battered glue-pots flying.

Flames were springing up here and there among the thick-fallen shavings by the time the carpenter and four of his largest trustyhands came clattering down their temporary stairs with roars of rage, hurling mallets as they came. If a foolblade got knocked senseless or lost a nose to his own foolishness, well that *too* was in the hands of the gods.

With a whoop Beldar Roaringhorn sent Taeros sprawling over a pile of boards. Emptying a small belt-flask in a single quaff, he spun around in a ruby-red swirl to slice through the stout rope lashings holding the lowest flight of the temporary stairs in place.

Under the weight of onrushing workers, that run of steps plunged to earth. So great was the force of its landing that it rebounded hard and high into the air, then slammed down again amidst splinterings of protest. Those crashes smote the ears almost as hard as the toppled workers hit the board-and-shaving-strewn floor. Almost.

One laborer struck a litter of lumber with a helpless curse that rose into a howl of fear as a trio of propped beams toppled over onto him. They slammed down on the man and then rolled away, leaving him bruised and groaning. Enraged, another trustyhand leaned down from the floor above to send a drop-bucket swinging hard at the back of Korvaun Helmfast's head.

Taeros saw this peril approaching on the end of its stout rope and lunged into a frantic dive that took a startled Korvaun safely to the floor with him. It was merest mischance that someone had left dressed boards atop a row of sawhorses there and that their sudden arrival dislodged the end horse, making the boards dance and rattle with force enough to spill the carpenter's crate of precious hand-forged longnails.

The noisy clatter of that outpouring swept the carpenter into white-hot, shrieking fury. He charged at Taeros and Korvaun heedless of obstacles.

Accordingly, several sawhorses and an entire handcart of wooden pulley-blocks were sent flying, sweeping several workers from their feet to slide and roll helplessly. One man's tumble took Starragar Jardeth's feet out from under him, and the watching gods alone willed that Starragar's flailing blade severed a vital anchor-binding of a scaffold still alive with laborers pounding along its boards and hastening down its ladders.

In a sudden and sickening cacophony of shrieking wood, a corner of that scaffold buckled and swung out from the building, spilling mallets, nails, boards, off-cuts, and shouting trustyhands down into Redcloak Lane, where, a staggering Malark Kothont could not help but observe, as he smote aside a furious laborer with the flat of his blade and puffed his way back into the flame-flickering heart of the deepest shavings where Taeros and Korvaun were enthusiastically thwacking a roaring carpenter with the flats of their own blades, a delighted crowd was beginning to gather.

"*Ho!*" Malark shouted sportingly as he came, his sword cutting the air with mock ferocity. Workers were fleeing in all directions now, having little taste for fencing sharp steel with battered hand-mallets.

As the worksite speedily emptied of cursing, sweating laborers and Malark bore down on the still-raging carpenter, the blare of a Watch-horn arose to the north: the single note of one patrol summoning another. Redcloak Lane would very soon host more

Watch officers than a bugbear had fleas.

Malark halted, abandoning his sport with a shrug. No one had been slain, though if this fool of a carpenter didn't stop snatching gouges and chisels from his belt and throwing them at Taeros Hawkwinter, *that* might well change . . .

Malark's speculation was abruptly cut short by a flying chisel. He ducked low then turned his dive into a somersault, bringing both of his boots up hard and fast into the carpenter's gut. They sank therein with satisfying thuds, hurling the retching man away into a pillar, which, being a fresh and temporary prop rather than a stoutly anchored timber, promptly gave way.

The slow but gathering-in-strength groan that followed was truly impressive and heralded the sagging of an entire section of still-charred ceiling. Gemcloaks scampered away with excited shouts but were forced to turn in swirlings of bright finery as the peg-popping, wood-twisting shiftings overhead caused the already leaning Redcloak Lane scaffolding to turn and crumple a little more.

Cries of excitement and alarm arose from the crowd, and the few of them who'd shown signs of drawing daggers or brandishing dock-hooks to join the fray drew hastily back.

The carpenter's belligerence seemed to have left him along with the contents of his stomach, and he now devoted himself to hastily crawling away, coughing, "Help!" and "Fire!" and "Call the Watch!" as he went.

Magnanimously Malark let him go, for there were brighter foes to vanquish—to whit, one Taeros Hawkwinter, a certain Korvaun Helmfast, and the never-to-be-overlooked Starragar Jardeth. With Beldar Roaringhorn at his side, the valiant Malark Kothont would now . . . and where *was* Beldar?

Malark caught sight of him through merrily rising flames. The ruby-cloaked Roaringhorn was happily fencing with Starragar, while Taeros and Korvaun raced to snatch and empty the workers' fire-buckets on the most enthusiastic of the conflagrations. Beldar, unaware or uncaring of such trifles, buried his blade deep in a pillar that Starragar had ducked behind.

The Jardeth took advantage of Beldar's frantic tugging to race up a short ladder, snatch another fire-bucket, and empty it over Beldar's head.

Thankfully it proved to be full of water and not pipe-ash and sand, and watching Waterdeep was treated to the sight of the leader of the Gemcloaks spitting water and roaring in damp fury.

Malark opened his mouth to bellow delightedly—and Waterdeep suddenly vanished in a dark, stunningly wet torrent of evil-smelling water.

The scion of House Kothont staggered blindly, clawed the bucket off his head, and glared angrily into the coldly smiling visage of a Watch officer. The man faced Malark with his sword drawn, its blade thrust through the handle of a second full bucket. The dozen hard-faced Watchmen looming behind his leather-armored shoulders held leveled halberds in their hands, and they were not smiling.

"Stand!" another Watchman bellowed from the far side of the building in the tones of one who is accustomed to obedience. "Stand, and down arms all! Reveal your names and business here to the Watch! All others, keep back and keep silence!"

"Stamp and quench!" the officer facing Malark snapped, without turning his head to look at his men. "In there now, swift as you can! Get those fires *out!*"

The Watchmen charged forward, more than one of them roughly jostling Malark. The officer took one slow step forward and curtly made a 'down arms' gesture to Malark.

Who spread his arms wide, splendid emerald cloak swirling, and asked, "Surely, goodman, you don't mean to separate a noble from his sword?"

The Watch officer's face went carefully expressionless. "Being an officer of the City Watch, lord, I never *mean* to do anything. I uphold the law, follow orders, and visit consequences on *those who do not.*"

He repeated the 'down arms' gesture. Malark shrugged and let his blade fall to the shavings-littered floor at his feet.

The Watch officer nodded curtly. *Good dog,* Malark thought, remembering one of his father's huntsmen nodding in exactly the same way to a hound he was training.

"And what might your name be? Lord . . .?"

"Kothont. Malark Kothont."

Many Watchmen were approaching through the littered building, forming a loose ring around the other Gemcloaks. The Watch officer nodded his head toward them without lowering his blade or taking his eyes off Malark. "And these bright-feathered birds: They're nobles, too?"

"Of course," Malark said airily, spreading his hands in an expansive gesture.

"Of course," the officer echoed, the merest thread of contempt in his level, carefully flat voice.

Catcalls and derisive comments were being shouted from the crowd, but by now there were more Watchmen than dock workers in Redcloak Lane, and when curt "stand away" orders were given, space was cleared.

The complaints of the carpenter rose into a roar as he and his men were included in that shoving of turned-sideways halberds. The ranking Watch commander held up a warning hand and growled, "Patience, goodman," in tones that promised dire consequences for disobedience. The carpenter fell silent.

The commander turned back to Beldar Roaringhorn, who with Taeros and the others had now been herded to stand with Malark Kothont. He made a swift, two-fingered circling gesture, and Watchmen scrambled to take up the Gemcloaks' weapons.

"I say—" Malark protested, and again the warning hand came up, commanding silence.

"Assault, damage to property, and fire-setting," the commander listed almost wearily. "Openly and in public, apparently with pranksome intent. Have you any explanation for this fool-headedness or good reason you should not face magisterial justice forthwith?"

With only the slightest of wincings Beldar stepped forward and gave the commander an easy "We're all reasonable men here" smile. Malark subsided, more than content to let his friend fly this particular hawk.

"Mere fun, nothing more! No harm was meant and little was done. On my honor as a Roaringhorn, we'll be happy to compensate the building's owner for any damage!"

Most of the Watch officers were eyeing the Gemcloaks as if they'd like to toss the young nobles into the nearest rat-infested dungeon, yet in a civilized city, money smoothed many rough roads, and men of means could send their stewards around to settle any unpleasantness.

On the other hand, Malark mused, perhaps the city was *too* civilized. In Waterdeep, things were done in sly roundabout ways that didn't suit him at all. In the wilderlands of his mother's kin, men *dealt* with matters, promptly and openly, with none of this whining dependence upon a council of anonymous rulers.

Here, a carpenter could glare at Malark with eyes holding deadly promise, and a nobleman could be deprived of his sword, yet knowing Waterdeep, most likely both of them would die not settling their differences blade to blade but eating a stew poisoned by an unseen aggrieved party.

The Watch commander made a gesture, and the Gemcloaks' weapons were proffered to them, hilts-first.

"Stand back, men," he said softly. "Restitution has been offered. These men are free to go."

Beldar sheathed his sword, and his companions followed suit. "We meant no harm," he repeated.

"Aye," the commander said dryly, his eyes boring into those of Beldar Roaringhorn like two contemptuous daggers. "Your sort never do."

CHAPTER TWO

Morning came slowly to Dock Ward. Its close-huddled buildings cast stubborn shadows the guttering street-lanterns did little to dispel. Here and there roosters caroled like conjurers summoning the sun. Muttered curses followed most of their crowings amid clatters of tools. Some folk who dwelt here had to rise early to earn coin enough to eat.

Mrelder headed for Redcloak Lane, marveling at the changes a year could bring. The last time he'd stumbled wearily along here, seeking his way back to Candlekeep, most of these buildings had been charred and smoking ruins.

The rebuilt structures had stone walls to twice a man's height, crowned with one or more stories of stout timber. Most roofs were of new thatch, but the fires hadn't been forgotten: there were a few runs of slate tiles too. Mrelder wondered how much such a roof would add to the cost of his new establishment.

He stopped where Candiera's Fine Shoes and Sandals had stood. Its rubble had been carted away, and a new timber frame soared to impressive heights above a repaired foundation of dressed stone. However, roofless openwork timbers kept a man a trifle damp and drafty, even in fabled Waterdeep.

One of the workers shifting and hammering boards in that littered interior saw him and strode over, mallet in hand.

"Have you business here?"

Mrelder smiled faintly. "I'd fondly hoped to be doing business here before the midsummer fairs, but it seems the work goes slowly."

The man's eyes widened. "Be you the sorcerer who bought out Candiera?"

"The same. Would you be Master Dyre?"

A passing trustyhand grinned at them. "If yer offering to magic him into Dyre, he'd probably take you up on it—leastwise, if'n he could keep his own nose." There were roars of laughter from workers all around.

"I take it Master Dyre's not here. May I . . . look about?"

The carpenter shrugged. "It's yours, bought and paid for. Don't be climbing the frames or pulling on any ropes, though; they're not secured proper."

Mrelder nodded. "Fair enough. I want a look around back to see what room we'll have for loading carts and such."

"Back there? Done, all but some carting away. Mind your step and take a torch—it's dark as Cyric's heart down by yon well."

"Oh? What befell the glowpaint?"

"Probably wore out. Everything does. I can tell you true there was no magic about the place when we started. Master Dyre always makes sure; says it costs him less coin to hire a wizard to spy out magic than to pay for his own burial if he blunders into an old ward."

"A prudent man," Mrelder observed.

Accepting a torch, he made his way through ankle-deep shavings to light it from a small fire in a copper brazier near the workers' glue pots, and picked his way on through the litter to the well house.

It, too, had changed. Beyond a new door, neatly dressed stone had replaced the old chipped steps. As the carpenter had said, the glowpaint was gone.

As Mrelder glanced at the well, his heart sank. It had a lid so new that the wood was still pale, the brass fasteners bright. Beside it, the old cover lay in a rotting heap.

There was no sign of the Candlekeep rune on those moldering shards. The magic was gone. The wood had probably crumbled when the enchantment was dispelled.

Mrelder sighed. No doubt spell-ways into that great fortress temple were crafted to vanish if any magic was worked on them.

Or perhaps the monks now believed they had reason to distrust him.

Mrelder shook his head. No, they had applauded his decision to apply himself to the study of sahuagin. After a year, when he'd declared his intent to fare forth to gather tales of sahuagin attacks and compile information about their magic and methods, the First Reader had given his personal approval and even modest funding. No, these doubts were his fancies, no more.

He lifted his torch high. To his astonishment, its flickering light fell on a fresh oval of solid stone wall. The tunnel was gone!

Mrelder rushed around the well to feel and then pound the stones—large, solid blocks, each so tightly fitted to its neighbor that he doubted a dainty lady's dagger could slip between them.

Mrelder stared around the well house in stunned disbelief and then turned, rushed up the stairs, and ran back through the worksite until he could catch the sleeve of a passing worker.

It was the carpenter, who blinked at the ferocity of Mrelder's question: "What happened to the well house?"

The carpenter frowned. "Dyre oversaw that rebuilding himself. The stonework should be tighter'n a dwarf moneylender."

"It is, in fact, too tight," Mrelder snapped.

The carpenter looked incredulous, so he invented quickly: "I plan to sell well-aged cheeses. They require a cool, damp place to ripen."

The man's face cleared. "Well, that's fine, then. You'll have a big root cellar yonder when we're done." He glanced swiftly about and then leaned close and murmured, "There was a tunnel in yon well house leading to gods-only know. 'Tis good fortune for you Master Dyre closed it off. What was found there, you don't want to have come a'calling."

Mrelder's heart thudded. He slipped a silver coin from his purse, turning his hand discreetly to show it to the carpenter alone. "A prudent man knows the dangers he avoids as well as those he faces."

"'Twas a token," the man said softly, his eyes on the coin. "From Those Who Watch, whose noses you *don't* want poking into your affairs."

"The token was black," Mrelder said softly, and the carpenter nodded.

Mrelder managed a smile and held out his hand. "My thanks for your help." They shook, and the silver changed palms.

With that, Mrelder waved farewell and strode away. On his return to Candlekeep a year ago, he'd sought in vain for the little black helm Piergeiron had given him, and in the end concluded it must have held some magic and so had been stripped from him by the defenses of the gate.

It seemed he'd dropped the charm in the well-tunnel, and the workers had taken it as a warning from the First Lord to keep away.

What to do now? Requesting the tunnel be re-opened might establish him as a man with ties to . . . well, to those whose noses were best kept out of common folks' business. *That* sort of reputation would draw attention he could ill afford.

By now it was bright morning, and the streets were filling quickly. Mrelder walked briskly, dodging the inevitable creaking hand-carts and sleepy-eyed, shuffling dockers as he made for the house he and his father were to share.

Golskyn had pointed out, sensibly enough, that they'd need more than one base in the city. For several tendays now his father's followers—mongrelmen who served the priest with hound-like devotion—had been busily connecting divers lodgings and storehouses with new tunnels. Most who served Golskyn couldn't walk any city openly and so had become well versed in the lore of dark places, including tunneling and hiding all traces of such work.

Mrelder would send some of them to Redcloak Lane when the harbor fogs rolled in and full darkness came to begin a tunnel between the root cellar the carpenter had pointed out and the stone passage where the tiny sahuagin lay waiting.

Thinking of what was to come, Mrelder felt himself smiling.

The sahuagin would regain its formidable size and find itself joining a certain young sorcerer in a new war.

More accurately, *selected parts* of the sahuagin would join with Mrelder.

△ △ △ △ △

"No work ever got done," Varandros Dyre growled at the two apprentices scurrying at his heels, "by a man who spends more time on his arse than his feet. *That's* why we go from site to site, afoot so the lads don't see us coming three streets off! And mark me, young Jivin, our little visits are why Dyre's Fine Walls and Dwellings can afford to hire the likes of you and Baraezym here—and why *I*, the gods help me, can afford the fine gowns my daughters so like to wear."

Dyre shouldered through the thickening crowds at the mouth of Redcloak Lane, clearing a path for his two 'prentices like a hard-driven coach. Not much stood in Varandros Dyre's path. The sheer energy of the man was enough to sweep aside obstacles and draw eyes to him.

Not that he was a pleasure to behold. Gray-haired and sharp of glance, Dyre had the sun-weathered hide and battered fingers of the Master Stoneworker he was, and his nose was so large that Baraezym, his older apprentice, had once described it as "the snout of a shark." Those words came into Jivin's mind whenever he glanced at his master, leaving him on the verge of grinning.

Jivin's life was hardly one of ease, but much could be learned from such a master. Building after building had been raised from the rubble of last year's fighting under the Dyre banner, and Baraezym and Jivin knew very well Varandros had taken them on because he needed men who could write, count coins and see approaching menaces and swindles, not trustyhands who could lay stones and hammer pegs and nails with keen-eyed skill. He already owned scores of those.

Baraezym and Jivin knew something else: Dyre was smarter than he liked to appear and had been testing them with deliberate ledger errors and casually "forgotten" coins left in coffers here and strongboxes there. He'd been watching to see if they'd keep even a single copper nib for themselves.

Like a storm wind or Mount Waterdeep, Varandros Dyre loomed up fierce and unyielding. Just now, he'd lifted his snout sharply to gaze down the crowded street, toward the distant scaffolding that was their destination.

"What boar-buttock-brained idiot braced *that* mess?" he snapped, rounding on them as if his two apprentices were personally responsible for the sloppy lashings. Without waiting for replies, he whirled around and set off at a speed that forced them to trot to keep up.

"Baraezym!" he growled, over his shoulder. "Tell Jivin what's wrong with that scaffolding!"

The older apprentice peered. "Uh, broken boards . . . loose lashings." He frowned. "It looks almost as if it *fell down*, or came close to, then got dragged back up into place with ropes and braced with a few boards. Everything's . . ."

Baraezym flung up both hands, as if his fingers could snatch the words he wanted from empty air. He succeeded only in knocking a hat off the head of a hurrying sailor on his right and unintentionally slapping the cheek of a heavily cloaked woman on his left.

The sailor cursed as he leaned and snatched his hat out of the air before it could fall and be lost. The woman spun around to lessen the force of Baraezym's blow and said huskily, "*Hey*, there! I charge good coin for that, y'know!"

Baraezym's stammered apologies were lost in his own hurried pursuit of his master, and in Dyre's fiercely approving, "*Exactly!* Yon work's sagged and been hauled back into place, rather than rebuilt properly! Oh, heads are going to *roll!*"

The master of Dyre's Fine Walls and Dwellings stopped dead in mid-stride, so suddenly that Jivin nearly slammed into him. The Shark was staring up, but barely had time to gape before broken boards came tumbling down through the air. Trailing a startled shout, a workman plunged after them.

From high above Redcloak Lane the man fell, mallet tumbling, and disappeared behind the crowd filling the street with their hand-carts and shoulder-perched baskets.

The crash and clatter was surprisingly loud, and heads turned all over Redcloak Lane. Varandros Dyre was already racing through the gawkers, spitting a stream of unfinished, crowded-atop-each-other curses. When he fetched up against a close-harnessed team of three mules, it was the mules that were brought to a rocking halt.

Their carter spat a curse at Dyre as the builder shoved his way past, but Dyre's roared reply was so fierce that the man recoiled. Baraezym and Jivin gave the startled man apologetic grins as they hastened after their master.

They burst free of the press of bodies to find Dyre in the midst of a ring of workers, grimly promising a groaning man at their feet his healing would be paid for, every last shard and dragon of it. The man smiled, nodded, and promptly slipped into sense-lessness.

Varandros Dyre looked up with a black storm brewing in his eyes. He gave the grizzle-bearded carpenter a glare that should have spat lightning.

"D'you call *that* scaffolding, Marlus? For once I trust you to raise woodworks alone, just once, and you—"

"'Twas nobles again!" a worker burst out. "Young louts with bright cloaks and blades! *Playing* at being swordsmen! They had our works that side right down, an' chased us with swords and tried to burn the place down, too! This side just slumped 'n' hung, and we spent so much time getting the other up again . . ."

Dyre's eyes never left those of the carpenter. "Is this true?" he asked quietly.

Marlus nodded, his own anger red and clear on his face. "Every word! Glue ruined, boards broken, everything thrown down, and they *laughed* at us and tried to sword us, like we were little goblins running about for their amusement!"

Jivin waited almost eagerly for the explosion. The Shark was, he thought, more terrifying when he was calm and quiet.

"And the Watch? Did they happen along, perchance?"

"They did," Marlus said heavily, "and broke it up. If they hadn't, we'd never have got the fires out."

"And they took our happy noble lads where?"

"Nowhere," another worker said sourly. "They let 'em all go. Oh, the Watchcaptain was as cold as winter ice, but they went free, for all that."

"I see," Dyre murmured, strolling forward into the building site as if idly enjoying a walk across a flower-meadow. Hands clasped behind his back, he ambled through shavings, scorch-marks, and hastily restacked lumber.

"Mark me, Jivin," he said softly and suddenly, never turning to check if his younger apprentice was right behind him or seeming to care that a ring of men were moving as if glued to his shoulders, intent on his every breath. "Mark me: this is the last time a pack of noble pups will sport with my hard-working men. Young idiots, too coin-heavy to work and too stupid and bone-idle to think of worthwhile spendings of their time . . . so they work mischief with Varandros Dyre, and *cost me coin*. Oh yes, this is enough, and more than enough."

Baraezym and Jivin exchanged unhappy glances, silently and instantly agreed on one thing: they feared this dangerously calm and quiet Varandros Dyre far more than the loudly authoritarian one.

Dyre's boot struck against something sharp amid the shavings. He bent and plucked up a slender, finely made dagger. Its pommel was shaped like a spear point transfixing a star, and on both sides of the spear-blade was a complicated monogram of curlicues and interlaced letters.

Varandros Dyre was neither herald nor calligrapher, but he was a master at looking past fancy trimmings to what lay beneath. "M-K," he murmured, and raised both of his eyebrows as he looked slowly around at his silent, gathered workers. "This belongs to none of you, I trust?"

There was a general rumble of denial, but it was hardly necessary. No one among them could afford so costly a weapon, and none were foolish enough to carry a dagger that could have tumbled from the pages of some fancy tome of heraldry. The shaped hilt was clearly adapted from the proud device of some house or other.

And proud houses could be traced.

Varandros Dyre smiled, slowly and unpleasantly. For the very first time in his life, Jivin did not envy the nobility.

CHAPTER THREE

'It goes against my sacred beliefs," Golskyn said sternly, "to waste good money and evil monsters."

Wrapped in his long, deep-hooded cloak, the old priest was striding along the docks at a pace Mrelder, though taller, was hard-pressed to match. His father had stepped off a ship from Chult only a few breaths ago but had already found a dozen ways to express disdain for Mrelder's plans.

"There'll *be* no waste!" the younger man protested. "I've studied sahuagin for over a year and read *all* the known lore. I've been trying spells—"

"*Trying spells!*" the priest echoed scornfully. "Better you should approach the most fearful gods known to man and monster and in holy fervor *demand* what you desire."

"I'm no priest!"

"As well I know! You had to be a *wizard,* mucking about with bat dung and bad poetry!"

The young man repressed a sigh. "No wizard, either. I'm a sorcerer, Father."

"The whim of the gods at your birthing, nothing to boast about. A man is what he makes of himself, and you are still no different from the boy who turned tail and fled ten years ago!"

Mrelder looked around for something—other than his own shortcomings—that might capture Golskyn's attention. "Look, Father! See yon colossus standing sentry on the mountain? 'Tis one of the famous Walking Statues of Waterdeep. When I was last here, it looked like a gigantic man. In honor of the victory over the sahuagin and as a warning to other would-be invaders, Waterdeep's archmage re-fashioned it into a sahuagin."

The priest nodded approvingly. "Man into monster. Perhaps I might find common cause with this archmage of yours."

Golskyn and Khelben Arunsun together. The thought left Mrelder unsure whether to laugh or shudder.

Spying the guild badge he'd been looking for, he hailed a passing carter and gave instructions for his father's strongchests to be delivered to their house.

The former rooming house wasn't far off. It had been secretly purchased by the Amalgamation Temple almost a year ago, after Mrelder had convinced Golskyn to turn his attention to the fabled City of Splendors. Several Temple followers had been living there for months preparing for this day.

His father set off after the cart without another word, leaving his son to hasten behind. The dockside streets were their usual crowded chaos, but Golskyn dodged as adroitly as any seasoned Dock Warder, his hood moving like the beak of a crow as he peered this way and that. Mrelder had no need to look inside it to know that his father's face would be as calm and set as old stone.

Mrelder often wondered what Lord Unity of the Amalgamation was thinking behind that stonelike mask. It was unlikely to be anything gentle, caring, or merciful. His father never had time to waste on such weaknesses.

♠ ♠ ♠ ♠ ♠

The last of the strongchests was vanishing inside the rooming house as they arrived. A tall man, close-wrapped in a cloak, barred their way at the door. He was unremarkable but for the breadth of his shoulders and the girth of his chest; when he squared himself, he almost filled the doorway.

This sentinel gave Golskyn and Mrelder a glance, and his eyes, of a gray so pale it was almost silver, took on a reverent gleam.

Quickly ushering them in, he shut and barred the door and then bowed low to Golskyn.

"Lord Unity," he murmured, "we've long awaited your arrival. You're well, I trust?"

"I am *better*," Golskyn said meaningfully. Sweeping back his hood, he touched the black patch covering his left eye. "You have learned well, Hoth. Your work is excellent. The grafts were a great success, as always." He gave Mrelder a sidelong glance and added, "With minor exceptions."

The big man bowed again. "I am gratified."

"And perhaps curious?" the priest asked slyly. He removed the patch, revealing a bulging crimson orb. His mismatched gaze swept the room and settled on a small table set with a light welcoming meal: fresh bread, a cold joint, a bowl of summer berries and a smaller bowl of clotted cream.

"Fresh jam would be a pleasant addition," Golskyn commented. The red orb glowed—and a thin crimson beam erupted from his eye.

A flash more fleeting than lightning erupted from the berries and left them at a seething boil.

Hoth exclaimed in delight. His cloak parted as the three pairs of arms that had been folded neatly across his chest and belly rose to applaud.

"You've achieved remarkable control," he said proudly.

"It was hard-won. Mastering a beholder's eye is no easy task." Golskyn turned to Mrelder. "Hear me well: what you propose will be nearly as difficult."

"I'm ready," his son insisted.

"So you've said, time and again. How many times should precious seed be sewn in soil too weak to see it sprout?"

Rage rose in Mrelder, almost choking him. He turned away quickly to hide his anger and made the movement into a doffing of his cloak. A hunchbacked mongrelman whose warty, toadlike head was topped by an improbable pair of fox ears stepped out of a doorway and padded silently forward to take the garment.

"Before you dismiss my notion, Father," he said, "come see the sahuagin." Stepping into an archway that pierced a very thick wall, Mrelder pressed the right two stones and swung open the door hidden in one side of the arch.

Wordlessly Hoth held out a lit lantern. Mrelder took it with a nod of thanks and led the way down a steep stair. The air was cool and smelled of damp earth and stone.

The descending way soon started to spiral, going as deep as two buildings atop each other, until it ended in a room that had lain dark and forgotten beneath the rooming house and, more than likely, several buildings earlier.

It was dark no longer. Hanging lanterns glimmered in a chamber large enough for more than twenty men to dwell in spacious comfort. A dozen mongrelmen awaited them, wearing the dark cloaks of acolytes of the Amalgamation.

Their reverent gazes followed Lord Unity as he strode slowly around the room, expressionlessly examining cages, metal-topped tables, shelves of weapons and tools and racked glass vials, and even small floor-drains underfoot that emptied into yet deeper places.

"We found this while digging the tunnel from Redcloak Lane," Mrelder said proudly. "There are two ways in: the stair we've just taken and a tunnel yonder. I trust it will serve you and Hoth well for the holy work ahead." Slapping the nearest wall, he added, "Private and defensible, these walls are more than three feet thick, of solid stone, with the streets of Waterdeep a long way above our heads."

Which means, he thought silently, *no one will be able to hear the screams.*

Golskyn turned. "As yet," he remarked almost idly, "I see no sahuagin."

Mrelder entered the tunnel and stepped into an alcove, lifting his lantern to light up a large raised cistern capped with iron bars. "At least twenty feet deep. Water storage, perhaps; this place was built as a hidden refuge."

Golskyn strolled over to take a closer look.

"'Ware, Father," Mrelder murmured.

As he spoke, four thick, green-scaled arms thrust up through the bars at Lord Unity's face, talons flexing to seize and rend. The old priest flung himself to the floor, rolling away with surprising agility.

He came up smiling. "A live sahuagin! Who'd have thought it possible?"

Mrelder bit back the urge to sarcastically thank his father for having such confidence in him and instead asked, "Shall we harvest the limb?"

Golskyn nodded.

Mrelder signaled to a ready trio of mongrelmen. One took a pinkfin from a large bucket, and another hefted a heavy chain, threaded through a metal ring in the ceiling directly over the cistern, that ended in a barbed hook. With deft brutality the first mongrelman transfixed the fish with the hook, and raised this squirming, dripping bait for all to see.

His two fellow acolytes faced each other across the cistern, each holding a docker's reach-claw: a metal rod ending in two open, claw-like metal pincers, fitted with a trigger-wire that controlled a spring holding the pincers open.

"Ingenious," Golskyn murmured, seeing what they meant to do. "Begin."

The cloaked acolytes started to chant. The strange result was more akin to nightmares than bardcraft, half-spoken and half-sung over a jagged, ever-changing rhythm.

Hoth drew his sword and extended it, long and slender, toward the chanting mongrelmen.

Then Golskyn began to sing, a thin thread of melody that twined around the chant, goading it to a higher pitch and intensity. Like foul incense it rose, prayers to gods whose names Mrelder still did not know.

Slowly Hoth's sword began to glow, not with heat but with a cruel, pale light: divine magic. Mrelder nodded to the acolytes by the cistern.

The mongrelman who'd baited the hook hauled on the chain, lowering the dying pinkfin to dangle over the iron bars, gasping and writhing.

The taloned hands lunged for the fish.

The mongrelmen flanking the cistern moved just as swiftly. A pair of triggers snapped, and iron claws clanged shut around sahuagin wrists.

Its hissing, snarling bellow of rage was almost lost in the swelling chant. Still singing, all the acolytes rushed forward to haul on one reach-claw, pulling one sahuagin arm well up through the bars. Tugging and singing, they managed to pull it flat against the iron grate. The manacled sahuagin thrashed and struggled but was overmatched.

Hoth strode close, glowing sword lifted on high. He hefted it, two of his hands on the hilt and one on each crosspiece, his thews rippling—and then brought the blade down.

Scales, flesh, and bone were shorn through as if they were so much butter, and the arm bounced on the stone floor, severed above the elbow. The cleanly sliced stump vanished back through the bars, and a bubbling wail of agony trailed away into the unseen waters.

Mrelder was already peeling off his tunic. He lay down quickly on one of the tables, extending his arm. Strong hands held it firmly in place as he closed his eyes and composed himself, silently reciting the mind-chant an old monk of Candlekeep had taught him.

It was working. He was drifting . . . down . . . deeper and darker, all sound fading. He was only dimly aware of the continuing chant now . . .

He'd spent hours practicing this, hoping that if his mind was settled just so, his body might accept the new limb.

White-hot pain exploded in Mrelder's skull like a fireball, dashing his wits and will to screaming froth in the void, tatters that writhed, faded . . . and were lost in the deepening, silent darkness.

🏰 🏰 🏰 🏰 🏰

Varandros Dyre leaned across his gleaming desk and snapped, "Be welcome!" with a fire in his eyes that betokened no good for someone.

All the men taking chairs in this unfamiliar upper office wondered just who Dyre held such ill will toward, and hoped they'd not be caught standing too close to whoever it was when the old Shark struck.

Dyre noticed Karrak Lhamphur eyeing the nearest of the small, gleaming forest of decanters on the curving table before the arc of guest-seats, and waved at it grandly. "Drink, friends!"

Lhamphur and Dorn Imdrael shot him similarly suspicious glances, but it was Lhamphur who spoke up. "What's the occasion, Var? And why here, in such secrecy, instead of at your grand little citadel on Nethpranter's Street? Something you don't want your 'prentices to hear?" He glanced around curiously. "What *is* this place, anyway? A new venture you want our coins for?"

The Shark's eyes flashed, and—just for a moment—the room sang with tension as every guest awaited the expected explosion.

Then Varandros Dyre smiled and slowly reached for one of the two decanters on his desk, and men breathed in the room again.

"No to your last, Master Smith! Dyre's Fine Walls and Dwellings owns this building free and clear, thanks to the successes we've all shared in this season. Just as Lhamphur's Locks and Gates recently acquired a warehouse for metals to meet the need for gates and hinges and doorplates, I find myself in need of a place to store cut and dressed stone. I can't just leave it lying about in the streets, now can I?"

This caused an overly eager eruption of chuckles from Dyre's closest friend, Hasmur Ghaunt, which thankfully distracted the Shark from noticing the expression that passed momentarily over the face of Jarago Whaelshod, the last-invited of his four guests. The proprietor of Whaelshod's Wagons privately held the view that to save sharing coin with him whenever possible, Varandros Dyre frequently did just that. The Watch usually came to Master Carters to inquire as to how piles of building-stones came to be blocking the narrow streets of the southerly wards of the city, rather than bothering the fastest-rising builder in Waterdeep.

"No," Dyre said heartily, "I don't want your coins, yet I *do* want to share some news with you, and the words we may exchange shouldn't be overheard by anyone. My home comes furnished with not only 'prentices but daughters and servants, whose hearing, I shouldn't have to tell any of you, can be far keener than even their tongues."

Some chuckles arose. Of the five men in the room, only Hasmur Ghaunt was unmarried, and only Dyre had buried a wife. All of them had been blasted, at one time or another, by the dragonlike temper of Goodwife Anleiss Lhamphur.

"My lasses'll be along later to bring us food to go with this death-to-thirst, but we'll hear them arrive and have to let them in: there'll be no listening at keyholes."

The four guests nodded. Jacks were drained and set down thoughtfully, and Dyre waved at his guests to have more and drink freely.

Surprisingly, it was the swift-to-roister Dorn Imdrael who put his hand over the top of his jack and suggested, "Before we all get roaring, suppose you tell us why we're here. I prefer to be prudent when giving my aye or nay."

Dyre nodded. "Well said. Of course." He looked meaningfully over at the closed and barred door they'd all come in by. It was the only door in the room.

His glance made Hasmur Ghaunt lean forward in almost breathless haste to gabble, "I barred the door like you said! And set the alarm-cord, too!"

Dyre nodded his thanks and planted his hairy, battered hands on the table. "Yestermorn," he began, "a man of mine was injured falling off a scaffold in Redcloak Lane."

His guests winced, frowned, and made sympathetic sounds. The days of hushing up deaths and maimings of workers were gone or going fast. A hurt man meant coin paid out for no work, and hard questions in the guildhall—or harder questions from the Watch.

"Boards broke and spilled him off works that had got all twisted the night before and near-fallen into Redcloak Lane."

"Wasn't that Marlus and his crew?" Lhamphur asked disbelievingly. "I thought he was one of the best—"

"He is. A pack of noble pups at play set their swords on him and his hammer-hands, and started fires, too! One scaffold came right down, but this second one they hauled back into place and braced, and I hardly blame them. But for the whim and grace of Tymora, and the Watch happening along in a timely manner *for once*, the whole place would have burned!"

There were gasps and whistles at that, and more than one man reached for a decanter.

"As you know," Dyre went on, his voice on the edge of a snarl, "this is hardly our first brush with Waterdhavian nobility."

Lhamphur pursed his lips. "They walked free?"

"They did. The Watch gave them cold words but let them go. Utterly unpunished. One of them made noises about restitution, and that was the end of it."

Whaelshod shook his head. "They've got to be stopped," he growled, and heads nodded around the room.

Dyre's was one of them, as the grim beginnings of a smile crept onto his face. Two seasons back, some idiot nobles had taken it into their heads that racing each other on their most wild-spirited horses from the Court of the White Bull to the South Gate was a daringly sporting thing to do. The fastest way out of the Court was down Salabar Street, and Whaelshod's Wagons stood on west-front Salabar. Everyone knew Jarago Whaelshod had lost beasts and harness and had one man injured.

"I don't know how prudent 'twould be to complain about it, though," Lhamphur said slowly, twirling his jack in his hands.

Dyre suppressed a knowing smile. Nobles bought the elaborate and expensive gates crafted by Master Smith Karrak Lhamphur, and nobles paid the highest coin for copies of keys made with utter discretion, which half the city knew to be Lhamphur's special skill and greatest source of income.

Instead of sneering, Dyre nodded. "Right you are, Karrak. We've complained before and gotten nowhere. I'm through complaining."

All of his guests looked up sharply. This time, Varandros Dyre *did* smile.

"Something must be done," he told them. "And mark me: this time, something *will* be done."

The proprietor of Ghaunt Thatching, normally Dyre's smiling and enthusiastically tail-wagging follower, frowned at his friend a little doubtfully. "Uhmm . . . Var? What d'you mean?"

Varandros Dyre sat back, regarded his guests over the large and battered ruin of his nose, drew in a deep breath, and began.

"Waterdeep's a city of coins, hard work, and the rise and fall of trade. How is it that we who sweat and strain for every last nib and shard suffer the antics of idle young men who ruin property and harm hard workers and *cost us all coin?*"

His voice had sharpened to match the fire in his eyes. Dyre drew himself up as firmly as Mount Waterdeep and answered himself. "Because we know speaking up or seeking justice is a waste of time and marks us as men to be hurt, ruined, or driven out of the city. Why? Because, deep down, we know the Masked Lords, who purportedly rule us all in fairness and *supposedly* number among their ranks many dungsweepers and humble crafters from Trades Ward garrets as well as master merchants and the occasional noble, are in truth *all* nobles or powerful mages! The Lords keep the city safe and firm-ruled and orderly not for the common weal but to guard the power they have—and they suffer none to rise and challenge it! The tales of humble folk wearing the Masks of Lordship are mere fancies intended to accomplish just one thing: to keep any Waterdhavian not nobly born from rising up against the rule of the Lords!"

He leaned forward again, eyes blazing. "Now, I've no more interest in ruling Waterdeep than the rest of you, but I have had it up to *here*—" He slashed one hand across his throat. "—with standing idly by, swallowing my lost coins and trying to smile into the foolish young faces of those who openly despise and ridicule us because of the names they happen to have been born with, while this goes on and on, and we await a *real* disaster! City blocks set aflame, scaffoldings falling with scores of good men on them . . . as our taxes rise year by year, those who're driven beyond prudent silence are savagely put down—"

There were grim nods across the room, as everyone remembered Thalamandar Master-of-Baldrics, and the body of Lhendrar the weaver being fished out of the harbor, and . . .

"—and the nobles grow more and more reckless and steeped in their depravities, as they jeer at us from behind the wall of faceless Lords! How many of them wear the Masks of Lords? *How many?*"

"True," Imdrael muttered, "all true, and said before, by many of us, even without . . ." He held up his jack in salute, to indicate the fine wine it held.

"True," Lhamphur echoed, "and to my mind almost all the Lords are probably nobles, yet pointing fingers at rot and corruption is one thing, and doing something about it is another. The doing is what can get us all killed."

"So what," Jaeger Whaelshod asked heavily, as if Lhamphur's words had been an actor's cue, "d'you want of us, Var?"

The Shark looked across his gleaming desk at them, juggling something in his large-fingered hands. Almost lazily, he tossed that something into the air.

It flashed back the light of the candle-lamps as it came. The merchants holding their jacks of wine, men of Waterdeep all, drew sharply back from what they saw in an instant was battle-steel, and let it bite deep into the table not far in front of Karrak Lhamphur and stand there quivering.

The weapon was a slender, finely made dagger with a curiously shaped pommel: a speartip topped by a star, bearing an ornate monogram on the sides of the spear blade.

"M . . . K," Lhamphur deciphered it frowningly. "Kothont."

"Dropped by one of them, in his haste to carve up Marlus," Dyre told them. "*They* don't hesitate to draw steel on *us.*"

The proprietor of Ghaunt Thatching had gone as pale as the linens his sisters were wont to hang across his balcony on Simples Street. Cradling his jack in trembling hands, he asked faintly, "But what do you want us to *do*, Var? Surely not—not—" He nodded at the dagger wordlessly, his meaning clear enough: *take up arms.*

Dyre smiled and shook his head. "Nothing so drastic. I want us to work together, friends, to make a new day dawn over Waterdeep. Let *us* be that 'New Day.' Not to butcher Lords, nor cause unrest in the streets, for how does that help hard-working merchants make coin? No, I've something simpler and fairer in mind: to make the folk of the streets demand, more and more loudly, until 'tis the Lords who'll have to agree to the changes we seek or draw their blades and show us all their true villainy."

Lhamphur looked very much like a man who had impatient oaths dancing ready on his tongue, but asked only, "*What* changes, Var?"

"I want the Masks to come off. Lords should vote openly, in front of anyone who wants to walk in off the street and watch, and I want the Lords to stand for election just like guildmasters—say, every ten summers."

Eyes narrowed, then brightened again.

"That's all?"

"But then everyone would know how they voted!"

"*Exactly.* Lords who rule unfairly, to fill their own purses, or to reward themselves and their rich noble friends, would have to answer to honest men."

Jarago Whaelshod set down his jack very carefully and announced, "That, friend Dyre, is a New Day I'll work to bring about."

"Aye! Me, too!"

"*Yes!*" Ghaunt shouted, coming to his feet for an instant before realizing how loudly he'd bellowed and freezing into silence, as stiff as the monument on a paladin's tomb.

"Oh, sit down," Dyre told him irritably. "There's no harm done, for there's none as can hear us here."

⚜ ⚜ ⚜ ⚜ ⚜

In the forehall at the bottom of the stairs, a slender hand deftly unhooked the alarm-cord. Three pairs of hastily bared feet ascended a few steps, and three heads bent nearer still, so as not to miss a single word from the locked room above.

Muttering an apology, Hasmur Ghaunt hastily sat down again, almost toppling a decanter.

Imdrael shot him a look of contempt and asked Dyre in a low, eager murmur, "So what will we of the New Day do, exactly?"

"Are you with me?" Dyre asked, just as eagerly. "Each and every one of you? Guild oath?"

His four guests almost fell over each other's tongues giving their emphatic oaths, two of them nicking palms and slapping down blood onto the table in the manner of their guilds. Decanters danced, and Dyre's smile grew.

"You know the Lords control the very sewers beneath our feet?"

Every Waterdhavian knew that, and the four merchants said so.

"Wherever the sewers don't run just to suit them in their spying and rushing bands of thugs here and there by night to silence unruly commoners, they cause passages to be dug. As a Master Stoneworker, I see much of the ways beneath the cobbles, and I swear to you: this is truth."

Four heads nodded—and from somewhere below came the sharp creak of a board, as if someone was on the stairs.

Five heads turned with frowns of alarm to listen intently.

And heard only silence.

The stillness stretched until Dyre stirred and muttered warningly, "For the words we've traded here this night, *we* could be the next unruly commoners to be silenced, so—"

"We must protect ourselves!" Imdrael hissed.

The Master Stoneworker smiled thinly. "I've already started doing precisely that."

From below came the hollow boom of the door-knocker. The men of the New Day flinched in unison, grabbing hastily for daggers.

"Dyre," Lhamphur snarled through suddenly streaming sweat, "if this is some sort of trap—"

The Shark flung the door wide, peered down the stairs, and turned back to his guests with a smile.

"Alarm-cord still stretched, door still closed, and—hear that giggling?—my gels at the door outside, with hot platters of something to make us all a little less fearful! Men, 'tis time to talk of the new buildings we'll raise together before the season's out, and those we must repair before they topple! No New Day talk around the ladies, mind!"

"We're not fools, Dyre," Whaelshod muttered under his breath.

"Oh, no?" Lhamphur whispered, his own knuckles white on the hilt of his still-sheathed dagger. "Let's hope not, or the heads that roll won't be the ones wearing the masks of the Lords of Waterdeep."

♠ ♠ ♠ ♠ ♠

You must find him, Piergeiron had said. *From what I've seen this day, I'm certain any father would rejoice in such a son.*

The First Lord's words echoed in Mrelder's mind, mocking him with the hope he'd cherished for more than a year. The *false* hope.

He knew. He had yet to open his eyes, but he knew the graft had been a failure.

There was a dull, phantom ache where his left arm had been. If the gods had granted Golskyn's prayers and found Mrelder a worthy host, he would now be aflame with searing pain. Not lightly did the monstrous gods award their favors.

A faint, unfriendly hiss came from somewhere beside him. Then another, slightly fainter.

Mrelder fought his way up through the darkness. As lantern-light flared before his eyes, he turned his head toward the hissings.

The dying sahuagin lay on a table beside him, its gills flaring weakly as it gasped out its last breaths. A foul scent came from the charred, blackened stumps that were all that remained of not one, but all four of its scaled arms.

Four times had the followers of Lord Unity attempted the graft, and four times Mrelder's body had refused to accept the gods-given improvement.

"My son lives," Golskyn said coldly, looming over Mrelder, "and the sahuagin dies." His tone left little doubt as to his opinion of this state of affairs.

"I ... I'm sorry," Mrelder managed to murmur.

"My sentiments precisely," his father replied, each word burning like acid. He drew a long dagger from its belt-sheath. "The mongrelmen follow me because I tell them they are *more,* not less. They enjoy the special favor of the True Gods. They are already well along the path only the strong may take. *They* are my children. I need no other."

Golskyn lifted the knife high.

This was it. His father's patience was at an end. Forlorn dreams and schemes flooded Mrelder's mind, a storm-flow of regret and loss. All would fade with him, thrown away in this dark cellar, all ...

One idea caught in the rush of thoughts, looming rather than being swept on. A moment later, it was joined by another—and fresh hope, as Mrelder realized the two notions could become one: the sahuagin-shaped Walking Statue and the Guardian's Gorget.

"There's another way," he gasped.

"To end your worthless life?"

"To gain the strength of mighty creatures!" Mrelder gasped excitedly, seeing it all now.

The priest's uncovered eye narrowed. "Explain."

Mrelder nodded, but the words he needed would not come. As his stupor faded, the pain came in waves. He reached across to the other table to pluck away a strip of the dying sahuagin's scales from one of its stumps. Holding up the ribbon of hide, he managed a single word: "Gorget."

For a long moment Mrelder prayed to any gods who might be listening that his father would remember the letters he'd written about Piergeiron and the Walking Statues, wherein he'd told

Golskyn about this wondrous magical piece of the First Lord's armor, enspelled to command the great constructs.

Golskyn lowered the knife. His uncovered eye regarded his son thoughtfully. "This has possibilities. *You* can do this? With your . . . sorcery?"

Mrelder nodded. Perhaps he could prove to Golskyn that magic and items that held it were worthy sources of power, and in doing so earn his father's respect.

And, not incidentally, save his own life.

CHAPTER FOUR

Naoni Dyre sang softly to herself as she spun the last few chips of amethyst into shining purple thread.

A hole in the kitchen doorframe held her distaff: a long-handled runcible spoon, both ladle and fork. Instead of wool or flax, it held a steadily diminishing pile of rough amethysts. Delicate purple fibers spilled between its narrow tines in a curtain of gossamer purple that drew down into a triangle. At the point of that triangle Naoni's deft, pale fingers were busily at work, drafting the fibers together and easing them onto the shaft of her spindle.

It was a simple drop spindle, a round, smooth stick ending in a flat wooden wheel and hung suspended by the fine purple thread. As it spun, its weight pulled the fibers from the gemstones, and the thread collected in a widening cone atop the wooden wheel.

It was no small skill, keeping the spindle moving at the perfect speed—not so fast that it broke the delicate thread nor so slow that it fell to the floor. To Naoni, the rhythm was as natural as breathing.

When the last of the gems slipped into thread, Naoni eased the spindle to the floor. She didn't fear a fall might shatter her work. Anything she spun became as strong and flexible as silk, for Naoni Dyre was a minor sorceress.

Hmmph. Minor indeed. The ability to spin nearly anything into thread was her lone gift.

"You, dear sister, need a spinning wheel."

A fond smile lit Naoni's face as she turned to greet Faendra. Her younger sister was the very image of their dead mother: a petite and pretty strawberry blonde, plump in all the right places, with blue, blue eyes that promised sunny afternoons, and a pert little nose that matched a smile that was never far from her lips.

"Spinning wheels are far too dear. What would Father say about such expense?" Naoni asked mildly.

Faendra propped fists on hips and thrust forth her chin in imitation of their father's manner. "Buy a proper wheel, girl, and stop spinning thread like a Calishite slave! Good tools will triple your coins, or may Waukeen damn me to the poorhouse," she growled, in tones as deep and gruff as she could manage.

They laughed together, but Naoni's mirth quickly faded to a sigh. Her father knew she spun and earned fair coin, but dismissed attempted talk about her work with a brusque, "What's yours is yours." He was far more interested in her ability to run the household with frugal efficiency.

"Perhaps it's time to consider a wheel," she said. "Jacintha would be pleased to have more gem thread."

Faendra eyed the glittering skeins carefully laid out on the sideboard. "What wouldn't I give for a gown of Jacintha's gemsilk!" she said wistfully. "Perhaps this time the gnome could pay you in cloth?"

"Little chance of that; most of gemsilk's value is the gems, not the labor."

The younger girl sniffed. "Oh? Who else can spin such thread?"

"I know of none other," Naoni admitted, "nor know I another weaver who has Jacintha's gift for weaving many sources together into cloth. If not for her, how would I have gems to weave? We're fortunate to have found each other; I've no quarrel with our arrangement."

"So be it," Faendra said lightly. "How soon can we be in the Warrens?"

"We can leave as soon as I finish this last skein." Naoni picked up a niddy-noddy, a simple wooden frame of three sticks, and began to wind the thread around it.

"*Niddy niddy noddy, two heads with one body,*" Faendra chanted, grinning. "You taught me that rhyme when you made your first frame. How old was I then, I wonder?"

"Seven winters," Naoni said softly. She'd begun spinning the year their mother died, leaving her, a lass of twelve winters, to run the household and raise a frolicsome little sister.

Her swift hands made short work of the winding. "If you'll summon Lark, we can leave."

"I'm here," announced a low-pitched voice.

The young woman who emerged from the buttery resembled her namesake: small, trim, and as brown as a meadow bird. Her long hair was gathered back into a single braid, and she wore a brown kirtle over a plain linen shift. A green ribbon bound her brows to hold back stray wisps of hair, and its two ends had been laced into her braid. A matching sash was tied around one of her bared arms. Her nose was perhaps too narrow and a bit overlong, and her bright brown eyes disconcertingly keen, but she was pleasant enough to look upon.

Naoni gave her a tentative smile. Her father, in keeping with their new-found affluence, had insisted they hire a servant, but his elder daughter was still not sure how a mistress should treat a hired lass.

Her sister had no such worries. To Faendra, every stranger was a friend yet unmet, and any girl living under her roof as good as a sister. She picked up a skein of glittering purple and draped it around Lark's shoulders.

"What say you? Wouldn't you love to wear a gemsilk gown?"

Lark carefully lifted the skein and set it aside. "For my work, in this heat? It'd be as wet as washrags by highsun."

"Don't be goose-witted. You wear such gowns to noble revels, not for cheesemaking!"

"I've been to many such," Lark replied, in a tone that implied her memories of revels were neither fond nor impressive.

"To serve, yes, but not on the arm of some handsome, wealthy young man!"

Lark's lips thinned. "I know my place and want no other."

"Let's wrap and bundle the skeins," Naoni said hastily. They all got on well enough, but Lark had little patience for Faendra's thinking: beauty was its own guild, and the business of its members was to charm all the world into doing their will.

Faendra gave her sister a sunny smile. "I'll just change my gown and freshen my hair." She danced out of the room, humming.

"She'll not reappear until the task is done," Lark murmured.

True enough, but such truths would sit ill with the master of the household. "My father would not like to hear it said that any Dyre shirks work," Naoni observed carefully.

"Then I'll say instead both Dyre sisters are willing workers," Lark replied dryly. "Naoni's willing to work—and Faendra's willing to let her."

Naoni smiled faintly, shook her head, and wrapped linen over her basket. "That's the last of it. It seems strange so much thread can be woven from a handful of gems."

"Stranger still you can do it at all."

Faendra reappeared, twirling to show off her new blue gown and slippers dyed to match. The bodice was fashionably tight, the sleeves thrice-puffed and slashed to best display her rounded, rosy arms, and the slim skirt hugged her hips and thighs before flaring out in a graceful sweep.

Naoni frowned, gray eyes stern. "You're dressed very fine for the Warrens. Is that wise?"

Her sister danced over to kiss Naoni on the tip of her nose and then spun away with a grin. "You worry overmuch. Let's be off!"

⛭ ⛭ ⛭ ⛭ ⛭

As the three girls made their way through Dock Ward, the streets were as crowded and bustling as usual, but no fights or spilled wagons drew crowds and slowed them. Even the everpresent handcarts were fewer and less precariously loaded than usual.

They were soon standing in a narrow alley that ended in a tangle of ramshackle buildings. Naoni tapped on a sagging door half-hidden behind a rotting pile of broken barrel-staves.

It swung open to flickering torchlight amid darkness and the familiar hard stares of a pair of halfling guards. Mostly hidden beyond the doorframe, they were dressed as human urchins, and their belts bore cheap, bright-painted leather scabbards. Despite their childish, harmless appearance, those scabbards held swords that were very real and very sharp.

"A fine afternoon to you both," Naoni said, hefting her covered basket. "I've business with Jacintha."

The guards nodded and silently drew back to let her pass. The three girls ducked inside, and Lark spread her hands, palms up, to show she bore no weapons.

"You, too," one hin said in a surprisingly gruff voice, nodding at Faendra. "Palms, pretty one?"

The younger Dyre sister rolled her eyes and held her arms out wide as if to ask "And where might I be hiding anything in this gown?"

The guard nodded, and the door was already being thrust closed behind them as Naoni handed the basket to Lark and took a torch from the guards' barrel. Lighting it from their wall-torch, she started along the tunnel.

The smell of damp stone arose strongly around the three, and they took care not to brush against the walls. The Warrens was one of Waterdeep's lesser-known neighborhoods. It had been centuries in the making, beginning with stone houses built along hilly streets. Betimes a higher floor would be added here, or a walkway built across a street from house to house there, and with the passing years stretches of streets were completely hidden from the sun, and many lowest floors became cellars. Rebuilding shored up the lower levels and worked upward from there, and beneath a few blocks of bustling Waterdeep, the slow result of this tireless reaching for the grander was a forgotten layer.

Many Small Folk dwelt here. Gnomes, halflings, and even the occasional dwarf found a congenial and discreet address amid the dark cellars and narrow tunnels of the Warrens.

The lasses passed several gnomes coming the other way, and polite nods were exchanged. Jacintha was so highly regarded that Naoni, by association, was counted among their own.

Soon they reached a familiar arched door. Twice as wide as it was tall, it stood open, letting out a rhythmic, slightly ragged clatter to echo in the tunnel.

A soft clack and sweep filled the room, swelling around the three lasses as they entered. Half a dozen looms clattered busily in the low-vaulted stone hall, but one slowed smoothly as the weaving-mistress left off her work and bustled over with a smile of welcome.

Jacintha was, as usual, too busy for additional pleasantries, taking the basket from Lark without pause to unwrap the skeins and hold them up into the lantern light.

She stared hard and nodded. "Fine, very fine."

Faendra had already wandered over to Jacintha's loom, which bore a silky, almost translucent amber fabric. Woven into it was a pattern of dragonflies with brilliant, glittering wings.

"How's this done?" she marveled, peering closely. "Many colors ... but *all* the threads, warp and weft, seem of one ..."

"And are," the gnome said briskly, "made from your sister's amber thread and silk I dyed to match. One drop of amber had a dragonfly trapped in it, as I recall. The pattern's none of my doing; it came of itself as I was weaving. 'Tis a pretty thing."

"Indeed it is," Faendra said longingly. Something brighter caught her eye. "What of *this?*" she asked, waving at a nearby glittering swath of red cloth.

The gnome smirked. "That'll become a nobleman's evening cloak. Take two paces to your left and gaze on it, letting your eyes lose focus."

Faendra did as she was bid, and after a moment burst out laughing. "There's a pattern: a male peacock, all a-strut!"

"Fitting for those who wear such things," Jacintha observed dryly, "and fitting amusement to those of us who don't."

She unstrung a pouch from her belt and handed it to Naoni. "Your coins are on one side, and the next gems to be spun on t'other. Peridot, a very fine pale green."

"That hue would suit Naoni, with her hair and eyes," hinted Faendra.

Her gaze slid to a bolt of shimmering blue that matched her own eyes, then moved to the pouch holding Naoni's payment, her meaning all too clear.

Naoni looked up from examining the gems to give her sister a warning glance. "A lovely green," she told Jacintha. "I'll enjoy spinning it."

It was the way of gnomes to remember faults, longings, and other weaknesses for future bargaining. Before Faendra could say anything else, her elder sister made swift work of the farewells and hustled her companions back out of the Warrens.

⚒ ⚒ ⚒ ⚒ ⚒

As Father expected her to know the sites where Dyre money or men were at work, Naoni led them up Redcloak Lane to check on the recent damage.

One entire run of scaffolding was a near-ruin. Faendra surveyed the bustling workmen and murmured, "I begin to see why Father was so a-fret."

Naoni frowned. "Even so, I dislike this talk of New Days and challenges to the Lords."

"Old men's foolishness," her sister said cheerfully, putting a lilt to her hips for the benefit of the watching laborers.

"Such talk's nothing new," Lark observed. "Common folk have always complained about nobles, and rumors about the Lords are as old as Mount Waterdeep itself."

Naoni nodded. "The Lords know their own work best."

Lark made a sound that was suspiciously like a sniff. "Some may be good, fine men behind those masks, but I'll warrant most of them are no better than they have to be. Still, Waterdeep goes along well enough, and I'd just as soon not shave the dog to spite its fleas."

"Perhaps Father wants to *be* a Lord," Faendra put in lightly. "I suppose many might be unhappy that Waterdeep's governed in secret, for how can they rise in power and influence unless they can see the path ahead?"

Naoni winced. Despite her frivolities, her sister saw people with disturbing clarity. Sudden fear rose in her: did Faendra know their mother's secret?

No, that was impossible, surely! Naoni had hidden those letters and journals *very* carefully. And well she had! In his current temper, Father needed no reminders of Ilyndeira Dyre's sad taste of Waterdhavian nobility.

Redcloak Lane was behind them now, and Faendra had strolled into a smaller crossway than Naoni would have chosen.

They almost brushed shoulders with a cluster of dockers arguing heatedly over ownership of a battered crate in their midst.

Naoni was only six or seven strides past the men when a realization struck her with a sudden chill.

The argument had fallen silent.

She glanced back. One man was only a few paces behind her, moving very quickly and quietly.

He gave her a grin that might have been charming if he'd still possessed most of his teeth. "What's in the pouch, pretty one? Let's have a look."

Naoni's heart started to pound. All six of the others were right behind the foremost one. Before she could cry out to Faendra and Lark, the men charged at her, and knives flashed in their hands.

🛡️ 🛡️ 🛡️ 🛡️ 🛡️

"That dagger was my favorite—or rather, the two of them were." Malark held out his hands: one empty, the other holding a dagger with an elaborate Kothont monogram. "Superbly balanced, very fine steel, and a matched pair. I'll have it back, and damn the cost."

Taeros grinned mockingly. "I'd wish you luck, but you'll need the kiss of Tymora herself to find it. By now your fang's probably been buried in several hearts—"

"All at once?" inquired Korvaun Helmfast, with a gentle smile.

"—in rapid succession," Taeros continued, "and thereafter sent to the bottom of the harbor, still hilt-deep in its last victim!"

"*You,*" Beldar growled, "spin too many wild tales. Malark

has the way of it. Someone at the worksite picked up his dagger, and will doubtless require some . . . persuasion to relinquish his prize."

"If we employ discretion, perhaps we could settle this with less 'persuasion,'" Korvaun said. "If we keep our tempers and guard our tongues, this could be easily resolved."

"Have you a temper to keep?" Taeros asked with mock incredulity. "I've seen no evidence of it."

Korvaun shrugged. "We won't learn if the workmen found Malark's dagger if we arrive with accusations and demands, but we might well start a small riot."

"Speaking of small riots," Malark interrupted urgently, "*look!*"

Three young women were running frantically toward them, with several rough-looking men pounding along hard on their heels.

Beldar's disgruntlement changed to dark glee as his sword sang out of its scabbard.

Malark ducked deftly aside to avoid getting cut, drew his own blade, and started down the alley toward the girls.

Beldar sprinted past him, eyes afire. "Gemcloaks!" he shouted as he went, Korvaun and Malark right at his heels. "The Gemcloaks are upon you!"

Which is when, of course, Taeros tripped on a loose cobble and fell on his face amid a swirl of amber.

Fortunate was the hero, he observed wryly, who writes his own story. If ever this tale were told, Taeros Hawkwinter would be foremost among the fair maidens' defenders. Until then, he'd have to acquit himself as best he could.

He picked himself up, drew his sword, and charged after his more nimble friends.

🦇 🦇 🦇 🦇 🦇

Hard fingers raked down Naoni's back, then snatched at her hair. Desperately she jerked her head away, clenching her teeth against the burst of pain as tresses tore.

She stumbled and almost went down, but a glimpse of Faendra's wide-eyed terror gave her new speed. She caught her sister's hand and pulled her along. Lark was several paces ahead, running like a rabbit. Then, suddenly, there were men with drawn swords shouting and running *toward* them, too!

"Oh, Lady Luck!" Naoni gasped, as a heavy hand fell on her shoulder and dragged her down. "Be with my Faen . . ."

She struck the cobbles, hard. The pouch at her belt slammed into her midriff, leaving her no breath at all. Writhing and sobbing, she looked frantically about for her sister.

There! Somehow Faendra had slipped past the onrushing men and was nearly to the main street. She'd be safe there.

Relief swept through Naoni. She was dimly aware of rough hands clawing at her belt and her hand, where it was clutching the heavy little bag. Her attacker was snarling promises of what he'd do to her if she didn't yield it up right quick, and—

Suddenly he was gone. A bloodstained cobblestone rolled past Naoni's hair-tangled gaze, and she saw a determined-looking Lark reaching down for another.

A man with a long, gleaming sword in his hand and a red cloak flapping—a cloak made of Jacintha's gem-fabric, woven from *her* thread!—sprang past Lark, soaring right over Naoni in a leap that snatched him from view.

"Have at you, miscreants!" a cultured voice rang out.

Naoni rolled out of the way of Red Cloak's companions. As she came up to her knees, she caught sight of one of the halfling guards from the Warrens. He winked at her as he darted past, a blur of dusty gray, to hamstring one of the ruffians.

The man screamed and went down, and his fellow behind him went pale and staggered hastily back out of the way as a second grandly garbed man sprang past Naoni, blue cloak swirling and blade flashing.

The thieves brandished knives and muttered curses as they hastily retreated. One fell heavily, tripping the man behind him. Naoni saw a leather thong slide out from behind his ankle, and the two halflings responsible for tripping him vanish behind the tangle of frantically struggling arms and dirty, hairy legs.

These must be guardians, sent by Jacintha to tail her home. She'd often been assured the Small Folk protected their own, but this was the first time she'd caught them at their work.

"Run, lowlife scum!" exulted one of their sword-waving rescuers, a red-bearded young giant in a green gemcloak with, oddly enough, a Moonshar accent. "Bested with barely a slash of my steel!"

"They weren't all that good at standing, let alone fighting," observed a dark-haired youth whose cultured tones were heavily laced with sarcasm. "No, Beldar, let them go. I believe we can trust the Watch to find *crawling* men."

Nobles. These must be nobles. Who else would speak of Watchmen with such weary disdain? Plenty of crafters and dockers hated the Watch, but Naoni had never heard them dismissed with *amusement* before.

A sword slid back into its sheath, and firm but gentle fingers were under Naoni's elbows, lifting her. She looked up into a handsome face framed by fair, short-shorn hair. The man's eyes were blue and kind, full of concern . . . and something more.

It took Naoni a moment to recognize that "something more" as the sort of look commonly directed at pretty Faendra.

"Are you hurt, my lady?"

She considered this, and the man's lips twitched.

"Had I asked how your companions fared, you'd have a ready answer," he said quietly. "In the midst of danger, you spared no thought for yourself."

"Well, there wasn't time, you see," she said lamely.

He smiled, not in mockery, but with genuine warmth, and beyond him, Naoni caught sight of a rising cobblestone, clenched in familiar work-reddened fingers.

"Lark, *no!*" she cried.

The man whirled, blue cloak swirling. Lark stepped deftly back and tossed her weapon down.

"My . . . yon goodwoman means no harm," Naoni said urgently, putting a staying hand on the man's sword arm.

"Oho!" the red-bearded man grinned knowingly, as the nobles gathered around.

She snatched her hand away. Her pouch might be heavy enough to tempt even these young blades—and didn't such highnoses come to Dock Ward to sport with lowborn lasses? Would the refusal of a damsel they'd just rescued be heeded?

Her younger sister was wandering back, pretty face cat-curious. Fear choked Naoni. Not Faendra! Never that!

"Lark meant no harm," she repeated hastily. "Can you say as much?"

"Aye," the fair-haired man told her firmly. "Korvaun's my name—Lord Korvaun Helmfast—and despite what some say about the habits of the nobility, I'm not in the habit of attacking women in the street."

"He speaks for himself," the red-bearded man said cheerfully, giving Faendra a good-natured wink.

Naoni's heart sank at the delight in her sister's face. Faen might have their mother's beauty, but that didn't mean she had to repeat Mother's mistakes!

The sardonic man sighed. "Malark, not *now!* Save the jests for ladies not so unsettled. Ah, forgive me: I am Lord Taeros Hawkwinter, this buffoon is Lord Malark Kothont, and our foremost battle-blade yonder is Lord Beldar Roaringhorn. Usually his tongue is as swift as his sword, but just now he seems at a most uncharacteristic lack for words. Collectively we're the Gemcloaks for, hem, obvious reasons. Are you unhurt?"

Naoni nodded, alarm fading. "Bruised, perhaps. They took nothing." She managed a smile. "I'm Naoni Dyre. This is my sister Faendra, and our servant Lark."

Faendra pointed at Naoni, her eyes bright. "*She* spun the gems that went into the cloaks you're wearing."

The one called Beldar frowned. "Crafters?"

"Lord Roaringhorn," Lark said, her voice like acid, "you seem surprised to learn we're respectable women."

The leader of the Gemcloaks reddened at her rebuke. "Forgive me, mistresses, but what do you hereabouts? *These* streets are no place for—"

"Folk who must go where their work takes them?" Lark's voice and gaze were now positively glacial. "What would *you* know of work?"

Beldar and Lark locked gazes. What passed between them only they knew, but it looked profoundly unpleasant. Naoni winced.

Gods above, we should be *thanking* these men, not insulting them! They seem pleasant enough, but they're nobles—and who knows what such grand folk might do if they take offense?

"We just came from one of my father's worksites," she said hastily. "It was badly damaged by some bold blades playing pranks."

The four nobles exchanged uneasy looks.

The one called Malark frowned. "Stands this, ah, site on Redcloak Lane?"

"It does."

Four throats were cleared in unison. "Good ladies," Lord Roaringhorn said stiffly, "you're probably not going to like these next words of mine well . . ."

"*That's* a certainty," Lark said under her breath, causing Faendra to giggle and Malark to grin.

Naoni sent both girls a quelling look and turned it into a warning frown when Malark offered his arm to Faendra. Ignoring her, Faendra slipped her hand into the crook of Lord Kothont's arm with an easy grace that suggested long practice in front of a mirror.

"Mistress Naoni," Korvaun Helmfast murmured gravely as he took her hand in both of his, "will you suffer our protection as you take us to your father? Those ruffians are not the only dangers in Dock Ward."

"Ah, of course, but why take you such an interest in us?" Then, belatedly, "My father?"

"Mistress," Lark said crisply, "these four fine noblemen are obviously responsible for the worksite damage. *And*, being men of honor, they're planning to make restitution. Isn't that so, Lord Roaringhorn?"

"It is," Beldar said stiffly.

"Then my two lady mistresses here will be happy to take you to the man you wish to see. No," she corrected herself, "the man you *need* to see. No one *wishes* to see Master Dyre in his present mood, but ... the gods don't always grant wishes." She looked at Naoni. "Does that cover it, mistress?"

"It does," she agreed absently. "Most thoroughly."

Lark firmly took Lord Hawkwinter's arm, leaving Beldar with no partner, and gave him a glare. "Have a care where you walk, Lord Roaringhorn. It would be a shame to spoil those fine boots."

Naoni opened her mouth to order Lark into silence, but the words stuck in her throat. The girl's loyalty meant much, and her judgment could hardly be faulted. Everything Naoni knew warned her to distrust these noblemen—even kindly Lord Helmfast.

She glanced up at his handsome face, and something leaped inside her.

Especially Korvaun Helmfast.

⚔ ⚔ ⚔ ⚔ ⚔

Varandros Dyre reached his front door as the third imperious volley of rapping began. Even before its sharp thunder befell, he was scowling.

Someone was ignoring a perfectly good bellpull and striking his knocker-plate with hard metal.

The Master Stonemason shook the old sword that lived in the stave-stand beside the door out of its sheath and kept one hand near it as he shot the bolts. He didn't take the blade into his hand to heft meaningfully lest the rapping—now crack-crack-cracking on his good door *again*, by Tempus!—prove to be the Watch.

Dyre swung the stout door wide and stood back, his hand hovering by his blade, and saw what waited beyond his threshold.

His eyes flashed even before his mouth dropped open.

His daughters stood outside with the housemaid and a seeming *army* of smiling, fashionably garbed young men. There was color in everyone's cheeks, and hair askew, and faces that looked as if they'd been laughing and were holding back mirth even now!

And looming right in front of him, in the elegantly gloved hand of one of these laughing young pups, was a dagger, reversed and raised to strike his knocker-plate once more.

It was the twin of the one he'd found at the worksite, monogram and all.

Dyre raised a hand sharply, cutting off Faendra's excited flood of explanation of how their lives had been so bravely *saved*, by these very—

"Enough, daughter. I'll be having a word with these . . . gentle-sirs," he growled at her, his fierce gaze brooking no argument.

Fire to match his own kindled briefly in those blue eyes—not for nothing was her name Dyre!—but Naoni placed a quelling hand on her sister's shoulder. Her gray eyes fixed on him in some sort of mute appeal. Before she could speak, the maid deftly herded both girls back from the doors and drew them firmly down the hall.

Dyre gave a curt nod of approval. Lark's wages were well spent; she at least had sense. Though in truth, he cared not if his daughters heard every word. Might be better for them if they did.

Varandros Dyre turned his back on the young nobles and strode around behind his desk to stand regarding them across its large, parchment-littered expanse. His gaze was not friendly.

Taeros saw Beldar looking askance at the untidy papers. So did the master of Dyre's Fine Walls and Dwellings.

"You seem unused to the litter of honest toil," Dyre said coldly. "Might I remind you that some of us in this fair city must work hard to *keep* Waterdeep fair?"

Shrewd eyes and ears weren't needed to conclude that the stonemason was simmering with rage, and Taeros raised a hand in a warning gesture to his fellows.

"It seems you protected my daughters and my maid, and I owe you the thanks any father must tender. Please accept it." Dyre did not trouble to make that 'please' anything but a command, and swept straight on.

"You must forgive me if I have some suspicions as to why such grand young lords, free in idleness to pursue any amusement that might occur to them and range freely from end to end of great Waterdeep, come to be in the vicinity of a certain worksite in the heart of highly unfashionable *Dock* Ward—a worksite that a band of young lordlings recently reduced to a shambles! In doing so, it seems they also found it *amusing* to sword honest workers, to say nothing of setting fires that might well have devastated more than a street or two of fair Waterdeep."

Dyre's words came out cold, clipped, and inexorable, like measured lash-blows. "And so damaging a scaffold that *another* worker fell from it this morn: a man who'll be maimed for life if healings fail."

Taeros saw his own guilt mirrored on his friends' faces. Before any of them could find the right words, Dyre planted his large hands on his desk, leaned forward with his eyes ablaze, and asked softly, "Now, would any of you know anything about this?"

Despite the desk, his shorter stature, and several paces of floor between them, the stonemason seemed to loom over the younger men.

Taeros swallowed. "Master Dyre, goodsir, I assure you, we'll ..."

The Mason Stonemason looked directly at him, and under the sudden fierce fire of his gaze and its comical juxtaposition with that huge snout of a nose, the Hawkwinter's mouth went dry.

"Sir," Malark said swiftly, "of course we'll make amends!"

"Of course," Beldar added grandly, reaching for his purse. "I am—"

"I *know* who you are, Lord Roaringhorn," Dyre said with a snarl, "and I know you'll pay for all you've done. I'll have the Black Robes make sure of that, whatever *your* intentions. I know our laws, which is why I'm not taking a blade to all of you, right now, and ending your foolishness for good! Waterdeep had more than enough of the haughty vandalism of Waterdhavian nobility *years* ago."

He drew himself up, becoming, if possible, even more imposing.

"I shall expect all of you to keep well away from my daughters henceforth, which should prove easy for you, my lords, because *they* spend their days in honest work. You have your grand houses to sport in, to say nothing of clubs my *lowborn* girls would not be allowed through the doors of, even if they had coins enough to waste."

The stonemason took a long breath and continued more calmly

but even more firmly, "My daughters will have to *earn* their places in Waterdhavian society, and I cannot think they'll be aided in achieving the station and success they deserve by consorting with ruffians, however nobly born, who amuse themselves by harming and beggaring others whenever they're not doing the dirty work of the Lords!"

Taeros blinked. Dirty work of the . . .?

The Gemcloaks scarcely had time to frown in puzzlement ere the Master Stoneworker came slowly around the edge of his desk, hands hanging loosely at his sides, ready for trouble.

"Nor am I alone in such views. I've friends among the guilds and shopkeepers who watch the antics of you and your like with far less than approval. Many eyes will have seen your arrival here, and tongues will wag as to why. A good part of the city—the working part—will be watching you lordlings very closely in days to come, to see if any 'accident' should befall me. Not because I am important, or for any love of me, but because time and again dissent has been quelled in Waterdeep through the silencing of overly loud critics, by accident after accident, and they won't stomach much more of it."

He took a step closer, and more than one noble hand drifted toward a swordhilt.

"So, my lords," Dyre added softly, his eyes still blazing, "let us understand each other very well. I will accept your apologies and your coins, and you will keep away from the women of my household, and take *very* great care that no further accidents befall me, Dyre's Fine Walls and Dwellings, or any of my worksites."

The stonemason's slow stalk forward brought him nose-to-chest with Beldar Roaringhorn, who said quietly, "Have done, goodsir. Your anger is understandable, but your slander of Waterdhavian nobility is both misplaced and repugnant. I—"

"Don't like to hear truth. Your sort never does. Right now the most important truth confronting you is this: I am a citizen of Waterdeep standing in my own house, and I'm far too angry to be prudent, so you'd best begone. *Now.* In due time my 'prentices will bring you an accounting, and you can send the coins back to me here."

Dyre pointed at the door, his hard gaze never leaving Beldar's eyes. Korvaun Helmfast moved to open it as swiftly and quietly as any servant.

Two young men stood just outside, their faces set and pale. Their matching tunics bore the stone-sprouting-a-fist badge of Dyre's Fine Walls and Dwellings. The stonemason's apprentices were clutching ready mattocks in their hands.

"Baraezym, Jivin," Varandros Dyre greeted them grimly. "Our guests are just departing. In peace, I trust. Mark their faces, for there may come a time when you'll need to know them."

The Gemcloaks had already begun to stride silently out, faces set, but Beldar turned his head sharply. "Goodman Dyre, just what do you mean by *that?*"

"I mean, lords," the Master Stonemason said flatly, "that a time will come when consequences can no longer be laughed away."

♦ ♦ ♦ ♦ ♦

Varandros Dyre watched, stone-faced, as the lordlings stalked away, fine cloaks swirling.

Then he whirled around so swiftly his apprentices jumped. Ignoring them, he peered around the hall for his daughters.

There was no sign of them, but the door to the kitchens was open, and the housemaid stood in it, steam curling from the covered serving platter in her hands. Her gaze was on the floor, and she was as still as a statue.

Dyre nodded approvingly. *Some* folk, at least, knew their places. He permitted himself a chuckle of satisfaction as he made the gesture that sent his apprentices hastening to close and bar the doors.

Lark kept her eyes down and wisely said nothing.

CHAPTER FIVE

'I don't understand." Faendra shook her red-gold curls in puzzlement as she thumped the dasher emphatically into the butter churn. "Father may be hard, but he's fair. It's not like him to condemn a man for the cut of his cloak."

Naoni glanced up from the piecrust she was crimping. "Father has no love for the noble houses. Best you remember that before you sigh over highnosed redbearded rogues."

"I'd much rather laugh than sigh, and Malark Kothont's a merry fellow. Though I suppose *some* girls," Faendra said slyly, "might prefer Korvaun Helmfast's golden hair and courtly manner."

Naoni felt her cheeks grow warm. Faendra's smile broadened into a grin, and Naoni hastened to speak of something else. "What if Father's right—if the Lords *are* all nobles and control the sewers *and* the thugs who lurk there? That puts Father's New Day squarely between the highest and the lowliest, and *that's* as dangerous as . . ."

"Pissing into lightning?" Lark suggested.

Naoni's chuckle was weak. "Father won't listen to us, and his friends are too cowed by his temper or dazzled by their New Day dreams. I—I don't know what to do."

"There's one who might," Lark said slowly, pushing the simmering stewpot back to a cooler spot on the stove and turning to face her mistresses. "Know you of Texter, the paladin?"

The Dyre girls exchanged glances, then shook their heads.

"He's that rarest of things: a good man. He . . . helped me, once." Lark's words came haltingly, not with her usual tart-tongued confidence. Naoni smiled encouragement.

"He travels, helping folk wherever he goes, seeking news of importance for Waterdeep. He speaks to the Lords."

The leisurely thumping of the butter churn halted abruptly as Faendra threw up her hands in exasperation. "Yes, of *course* we must tell him all! Let's bring the Lords right to Father's door and save them the trouble of discovering his foolishness on their own!"

"I said he speaks to the Lords," Lark said quietly. "Texter knows how to keep a secret. I trust him, and I can say that about no other man."

Naoni frowned. She'd never met a paladin, but everyone knew they were upright men, holy warriors who could not break their stern codes without losing the blessing of their god and their own powers into the bargain. Moreover, Lark had good sense, and never before had she spoken so well of any man.

"You can talk to this Texter, and he'll advise you?"

"He travels much, but messages can be got to him. There's a hidden place in the Westwind Villa in Sea Ward."

Faendra tugged off the soft gloves she wore to keep churning from roughening her hands. "I know that place! The great hall there can hold half the nobles in the city—and will, at a grand revel morrow-night!"

Naoni raised an eyebrow. "And you learned this *how?*"

Her sister grinned. "A tiny shop on Sails Street sells ladies' cast-offs; betimes I talk to the maids bringing the gowns in."

"Stolen?" Naoni demanded, aghast.

"Rest easy! Some high ladies give their old gowns to their maids—as if the girls have any place to wear them! Fine stuff, nevertheless, that can be pulled apart and made over. I'll show you."

Faendra flitted from the room and in short order returned, bearing an armful of rich green.

"Off with your kirtle and shift, Lark," she ordered. "The bodice is too slim-cut for me, but it should fit you well enough. It goes on thus, this side to the front."

The maid sighed but peeled off her clothes and reached for the dress. Sliding it on, she checked to make sure her ribbon was still in place around her left arm and looked inquiringly at Faendra. "Where's the rest of it?"

The younger Dyre sister laughed merrily as she came forward to tighten the side-lacings and smooth the neckline into place. "This is all there is! No sleeves, you see, and the back's *supposed* to be open to the waist. It fits the hips snugly, but the skirt will flare out full when you turn. 'Tis meant for dancing."

Naoni stared in wonderment. "This is your design, Faen? *Your* work?"

Her sister nodded happily. "I've always been handy with a needle, and making over a gown's more pleasant work than hemming linens. Giandra the dressmaker stocks ready clothes for ladies who haven't time to order them made. She's already bought two of my gowns and will happily take more."

Looking as surprised as Naoni, Lark started to slip off the gown.

"Wait!" Faendra commanded, clapping her hands excitedly. "You can wear this to the revel at Westwind! You can go as a grand lady, and leave your message for Texter!"

"I've a better idea," Lark said dryly. "I'll go to Sea Ward after my work here is done and ask at the Westwind if they're hiring extra servants. For the big revels, they usually do."

"Why be a servant when you can go as a lady?"

A stubborn expression crossed Lark's face. "I don't like pretending to be other than I am."

Naoni put a hand on Faendra's arm to still her, and said, "I quite agree, but I overheard Master Whaelshod talking with my father and learned the Westwind changed hands recently. It now belongs to Elaith Craulnober, a rather *sinister* elf better known to the city as 'the Serpent.' He's been away from Waterdeep for a few seasons."

She leaned forward and murmured, "Master Whaelshod said this elf had a secret partnership with Lady Thann. She died two moons past, and Craulnober's returned to sort out his affairs." Naoni looked from Lark to her sister. "Their ah, connection's not widely known; you'd do best to keep this quiet."

Faendra's eyes grew round. "I've heard about the Serpent. *This* is the company your paladin keeps?"

Lark shrugged. "Not from choice, I'll warrant. In Waterdeep a man may choose his friend, but not the Lords who rule."

"Surely not! You don't think . . ."

"As I said, some of the Lords are no better than they have to be. Mayhap the elf is among them; who can say? All I know is that someone in the Westwind can get messages to Texter, or perhaps my notes are carried by magic, untouched by any hands but Texter's and mine."

"You must wear the gown," Naoni said softly, "and attend as a noble lady from afar. You'll get in more easily with less scrutiny. Elaith Craulnober's far more likely to be particular about his servants than his guests."

The maid sniffed. "As he's inviting nobility, that goes without saying."

As he stepped out of the midst of the comforting bulk of the House Helmfast bodyguards, Korvaun Helmfast felt suddenly alone.

Mirt's Mansion loomed before him like a scowling fortress, all dark, stern stone save for a cascade of green to his right, where its gardens climbed a rocky shoulder of Mount Waterdeep.

Straight before Korvaun, down an avenue formed by two rows of rune-spangled warding pillars thrice his height, the mansion's grand stair began. At its head the moneylender's guards were waiting for him. Four of them, standing impassively in full plate armor, two on each side of the broad black double doors, heavy-gauntleted arms folded across their chests.

Korvaun raised one eyebrow at the motionless full-face helms above him—or rather, at the complete lack of eye slits or visor openings in those unbroken, gleaming metal ovals. How did they see? Or were they but statues?

Seabirds squawked in the none-too-fresh breeze coming off the harbor, and his eyebrow rose still farther. If they were statues, what kept the bird-dung off them?

He took a stride forward. As he did so, the guards moved too, gliding a step sideways and putting hands on swordhilts, all in precise unison and utter silence.

Ah. Illusions or helmed horrors. My, but moneylenders were doing well in Waterdeep, these days.

"So," he asked, taking another step, "is there a password?"

The doors emitted a gentle feminine chuckle . . . or no: there was a sudden, ghostly shimmering in the air just in front of the doors, and the silvery shadow of a tall, gracefully slender lady—for Korvaun had measured folk at a glance for years, and this woman could be no less than a lady—suddenly stood before him. He could see the four impassive guards through her, and in fact she was *protruding* through them. Korvaun watched tiny blue motes of light, like sparks turned the hue of moonlight, dance along the line where ghost-shadow met gleaming blue armor, and noticed her flowing gown did not ripple in response to the harbor breeze but to some other, unfelt wind of its own. A ghost wind.

"Well met, Lady Ghost Wind," he said, in as friendly and respectful a voice as he could manage. Thanks to several maiden aunts, Korvaun Helmfast could sound *very* respectful when he needed to. "My name is Korvaun Helmfast, and I seek audience with Mirt, commonly called the Moneylender."

The ghostly lady smiled. "Ghost Wind is a better name than some have given me." She looked down the stair past Korvaun at his waiting bodyguard. "I trust you don't intend to bring all of your bullyblades inside our doors."

Korvaun bowed to her, turned, and made a certain signal. "You trust rightly, Lady. I'll proceed alone."

"Then be welcome. What you'll feel on the threshold within is no attack but a probing. Ascend the stair, and Mirt will doubtless find you."

She winked into nothingness even before her words ended. The helmed horrors stepped back to their former positions as the doors beyond them parted and drew inward, revealing a cavernous forehall beyond.

"Impressive, I'll grant," Korvaun murmured, as he crossed the threshold.

The lofty-domed forehall of Mirt's Mansion was smaller and far less ornate than most nobles' abodes, and far more welcoming. Free of clutter and ornate adornment, it didn't strive to impress the eye, yet everything was well-made. It was not a showplace but a home, of someone wealthy and pleasure-loving and yet no-nonsense.

Another eight helmed horrors awaited Korvaun, four on either side this time. As he stepped forward, he felt the probing the ghostly lady had warned him about, like a tingling haze in the air. He was suddenly surrounded by blue smoke so thin he could barely see it, and so acrawl with power that he was shuddering.

The youngest Lord Helmfast hesitated as radiances flickered and grew stronger all around him, and his hands and face went numb. He decided to walk on. What sort of probing was this? The surging tinglings coiled most strongly around the rings on his fingers and the slender sword he wore, but seemed to ignore his dagger. Most curious.

Then it was all gone, fallen away as if it had never been, and he was passing between the motionless helmed horrors and traversing empty flagstones toward the stair. Before him, massive turned wooden posts like the deck-bollards of a great ship held up stairs as finely made as the flights in any villa or mansion he'd ever seen, but far plainer.

Faint kitchen noises—and now a waft of cooking, too—came from behind some of the doors he was leaving behind as he ascended, but he still saw no sign of a living person.

Some folk of Waterdeep spoke of Mirt's Mansion as a sort of vast prison or series of bloodstained torture chambers, where folk who'd been unwise or desperate enough to fall into his clutches screamed out their pain as he cut what he was owed out of their flesh. Others held that it was as gray and drab and graspingly humorless as any moneylender must be, and still others . . .

Had obviously never been here, any of them. None had walked along a thick blue fine-weave rug as long as any Waterdhavian noble villa might boast, in a white-walled passage whose sides curved up and around overhead in a smooth, unbroken arch. Korvaun strode softly along it, past several closed doors: broad, plain-plank affairs rather than the gaudily carved entries of snarling lion faces and suchlike favored by most rising-coin merchants. He was heading for what must be a solar ahead, where the passage opened out, sunlight streamed down from above, and plants flowered in profusion.

Fine plants, some in hanging baskets. Dodging amongst them was a fat, puffing man in flopping boots and seaman's breeches held up by both braces and the broadest belt Korvaun had ever seen. But then, he'd seen very few bellies that bulged and strained above and over belts with quite the quivering enthusiasm Mirt's did.

Just now, the infamous moneylender was watering his plants with a shower of sweat as he stamped, parried, and scrambled. Mirt was grunting and wheezing like a tired cart-ox as he fenced with a petite lady in dark leathers, whose hair danced behind her like the mane of a proud horse.

My, what a beauty! Korvaun watched her in open admiration and found his gaze drawn to the quickening skirl and clash of blades as Mirt groaned, sputtered, and cursed his way right out of view, driving his lovely opponent back through the greenery.

There followed a sudden lionlike roar of dismay and a tinkling of merry feminine laughter. Korvaun followed the sounds into the warm, damp air of the solar.

Both combatants were regarding him with interest before he could even draw breath to speak. Rings on their fingers glowed in sudden readiness. Korvaun tried a smile.

"I . . . offer no menace to you or to any in this fair house. I'm

Korvaun Helmfast of House Helmfast, here to crave audience on matters of business with the famous Mirt the Moneylender."

Mirt grunted, wiped one fat-fingered hand across his brow, and leaned on his sword as if it was a dung-spade. Korvaun managed not to wince.

"A flatterer, eh? Ye *must* be desperate."

Korvaun found himself at a loss for words. *Well, that was quick.*

"I've some need for coin, yes," he managed, uncomfortably aware of dancing mirth in the woman's eyes, "yet I've come here rather than just emptying the nearest family coffer because I find myself also in need of some advice."

The shaggy-mustached head lifted from its hard-breathing rest on the pommel of the sword, its owner frowning in sudden interest. "Well, now. Have ye, indeed?"

A hand like a gnarled, hairy-knuckled shovel waved Korvaun toward a door.

"Rest yerself in there, my young friend, an' we'll sport together awhile. Asper will find us something to drink—something unpoisoned, I hope."

Asper gave him a dazzling smile, tossed her blade onto a cushion, and dived head-first down a hitherto-hidden slide. The broad leaves of a sea-mist flower, large enough to conceal several such floor openings, danced in her wake.

Aware of Mirt's scrutiny, Korvaun repressed the urge to shake his head in bemusement as he went to the indicated door. Unlike a noble villa, indeed. The man most of Waterdeep called the Old Wolf fell into step behind him.

"So, young Helmfast, how's your mother these days?"

⚓ ⚓ ⚓ ⚓ ⚓

Gods, but she was beautiful. Not in the overpainted, gilded, exquisitely coiffed manner of noble matrons, nor yet in the slyly wanton lushness of the best tavern dancers, but ... like a graceful wisp of a temple dancer, yet with something the imp about her, too, in her dark leathers.

Asper gave Korvaun a smile that made him blush as she handed him a decanter to match the one she'd given Mirt, stopper and all, and trotted out of the room, unstrapping and unbuckling as she went.

"She's gone down to the pool to bathe, an' there's no one else this end of the house," Mirt grunted, from where he was lounging in an old wreck of a chair with his feet up on a matching ruin of a footstool. He waved Korvaun to more catastrophes of furniture. "So speak freely. An' soon."

Korvaun lowered himself gingerly onto a decrepit chair. It creaked, but held firm. "Goodsir, I'm here because I need to settle a debt we—*I've* just incurred, to a certain Master Stone—"

"Nay, nay, tell me nothing, young lord! I needn't know an' don't *want* to know, for I cannot tell excited Guardsmen or dogs of the Watch what you've never spoken of. Besides, I know all about your little swordsclang with Varandros Dyre, an'—"

"You do?" Korvaun blurted, too astonished to stop himself.

Keen old eyes met his from under bristling brows. "Tymora keep ye, is each new generation born blind? As ye strut about the city, young cockerel, has it never occurred to ye that your every spit and belch an' casual insult is marked, an' remembered, an' told about to someone else?"

"What? By *who?*"

"By whom, lad, by *whom*. Ye don't want to sound unlettered. How d'ye think street urchins earn coppers enough for a daily gnaw-bun, hey? By running an' telling some merchant ye're strolling down *his* lane, or some gossip-monger who wants to Know All, an' resell some of it for brighter coin . . . or some creditor, that ye've wandered within reach at last."

Mirt swallowed most of the contents of his decanter at a single gulp without apparent effect and growled, "Yet ye spoke of having coin enough not to need my hand a-clutching at your purse, or if it falls empty, something else ye keep dangling rather near it."

Korvaun frowned. "I really came here for advice," he said quietly. Lifting his decanter, he peered into its depths, and his frown deepened.

"Drink," Mirt bade gruffly. "'Tis fine. Nothing but the finest horsepiss do we serve young noble visitors wise enough to know how dunderheaded they are! I grow older and thirstier by the breath, so out with it, lad: what troubles ye?"

Korvaun grimaced. "Dyre's furious with us. He said all of us reach a time when consequences can no longer be laughed away, and that his friends—all the merchants and shopkeepers of the city—would be watching us. He made it sound like the city was two steps away from rising to butcher all nobles!"

Mirt took a swig from his decanter, sighed in appreciation, and asked it, "Did he, now? How unusually candid of him. Ye should be grateful he managed to speak so bluntly, instead of trailing off into cursing the way most of us coarse lowborn do. I hope ye remembered more of his words than just that much."

Korvaun found that his mouth had fallen open. Uncomfortably aware of the weight of the Old Wolf's gaze, Korvaun murmured, "I'd never considered before that the commoners might get angry at, well, the way of things."

Mirt's gaze turned mocking, and Korvaun found himself burning with embarrassment.

"I mean, at what we young nobles have always done—pranks and swordplay and jollity. The common folk always just seemed to—"

"Get out of the way as best they could, an' otherwise just stand and take it?"

"Well, yes. Exactly. And yet I see it, now: they're *right* to be furious. We smash what they can ill afford to lose, and our jests mock them even when we don't mean to ... and yet most of the time we do."

Mirt nodded. "The road to being deeply loved, no?"

"No," Korvaun agreed a little grimly, and drank.

Liquid fire promptly ran up his nose as well as down his gullet, and left him sputtering.

The Old Wolf chuckled, deftly plucked the decanter from failing Helmfast hands, and dealt Korvaun a slap on the back that would have led to prompt face-first disaster if he hadn't also raised the knuckles of his decanter-holding hand like a wall in front of Korvaun's chest.

Korvaun wiped away tears and croaked, "What *is* this . . . stuff?"

"Firebelly. 'Tis all the rage in the pirate ports, an' goes well with the strongest cheese. Makes your breath sweet, clears out the pipes—as ye've found—an' is very good for ye."

Through still-watery eyes Korvaun found Mirt grinning at him, and gasped, "Are you drinking it, too?"

"Of course I am, ye silly man; I have *some* professional ethics. So it's dawned on ye at last that the common folk of our fair city might be discontented an' have cause to be. An' now?"

"An uprising would be terrible. It must be forestalled, and you . . . are of common birth, wise to the streets, and yet are . . . well, widely rumored to be—"

Mirt's eyes were bright and steady, offering no aid at all, and Korvaun wallowed in blushing embarrassment for a breath or two ere he managed to blurt: "—a Lord of Waterdeep!"

"Well, now. Rumors can be such ugly things, can they not?"

"So can truths," Korvaun told him quietly. "Nobles learn that much, at least. Even when secrets . . ." He paused, wondering just how to say what was in his thoughts.

"Are such fun, an' the game that all your elders are playing?" Mirt asked, his voice very dry.

Their gazes met squarely. After a moment, Korvaun nodded.

"Merchants are no different from nobles when it comes to secrets," the Old Wolf said gruffly, reaching down behind his chair to bring up a second decanter. "'Tis just that more of our secrets are about money. Nobles have more idle time to play at pride an' betrayal, but your biggest, sharpest secrets are all about coins, too. Inheritance, hidden debts, obligations, trade-ties gone wrong; all of that."

"All of that," Korvaun agreed. "So what should be done—no, what can *I* do—to take the commoners a step back from their anger?"

Mirt unstoppered his new decanter, sniffed it, and asked the stopper curiously, "Why should ye do anything?"

"Well, if we nobles are the cause, we must be the ones to make amends, and it seems fairly clearly that we *are* the cause."

"Ye've taken the first stride already, young lord: ye've admitted that, an' seen Waterdeep differently because of it. Now, if ye could bring your young friends around to the same view ..."

"I'll do that!" Korvaun said with sudden fire. "I'll go and tell—"

"*No*," Mirt growled, "ye'll not."

The youngest Lord Helmfast blinked at him. "Whyever not?"

"No one ever convinced a hot-headed young noble of anything—at least, not one who still keeps his brains in his codpiece an' hasn't yet had his teeth handed back to him by the world—by *talking* to him. Ye rush in with your jaw flapping, an' they'll listen an' think poor Korvaun's gone straight into gods-mazed idiocy, an' can safely be ridiculed or humored but either way *ignored*. Events have to bring your fellow lordlings around to seeing this for themselves."

" 'Events'? Like a city-wide riot?"

The retort brought a slow smile to Mirt's lips. "No, that'd make them see foes to stick their fancy blades through. I was thinking more the sort of 'hard lesson' events that knock sense into us all, events that sometimes—just sometimes, mind ye—can be nudged into happening by, well, by a young nobleman who's almost half as clever as he thinks he is. The sort of events that your mother an' every other woman her age learned long ago."

Korvaun frowned. "I *beg* your—?"

"Nay, ye do nothing of the kind. Ye look for a challenge, if ye beg my pardon or anything else in *that* tone. Stop thinking with your pride for just a breath an' see what I'm saying: now, don't all the noble ladies ye know, young and old, *arrange* things to make their menfolk or brothers or sons react in some way they'd like? Get angry an' insist on something, mayhap? Or regard some matter as touching the honor of the House, an' thus demanding the opposite response from them than they'd said they'd give, a little earlier?"

Korvaun nodded. "I see," he said, and did. "Yes."

"Good. The gods smile on us both this day," Mirt said briskly. "Now, how many coins d'ye want?"

"I know not, yet. Master Dyre said he'd send us an accounting."

"An' ye can send word to me, an' I'll have coins or tradebars or both ready here for your hands—*your* hands, mind, not some servant or fellow lordling—to claim."

Mirt's second decanter was almost empty. Korvaun regarded him in some amazement. He was fat, yes, but this firebelly stuff! The man should be slurring his words at least by now! Korvaun started to stammer thanks.

One large and hairy hand shot out in a silencing wave. "'Tis the least I can do to help such a rare breed: a noble who sees the city so clearly an' *cares* about what meets his eyes. Yet I can do something more, an' believe I will. If Waterdeep needed ye, would ye answer the call?"

Korvaun blinked. "But of course—"

That large, silencing hand worked its power again. "If *I* asked ye to do a service—large or small, perilous or seemingly silly—for our city, would ye? Dropping all else an' with no thought of fame nor reward?"

The youngest Lord Helmfast met the old moneylender's gaze squarely and said quietly, "Yes. This I swear."

"Good. Fix in your memory, then, two words: 'searchingstar' and 'stormbird.' Got them?"

"I—searchingstar?"

"Aye, and stormbird."

Korvaun nodded.

"Good," the Old Wolf said again. "Now remember also this: if a stranger says 'searchingstar' to ye, ye're to get yourself here as fast as your legs can bring you an' say 'searchingstar' to whoever answers the door. If some stranger instead says 'stormbird' to ye, do the same—but bring whatever friend ye've confided in."

"Friend? You suggest I'd confide in—"

Mirt made a rude sound. "However hard ye swear to the

contrary, here an' now, ye'll tell a friend all about this. Young, excited lads always do."

"I—"

Mirt's hand went up again. "Spare me your protests, but mind ye tell someone who can hold his tongue, or ye'll discover the hard way that I've never seen ye before, an' this little chat never happened."

Korvaun nodded. "I quite understand."

"There's something else ye should know, wise young noble, something to tell ye not to always trust in what ye see."

Mirt brought something else up from behind his battered chair: something small enough to fit in his palm. It gleamed, yet bent easily in Mirt's stubby fingers—but slipped back into its former shape as he shifted his grip. It looked like a miniature shield, with a flat top and sides but a rounded bottom, or at least it did until Mirt turned it the other way up and held it forth. Leather thongs dangled from it, making it now look more like an eyepatch than anything else.

"This," Mirt said simply, "is a slipshield. Touch it."

"A what?"

"A little secret of the city. Touch it."

Hesitantly, Korvaun did as he was bid. It felt . . . hard. Like wood, solid and smooth, neither hot nor cold.

Mirt had muttered something, and now drew back, fastened the thongs loosely around his arm, pushed the little shield against his arm with one finger, and murmured something else Korvaun couldn't hear.

The Old Wolf's features melted, blurred—and Korvaun was looking at himself.

"Aren't I handsome?" his own voice asked him. "Give a young noble a kiss? No? Look down at your hands."

Korvaun did so—and discovered to his horror that they were hairy and knobby-knuckled, with stubby fingers and calluses. They were the hands that had waved him to silence and hefted decanters. Mirt's hands.

He looked up at his double, but its shape was blurring, and his own hands were, too. Then the image of Korvaun was gone, and the stout, shaggy old moneylender was holding the little shield in his hand and grinning at him. Korvaun quickly looked down. His own hands were back, too. So the slipshield was a device that let two men trade shapes.

"Let that be the secret I'll test your keeping of," Mirt said as he dropped the shield into Korvaun's palm. "Now be off with ye, before your bodyguards reluctantly decide something's happened to ye and they'd better start earning their pay. Back on the streets with ye, an' back to getting rich. From the day ye pick up my coins, ye've a year to pay me back."

Korvaun discovered his mouth was still agape. He closed it hastily to stammer his thanks.

Mirt snorted and showed him to the door, slapping the unfinished firebelly decanter into his hand. "A gift. Ye'll be needing it, Lord Helmfast."

Korvaun managed a smile. "You speak with conviction. Are you a seer?"

The moneylender snorted. "Ye're tryin' to do the right thing, lad. D'ye think to be the first man who won't be punished for it?"

⚓ ⚓ ⚓ ⚓ ⚓

Mirt sneezed again and slashed aside another black, clinging armful of cobwebs. Well, 'twasn't as if this tunnel got used every day. The lantern in his hand was getting uncomfortably warm, so he must be almost there by now.

Aye, *there*'twas. And at least he wasn't making this trip at the dead puffing run, with some disaster or other rocking the city above him. 'Twas good some of the young noble pups were finally showing signs of taking up the mantle of responsibility. At last. At far too long and bleeding last.

And wonder of the gods, if young Helmfast wasn't actually seeing for himself that the common folk had true cause for complaint!

Mirt passed his hand along the wall at ankle height, and was rewarded with a momentary glow. Aye, right here.

He trailed his fingertips up the rough stone to the familiar knobs, curled his palm around one of them in such a way that his fingertips pressed onto the stones in spread array, and a door-sized oval of wall abruptly swung inward, revealing faint blue gloom beyond.

Mirt stepped through, to be greeted by the sound of a young lass choking.

The duty apprentice was seated at the usual desk, with a glow-stone resting on the pages of what might be a spellbook but then again might just be a heaving-bosoms chapbook. She'd dropped both book and stone in haste as the opening of the seldom-used secret door startled her, and grabbed for a ready wand beneath the still-bouncing book.

That wild grab had forced her to hastily swing her feet down from their perch on the far end of the desk, and her fashionable boots had brained her backup—who was now slumping senseless to the floor. So much for Tower guardroom rules about the backup sentinel watching from no closer than the far doorway.

Mirt put away his growing grin and set down his lantern as it became clear the tangle-haired young mage was in real trouble. The wand shook in her hand, and she was making strange gargling, mewing sounds as she spat out too little of a hot-mussels-and-gravy bun.

Mirt could lurch forward with surprising speed when he had to, and in a trice he'd snatched the wand from her trembling hand and flung it aside, then come around the desk and laid hold of one booted ankle. Thankfully these slender, high pointy-toed jobs didn't come off all that easily, so he could do *this*:

He hauled hard, put a foot on her stool, pushed off as if he was starting to climb a steep stair—and the choking apprentice was suddenly upside down.

Her fashionable skirts fell away to reveal old petticoats with holes in them and a stained undersash that wasn't much cleaner than Mirt's own customary clout. Her face promptly changed from trying to turn blue to also trying to blush crimson at the same time.

The Old Wolf shook the lass once, vigorously, then thumped her on the back hard enough to make her limbs bounce and flail like a rag doll's.

"This'll clear your pipes!" he announced heartily, watching hot mussels, gravy, and half-chewed bread shoot past his boots. Before she could even begin to sob for breath, he threw her up into the air, caught her waist in both hands, and spun her upright like a wheel.

She was taller and more gangly than Asper, and Mirt got an unintentional elbow in his face for his pains, but in another moment she was coughing and crying all over her desk, with Mirt resting one hand on her flank to keep her standing.

It took her some time to recover her breath, and Mirt passed it by reading her book—it *was* a heaving-bosoms affair, by Sharess!—aloud.

"'The bruising strength of his grip made her gasp, and even as she twisted furiously away, cursing her silks for their lack of handy daggers, she knew she'd been dangerously—possibly fatally—wrong about him.'

"'A moment later, her fingers found what they'd been straining for ... and a moment after that, he knew it too.'"

Mirt chuckled. "Ho-ho, but this is ripe stuff!" He thumbed a few pages, ate the discarded end of her bun with lip-smacking enjoyment, then glanced at still-heaving shoulders and asked, "Are ye all right yet, lass?"

"M-my ... my ..." She was still fighting for breath and turning to face him slowly, hands far from her belt dagger—or the one strapped to her ankle that Mirt's rough medicine had just revealed.

"Wand? 'Tis under my boot—and staying there, until ye settle down."

"Who *are* you?"

Mirt grinned at what he could see of the tear-streaked face through all the hair. "Call me Elminster—and get me Laeral straightaway, aye?"

Large, dark eyes goggled at him as frantic fingers dragged

hair out of the way, then the still-raw voice that went with them managed to stammer, "The L-Lady Laeral is, uh, elsewhere at the moment."

"Then," Mirt growled grandly, "I suppose Old Windbag—Khelben, to ye—will have to do."

A strange expression crossed the guard-prentice's face as mirth rose to join anger and embarrassment. Abruptly she gasped, "Stay here!" and rushed out of the room, looking even more like she was struggling not to laugh.

Mirt waited for her to look back and then disappear around the first bend of the ascending stair. Then he set off after her. He knew where she was almost certainly heading.

A short but wheezing journey later, they arrived more or less together at a certain door, where the guard-prentice gave Mirt an angry, helpless glare, and whispered something to its latch, almost as if she was kissing it.

The door clicked and moved a little, as if a lock had been released, and the apprentice quickly stepped forward, whirling to slam it shut again—and discovered that the fat stranger had somehow crossed three paces of passage and got not just his foot, but an entire leg through the door in her wake, and there was just no way she was going to be able to get it closed.

The rest of Mirt followed his bold leg into the chamber, favoring her with a fond grin. "Shouldn't ye be getting back to your post?"

The mage drew herself up to say something really blistering—and someone else said an oath for her, a long and heartfelt string of obscenities that owed so much to spell-inferences and references to wizards long dead that its heat was quite lost in its own bewildering grandeur.

"I love ye, too," Mirt replied affably, as the Lord Mage of Waterdeep came toward them like a thundercloud, with the chaos of collapsing spells singing and lashing across the vast chamber behind him like wildly whipping mooring ropes flung by a storm—ropes that glowed and spat showers of sparks and flung lightnings, that is.

So large was that room that it should not have been able to fit inside the neighborhood, let alone the slender girth of Blackstaff Tower—yet most of it was occupied by a gigantic stone head that any Waterdhavian would know at a glance as belonging to one of the Walking Statues of Waterdeep. Mirt knew Khelben was "bringing them all in" this month to augment their enchantments, but couldn't identify any of the strangeness in the air around the head as more than just "powerful magic."

There were glowing golden lines of force, now drifting slowly to the floor. Along and above some of them were elaborate runes and words, written in flowing script on the empty air, and here and there Mirt could even see tiny gemstones and winking motes of light orbiting a few of the sigils. It looked like hours of work to him ... and by the expression adorning the Blackstaff's face, probably was.

From somewhere down near her boots the guard-prentice found her voice. It emerged quavering dangerously, but quite loud enough. "S-sorry, Lord Master. I bring Elminster, who craves audience with you."

The exhaustion, loss, and rage warring on Khelben's face twisted into something like incredulity. "*That's* not Elminster! Idiot lass! He's not *nearly* so handsome!"

The apprentice recoiled from her master's anger but glanced helplessly at the fat, spiderweb-covered bulk of Mirt. Her face changed. She struggled again for a moment, as if she was going to choke anew, and then burst into helpless giggles.

With the last of his great web of spells crashing soundlessly to the floor behind him, Khelben "Blackstaff" Arunsun clasped his hands behind his back, gave his helpless apprentice a disgusted look, and swung his glare back to Mirt.

"Well, whatever do you want?"

🏰 🏰 🏰 🏰 🏰

Mrelder nodded thanks to the wench as she set down the latest round of ale.

The dozen men in the booth with him—apprentices, daycoin-men, and hireswords, strangers all—took up the tankards and drank deeply.

His offer of a free highsun meal with drink had bought him their time, and a few sly hints about a rich, fat, easily plucked pigeon of a merchant had won their close attention.

The theft he was hiring them for was pure fancy, of course. The men in the booth would probably always wonder how the plot had unraveled but would have no doubts about the fate of the man who'd hired them—or rather, the man whose face Mrelder currently wore. That unfortunate would be found dead in an alley before nightfall. Golskyn's mongrelmen would make sure of it.

Mrelder set down his tankard and tried not to be seen scratching. His father's spells had reattached his arm, but the fingers always felt numb, now, and the rest of it *itched* damnably. "Our time draws to a close. Questions?"

"What of the Watch?" asked a sell-sword.

The disguised sorcerer put on a grim face. "Greater concerns ride them than what we offer."

Uneasy glances were exchanged. "There's trouble in the city?"

"Trouble enough," Mrelder told them. "'Tis whispered Lord Piergeiron's passed into the Halls of Tempus."

"The Open Lord, dead?" someone gasped incredulously.

His neighbor gave him a sharp elbow. "How else d'ye get there, fool? And when the answer comes, try not to shout it *quite* so loud!"

"Aye," Mrelder said in a grim whisper. "The Lords're keeping it secret. Until they let it be known, I'd be taking it as a favor if you'd keep it secret too."

Every one of the dozen grunted agreement, but every last one of them drained their tankards in haste and looked to him for dismissal. Mrelder doubted their eagerness to depart came from any desire to return to work. He waved them away, hiding his smile with his ale.

By day's end, Dock Ward would be buzzing with the rumor of Piergeiron's death.

CHAPTER SIX

A trio of revel-bound matrons bustled past Lark, their feathered cloaks aswirl in the evening breeze. Self-satisfied confidence wafted from them like perfume—never mind that they resembled a gaggle of fattened geese. Lark batted away an errant feather and fought down a moment of panic.

"Gods going *sideways*," she murmured under her breath. "I don't know if I can go through with this."

Stars twinkled over elegant Sea Ward, and the night air was turning cool. Lark had surreptitiously tossed her old cloak over one of the ornamental spires adorning a grand railing two blocks back, and the breeze ghosting past her bared shoulders made her shiver.

She suppressed an urge to tug at the low-cut bodice. Faendra's gown was absent from much of her upperworks and clung to her hips as if it was dripping wet. Lark had never stepped out of doors in such scant garb, nor, for that matter, had her mother. This was a strange city, to be sure, where fine ladies showed the world more flesh than Luskan's dockside whores!

But then, Lark thought cynically, judging by the gems on lavish display around her, these noblewomen got a better price for their . . . wares.

Jewels sparkled in the night as women—and men, for that matter—alighted from gilded coaches. They swept down the street toward Westwind Villa in a grand promenade to the strains of hired minstrelsy.

Strolling with them but feeling very alone, Lark kept her head high and looked at no one. The gazes of the villa guards, standing silently in their dark finery on every step, felt heavy and suspicious. She reminded herself not to look too closely at them as she ascended the broad white marble steps. Nobles seldom noticed those who served.

Don't hurry. Hold your gown up as if you're used to doing it, and DON'T HURRY. Only a few steps more.

At the head of the stair, tall and many-paneled doors stood open to reveal golden light and revelry beyond. She could hear the announcements now over a rising hubbub of chatter and mirth.

"Lord and Lady Gauntyl," the doorwarden declaimed haughtily. Everyone ascended another step. She was the only one climbing the steps alone. Lark swallowed hard.

"Lord and Lady Thongolir," the warden said grandly.

Another step. Lark reminded herself that the Texter had thought she was worth the price of her freedom and good enough to serve him still, in the small, secret way hidden beneath her belt, inside her gown.

"Lord Ulboth Tchazzam, and the Lone Lady Carina Tchazzam," the doorwarden announced, his voice rolling out into the vast, growing din of revelry. Ah. They'd be brother and sister, not a couple.

One of the guards on the topmost step was peering at her suspiciously. *Oh, Lady Luck, be with me now!*

Lark forced herself to raise her chin a trifle more and kept her eyes cool and the faint half-smile she'd learned so long ago on her lips.

"Lord and Lady Manthar."

Then she was on the top step, and the doorwarden was giving her a faint frown.

She turned her head just far enough to give him her half-smile and murmured, "Lady Evenmoon, of the Evenmoons of Tashluta." That should be far enough away that she wouldn't have to fear dozens of Tashlutans loudly proclaiming her an impostor, and it certainly sounded better than: *A tavern wench from Luskan, daughter of a dockside trull, in a borrowed gown.*

There was a moment of silence as the doorwarden traded glances with two men in lace-wristed finery inside the great door—men a head taller than most.

Oh, *gods!* Should she've said "I am expected," or mentioned Craulnober's name? Should she—

"Lady Evenmoon, of the Evenmoons of Tashluta," the doorwarden proclaimed, raising his grand voice just a trifle to give it a thread of excitement: A guest from afar!

A few heads turned amid the glittering chaos of elegant men and women standing talking amid deftly drifting servants with trays of tallglasses, but the overall din continued unabated.

Lady Lark Evenmoon of Tashluta let fall the hem of her gown with an elegant flick of her wrist and strode forward across gleaming emptiness toward those suddenly much needed drinks as haughtily and as gracefully as if she'd been doing it all her life.

♠   ♠   ♠   ♠   ♠

"Korvaun's coming, surely?" frowned Beldar, surveying the glittering throng.

"He sent a servant with his regrets. Family business, apparently," Taeros murmured. "An odd excuse for a younger son whose proper business is carousing with his friends and tempting his parents to disown him. I've been threatened with that very fate thrice this tenday."

"Only thrice?" Beldar struck a pose and examined his fingernails as haughtily as an undefeated swordmaster. "Then my record, goodsir, stands."

Taeros smirked. "I'll continue my quest to unseat you, of course, but if our Korvaun continues to display such unseemly responsibility, he may take himself out of the fray entirely."

"Tragic," Malark declaimed, on the edge of mock tears. "Simply tragic. Just the three of us then." He rolled his eyes. "How shall we console our lonely selves?"

"In the usual manner, I expect," Beldar observed dryly. "Now remember, my gallant Gemcloaks: utter nothing about our host that you'd not say to his face. He's doubtless using one of those spells that lets you hear your name spoken, what words are said with it, and any reply."

Malark's eyebrows shot up. "I'll curse him inwardly then. What's he throwing this hurlygowns-prance for, anyway? To show us all he has spare coins enough to rent a villa just for a fling? Or to remind us all what jaded low-life dogs we all are, that he can jerk the leash and we'll come running in hopes we'll see the infamous Serpent do something infamous?"

"My guess," Taeros Hawkwinter told the backs of his fingers confidentially, as he inspected them for missed blotches of ink, "is that the far-traveled Lord Craulnober wants to show himself once more on the social ramparts of Waterdeep, to remind the, ah, darkest such ramparts that should they feel the need to hire someone to do something a little *shady*, he's . . . right here. Handy, as it were."

"Chatoyant," Beldar said grandly. "Simply *chatoyant*. Let's make our grand entrance before all the best wine's gone."

⛭ ⛭ ⛭ ⛭ ⛭

"So of course I told him to get on his horse and ride right *back* to Myratma—and take his hairy-rumped harem with him, too!"

Men guffawed and wheezed, and women tittered far too loudly and threw their heads back to let the conjured glowflames catch the full dazzle of the gems dripping from their earlobes and around their throats. Lark deftly slid her shoulder out from under an idly reaching hand.

"By Tempus, you take the maiden, Braerard! Fancy some dirt-neck from *Tethyr* thinking he can just ride through our gates and start acting as if he *owned* the place! Does he think we give two thin nibs if he calls himself a 'duke,' or some such? They'll be rolling in here calling themselves 'emperors,' next!"

Lark smiled absently at nothing at all and drifted on, trying not to look as if she was in any haste. More than one servant had already given her a puzzled look—as if they'd seen her before but couldn't quite place where. In Waterdeep, that could lead to a cry of "thief." She certainly wasn't the first person to come to a revel uninvited for purposes other than dancing and boasting.

Sun on the Mountain, but these old men thought well themselves! Judging by all the red faces and quivering jowls and—and *wattles*, most of them seemed to have mastered eating long ago, but judging from their vapid, vainglorious chatter, not much else.

Their gossip was a trifle more interesting than servants' talk, but of course that was because she wasn't familiar with most of the names and little catch-phrases yet. It didn't sound much subtler or grander than the boastful backstairs talk she was accustomed to.

"Brokengulf?" someone roared drunkenly. "Is that you?"

"Aye, what's left of me!" came the equally sodden response.

That jest, Lark thought sourly, was nearly as old as the man using it.

Come to think on it, there weren't a lot of young nobles here, beyond a few girls trailing their mothers around like pale-faced, gem-drenched lapdogs. As yet Lark had seen no sign of the handsome Elaith Craulnober—or any elves for that matter, moon or otherwise.

Suddenly Lark froze. Across a glittering expanse of flashing, winking gemstones displayed by women who apparently believed no one should be seen in public wearing less than half her own weight in gaudy jewelry, she saw three of the Gemcloaks absently taking tallglasses and crowns of smoked mussels off passing platters as they strolled together. They looked uniformly bored.

In that boredom lay danger; they'd be looking around for something to amuse themselves. Lark faded a few steps to the left to hide herself behind someone, and so brought herself into the lee of two red-faced, bristle-mustached old patriarchs in full spittle-spraying career. Lost in their jovial roarings, they were both clutching huge goblets in each hand and flicking flash-snuff rings all too often. Through the resulting threads of smoke they peered at her, leered in unison, and reached out together (transferring their goblets to one hand with a deftness that bespoke long practice), intent upon fondling the newcomer.

Lark stepped out of reach, seized with a wild urge to snatch those four goblets, empty them over the dyed and powdered coiffures of their owners, and then use the massive metal cups to do a little fondling of her own—hard, and where it would hurt.

The two promptly forgot her. "Scared?" one of them bellowed. "By *Bane*, sir, we were! Guides didn't last two breaths before they were off like spring rabbits, shrieking like a lot of gels seeing Piergeiron in the baths! Second night out, and us left alone, with all our food and kit gone with 'em! That's when we found the tracks, of course! And the blood!"

"Dragon?"

"*Dragons*. Three of 'em, at least! Big ones. Talons as long as my arm, and—"

Someone was grinning at her around a dragonslaying elbow. Lark blinked and then swallowed again.

It was the redbearded Lord Kothont. Malark, that was his name. His eyes were shining almost as brightly as his emerald cloak.

"Well, well! You *do* look familiar, Lady—?"

"Battle-axe," Lark told him smoothly. "Old Lady Battle-axe."

Malark's eyes twinkled. "Am I to take it that both edges of your tongue are as sharp as the weapon you refer to?"

"You may take it elsewhere, my lord," Lark told the back of her hand airily. "I give you fair warning—I've been told betimes that my knee is as sharp and as swift as any weapon you might care to name."

"Ho ho!" Malark chuckled, genuinely amused. "I take great care in naming my weapons, to be sure, but I like even more the names friendly ladies give them."

Lark gave him a very direct stare and murmured, "So go to your friendly ladies and collect some new names. I fear you'll acquire nothing so useful from me." She let him see a twinkle in her gaze to go with her bright and brittle smile to leave him nothing to flare into anger over.

Yet it seemed Lord Kothont was far from anger. He saluted her with something that might have been admiration in his eyes and cocked his head to give her an almost fond smile. "You offer rare sport, My Lady Battle-axe. I look forward to renewing our converse at revels to come—many of them, I hope—yet it seems your desires lie elsewhere this night."

"You should presume nothing as to my desires," she said coolly. "They are not one whit as obvious as you deem them to be."

She lifted her chin and stared him down, prompted by a surge of pride beyond anything she'd known before. She would not run from this man or any other. It was essential that she stand her ground, that it would be he who moved away.

Malark laughed almost as if he knew that too, gave her a wave of his hand, and strolled off—leaving Lark suddenly aware of two bloodshot, rather frowning gazes.

"*You're* not Lady Battle-axe," Old Dragonslayer said accusingly. "Rode her back in oh-six. Impudent young wetbottom."

The two old warriors then turned their backs on her, leaving Lark wondering if they meant she was impudent—which seemed most likely—or Lady Battle-axe had been, back in oh-six. *1306?* Gods above!

Suddenly in great need of a drink, Lark headed for the nearest platter. The liveried, carefully expressionless servant bearing it would have orders to circle back to wherever the pouring-pantry was when less than a fifth of the drinkables were left, and his load was approaching that now.

Her progress was halted abruptly by a familiar, dark-eyed gaze. Beldar Roaringhorn had lifted his head from the excited gabble of a green-haired matron—*Sune look away, WHERE do these women get such dyes? Or the blind idiocy to think such hues flatter them?*—to stare right at her.

She froze for a moment, and then realized she dare not show such a reaction. She forced herself to stroll casually forward and claim a glass from the tray. Sipping at the wine, Lark stole a glance at the Roaringhorn lordling. Yes, he was still looking her way.

So was Lord Hawkwinter—Taeros—standing at Beldar's shoulder, but Lark realized their regard held nothing more threatening than mild interest. There was no hint of recognition on either face, even though Beldar had met her twice before, under circumstances she considered memorable.

She let out a small sigh of relief. They were probably among the legions of nobles who didn't look closely at female servants who weren't thrusting bared charms under their noses. As a "noble guest," she was apparently worthy of closer scrutiny. Moreover, she was their age, and if no buxom beauty, a "stranger from afar" offered some small novelty.

Despite her tense nervousness, Lark understood their boredom. If this was what nobles did at revels, 'twas hardly better than the interminable orations of the worst opinionated windbag merchants who came around the shops—and those men at least had work to do that would eventually call them away, and their blustering and whinings with them.

Malark Kothont was well on his way back to rejoin his friends, and Lark decided it would be very much for the best if she was no longer in view when he reached them. Any comment about the young lass with the delightfully sharp tongue would draw attention she'd rather avoid.

"I don't believe you've ever met the third Lone Lady Ammakyl," someone gushed nearby, and Lark rolled her eyes and moved away. *Three* maiden aunts at once? *That* would be a delightful household to work for!

"Ohhh, *yes*, ahahahaha!" a man brayed, loudly and falsely enough to make Lark wince.

And wince again at her own stupidity. Gods above, had she lost her wits along with her own clothes? As a servant, she had the sense to keep her thoughts from her face. She twisted her lips into a vapid smile and lowered her bared shoulders into a more relaxed posture.

The great vaulted hall was filling up rapidly, which meant that some of the early arrivals, who wanted to avoid rivals or cut dead those with whom they were feuding, would soon start to leave. This didn't have the feel of a relaxed revel, where debauchery might soon break out. The grand folk of Waterdeep were uneasy because their not-yet-seen host was Elaith Craulnober, the notorious Serpent.

Right now might be her best chance to slip away. She was to leave her report in the study that overlooked the grand hall from the seaward side—and this had to be the grand hall.

She caught up to the servant, left her emptied tallglass on his platter and deftly procured a tallglass of something she could at least see through, and tilted her head back to idly survey the hall as she sipped.

Quite used to such self-absorbed behavior, the servant slipped around her and moved on, with neither of them having so much as glanced at each other's faces, which was a good thing, because the man's dwindling form looked familiar. She'd probably worked alongside him, cleaning up after some other revel elsewhere.

Lark raised her glance and her glass again—and spotted what she was looking for. The hall sported a promenade or continuous balcony, overlooking the crowded floor from all sides, and a second level above that of separately jutting balconies. One of them, on the seaward side, was larger than most and was glassed in. All was in darkness on both of those upper levels; the Serpent obviously wanted his guests to crowd and mingle beneath the glowflames and the chandeliers, to make it clear to all just how many of Waterdeep's best and brightest his invitation could bring.

"Eltorchul! *Eltorchul!* Hoy, Bunny-Ears! *Over here!*"

Lark winced at the deafening bellow and swiftly turned her back. If people looked this way, she would just as soon have them look at her bared back than her face. There were none in this city who'd recognize it, as she wasn't in the habit of baring her spine in noble mansions or anywhere else.

"Why, I was *talking* to Lady Hiilgauntlet just the other day, ahaha, and *she* told me—"

Lark began drifting toward the seaward wall. Now if I was an ascending staircase, where would I be? Close enough to a garderobe to serve as an excuse, it was to be hoped . . .

"What a *sly* little snake you are, Bedeira. How many hang-tongued men have you demolished as thoroughly as you did poor Laeburl, I wonder?"

"Forty-six, my lord," came the gloating reply. "Care to be my forty-seventh?"

Lark's progress thankfully took her out of hearing whatever reply Bedeira was offered—and even more thankfully, showed her broad stone steps, flanked by suits of armor far too ancient to have living men inside them, within the third archway in the wall before her. The light was dimmer here, and inevitably the gossip was more whispered and vicious—and some hands were wandering.

Lark stepped around a couple so lost in rapture that the feminine half of it was using her chin to hold up her own gathered gown. Beyond them was the arch that opened onto the stairway.

Glass in hand and affecting the frown of a well-bred lady who was beginning to feel some urgency in a search for the nearest garderobe, she stepped through the arch, glanced up the stair, and discovered something else.

There was not a guard to be seen, and over a landing far above her hung the paired blue and red lanterns that proclaimed: Garderobe Here.

Gasping a relief she didn't quite feel, Lark started up the stairs.

▲ ▲ ▲ ▲ ▲

"You look as bored as I feel," Taeros murmured to Beldar, deftly avoiding a drunken Brokengulf maiden aunt. The aging beldame seemed bent on changing that status before the evening was out; she reeled past, twittering and clutching at all and sundry.

Beldar inspected the dregs in his latest goblet and told them, "I am hideously bored. One thinks of the notorious Serpent with the spice of danger, not-so-veiled elven insults, a whiff of things illicit—and a lot more elverquisst than I've seen yet." He waved a hand to indicate the room all around and added, "But this... this is our parents, chattering about their petty politics and intrigues. As harbor-filling usual."

To underscore his judgment, Beldar nodded his head toward old Laranthavurr Irlingstar just as the craggy-faced old bore's monocle made another of its inevitable plunges from its cheek-top perch into the grotesquely large snifter in the eldest Irlingstar uncle's hand. Droplets of luminous green liquid arced up in all directions in the wake of its loud "plop," and Aeramacrista Gauntyl, whom he'd been lecturing about proper precedence when dealing with "those new-coin think-far-too-well-of-themselves visitors from Amn," drew hastily back from the shower with a little crow of alarm that she clumsily transformed into a titter.

Her retreat caused her to jostle Mornarra Cassalantar. Exaggerated exception was taken. Cutting words erupted.

Taeros rolled his eyes.

Beldar was rather gloomily regarding a glistening emerald droplet that had just landed on the back of his hand. "Calishite aumbruril. *How* three decades back!"

Taeros chuckled rueful agreement. "Shall we flit elsewhere, then?"

"Decidedly. There's a dance on at the Slow Cheese. Find Malark, will you?"

"Consider him found. Behold our royal blade—besieged, as usual."

Taeros pointed with his fresh goblet at a solid ring of noble matrons, all waving ring-laden hands expressively and spouting nonsense as fast as they could draw breath. The two Gemcloaks could just see Malark's rather weary smile over the fantastic coiffures of the shortest noblewomen. It seemed silver galleons were fashionable at the moment, for no less than three such vessels were sailing through cranial waves of artfully dyed, pinned, and stiffened hair.

As they watched, Malark's smile slid just a trifle more. Taeros made a sympathetic sound, tossed his goblet in the general direction of the nearest servant, and strode into the press of loud laughter, overwhelming perfumes, and glittering, gleaming "my taste is even worse *and* more expensive than thine" garments. Trills of alarm erupted and flower-bedecked fans swatted at him, but he forged on.

"Come, Lord Kothont," Taeros announced firmly, arriving at his destination, "'tis past time we attended to your prize pegasus. You *know* the poor thing goes mad if you don't dose it by four bells past dusk!"

"Goes mad?" one matron crowed delightedly. "How so, young sir?"

"Dose it?" another shrilled, her plump face gleaming with the avid fascination of one whose own ills were legion, endlessly fascinating, and entirely imaginary. "What *sort* of medicine?"

Malark was already grinning helplessly at the fancy Taeros was so glibly spinning and continued to do so as the youngest Lord Hawkwinter laid hands on his shoulder and started steering him out of his twittering prison.

"A secret distillation," Taeros confided grimly.

"Secrets, my lord? Come now! You dare keep no secrets from *us*, your elders and betters!"

"Very well," Taeros said sweetly, turning to survey the bright-eyed host of over painted faces as Beldar, not quite wearing a smirk, took Malark's other arm. "'Tis a distillation of . . . *the blood of noblewomen.*"

They departed amid a noisy chaos of scandalized exclamations, delighted laughter, and uncertain mirth. Taeros suspected Malark would have slightly more breathing room at the next revel he attended.

By the lopsided grin on his face, Malark evidently thought so too. "Couldn't you have said the blood of *old* noblewomen?"

🏰 🏰 🏰 🏰 🏰

By the giggles issuing from within, the garderobe was being used for other than its usual form of relief. Good, that gave her a handy excuse. Lark strolled idly on into the darkness to look over the promenade rail and noticed the three Gemcloaks making their way to the doors. Good and *better.*

She faded back from the rail with the air of someone killing time in casual boredom toward the flight of steps up to the second level. She was almost underneath the study now, if she was right about which room it was. Ribbed vaulting soared from spindles to carved bosses and supporting statues. Lark spared their shadowed beauties no more than a passing glance, because no bored young noblewoman would have done any differently.

She strolled along the promenade and oh-so-casually ascended the second stair. The reign of darkness and silence continued.

Fur rugs covered the landing at the top of the stair, and their whiteness glowed slightly in a faint blue radiance issuing from the open door of the study, immediately to her right.

Lark swallowed. Could things be this easy? Surely not.

It was hard to maintain her casual air, and harder still to stroll on thick furs, but she thought she managed it, passing the door and glancing in as she did so.

The glow was coming from a large map or chart spread out on a desk, and was strong enough to show her a chair and a crammed bookshelf beyond. There was overstuffed seating on the far side of the desk, some sort of large but tidy potted plant, and so far as she could tell in the gloom, no one in the room.

Raising her eyebrows in what she hoped was a look of languid interest, Lark went to the doorway. If that desk had a carved ship-under-sail medallion on its far side, it was the place Texter wanted the report left. She smoothed her gown and felt beneath it the reassuring stiffness of the message written in Naoni's neat, careful hand.

Lark slipped through the door and walked boldly across the soft, deep rugs. As she neared the desk, she noted that the parchment on the table was creased with many rectangular folds—too creased to be parchment, come to think of it, because it hadn't cracked. It showed a finely drawn labyrinth of chambers and passages—more of the latter than the former—like some vast dungeon. Fascinating, but she dare not spend the time to look at it properly. Maps were valuable, dangerous things. She'd seen sailors and treasure-seekers alike kill each other over the possession of an ink-scrawled canvas scrap. If she were caught here studying a map, no explanation would suffice.

She strolled past the desk to the window overlooking the grand hall. "Well," she announced idly, "*this* is quite a view. Not that it makes those tail feathers on Lady Eirontalar's hat any more attractive, seen from above."

She turned back to face the desk. *Yes!* There was the ship medallion. A quick glance assured her she was alone.

Lark went to her knees in a flash, touched the sail of the ship, felt the medallion drop open like a flap, and ran her hand up under her gown and snatched out the report. Slipping it behind the medallion, she closed the little panel again and straightened up—

To stare straight into the coldly amused eyes of a slender moon elf in a dark, jeweled doublet and hose, who was leaning against the doorframe with one hand resting comfortably on the hilt of a long, slender sword. His other hand toyed with a drawn dagger whose blade was little more than a needle.

A needle as long and glittering as Lark's forearm.

"Lady Eirontalar's headwear is indeed quite gaudy," Elaith Craulnober said in singularly rich, musical tones, "but her presumption is more than matched by other ladies here in my house this night. Wouldn't you agree?"

🏰 🏰 🏰 🏰 🏰

The Slow Cheese was neither the grandest festhall in Waterdeep nor the largest, and even a blind and none too choosy man would not have deemed its dancers as anywhere near the best, but it was all the rage at the moment for the very novelty of its newness and for its hanging balconies.

The Gemcloaks were crowded into one of them now, overlooking the oval stage where dancers were disrobing in a succession of little mime-plays of true love, roguery, and elopement, to the accompaniment of some pleasant but rather wandering airs performed on lute, harp, and string-of-bells.

Not that anyone could hear much of it through the lusty roars of inebriated patrons shouting bawdy suggestions down at the stage, the rumble of converse, and the groaning of overloaded balconies. The Cheese was packed this night.

Malark helped himself to another generous slice of peppered Tharsultan cheese from the little "castle" of cheeses on the table in their midst. Exotic cheeses were the house gimmick, all of them strongly seasoned enough to make even iron-throated patrons order more drink.

"Thirsty?" Beldar inquired mockingly, watching Malark's eyes fasten in amazement on a particular display of bulbous flesh below.

Their own prized perch was one of dozens of small, elaborately filigreed and obscenely carved balconies that jutted so far out over the stage that they were barely a man's height above the heads of the dancers. All around the Gemcloaks, it was raining, a constant flashing fall of coins being dropped from balconies, aimed with greater or lesser degrees of lubricated skill to plunge down bosoms below. Wise dancers at the Cheese kept their mouths shut when on stage; one could choke on a freshly minted silver shard.

Malark delightedly watched some of those coins find their plunging destinations and others just miss and bounce, ricocheting most amusingly. One of them stuck, just for a moment, half-up a dancer's nose—and the roar of laughter that swept through the Cheese was deafening.

The balconies shook and quivered under the Gemcloaks—and under everyone else, by the feel of it, as drunken patrons started to clap rhythmically. The dancers obliged by hiking what little skirts they wore to kick in time, and the very stage swayed.

"Magic?" Beldar muttered. "'Tis like being on a ship fighting high seas in the harbor!"

"Hoy!" Taeros exclaimed suddenly, slapping his friend's arm. "Look! Isn't that Jessra Belabranta?"

He was pointing at the next balcony, barely the stretch of two long arms away. His gesture was noticed by its occupants, who waved and grinned back.

Beldar and Malark looked, and momentarily forgot the balcony-shaking dancers below.

Jessra Belabranta was widely held to be the silliest and most slow-witted of the Belabranta sisters—as well as the fattest. Her natural endowments were ample in all directions, and she was proudly displaying a pair of them to everyone in the festhall at the moment.

Jessra had evidently just acquired a mer-scale bustier—a garment simply dripping with thumb-sized, teardrop-shaped deep sea pearls of the sort reputed to be the exclusive "catch" of certain pirates of the Nelanther. She obviously wanted all Waterdeep to see those pearls, and the designer of her new garment understood that teardrop sea pearls are best displayed dangling from something and so designed the bustier to reveal to all the watching world the magnificent frontage of the wearer.

Jessra's frontage was . . . expansive, and the gems she'd glued all over them in a random array did nothing to detract from this.

She was also obviously of the school of taste that believes too much is better and had just tossed a pinch of glow-dust over her bosom. The effect was very much as if a lantern had been lit atop two . . . two . . .

Taeros whirled around to face Beldar, swept a flurry of cheeses off the little table, and with a finger wrote in the revealed dust beneath: *Two blind whales trying to out-leap each other!*

Beldar stared down at the symbols—a code they'd not used since they were young boys together, bored beyond yawns at the same revels. Then it all came back to him. He looked up again at Jessra Belabranta and whooped with helpless laughter.

Taeros promptly joined in, almost choking with mirth, as Malark sat there grinning at them and rolling his eyes.

Jessra cast them a slightly annoyed look through the trembling din of the sort that asks, "And just what do you find so *amusing?*"

That, of course, only made Beldar laugh all the harder, slapping the table hard.

As if that had been the proverbial last stroke of a woodsman's axe, the table fell through the balcony floor. The slowly building groan of wood that followed was almost deafening, and a startled Taeros stood and spun around in time to see . . .

All the balconies swaying, sliding, their support-pillars leaning . . .

Boards popped free, folk screamed, and patrons toppled helplessly over the low balcony rails.

Then everything was falling, with an enthusiastic roar.

CHAPTER SEVEN

Elaith Craulnober lounged against the doorpost, watching the fear that had leaped into the young woman's eyes. Apparently she wasn't a complete fool. He had yet to ascertain, however, exactly what she was.

He watched as she gathered herself with admirable speed. Her panic faded, and her softly curving smile of invitation was more subtle than most he'd received this night from fine Waterdhavian ladies. The dock whores of Luskan evidently bred a finer class of trollop.

"In truth, Lord Craulnober," she breathed, "I was hoping you'd follow me here."

The elf smiled. "You're pretty enough, by human standards, to add temptation to that offer," he said dryly, "but I can hardly leave my guests long enough to make a tryst worth my while or yours."

She cocked her head to one side. "Strange words from one who's not yet appeared among his guests."

"Oh? Who can say with assurance that I have not?"

The girl calmly made no answer. Some of Elaith's guests had responded to similar suggestions with barely disguised panic. Their eyes had grown wide and wild as they took hasty inventory of what they'd said, and to whom, and in whose hearing. This girl knew she'd committed no indiscretion. She'd said or done nothing, save intruding here, to offend her notorious host. That alone made her a rarity among his guests.

He regarded the girl with something approaching interest. "You must have been wandering about alone for quite some time to not have heard the whispers in the great hall."

"You'll have to be more specific, my lord," she replied. "Waterdeep knows no shortage of rumors."

"True enough. I'm not so thoughtless and inattentive a host as you suppose. While it's true I've not entered the great hall—at least, not as you see me now—I've received several of my guests at brief private meetings."

She nodded, understanding at once. "They leave your presence speaking of things you'd like to hear said when nobles talk with nobles, rather than making idle chat about the cut of your clothes and the quality of your wine."

"Well said," he told her approvingly.

"And, of course, the nobles of Waterdeep being what they are, those who were given an audience will lord it over those who weren't," she added. "I'd wager gold against copper that within a tenday, half of those spurned will seek you out. Whatever the business at hand, you'll get a better offer from the come-lately folk than from those you spoke with tonight."

The elf's silver brows rose. "Well said, indeed. You know the fair flower of our citizenry well for a foreigner."

He allowed himself a certain dark pleasure at the sudden panic that flashed into her eyes. "You must be enjoying our sea breezes, Lady Evenmoon. Tashluta's very warm during the Flamerule moon."

If the girl harbored any uncertainty about this matter, she hid it well. "Warmer than in winter, certainly."

Elaith chuckled at her deft parry. He swept one hand lightly toward her, subtly unleashing a minor spell. "Please be seated. Not on the carpet, preferably, though I can see why you were on the floor when I entered the room."

Her eyes were wary as she moved away from the desk and took the chair he'd indicated. "I'm not sure I understand, my lord."

"Why, you've lost an ornament, of course."

The girl's hand immediately went to the green ribbon around

her left arm—precisely the response Elaith had anticipated. He suppressed a smile. Toying with this girl was the most pleasure he'd had all evening.

"I was speaking of your earring," he said lightly. Striding around behind the desk, he plucked from the carpet a hoop of silver wire, from which was suspended an intricately knotted web of gem-like threads.

The girl's brown eyes widened and her hand lifted to her ear. She'd not felt the earring vanish with his simple theft-spell.

"Thank you," she said, accepting the pretty thing.

Her eyes followed him as he went directly to the hiding place and touched the carved wood in precisely the spot that released the hidden panel.

The young woman relaxed noticeably, hardly the response he'd expected from someone whose secret message had just been intercepted.

Elaith skimmed the note, a report about some merchants seeking to unmask the Lords of Waterdeep. From its tone, it was apparent that this girl, or someone who paid her hire, was an agent of one of the Lords. He raised his eyes from it to meet her watchful gaze.

"For whom are you working, girl?"

Uncertainty flickered over her face, swiftly blossoming into suspicion. Elaith realized, to his surprise and delight, that she assumed *he* was her contact!

Logical enough, being as he'd shown familiarity with the hiding place. Folk who knew little of magic seldom stopped to think about the precautions taken by those who did. Elaith knew of every magic in this villa, including those borne by each of his guests. Magical toys of his own collected such information.

"Who do you work for?" he repeated, phrasing his query in less formal terms and, not incidentally, in a manner one of his magical devices would recognize.

He glanced at one of several portraits hanging on the wall. The nondescript image shifted, taking on the features of Texter the paladin—an image taken from the girl's thoughts.

Well, well. Little surprise there; Texter had long been on Elaith's private short list of suspected Lords. The paladin's business often took him north, and he was the sort to rescue maidens in distress. No doubt he'd extricated this girl from the clutches of a rough-handed patron, thinking her a set-upon serving girl.

"A reasonable question," he continued, staring into her increasingly suspicious face, "given your former employment. Our good friend Texter holds a far more optimistic view of human nature than I do."

Color drained from the girl's face. "What do you know of that?" she whispered.

In a heartbeat, he was standing over her, dangling the ribbon from her arm tauntingly before her eyes. Too late, she slapped a hand over the small brand burned into her upper arm.

"A mark of indenture," Elaith said softly, recognizing the shape of the old scar. "All too common on the docks of barbarous Luskan. Your mother was a tavern slut and owed more than she could ever hope to repay on her own. She no doubt rejoiced when her belly swelled with a ten-fathered bastard, and sold the babe at birth. I doubt you were much past childhood when you started plying your mother's trade."

To her credit, the girl did not weep or plead with him to stop. A question burned in her eyes, more painful to her than her revealed shame. "Did he tell you?"

Elaith did not need to ask whom she meant. Something held him back from naming the paladin as his source. His reticence was not, he told himself, prompted by a desire to save the girl from disillusionment and pain. It was merely—practical. Let her believe in her Texter's shining honor, and so let her continue to send and receive messages. Messages the Serpent would intercept and profit from.

"I have some ... small magical skills," he murmured, giving her his softest smile. "You may rest assured: *Texter* did not betray you."

The emphasis was not lost on her. "But you might."

"If it affords me an advantage, certainly. That's why I make it a point to know the secrets of everyone in my employ."

She frowned, lips thinning.

"It's not escaped my notice that you've avoided your first trade since arriving in Waterdeep—in fact, you seem to want nothing much to do with men."

He let the ribbon drift down, and watched her snatch it deftly out of the air before adding dryly, "It would gladden my heart if more elven females would emulate your good judgment in such matters."

"I want nothing to do with male elves, either," Lark said bluntly.

He smiled, faintly amused by her presumption. "You'll have no quarrel from me on that score; it's hardly the service I require from you."

The girl shook her head. "I owe a debt of honor to Texter. It's him I'll serve, and no other."

"Is that so?" he asked mildly. "Whom would you serve if your tawdry past became common knowledge? The working-class respectability so dear to Master Dyre would demand you be summarily dismissed and loudly denounced. You'd be hard-pressed to find another position among respectable folk."

She regarded him with a mixture of anger and uncertainly, but said nothing. Merely watched him, eyes larger and darker. Waiting to hear her fate.

Elaith smiled pleasantly. "You wish to leave your past behind. Commendable." *Time to twist the knife.* "Also understandable. I can see how this knowledge could color your working relationship with an upstanding man like Texter."

"You son of a snake," she said softly.

Elaith's smile never faltered. "I'll ask you one more time: Who are you working for?"

A long, heavy silence followed as Lark wrestled with herself under his interested eye. Then she took a long breath and squared her shoulders.

"You," she said heavily.

The elf took her at her word. How could he not? The portrait of Texter had shifted again, and his own handsome face gazed out of the frame, amber eyes gleaming over a smile of supreme satisfaction.

🏰 🏰 🏰 🏰 🏰

The rumble and roar of falling timber was all around, unseen in swirling, choking dust.

"Taeros!" came a familiar Roaringhorn bellow. "Malark!"

Taeros knew Beldar was nearby, somewhere *that* way ... but "that way" was all dust, fallen wood, and leaning beams.

Lanterns and candles had crashed down everywhere to start little leaping fires, and their flickering glows showed Lord Hawkwinter a swaying, swinging chaos of ropes and beams. Smoke was rolling and eddying energetically—and all around him wood was *screaming*.

Taeros wouldn't have believed splintering, rending wood could scream, but then, he hadn't known it could groan, either.

It was doing both right now, even more loudly than the frantic, sobbing screams of women blundering about in the alarmingly leaning labyrinth of pillars and sagging balconies. Men were shouting and coughing, and at least one fool had drawn a sword and was slashing wildly as he came staggering through the dusty gloom, as if sharp steel could slaughter dust.

As Taeros struggled to his feet, the remains of someone's chair and table falling away from his bruised shoulders, a balcony tore free and plunged to the stage with a thunderous crash. In an instant, the man waving the sword was smashed into a bloody smear on those shattered, bouncing boards.

Taeros saw that sword, still clutched by the severed ruin of a forearm, clatter to the floor near Malark, who was having troubles of his own amid much splintered furniture. Then roiling dust hid Lord Kothont again.

Curses and thuds heralded someone wearing a splendid scarlet-and-gold tunic, not Malark's emerald gemfire, who came stumbling out of the dust. The man clawed his way past Taeros, trailing a stream of curses and half-dragging someone long-haired and presumably feminine whose slender shoulder slammed into Beldar with force enough to stop a Roaringhorn bellow in mid-roar, and leave Beldar retching on his knees.

Well, at least Taeros now knew where *that* friend was. He turned toward Beldar, but—

Another balcony fell, with a splintering, floor-shaking crash. And then another.

Taeros fought for balance on floorboards that were suddenly rising and falling like waves rolling into the harbor.

The next crash was a long, rolling, ear-hammering chaos, and Taeros saw a ceiling-beam, wreathed in flames, plunge to the floor. Dust rose like a wall.

As the echoes of its rolling faded, he became aware that someone was shouting—someone familiar. Beldar had found his breath again.

"Get out! Come *on!* We've *got* to get out!"

Taeros turned, staggering as loose boards shifted under his boots, and then glanced back. Had Malark—?

Other patrons were thundering past, running blindly. Some slammed into already trembling pillars and reeled sideways or fell senseless.

Flames flared as a fallen curtain ignited, and Taeros could suddenly see the stage again, where blood lay in pools and still, huddled forms were sprawled under tangles of jagged wood.

"Malark?" Taeros shouted, peering at where his friend had been. Dust swirled thickly there, but he thought he saw a glimmer of green.

He started forward—and fell hard as something else collapsed, far off in the gloom, and the floor bounced and rippled again.

More grandly garbed folk came running out of the smoke and dust, wild-eyed and staggering. Among them, a woman who wore a tiara and dripped with jewels was cursing like a sailor as she tried to twist and tear free of three or four terrified serving-girls who were clinging to her long sleeves and trailing gown.

"Let *go!*" the woman spat. Cloth tore with a long snarl of protest, baring her legs, and a mewling trio of maids crashed to their knees in the wreckage.

Weeping with fear and rage, the woman ran on, spraying jewels in her wake like hailstones. Across much dust and chaos, Taeros finally caught sight of Malark's familiar grin—directed not at him, but at a servant-lass who was clinging to him, sobbing and trembling.

As they emerged fully from the dense smoke, Lord Kothont put her gently away from him and gave her a little shove in the direction of the door. She stumbled, then caught herself and darted toward safety. Malark nodded in satisfaction, then reached down to pluck up one of the three terrified maids.

And then, with a crash like the hammer of Gond coming down on his Greatforge, three or four ceiling-beams came down right in front of Taeros, hurling him helplessly back, arms flailing, into—something hard yet yielding that cursed as it collapsed under him.

"Hawkwinter?" whoever it was snarled. "That you?"

"Beldar!" Taeros gasped, fighting for breath. His arm was numb, one of his knees was burning as if afire, and—

"*Up*, and out of this!" Beldar growled, rising up under Taeros like a harbor wave. His snarling strength hauled them both to their feet, and they swayed together as more beams fell. Then the young flower of House Roaringhorn snatched, heaved, and broke into a stumbling run, Taeros Hawkwinter bobbing along on his shoulder like a sack of meal.

"Malark—"

"Can fend for his bloody self," Beldar panted. "Much good we'll be ... to him ... flat as ... fish-heads underfoot ... on the docks. 'Sides, have you ever known Malark not slide out of *anything?*"

Taeros couldn't find breath for a reply as he was hustled along, bouncing jaw biting his own tongue repeatedly, but he didn't have to. Malark would come out unscathed. Malark always did.

⚒ ⚒ ⚒ ⚒ ⚒

He couldn't stop coughing.

On his knees on the dirty cobbles, Taeros hacked and spat and heaved, shoulders shaking, until a grim-jawed Beldar slapped his back hard enough to drive him nose down onto the stones, which promptly rattled and shook hard enough to numb a Hawkwinter chin and send its owner rolling helplessly over onto his side, still coughing.

"What was—?" he managed to ask.

"The last of the Slow Cheese," Beldar Roaringhorn snapped, in a voice that promised brutal death to someone, and soon. "Going down flat."

"M-Malark?"

"Under it, somewhere." Beldar thrust something under his friend's nose.

Taeros blinked at it, fighting for breath.

"This," Beldar growled, "was stuck to a spar that was flung into the air just after I carried you over here—and damned near skewered me coming down. It was stuck there with blood."

Taeros stared at what his friend was holding: A blood-smeared scrap of emerald green gemweave, cloth that in all Waterdeep, only Malark Kothont could have been wearing.

CHAPTER EIGHT

The first rumble and roar brought Golskyn from his bed, coverlets flying. He hurried to the window of their upper room and gazed up into the midnight sky, his uncovered eye searching the stars with open longing.

"A dragon's heart," he said wistfully. "Now *that* would be a true test of a man's strength!"

Mrelder stumbled to his father's side, rubbing sleep from his eyes. His thoughts were not of dragon flight, nor the wondrous challenge of capturing, dismembering, and incorporating that greatest of creatures. He thought instead of the city all around and the folk who dwelt in it. Fresh rumblings drew his gaze.

"A building's fallen!" He pointed. "Look, there: Dust rising. Flames now, too."

Golskyn peered. "Dragonfire?" he asked hopefully, not ready to relinquish his fond hope.

"No dragons," his son murmured.

Mrelder thought he might know the cause of the collapse. The mongrelmen had tunneled thereabouts to link to the cellars of another of Golskyn's buildings. Lord Unity wasn't the only priest of monstrous gods in Waterdeep, but he was new to Waterdhavians, and undeniably impressive. Folk were flocking to his hidden rituals, and the traffic beneath Waterdeep's streets was rapidly increasing. If one foundation had been so weakened, what else might soon fall?

Once the rubble was cleared, that tunnel would be discovered, and then—

The sharp, suspicious glare of his father's uncovered eye suddenly blocked Mrelder's view.

"You know something of this," Golskyn snapped. It was not a question.

Mrelder's thoughts raced. Nothing less than a solution would serve; Golskyn had no patience for unsolved problems.

"Well?"

A map of the city sewers came suddenly to mind, and with it his answer.

"I had the mongrelmen undermine yon building's foundation," Mrelder lied. Golskyn scowled, and his son added hastily, "Their work runs *very* close to a long established sewer-run. It'll be short work to breach what's between them and use the dirt and stone to block off one end of our passage, keeping it secret."

"And the *other* end?"

"Leads to an old warehouse, half-full of the rubble of our diggings."

Golskyn's scowl remained. "I like this *not*. Too high a risk."

"How so? Investigation will show only that someone's extending tunnels. Most Waterdhavians believe the Lords control the tunnels, so the Lords'll be blamed. The more troubles Lord Piergeiron must answer for, the more frequently he'll be out among the people—and the more opportunities we'll have to lay hands on the Guardian's Gorget."

"And this warehouse?"

A genuine smile spread across Mrelder's face. "I won it at dice—no coin changed hands, no papers—from an old, retired merchant. He had no family, and, ahem, died suddenly. Shortly after our game."

"He'd no parts worth keeping, I'll warrant," Golskyn muttered predictably, in his usual response to news of death, dismemberment, or murder.

"Alas, none. Heirs and mourners: None again. If anyone wonders who owns the warehouse, the law's clear: as he had no heirs, it's now city property. Another finger pointing at the Lords."

Lord Unity's scowl was gone. "You've given this hard thought."

Mrelder nodded. "Once the 'why' of this collapse is known, citizens'll be ready enough to blame tunneling for other downfalls."

"There are *other* buildings down?"

"Not yet." Mrelder smiled. "Before dawn, another building will fall. Far from here, so no hint of suspicion comes to our doors."

Golskyn actually smiled. "Your sorcery will cause this?"

Mrelder bowed.

The priest squinted at the sky. "You'd best get on with it, my son. Dawn is but three bells away."

My son. Mrelder turned away to hide his blushing smile. He'd never thought to hear those words spoken so casually, much less with something approaching pride. He'd felt such happiness only once before, but then it had been Lord Piergeiron who'd looked on him with warmth and called him friend.

The sorcerer put that fond memory firmly out of his mind and strode across the room to his clothes. It was time to go out and spread dissent and destruction in Lord Piergeiron's Waterdeep.

🏰 🏰 🏰 🏰 🏰

The guards on the Palace steps gave Mrelder hard, steady stares, but let him pass.

The guards inside challenged him, and no wonder. The mists weren't off the harbor yet; it was early indeed to have honest business at the Palace.

However, it seemed the polite note he'd sent Piergeiron yestereve, mentioning his own arrival in Waterdeep and inquiring after the First Lord's health, had done its work well. Merely giving his name had the guards nodding respectfully and waving him toward a servant in a fine tabard.

"The First Lord bids you welcome and wishes Waterdeep had more friends of your mettle," that man said approvingly, as he waved Mrelder smoothly through a door that looked like most of the others in that long, lofty hall.

Morningfeast for Piergeiron was evidently a hearty serve-yourself affair. Steam was rising from platters on a sideboard, where about a dozen grandly dressed, important looking men with serious, frowning faces were forking sausages and smoked silverfin into wooden bowls, and plucking boiled eggs out of a sea of spiced butter. They looked as if they were expecting grim doom to strike them down before highsun, and had little desire to meet it with empty bellies.

The First Lord looked up from a stack of papers a clerk had just put in front of him, smiled broadly, and waved Mrelder to the sideboard.

Mredler grinned back. Whatever his father's intended dooms for Waterdeep or anyone who stood in his way—and the First Lord of Waterdeep could hardly help but do that—he found it impossible to dislike this man.

"We can talk soon," Piergeiron promised, taking a quill the clerk was already holding out to him.

The son of Lord Unity joined the men at the sideboard, who all gave him silent "And you are—?" frowns. He found himself nose to nose with sleepy-eyed City Guard officers, a few softly gliding courtiers, and several grumpy looking Watchful Order wizards.

Mrelder's stomach rumbled. Several of the guardsmen were heaping their bowls to precarious heights, so he didn't stint in filling his own, ere he sat with the others at the long table. He had the far end from Piergeiron, of course, but as he dug into fried mushrooms dripping with some sort of sauce and gratefully received a drinking-jack of warmed zzar from a deft servant, he gathered from the speed with which the others were eating that they'd soon be out the doors to their duties.

So it proved, and Mrelder was just sitting back from his last few sausages with a sigh of contentment—gods of Amalgamation, it'd been *years* since he'd eaten this well!—when the oldest-looking wizard sat down right beside him and asked quietly, "And you are—?"

"Mrelder. I—"

"Fought beside the Lord Piergeiron in defense of the city, and are his personal friend, yes," the wizard said smoothly, his dark old eyes keen and bright. "Perhaps I should have added the words, 'here for' to my question, thus: And you are here for—?"

"Ah, to thank the Lord for his advice, and tell him I found my father, just as he suggested. And to give him a gift."

"Aha. What *sort* of a gift?" Two rings on the wizard's fingers winked into life.

Mrelder had expected this but put a puzzled frown on his face as he dug into his belt pouch. Retrieving the small copper coin he and two Amalgamation acolytes had done so much hasty work on, he put it on the table.

The mage peered at it suspiciously. Its origins were evident if one examined it closely enough, but it now had the shape of a small copper shield bearing, in an arc, the words: "All Perils Defeated."

The wizard held a hand above the badge. A third ring kindled into life, and he gave Mrelder an unfriendly look. Taking up a fork left behind in someone's bowl, he carefully turned the little shield over and read aloud its obverse: "To the Open Lord of Waterdeep, in deepest respect, from admirers at Candlekeep."

"Fine folk, all! Well met, friend Mrelder!"

The sorcerer sprang up to greet his host. Piergeiron, it seemed, could move as silently as a cat when he wanted to. They grasped sword-forearms, in the greeting of one trusted warrior to another.

"You found your father?"

Gods, he remembered!

Mrelder found himself grinning widely. "Yes, Lord, and I wanted to thank you in person for your advice. We're reconciled."

In our own manner, at least.

"Good! Good! So what's got Tarthus here so suspicious?"

"I—I'm afraid I was bold enough, Lord, to bring you a gift, on behalf of all who came from Candlekeep to fight for you that day. We'd be honored—"

"As will I!" Piergeiron said heartily.

"There're no spells on it, Lord," the mage murmured, "but prudence demands ..."

"Of course, of course."

Mrelder carefully kept all trace of a smile off his face. Not a spell, but a spell focus, by which Mrelder, who'd so painstakingly engraved the cruder of the two messages it bore, could with a swift spell of his own easily track Piergeiron's whereabouts.

The Open Lord took up the shield and admired it with pure, simple pleasure. "All Perils Defeated, eh? I wish I could measure up to that. Still, let it be my goal and be ever with me." He turned it in his palm. "Made from a copper piece. Clever." He fixed Mrelder with that disconcertingly direct gaze and said simply, "Thank you. This is a princely gift."

Mrelder knew he was blushing. Boldly, before he lost his nerve and the chance, he stood up, took the little badge from the Open Lord of Waterdeep, and went down the table to where Piergeiron's war-helm sat, holding down stacks of papers still awaiting the Paladin's signature.

Slipping the point of the shield firmly under the edge of the brow-guard that surmounted the helm's eye-slits, he settled it in place, centered over the nose guard. "There!"

Piergeiron grinned again. "Now, *that* I shall be proud to wear." His grin faded. "Though hopefully not soon. Waterdeep enjoys a hard-won peace."

Mrelder put the helm down carefully and came back down the table, aware of the wizard's thoughtful scrutiny. Tarthus had doubtless noticed the spell of binding Mrelder had cast on the shield earlier, to keep it affixed wherever it was put. No matter: There was no magic more harmless.

"Peace is always my hope, too," the young sorcerer said quietly, "yet strangely, Lord, the mood in the city now seems darker than when folk were fighting beasts from the sea. If I may speak bluntly: I've been in cities in the South where unrest was strong, and this has the same feel."

Piergeiron nodded. "You see and speak truth, lad." He strode back down the table, frowning. "Waterdhavians work together against clear peril," he added slowly, "but not in times of prosperity."

Mrelder spread his hands. "Why not remind citizens that in the thrust and parry of trade, Waterdeep is in one sense always at war? Some folk only see a battle when blades are bared and blood flows."

Tarthus was frowning at Mrelder now, too. "What sort of reminder?"

Keeping his eyes on Piergeiron, Mrelder waved at the war-helm.

"Put on your armor. Be seen only clad in battle-steel, sword at your side, awakening not fear but remembrances of victories and sacrifices—a rebuke to those distracted by foolish trifles and an reminder to all of the precious cost of what they enjoy."

"You," Piergeiron replied slowly, "are a lad no longer, but well on your way to being a graybearded sage."

He strode to where he could snatch up his helm and did so, smiling at its gleaming curves. "I've always preferred honest battle-steel, even with its heat and discomfort, to walking about in whatever foppish nonsense is currently in fashion."

Mrelder nodded. "Folk know you in your armor, and it's probably best if you're seen and recognized all over the city. I heard more than a little unhappy talk in Dock Ward this morn that you were dead or gone from Waterdeep, and tax collectors were inventing their own orders and charges in your name." He spread his hands. "We of Candlekeep have a proverb: If a thing is said often enough, fools aplenty will believe it to be true."

The First Lord and his wizard exchanged a quick glance. "Graybeard indeed," murmured Piergeiron.

⚓ ⚓ ⚓ ⚓ ⚓

Tarthus drew his cloak around himself. The wind on the high balcony was, as usual, as cold as a knife blade. Piergeiron had stopped looking at the new badge on his helm at last, and was gazing out over the city. The wizard kept silent, waiting for what he knew would come.

"Well, Tarthus?"

"Some things the lad kept from you. I doubt his meeting with his father went as well as he wanted you to believe."

Piergeiron sighed. "Hardly unusual, I'm afraid, and tells us nothing sinister about young Mrelder. So they're saying I'm dead again, are they?"

Tarthus had been the Open Lord's spell-guard for a long time, but he was still a senior Watchful Order member and kept himself well informed. "Though it seemed a rather heavy-handed urging on the lad's part, he spoke truth. They *are* saying you're dead down on the docks, and of course, that all manner of villains and impostors are signing your name to decrees and running the city just as they see fit."

Piergeiron's smile was wintry. "Who would these villains and impostors be?"

"We of the Castle. Every last belted noble in every last mansion and crypt in the city. The secret cabal of wizards who've ruled Waterdeep these past three eons. Dragons using spells to take the faces of humans. A legion comprised solely of Elminster's bastard offspring. Take thy pick."

The Open Lord of Waterdeep sighed and clapped his war-helm onto his head. "None of those, thanks. Let's go find my armor, and you can check it for sinister spells, too."

"Of course, Lord," the wizard replied calmly. "Someone may have cast some since I last checked it, yestermorn."

🏰 🏰 🏰 🏰 🏰

The door thudded sullenly against the wall of Varandros Dyre's new meeting chamber, and a sleepy-eyed Karrak Lhamphur lurched into the room.

"You're late," Jarago Whaelshod growled. "*My* working day begins three bells before dawn, not one."

"Work a little harder, so as to enjoy the successes I have," Karrak Lhamphur flung back, "and you can sleep in just as late as I do!"

Whaelshod grumbled wordlessly, turned his heavy-lidded

gaze to their host, and barked, "Well? We had to wait until this sluggard got here for *what*, exactly?"

Varandros Dyre looked less than bright-eyed himself this morning. "Two buildings collapsed last night," he said grimly.

Lhamphur frowned. "You're blaming *those* on the Lords and nobles? I doubt they even know what holds buildings *up*, let alone what makes them fall down! That's why they hire the likes of us, no?"

"They didn't hire *me* to dig tunnels that aren't on my maps," Dyre snapped back, "and how else d'you think the collapses occurred? Both buildings fell *into* something."

"Like a pit that shouldn't have been there," Hasmur Ghaunt put in nervously.

Dorn Imdrael drank the last of his steaming broth and waved his tankard. "Thanks for this, Var. It's hard for a man to think on an empty stomach."

Turning to Whaelshod and Lhamphur, he pointedly eyed their still full mugs and asked quietly, "Who else could pay for a tunnel without the rest of us knowing about it? Or do the digging, without all the city gossiping about it? There's a warehouse by the docks full of dirt up to the rafters. Doubtless it's where someone stored what they dug out of a secret tunnel—and I *can't* believe the Watch and the Guard *and* the Watchful Order are all such idiots they don't notice when something like that's going on. No, Var's right: the Lords are to blame for this."

"Well said," Ghaunt agreed hastily, looking at Varandros.

Dyre bared teeth in what might have been a smile. "*Thank* you, Dorn. I say again: we must learn who wears the Lords' masks . . . and one way or another, see that the *real* incompetents among them get replaced."

"'One way or another'?" Imdrael echoed. "Var, we must be *very* careful. Even if we do nothing that makes anyone decide to put a blade through us, we'd be wise to remember that old saying about toes."

Jarago Whaelshod scowled, in no mood to play games this morning. "What old saying?"

"Be careful which toes you step on now, lest they be connected to the arse you must kiss on the morrow."

Karrak Lhamphur waved away those words with an impatient hand. "How exactly do we set about learning who's a Lord?"

"Watch over Mirt's Mansion from now on, to see just who comes and goes, because . . ."

"I know!" Hasmur interrupted excitedly. "Because *everyone* knows Mirt's a Lord!"

♛ ♛ ♛ ♛ ♛

Naoni silently closed the well-oiled door, turned her key in its lock with slow, exacting care, and sat down with Faendra and Lark around the broth pot. A warm, rich-smelling mist was rising from it in the chill of approaching dawn, but they left their mugs untouched, staring at each other with identical looks of dismay.

"And so it starts," she whispered. "Father's striding right down the path that can take them all to their deaths."

"And us with them," Lark said quietly.

Faendra turned wide eyes on them both and asked forlornly, "So what do we *do?*"

Naoni rose and began to pace, her thoughts flying. "Hasmur Ghaunt's the one to work on. The others are much too clever. We leave them be until we've learned things from Ghaunt that we can 'let slip' to make the others think Father's brought us into his confidence. Your task, Faen!"

Her sister smiled sweetly, lashes fluttering over guileless blue eyes. "Dear Hasmur," she murmured. "So very wise, so handsome—"

"Don't fluster him overmuch," Lark warned, "or the poor man won't be able to stammer a word. We need to know, as things unfold, just how far each of them is willing to go."

Boots thundered faintly down the stairs within, and Lark hissed, "Lean back and look sleepy!"

They barely had time to do so ere the lock rattled and the door grated open. Jarago Whaelshod glared out suspiciously. Seeing naught but three sleepy girls huddled in their cloaks, he nodded in grim satisfaction and strode out and away down the street without a word.

Lhamphur and Imdrael were hardly slower, though both returned their tankards with murmured thanks.

Then Hasmur Ghaunt was blinking out at the brightening dawn. Alone. The girls exchanged glances.

Naoni quickly slipped past Master Ghaunt and up the stairs to forestall her father's departure for a few breaths, and Lark knelt to tend the fire. Faendra stepped to Hasmur Ghaunt's side with an understanding smile and murmured, "I know how upsetting this must be for a man as wise as you."

Ghaunt blinked at her, then blushed at the thought such a lovely young lass would know something about him. Had she—no, surely not—said "wise"? He cleared his throat. "'This'?"

"This business with the Lords," Faendra said, eyes demurely downcast. "You've always been the most *understanding* of Father's friends. I know he trusts you more than anyone else in the New Day."

Her gaze lifted to Ghaunt's face as it drained of color. "New—? How—?" he croaked.

Faendra patted his arm, then took it and walked him a little away from the doors, snuggling against him. Trembling against her soft warmth, Hasmur Ghaunt made the mistake of looking into her blue, blue eyes and was lost.

"Father tells us everything, since Mother died," Faendra told him a little sadly. "I know he was worried that Whaelshod and Lhamphur didn't believe him. Did he tell *you* why he thinks the Lords are watching him?"

Master Ghaunt blinked. "Y-yes. He showed us all."

"Showed you?"

Faendra raised her eyebrows and turned her face to his in mute appeal, and Hasmur Ghaunt blushed vividly and stammered, "Y-you're right: Jarago pressed him to say why he's so sure the Lords are watching him, and Var—uh, your father, showed us a little charm he found in a tunnel near one of his worksites: A Black Helm token, of the sort Lord Piergeiron passes out as marks of his favor!"

"In a tunnel," Faendra echoed soothingly, looking very serious.

"Aye—yes—err—ah, a tunnel your father swore wasn't on any map he, a master stonemason, has access to, so . . ."

"So it must be one of the secret tunnels the Lords use to keep an eye on honest men like you and Father," Faendra breathed, her wide eyes very close to Ghaunt's.

He trembled in her grasp like a rabbit on the verge of fleeing. Then there was a familiar roar from behind them both, and Master Hasmur Ghaunt tore free with a high-pitched stammer of apologies and fled, gone down the street in a scampering instant.

"Stop *teasing* the man, Faen!" Varandros Dyre growled, stamping up to his favorite daughter. "You've been making men blush like lasses since your twelfth winter, but Ghaunt has work to do, and 'tisn't seemly, a daughter of mine reducing a grown man to gabbling, in a public street!"

"Father," Faendra said reproachfully. "That's hardly fair! Master Ghaunt's like an uncle to us. He's the only one who has time for our jokes, and he's polite when we—"

"Yes, *yes*," her father agreed curtly. "Now get in there and clean the place up! Mind you bar the door and keep behind it, and have the place spotless before highsun; I'll send some of my men then to escort you home. You're *not* to go traipsing around on your own. What with footpads and wandering nobles, this ward isn't safe for young gels to be flouncing through unguarded!"

Faendra knew when it was time to meekly agree—whatever her actual intentions might be—and give her father a quick hug and kiss. This was one such time.

Then he was off down the street like a thunderstorm afoot, and she and Lark were settling the bar into place.

Naoni came down the last few steps, her face thoughtful. "I recall once," she said slowly, "Father having dealings with an old tunnel-repairer, one Thandar Buckblade. Remember, Faen?"

Faendra shook her head. "Father has dealings with lots of old men. I get tired of their winks and leers. Some are so old they can't even whistle, and they just *wheeze* at me!"

Lark rolled her eyes. "Don't be so quick to dismiss old men. There can be snow on the roof *and* fire in the loins."

"This Buckblade," Naoni said firmly, "was a dwarf of Dock Ward. Father said he knew everything under the cobbles of the city. *Everything.* He retired years ago."

Lark frowned. "And you think we should go and ask this Buckblade about the Lords' secret tunnels? If he was in the habit of giving away the Lords' secrets, how did he live long enough to retire?"

"Perhaps his reaction will tell us something."

"And if he gets angry and demands to know where you got this foolheaded notion?"

"I . . . I'll tell him I overheard Mirt the Moneylender talking about the tunnels when he was drunk—and claiming he was a Lord, too!"

Lark shrugged to the accompaniment of Faendra's long, low whistle of appreciation, and said reluctantly, "That should work, but make it his *servant*, not Mirt himself. Who'd believe the Old Wolf a loose-tongued drunkard?" When Naoni nodded, she added, "So where exactly do we find this dwarf?"

"On our shopping next morn, we can ask some of the men Father trades with if they know where Buckblade lives, and then go see him after our highsun rounds the day after."

Faendra's nod was as eager as her grin was wide.

"Mistresses, it seems adventure awaits," Lark said dryly, "but first things first: While fortune may favor the bold, masters *pay* the tidy and hardworking. Hand me that mop."

CHAPTER NINE

Korvaun unlocked the clubhouse door and held it open for the trio who'd followed him up the stairs, carrying fresh provender for the Gemcloaks' morningfeast. His friends had agreed to meet here first thing in the morning, which to them of course meant "shortly before highsun." Accordingly, Korvaun had ordered a spread of cold food commonly served at both morning and afternoon meals: breads, cheeses, sliced roasts, berry tarts, and cool ale.

His thanks and coins swiftly saw the baker's man and the provender shop delivery lad off, so he could supervise the placement of the ale.

The brew had been carried up by the brewer's apprentice, a boy of perhaps thirteen winters, who lingered after the handkeg was settled on the coldsmoke rack, staring at wisps of cold steam rising from the rack's copper basin.

"How's that done?" he demanded, too fascinated to remember proper deference to nobility.

"Handy magic." Korvaun plucked up the vial of coldsmoke liquid. "A few drops of this in the basin—so—creates enough cold air to cool a cask this size for two days."

A frigid cloud rose from the basin, and the copper fittings of the barrel misted over at once. The boy peered with bright-eyed interest, and Korvaun thought of his own boyhood. He remembered intense impatience when lessons ran overlong, but he'd been fortunate to have had the opportunity to learn. There'd be no books, lessons, or boring tutors for this lad.

The apprentice waved at the vial. "What if you get that on your hand?"

Korvaun smiled. "Well asked; I'm sure Nipvar Tattersky—the alchemist who devised coldsmoke—wishes he'd had your foresight. His best mouser tipped over a vial and was frozen alive, as stiff as wood. Master Tattersky's exceedingly fond of his cats, and spent days seeking a priest willing to beseech the gods on behalf of a cat. He altered his potion, so now it works only while touching copper."

The lad was frowning but also nodding slowly.

On impulse Korvaun asked, "Why do you suppose he chose copper?"

The apprentice looked at him. "I'd say he didn't want coldsmoke used as a weapon or *on* weapons so warriors could freeze foes at a touch. No one fights with copper blades, but coopers use it all the time."

The youngest Lord Helmfast nodded, impressed. This lad was as bright as new coin, utterly wasted as a brewer's drudge. "How came you to Master Drinder?"

The lad shrugged. "My father knows Drinder, or you might say he knows his ale. Da's powerful fond of it and likes to chide me for the six tenday's drinking lost to my apprentice fee."

Outrage flooded Korvaun. "Your father sold you for two months of ale?"

The boy's jaw dropped. He stared at Korvaun and then whooped with laughter. "Oh-hoho, that's rich! A *master* don't pay the apprentice fee! It's the 'prentice as pays *him*—and thanks him for the privilege!"

"I see." That made sense, given that an apprenticeship was a crafter's education. "If you could do anything, would you have apprenticed to a brewer?"

The lad gave Korvaun a puzzled frown. The thought of choosing a livelihood was obviously new to him. "There's a lot to brewing," he said slowly, "but Master Drinder says I need only know what he sees fit to tell me, which isn't much more than fetch this, mop that."

"You and Master Tattersky would get on well. His lament is that his new apprentice is content to do what he's told but hasn't the wits to wonder why. The alchemist values an inquisitive nature, which most likely explains his affinity for cats."

"Master Drinder doesn't like cats *or* questions. He says too much thinking sours ale."

Korvaun corked the vial and handed it to the lad. "Take this to your master, and instruct him in its use. It might be of benefit to him in brewing, and—who knows?—perhaps the brewer and the alchemist might find themselves engaging in mutually beneficial trade. Of more than one kind."

The boy was quick to grasp the unspoken, and his eyes widened with the wonder of new possibilities. Korvaun watched the dawning of hope with pleasure and dropped a large handful of coins into the lad's hand. "For your apprentice fee," he said softly, touching a finger to his lips to counsel secrecy.

Eyes shining, the boy nodded and knelt to Korvaun as one does to kings. Springing up, he ran down the stairs in a joyful clatter of boots.

"You're a good man, my friend," a voice observed quietly. "The best of us all."

Korvaun looked up, startled. Wary alarm melted into pleasure at the sight of Roldo Thongolir. His long-absent friend was lounging against the doorpost, smiling wistfully. Roldo was sunbrown from long hours riding under summer skies, and his blue eyes were weary. He'd always been shorter, slighter, and less flamboyant than his friends, but he wore his new gemweave cloak proudly. Its soft rose caught the light, glowing like a cloud at sunrise.

Grinning in real delight, Korvaun strode forward and pulled his friend into a back-thumping hug. "Welcome home! I didn't hear you come up."

"You were too engrossed in arranging that lad's future. When did the Helmfasts leave off shipping to become champions of the common man?"

"Weren't champions once those who gave aid wherever it was needed?"

The Thongolir heir chuckled. "You sound like Taeros talking of knights and heroes. Speaking of whom, it seems our sharp-tongued friend's been busy."

"Oh?"

"Aye. I've just come from the print shop, where the ink was drying on his latest broadsheets. The cryers' lads came to take them round the taverns. Fur'll fly before day's end."

Korvaun sighed. "Our Taeros can offend people more efficiently than a flatulent half-orc in a public bath."

Roldo smirked. "His is a rare gift—Lathander be praised for that!"

The youngest Lord Helmfast nodded in full agreement. "How was your wedding promenade?" he asked, knowing he must.

His friend's smile slipped. "I always enjoy Silverymoon. The minstrelsy and plays are better than ever! I held dawn vigil at Rhyester's Matins; it fills with rainbows when the light of morning touches its windows. Extraordinary." He plucked at his rose-quartz cloak. "I'll wear this when next I worship there, and see if the faithful mistake me for the next Mornmaster!"

Korvaun nodded. 'Twas said that laying the right "sign" of the god on that temple's altar would show the devout of Lathander their next leader, or some such. "And Sarintha?"

"She was pleased with the trip."

"It augers well for your union," Korvaun observed carefully, "that you find enjoyment in mutual interests."

Roldo smiled faintly. "As to that, my lady's already showing promise of a steady hand at the Thongolir helm. Father's pleased with several ingenious plans she's devised to increase trade with Silverymoon."

"I'm surprised to learn Silverymoon lacks either scribes or books."

"They've both in plenty. In fact ..." Roldo reached into his belt-satchel and took out a volume bound in purple leather and stamped in gold: *Dynasty of Dragons: The First Thousand Obarskyr Years.* "I found a tome The Hawkwinter has long sought."

"Ah, he'll be pleased."

"Oddly enough, 'twas Sarintha who acquired this. She was busy indeed during our time in Silverymoon."

"Oh? What schemes hath the fair Sarintha hatched?" Korvaun asked, not without genuine interest.

Sarintha Thann was the granddaughter of the redoubtable Lady Cassandra and had inherited that lady's shrewd business sense as well as her blonde beauty. The unfolding of Sarintha's plans for the Thongolir calligraphy, limning, and printing businesses would be worth watching.

Roldo smiled a little ruefully. "We're now in the trade of printing music, and off to a promising start. The lutemaster at the House of the Harp is something of a legend, a half-elf of the old bardic tradition: memory only, nothing written. Sarintha won him over with personal charm and samples of family calligraphy; he's agreed to allow his work to be set down in a fine Thongolir tome. Each page carved and block-printed, and for the coin-heavy, copies with hand-painted borders. Demand swells already, with not a single page printed."

"Then we'll drink to its success." Korvaun strode to the keg and drew two tankards. "To the union of Roldo and Sarintha, and to your new business venture."

Roldo lifted an eyebrow and his tankard together. They drank in silence, and it was almost a relief when swift footfalls on the stairs heralded the arrival of another Gemcloak.

Starragar Jardeth stumbled into the room, face even paler than usual. His air of quiet elegance was absent, and his garb uncharacteristically disheveled. His hematite cloak was twisted around and hanging over one shoulder, and his black jerkin gaped from shoulder to opposite hip, slashed open to reveal his tunic beneath. A tunic smeared with dirt and—

Korvaun's eyes narrowed. "Scods, man! Is that blood?"

"Aye," Starragar said grimly. "Who'd have thought a made-from-scrap fang could cut so well?"

"Sit," instructed Korvaun, pointing to a chair. "I'll get a healer."

Starragar flopped into it with a groan. "No need. A good jerkin reduced to rags, but I've naught but a scratch."

"What befell?"

"I was out dicing with the Eagleshield twins last night. By the time they ran out of coin it was so late we took rooms above the tavern. Come morning, they insisted on seeing me safely here, and for that I owe them my life. We were set upon by ruffians. Like all Eagleshields, they're keen brawlers and leaped right into the fray—so they took the worst of it."

"Badly hurt? Did the Watch come?" demanded Roldo.

Starragar looked up. "You're back," he said flatly. "Welcome home, and so on. Aye, to both: the twins'll mend, but not soon. The Watch came—again, not soon. Once come, they didn't move to protect us any too swiftly, either. Is there more of that ale?"

Korvaun filled a tankard to the brim. A thunder of booted feet below bespoke more arrivals, so he filled another three.

"A sad day, when Waterdeep's lowlives run in packs like wild dogs," Starragar grumbled. "'Tis time to run blades up a few backsides to teach some lessons!"

"Hear, hear!" Roldo echoed, raising his tankard.

Korvaun frowned. "What lessons?"

Starragar looked up from his ale. "Quelling talk of the Lords all being nobles working hard to enrich nobles, for a start. You should hear what they're snarling in the taverns! Some hold the Lords—yes, the Masked flaming Lords of Waterdeep!—to blame for the festhall collapse!"

Roldo frowned. "Festhall?"

"The Slow Cheese," Beldar Roaringhorn snapped, striding into the room to clasp Roldo's forearms in welcome. He continued straight to the three tankards, drained one without pausing for breath, and stared at the other two. After a moment, he picked up a second and drained it just as quickly.

Korvaun regarded him in puzzlement. Accustomed to servants, Beldar seldom gave thought to menial tasks but was as attentive to his friends' comforts as his own. It was unlike him to help himself to a tankard obviously meant for someone else.

"News travels fast," Taeros observed, limping into the room

and leaning hard on a silver-handled cane. Sinking into a chair, he grimaced as he stretched one leg out before him. "Alas, faster than I do."

Korvaun frowned. "What befell?"

"An unfortunate choice of words," Taeros replied in a strangely flat voice. "The Slow Cheese fell. We three were inside at the time."

"Three? So where's Malark?"

"Dead," Beldar said bluntly.

A heavy silence descended.

"I left him," the youngest Lord Roaringhorn added angrily. "I left him there, and the whole damned festhall fell on top of him."

Taeros stirred. "If there's blame in this, Beldar should shoulder none of it. He was occupied with matters of lesser importance in the grand schemes of the gods, namely, carrying me to safety." His voice broke. "Don't think me ungrateful—never that—but Malark was worth two of me."

"As to that, Malark *outweighed* two of you," Korvaun pointed out, his voice gentle. "If Beldar had left you lie to help Malark, all three of you might have perished, and Faerûn would be poorer by two good men."

"The matter before us now," Starragar said grimly, "is avenging our friend's death."

Roldo gripped his swordhilt. "I'm ready." He looked to Beldar, awaiting their leader's word.

Roaringhorn set down his tankard and smoothed foam from his mustache before turning to Starragar. "You'd know the men who attacked you if you saw them again?"

Starragar's lips tightened in a deadly smile. He nodded and held out a hand, palm down. Beldar strode over and put his hand atop Starragar's. Roldo followed suit, and the three waited for Taeros, who fought to rise from his chair with the unfamiliar assistance of the cane.

Korvaun frowned. "Might I remind you that these men did not kill Malark? They should be reported to the Watch, certainly, but not hunted down merely because we can't take vengeance on a fallen *building*."

Taeros gave up the struggle and fell back into his chair. "So, you suggest?"

"Caution. Whatever we do shouldn't embrace bloodletting in the streets."

Roldo's hand rose from the clasp to hover uncertainly. "Then what?"

"I know not," Korvaun admitted. "Yet."

He watched his friends' hands slide part and found himself transfixed by Beldar's dark glare. Worse than the anger in those Roaringhorn eyes were the uncertain looks of the other Gemcloaks. He'd challenged Beldar's hitherto undisputed leadership, but offered no path of his own.

Yet.

🏰 🏰 🏰 🏰 🏰

As Taeros Hawkwinter limped between the last pair of impassive, gleaming-armored guards, he cast swift glances at the four men who'd walked the length of the grand hall in perfect step with him, limp and all.

No man, he swore silently, had ever been gods-blessed with better friends than these. When his father's grim old manservant had stepped into the Gemcloaks' clubhouse bearing Eremoes Hawkwinter's summons, the Gemcloaks had insisted on accompanying Taeros, though they'd all felt the sharp tongue of the Hawkwinter patriarch before and knew what was coming.

Taeros swallowed. The painted shield that had for years hung over the door of his father's office, displaying the Hawkwinter arms, had been replaced by a bright new tapestry. Its royal blue field positively glowed around the black silhouettes of two mailed fists holding wind-tossed banners. A large silver star gleamed high in one corner.

They stopped together before it. Beldar was already scowling. "Real silver, look you! That gnome weaver will answer for this! She swore to sell gemweave to me alone until spring."

"Silver's not a gem," Starragar pointed out, predictably contrary.

"Nevertheless," Beldar muttered.

Taeros knew stalling when he heard it. "Wait for me here, lads. If I'm not out in three bells, go in and offer to bury what's left of me."

Four mouths opened to protest, but he flung up his hand to silence them. "We've just lost Malark, and none of you are minded to shrug away unearned abuse today. It'll be hard enough for me in there, and I deserve the accolades my loving father heaps upon me." He lifted one black brow. "And need I remind you we stand in a garrisoned armory, full of loyal Hawkwinter men impatient of any challenge to their employer's will and well-being?"

"Good points all." Beldar clapped his friend's shoulder. "We'll wait here."

Taeros gave Beldar his cane to hold, squared his shoulders, and pushed open one of the great metalshod doors.

His father looked up, face darkening. His briefest of glances at the three men flanking Lord Hawkwinter's desk—veteran warcaptains who'd been in Hawkwinter employ as long as Taeros could remember—had them bowing in silence and striding out past Taeros without a glance.

The youngest Lord Hawkwinter tried to match their confident swagger as he advanced on the desk, but his swollen knee throbbed with every step.

"Limp if you must," his father growled. "No sense doing more damage to that knee."

Taeros came to an abrupt halt. "You've heard about the festhall."

"The Slow Cheese," Eremoes Hawkwinter snapped in disgust. "A low alehouse where 'dancers' disrobe while drunken emptyheads toss coins at them. No fitting place for a noble of Waterdeep to die. Better a man of honor die of heartstop riding some unmarried lass—at least then his family can claim he died trying to extend their lineage!"

"I'm sure Lord Goldbeard regrets the *fact* of his son's death more than the *manner* of it," Taeros replied in acid tones.

Eremoes waved a dismissive hand. "The Kothonts are herders and trappers, not men of battle. Better's expected of you."

His son bowed. "Then give me your blessing, Father, and I'll set out forthwith to study upon a more glorious end."

"Still your tongue!" Lord Eremoes Hawkwinter roared. "It's barely highsun, and your foolish words this morn will last us all season!" He snatched up a sheet of bright new parchment. Through the closed door, Taeros heard Roldo groan; the Thongolir heir knew only too well what was coming.

"A broadsheet, Father? Since when do you heed anonymous scribblings?"

"Since I received on good authority the name of he who printed this—this rhyming dung, and more importantly, the fool who *paid* for that printing." Lord Hawkwinter shook the broadsheet.

"That fool," he added sourly, making the parchment rattle, "seems to be me. Now, is this your work, or hired you some *other* half-wit to pen it?"

Taeros bowed sardonically. "'Tis mine own. Merely a small tribute to the royalty of Cormyr; no harm in it, Father."

"*Tribute!* Since when is any man increased through another's ridicule?" Clearing his throat, Lord Hawkwinter read aloud:

> *When great Azoun fell dragon-doomed*
> *And princess mage lay dying,*
> *In steel-clad Regent's peerless arms*
> *The next great king was lying.*
>
> *But when OUR Lordship's heir is crowned,*
> *It's likely they'll have found her*
> *In converse with some paramour—*
> *Both flatter than a flounder.*

Taeros nodded. Catchy, mildly clever: Cormyr's stability compared to Waterdeep's energetic street-scandals. The infant king cradled in the arms of his warrior aunt contrasted ironically with what dignitaries might well find if they went looking to crown Piergeiron's roving, fun-loving daughter. No one in all Waterdeep expected her to succeed the Paladin—a point that had apparently sailed over his father's head with room to spare.

Wherefore an explanation would probably fail, but he must try. "Piergeiron's daughter—"

"Is none of your concern!" thundered Eremoes, his fist slamming down onto his desk. "She can do whatever she sees fit, in whatever bed suits her fancy, and Waterdeep's none the less for it! We've no hereditary monarchy—or have you forgotten that merest of details?"

"I strive daily to reach that happy oblivion," Taeros replied coolly. "The Obarskyr dynasty has endured a thousand years, but what awaits Waterdeep when the Open Lord's reign is done?"

"Well, we're about to find out, aren't we?"

Taeros felt suddenly cold. "Lord Piergeiron's *dead?*"

His father nodded grimly. "So 'tis said. The city's always awash in such rumors, but this news is racing through the ranks of the Castle itself. True or not, when warriors think their leader's dead, a door opens that's seldom shut again without bloodshed."

Taeros swallowed. "No one will believe House Hawkwinter foments rebellion against the Masked Lords," he said tentatively.

"Won't they? Tell me, how many men-at-arms can any noble house maintain?"

"No more than seventy, by decree of the Lords."

"And how many swords are hired through us every tenday?"

"I—I don't know."

"Of course not." Eremoes crushed the broadsheet in his hand. "You've *far* more important matters to attend to, such as, perhaps, the forcible establishment of a Hawkwinter ruling dynasty? I've made inquiries—it seems this isn't your first foray into scurrilous politics."

Taeros sank into the nearest chair. "How could anyone draw such conclusions from a few humorous verses?"

"This wouldn't be the first time swift and foolish words have been used to sway small minds and herd crowds like cattle. You call for a dynasty; what man does that, but to advance his own line? Even if no one accuses us of ruling ambitions, many will likely ponder the wisdom of allowing *any* one family so much control over men of the sword—the hiring of which is, may I remind you, the family business?"

Taeros sat in silence for a long moment. "My rebuke is well deserved," he said quietly.

His father nodded curtly. "I don't need your apologies, Taeros, I need you to *think*." He picked up a scroll and added, in a softer voice, "This came for you."

The seal was broken. Taeros decided not to comment on that breach of privacy. It was a swiftly written notice announcing that Malark's funeral would be held *that very day*.

"You were right about Lord Goldbeard," he told his father wearily. "The Kothonts are ashamed of Malark's death, though he died a hero. His last act was helping a servant girl. He died trying to save her."

Lord Hawkwinter's expression was unreadable. "Is that a hero to you, or is this?" He waved the ruined broadsheet. "Dragonslaying, royal blood . . ."

Taeros stared at the crumpled parchment. "I ... I don't know."

Lord Eremoes Hawkwinter sighed, massive shoulders rising and falling. "You might have less sense than the gods gave to sheep, son, but at least you're honest." He waved a hand. "Go then, and honor your friend as best you can."

CHAPTER TEN

The last rays of the sun were slanting through the trees, bathing the City of the Dead in warm, golden light. Walking in its serenity, Taeros Hawkwinter couldn't deny the Deadrest's beauty, even in his current mood.

No other spot in all Waterdeep had been so touched by artists. The finest sculptors of many lands had crafted wondrous statues and adorned the flanks of soaring monuments with intricate carvings. The inside walls of many tombs were painted with vast and lush scenes, and there were living artworks, too: small floral bowers and ponds full of bright fish. Beautiful pavilions beckoned not only those who came to mourn or contemplate but also folk who sought green pleasantness for outdoor dining or trysts. Children were wont to run and play among the tombs, their voices hushed by awe and by subtle enchantments . . . and the rare druid arriving in Waterdeep would be drawn to the old trees and quiet groves. Pixies and sprites were rumored to dwell here.

As were other, darker creatures. The high, magic-mortared cemetery walls weren't just to keep out vandals and tomb-robbers. They also, it was whispered, kept in night-hunting monsters and unquiet dead.

The gates in those walls would be closed at twilight, so there was little time for a full funeral. Malark Kothont, noble of Waterdeep and blood-kin to royalty, would be laid to rest with only slightly more ceremony than that afforded a favorite hound.

Taeros glanced at the western sky. Sunset was already approaching; the burial would be swift indeed.

His gaze fell on a familiar face: a small, slender lass with snapping brown eyes, walking with another girl. Who—ah, yes, the maidservant of Dyre's pretty daughters. Named for a bird . . . Raven? Wren? Lark—yes, Lark.

He fell back a pace, waving his friends to walk on. "I'd not thought to find you here, Mistress Lark."

She regarded him thoughtfully. "Nor had I expected an invitation."

"From?"

Lark nodded at the backs of the four Gemcloaks Taeros had been walking with. "Lord Helmfast came this afternoon to the Rearing Hippocampus. I serve betimes in the dining hall there. He asked me to find the woman your friend saved." She smiled reassuringly at the wan, fragile-looking lass clasping her arm.

Taeros also gave the timorous girl a faint smile, wondering what Beldar would make of this. Usually such timely gestures were his doing . . . but perhaps the youngest Lord Roaringhorn was as much unsettled by Malark's death as a certain Taeros Hawkwinter.

"He seemed a good man, your friend," Lark said quietly.

Taeros looked at her, startled. "You knew Malark?"

"We shared words at a revel. Very fond of women, he was, but less obnoxious about it than most."

He snorted. "Thus you define a 'good man'?"

"I haven't met many who were better," was the flat reply.

Taeros nodded in full agreement, though he suspected he and the maid saw different meanings in those words.

They walked together in silence the rest of the way to join the mourners gathering at the Kothont tomb. Some noble families had their own crypts at country mansions or beneath their city villas, but deceased Kothonts slept in the City of the Dead, in a small fortress of white marble hung about with banners of Kothont green. A constellation of silver-plated stars, echoing the Kothont arms, gleamed on its domed roof in a grand, even ostentatious display that Malark had poked sly fun at in life.

All stood silent as the plain oak casket was carried to the threshold of the open tomb. By custom, final tributes would be said at the door.

Long moments passed, and no one spoke. Alauos Kothont—known to all Waterdeep as Lord Goldbeard—stood with head bowed and tears running unchecked into his famous red-gold beard, a beard not quite as long or luxuriant as his son's had been. How often had the Gemcloaks teased Malark about this family affectation, calling him a long-legged dwarf and more? Never once had their good-natured friend taken offense. He was a good man, the best of them all! Why would no one say so?

Taeros swallowed. Why couldn't *he* say so?

The silence became strained. Grim looks passed between Korvaun and Beldar. Taeros watched them both. It had always been Beldar who spoke and Korvaun who quietly arranged. Longstanding habits were not easily broken.

Finally Korvaun stepped forward and put his hands on the polished oak. "The measure of a man," he said in a raw voice, "is often found in the worth he accords those around him. Malark saw good in everyone and was ever swift with kind words and gentle jests. He died not obeying some great lord in battle, but aiding a frightened lass."

Korvaun's gaze turned to the girl standing with Lark, and he walked to her, smiling in reassurance. Yet only Lark's arm around the girl's waist kept her from shrinking away, so overwhelmed was she by the eyes of so many grand folk turning upon her.

To the astonishment of all, Korvaun went down on one knee before the girl and took her small, work-roughened hand in his. "Melia Brewer, never forget your worth. A good man valued your life more highly than his own."

He lifted her hand to his lips in tribute then rose and looked slowly around at the gathered mourners. "The same can be said of all here. A good man called us brother, cousin, father, or friend. Malark Kothont called *me* his friend. If that's the only tribute said at my burial, I'll need no other, and rest content."

Taeros blinked moist eyes and watched as Lord Goldbeard placed his hand on the casket. There was no time for more farewell than that.

On a nearby knoll stood a memorial graven with the curving runes of elvish Espruar. The leaves of the tree sheltering it were turning blue, a sure sign of coming night. The Elven Ghost Tree—by day an oak, at night form-shifting into an Evermeet blueleaf, a tree well loved by the elves buried among its roots. There were strange tales aplenty told about it . . . and what if all the *other* tales told of the City of the Dead were true?

Taeros fell into line, taking his place among those shuffling quickly past Malark's casket to bestow the customary farewell—and make a quick escape.

✦ ✦ ✦ ✦ ✦

The dining hall of the Rearing Hippocampus wasn't a place any of the Gemcloaks would normally have chosen for an evening gathering. It lacked the dazzling splendor and pretensions of highcoin houses, the sly exclusivity of daring clubs and festhalls, and the raw fun of the Dock Ward dives.

What it did have, as Taeros had successfully argued, was zzar laced with stronger drinks to achieve a potency that matched their collective need to remember Malark over something far stronger than ale. It also happened to be the inn where Lark worked, though neither Taeros nor Korvaun mentioned this to the other three remaining Gemcloaks.

Lark was waiting tables right now. She came around to theirs with a well-laden tray and briskly replaced their empty glasses with full ones. Taeros found his gaze following her as she walked away.

"This," Beldar announced, raising his tallglass, "is a more fitting tribute to our fallen friend. Wine, pretty women, and frivolous sport—that's a send-off Malark would appreciate!"

Glasses were raised in their third or fourth toast. Taeros drained his in a single stinging swallow, grimaced, and gasped, "I thought Korvaun's words well said. He took the burden none of us cared to lift and deserves no chiding for it."

"I take no offence," the Helmfast scion said quietly. "Malark was fond of revelry. It's fitting we celebrate his life as he lived it."

"Hear, hear!" Roldo echoed, waving his tallglass. It hadn't escaped Taeros's notice that the Thongolir heir had drunk sparingly, not much more than wetting his lips with each toast. Roldo was wont to talk overmuch in his cups and probably feared what he might say if he drank freely on the night of Malark's funeral.

Beldar had no such qualms. Their leader waved his empty glass imperiously on high. Lark promptly arrived with a serving tray in one hand and a bottle of zzar in the other, and began pouring.

"Leave the bottle," Beldar ordered, not glancing up. "Yes, yes, Korvaun did well. Just as he said, I consider myself honored to have been counted among Malark's friends." He shook his head. "But what an appalling *waste!* Was it really meet to elevate a serving slut—a whey-faced chit with no grace and less bosom—to the same honor as noble friends and family?"

"If, my lord," an acid-laced female voice inquired, "the lass sported breasts larger than your head, would you find her more worthy of Lord Kothont's sacrifice and your *regard?*"

Taeros stared at Lark in both curiosity and horror. Serving wenches, even those pleasing to the eye and possessed of a swift and entertaining wit, simply did not intrude upon patrons' conversations—and certainly not with a rebuke!

Beldar gave Lark a drunken glare. "Sported? Aye, she might then be worthy of *sport*, if not the high honor Korvaun offered."

The servant regarded him for a moment. Then she set the bottle of zzar on the table with exaggerated care, turned to leave—and whirled back, serving tray held high in both hands. Before anyone could do more than gape, she brought it down on Beldar's head with a ringing clang.

He crashed to the floor, chair and all. Lark spun away and marched straight out of the Hippocampus, tossing the bent platter to the floor and her apron to the indignantly sputtering master of the hall as she went.

Chairs scraped as the Gemcloaks sprang to help their fallen leader. Korvaun, who'd been seated next to Beldar, did most of the honors, raising the dazed Lord Roaringhorn to his feet and briskly brushing floor-reeds from Beldar's ruby cloak. "Are you unhurt?"

Beldar explored his scalp with tentative fingers and nodded.

"Good," Korvaun said politely—and punched Beldar in the jaw, hard. The youngest Lord Roaringhorn reeled back, stumbled over Lark's twisted serving-tray, and found the floor once more.

As the hallmaster stared, aghast, Lord Korvaun Helmfast strode quickly to the front door, his sapphire cloak swirling around him like a stormcloud.

This time Beldar stayed down, groaning and unaided, as Taeros, Starragar, and Roldo stared open-mouthed at their departing friend's back.

"Thank you, Hoth," Mrelder murmured, when it became clear his father wasn't going to say anything at all.

The tall man bowed silently and departed, leaving Mrelder and his father alone in Golskyn's office with the tankards of hot cider Hoth had brought. The priest gestured imperiously, bidding Mrelder to go and bolt the door.

When he turned back from doing that, Golskyn of the Gods was sitting at his desk looking out the windows at the dawn, warming his hands around his tankard. "You have been here longer than the rest of us," he said abruptly, "and so seen more of this city of greed and bustle. Moreover, you are still of an age where dreams and fancies flourish, so tell me something of your thoughts: What should we of the Amalgamation strive for? Speak freely."

Mrelder's jaw dropped.

His father's gaze never left the street below, but the thin smile on Golskyn's hard, lordly face told Mrelder he'd seen his son's astonishment.

"Waterdeep," Mrelder said slowly, "is a city of secrets and strivings. Men clash daily with wits and coins—and too often with daggers and worse. Buy this, sell that, swindle and cajole and misrepresent: Folk here spend their lives chasing coins."

He waved at the busy street outside, where carters were calling their wares amid rumbling wagons and hurrying folk. "Many dream of great wealth, even when they know it's forever beyond their grasp. Some slave their days away grumbling or resigned to their lot, but a great many here have the fire and ambition I've always seen in you, Father—though not your wits or perception."

"How so?"

"They seek an edge, an advantage over others, some first step or hold on power that'll bring them a shade closer to making their dreams real. Waterdeep holds a lot of *doers*, not just dreamers."

Golskyn nodded. "And this means . . . ?"

His father actually seemed to be taking his words seriously! Desperate not to put a word wrong, Mrelder took a deep breath and burst out, "Folk so eager for riches offer themselves, often without realizing they're doing so. They leap at chances, for fear of missing the trail to riches. They never want to refuse or turn away from what could be their way to power. They all like to *think* they're cleverer than their fellows, but time and again someone crafts a new swindle, and jack after lass falls for it: They can't resist."

Golskyn sipped his cider. "So if we say and do the right things, we can 'use' a large number of these coin-hungry schemers. To what end?"

"I'm not certain. Yet this unrest, the anger against the Lords and the nobles, these snarls in the taverns over the falling buildings . . . all can be turned to our advantage. The city's more restless than I've ever seen it before."

His father turned an amused eye Mrelder's way, and the sorcerer hastily amended, "Not that I've seen all that many years passing in Waterdeep, I'll grant, but graybearded Waterdhavians are saying it in the streets and alehouses, and goodwives in the shops agree with them."

"So this city is, as they say, ripe for the plucking," Golskyn murmured. "Whereas any hothead can set men to swords out and shouting in the streets, superior beings can control, or at least steer what unfolds, to achieve intended ends."

"Exactly," Mrelder agreed, a little too enthusiastically.

Golskyn was suddenly facing him, his uncovered eye as cold and hard as ever. "And so, my son of such wisdom and keen perception, what plans have you thought through to take advantage of this rare opportunity?"

Mrelder swallowed, aware that he was on dangerous ground. He said cautiously, "The grafts, Father, are valuable. If we can master them, they improve us."

Golskyn's smile was wintry. "And?"

"Yet they are by definition limited to we who already believe in Amalgamation, who revere you for your vision and try to enact your desires."

The priest waved impatiently at Mrelder to continue.

"More can be accomplished by improving others—*if*, through these improvements, we achieve a measure of control over those persons we ... augment."

Golskyn nodded. "We gain tools, whether they know their servitude or not, and thus increase our reach and power. Continue."

Mrelder took his first sip of cider, more to look away from his father's piercing gaze than to slake any thirst. "Perhaps," he told his tankard carefully, "it's this control that's most useful to us, not the improvements themselves. I say nothing against the gods, mind, or the rightfulness of augmenting ourselves as they guide us to; I speak now only of others, non-believers. Nor am I necessarily saying such persons should remain non-believers ... only that control itself is valuable and that there are other ways to achieve control than through—"

"Cutting useful bits from beasts most would deem 'monsters'?" Golskyn's tone was cold. "So you look no higher than an alley-thug who seeks to gather a gang around him and so feel powerful? Tell me, O wise young one: What sense is there in controlling fools and weaklings?"

"They can go places and do things that augmented men cannot. If I'd gained and mastered that sahuagin arm, I wouldn't have been allowed anywhere near Lord Piergeiron. I'd have been wrestled down and carried off for his guardwizard to mind-ream!"

"Until you prove yourself before the gods," Golskyn said icily, "you are like all other men and so can serve me as the unsuspicious envoy you champion. I have one weakling; why do I require others?"

"But Father—"

"But son," Golskyn mocked him, "you can find words to do no more than feebly try to justify your own failures. You see Waterdeep well enough but still fail to see yourself. Has your vaunted sorcery brought us one of the Walking Statues yet? And if it did, how would you then protect the rest of us against the alerted Watchful Order or this Lord Mage of Waterdeep everyone whispers of with awe? Or the energetic buffoons of the local Watch, who can call the clanking-armored Guard out to march on us from all sides, to say nothing of fly down at our very heads? Have you a plan to defeat them all? Or some mighty spell you've been hiding from me?"

Mrelder flushed, anger rising. Again his father was dismissing him with scorn. He should have known not to expect more. Hope, it seemed, was the latest of Golskyn's victims.

"Go and scheme some more," Golskyn of the Gods decreed coldly, pointing at the door, "and come up with something *useful*."

🦇 🦇 🦇 🦇 🦇

The Meadows were lovely on a midsummer morn, fragrant with flowers, sweet grasses, and swift-drying dew. The cleared lands east of Waterdeep's walls were a fine hunting ground. Pheasants and grouse nested in plenty in the tall, wind-rippled grass, and plump hares were easy prey for the bright-feathered hawks of nobles.

Taeros and Korvaun rode without speaking, their glossy mounts trotting briskly. Korvaun's invitation had come by messenger late the night before. Taeros had agreed to come riding at this ungodly hour—a mere two bells past dawn—mostly out of curiosity. On the pommel of his black mare's saddle rode a hooded peahawk very nearly identical to the bird perched on Korvaun's golden, white-maned stallion. The blue and green plumage of his friend's bird was perhaps a shade more brilliant, but his, Taeros thought, was more pleasingly marked.

He waited as long as he could before raising the subject that had no doubt prompted this outing. "You're seldom as angry as you were last night," he observed, as they halted on a little hillock they'd flown their hawks from hundreds of times before. "How did Beldar so offend you?"

Korvaun unhooded his hawk and undid its jesses. The bright little raptor immediately hopped onto his gloved wrist, and he tossed her into the air.

"Beldar's a fine lad, make no mistake," Korvaun said slowly, watching his hawk wing happily into the sky, "but he can be far too swift and loud in dismissal of common folk."

Taeros echoed Korvaun's words over the casket: "The measure of a man is the worth he accords those around him."

Korvaun's smile was faint. "You don't sound convinced."

"I agree in the main," Taeros replied cautiously, "and 'twas certainly tactless of Beldar to make such remarks in the presence of a servant girl." He turned his head suddenly from following the flight of the hawk to add slyly, "Especially a little brown lark in the employ of a white dove."

Korvaun flushed, and Taeros whooped with laughter. "Aye, I *thought* you paid rather close court to the elder Dyre lass. Though, forgive me, she seems . . . singularly lacking in color, despite her red hair."

"No woman is half so fair in my eyes," Korvaun said earnestly, "Naoni has a quiet and restful spirit, yet she's quick to see what needs doing. She's swifter to think of others than of herself, and as kindhearted as she is sensible."

Kindhearted? Sensible? Not words that sprang to the mind of Taeros Hawkwinter when he daydreamed of feminine perfection, but then, feminine *im*perfection was more to his liking. Take the servant girl, now: Lark was no more a beauty than was her mistress, but Taeros admired the keen edge of her tongue.

"Her hands are touched by Mystra Herself," Korvaun went on. "Only a blessed-of-the-goddess could spin gems into thread. Pretty

Faendra says Naoni could spin broken dreams whole, if she took it in mind to do so."

"Perhaps so, but her father, the so-fierce stonemason, will have your guts for his next set of garters if you lay hand on the girl."

"I'm not worried about Master Dyre," Korvaun said quietly. "Naoni's her own mistress. Alas, there the matter ends: she stands adamant against any notion of romance."

Taeros regarded his friend with amused fascination. "And you know this how?"

"I've sent her letters respectfully requesting her company. She declined, with equal respect."

"You've sent letters," Taeros echoed disbelievingly. "Have you never heard bards sing 'faint hearts ne'er won fair prize?' Seek her out, man! Chase her down!"

He shook his fist in emphasis, drawing a squawk from the hooded peahawk perched on it.

"Was that my intent, I'd need a bigger bird," Korvaun said dryly.

Taeros chuckled. "What I *meant* was, woo her more heartily! Flowers and gifts, pretty words and poetry."

Korvaun roared out laughter. "Oh, and who's to be my poet? *You?*"

Taeros grew a slow grin. "Perhaps you're wise not to be employ me as your envoy. Even so, you should *speak* to the girl at least."

Korvaun started to nod—and his hawk suddenly plunged to the meadow, disappearing into the grass. He kicked his steed toward her.

"Fly your hawk!" he called back. "Mornings this fine are meant for hunting!"

"Precisely, Korvaun," Taeros murmured, releasing his bird. "Precisely."

She circled twice, then stooped—and almost immediately rose with a small, long-tailed grouse in her talons.

Taeros stowed the kill in his game satchel and fed his little hunter her reward from the vial of diced giblets his hawkmaster always provided.

The Helmfast had dismounted to collect the plump hare his hawk had slain, but sent her flying again without reward—a sure sign that something other than the morning's hunt, perhaps something other than wooing the fair Naoni—rode his thoughts and heart.

"Your mind seems a crowded place this morn," Taeros said quietly.

Korvaun swung back into his saddle. "Your father told you the talk of Lord Piergeiron's death?"

"Rumors—and like most such, more smoke than embers."

"I think the tales false, too, yet they're troubling nonetheless."

Taeros chuckled in bewilderment. "You've never shown the *slightest* interest in politics! Why now?"

"It's time," Korvaun said simply and whistled his hawk down from the skies.

Taeros pondered that reply as they rode back to the city. Try as he might, he could think of none better.

⚜ ⚜ ⚜ ⚜ ⚜

Later that morning, the youngest scions of Houses Helmfast and Hawkwinter traded glances in front of a heap of rotten barrel-staves and a small, sagging door beyond it, an inauspicious ending to a narrow alley.

Korvaun shrugged and tapped on the door. There was no response.

He rapped more firmly. Still nothing.

Exchanging glances with Taeros again, the youngest Lord Helmfast shrugged. "The lad who sold this destination is doubtless snickering with his friends about now."

Whereupon the door swung open, and the two nobles found themselves face to face—or more accurately, waist to face—with a pair of grim-looking halflings who held daggers ready. They looked not at all like the plump, complacent Small Folk the Gemcloaks betimes saw drinking in the more squalid taverns: These two were lean, sharp-featured, and coldly alert.

The curly head of a third halfling thrust between the two guards, eyeing the nobles' glittering cloaks. "Gemweave; you'd be the Tall Folk who blundered by to 'save' the Dyre lasses and Lark a few days past. Your intentions are appreciated, even if your assistance was unnecessary."

Taeros blinked. " 'Unnecessary'? Three unarmed girls are hardly a battle-match for half a dozen roughblades!"

"Perhaps not, but so few are no match for Mistress Dyre's guard."

"I saw no guard in that alley!"

The curly-haired hin grinned. "We do our work well, then, don't we?"

Korvaun drew a deep breath and tried again. "I'd like to speak with Mistress Naomi Dyre. We were told she might be found here."

"What business have you with Mistress Dyre?" one of the guards demanded. His voice was low, gruff, and unfriendly.

"Take ease, good fellow. We mean her no harm."

The guard sniffed. "You couldn't harm her if you tried. Not in here, not anywhere in the city."

"Then you've no cause to object," Taeros pointed out, reasonably enough.

The curly-haired halfling studied Korvaun for a long moment. "She's not here," he said slowly, "but there *is* something within that you should see."

Taeros peered into the dimness beyond the doorway. "What is this place?"

"The Warrens, home to most Small Folk in Waterdeep," the hin replied. "Take a torch."

The nobles traded looks, shrugged, lit a torch each, and followed their guide.

"This tunnel's cobbled," Taeros muttered, stamping his boot.

"Used to be a street. You Tall Folk kept building up and up 'til this level got forgotten. Through here."

The hin led the Gemcloaks into a small room where seven well-armed halflings lounged at small tables, drinking and dicing. They came to sudden, silent alertness at the sight of the humans.

"I need to show them something in Mistress Dyre's safe-box," said their guide.

One of the guards went to a wall and busied herself with a complicated set of locks as two others stood like a wall to block the visitors' view of what she did.

When the door swung open, their guide ushered the nobles into the low-vaulted cellar beyond. Selecting a metal box from shelves of seemingly identical boxes, he took a single sheet of parchment from it and handed the page to Korvaun. "You're the one who's needing to see this."

The young noble read silently. Something like sorrow stole into his eyes, and he silently handed the parchment back.

"You'll not be coming back," the hin said. It wasn't quite a question.

"No," Korvaun agreed quietly. Nodding his thanks to the halfling, he strode quickly from the room.

Taeros hastened after his friend, curiosity aflame, yet Korvaun was silent until they were out of the Warrens and blinking in the bright light of approaching highsun.

Then he said two words: "Thank you."

A black Hawkwinter eyebrow lifted in inquiry.

Korvaun smiled faintly. "For not asking. I can only imagine what that silence cost you."

Taeros draped an arm about his friend's shoulders. "No sacrifice too great for friendship," he said grandly. "Besides, when all's known, won't it make a grand broadsheet ballad?"

"I'd not do that, were I you—not for fear of my wrath, but of unseen Small Folk blades."

The Hawkwinter chuckled but cast a quick glance into the alley shadows all around. He'd never before thought to check small places for lurking danger. Waterdeep held far more than his life, much less his fancies, had thus far revealed.

Deep waters, indeed!

CHAPTER ELEVEN

One of the things that made the library Taeros Hawkwinter's favorite room in all Hawkwinter House—gods strike that, in all Waterdeep and the wider world beyond—was that it had a door that locked.

He set that lock now and turned to regard the principal reason this was his favorite place, "the refuge of my soul," as he'd declared it grandly to himself one summer evening years ago: his books. Rows and rows of them, precious tomes that had cost more than he'd ever in his life spend on gems or clothing, no matter how often fashions changed.

Taeros ran a hand caressingly across the gilded, tooled, *familiar* spines of his treasures—tales of great men and women, of heroic deeds and glorious quests, the very fire, heart, and glory of what it was to be human. To *matter.*

Here was Aldimer's *Histories of the Heroes,* and there *The Glory of the Dragon,* Danchas the Scribe's glowing history of Azoun IV of Cormyr.

The Purple Dragon. Dead now, swept away in fittingly heroic sacrifice, dying in battle to save his realm, hewing down a dragon on a blood-drenched field.

What wouldn't he give to serve a man such as Azoun! Oh, not a king, but a leader whose name men murmured in genuine awe, a man so loved that those who wore his colors would unhesitatingly throw their lives away in his cause. To see that fierce loyalty like a flame in their eyes, to hear your lord's name chanted because the very sound of it bolstered courage and gave a sense of purpose.

Now, more than ever, Waterdeep needed such heroes—and to be shaken by the throat to open eyes and *follow* them, too. To lift Waterdhavian attention from daily coin-grubbing or the cut-and-thrust of proud noble rivalries, and look upon . . .

Taeros snorted aloud. Who? No faces came to mind. And who was he to tell Waterdeep what it needed, and be heeded? After all, what great deeds had he done?

He glanced at the locked, chained-to-the-table box wherein lay the precious parchments that would someday become *Deep Waters*.

Nothing, yet. Nothing beyond pondering things a trifle deeper than the frivolities that consumed the lives of his friends and their noble elders, especially the older nobles. Arrogant, feuding emptyheads and gossips, wasteful, cruel, selfish, malicious when crossed . . .

Enough. Suffice to say that he could point at nothing in all that parade of smeering faces and proud names to admire and emulate. Not one thing.

So what would befall if Piergeiron was truly gone and Waterdeep left lordless? Oh, Masked Lords abounded, but what of the tall, striding figure in armor at whom citizens could roar approval?

How went the song? *Empty throne at the Palace . . .*

As he tried to recall words for that tune, an angry face swim up in memory to glare at Taeros: Varandros Dyre, standing behind his desk glowering at them all.

The more Taeros pondered that stonemason's anger, and Dyre's snarls of a "New Day," the more sense the man seemed to make.

Not that Varandros Dyre was any sort of hero. A hard, grasping man, full of bile and indignation, and lowborn to boot.

Yet heroes were just his own fascination, and it was *so* typically noble a mistake to let one's own enthusiasms and views blind one to everything else. Perhaps, in crowded, bustling Waterdeep, it was men such as Dyre who could get things done. Small men, effecting small changes. Coin by coin, deal by deal ... small tugs at the tiller of the great ship of a city, turning it slowly and ponderously on into a new sunrise, and ... a New Day.

Taeros Hawkwinter snorted again. If Varandros bleeding Dyre could turn Waterdeep, so could the youngest, hitherto most idle flower of the Hawkwinters.

With Piergeiron dead or alive but with folk thinking he might be, it was time for change. The city needed a man to become a hero, or at least take the first longbooted stride toward glory.

Beldar. Beldar Roaringhorn, who'd always been at the fore in the Gemcloaks' adventures, and in settling their disputes. He'd never become "the" Lord Roaringhorn unless at least three cousins died first, but his kin weren't blind to his gifts. They'd noticed his quick wits and swift tongue and set him to studying law, the better to aid them in dancing around it. Beldar, of course, had excelled, and when inclined, he could argue a Black Robe to a standstill.

Beldar must be Waterdeep's tall man in armor! He was as strong of arm as he was keen of wit, the best blade among the Gemcloaks, and a skilled rider. The Roaringhorns bred racehorses and battle steeds, and Beldar had learned to ride almost before he could walk. Taeros could easily picture him in a high saddle, swinging a blood-drenched sword and bellowing Waterdeep's greatness in the thick of battle ...

He was handsome, too, with an infectious energy and a gift for the grand gesture, and there was something more. Since boyhood, he'd carried himself with the confidence of one destined for great things. Because Beldar believed that, so did his friends. In time, so might others.

Belief was a powerful thing. Enough of it could turn a demon into a god. Of course, a man who lacked the gifts and personal discipline to support a lofty opinion of himself was no more than a buffoon, but Beldar had that discipline. He listened to his friends, and if those friends included wise Korvaun and—ahem—one Taeros ...

Yes! There was no time to waste. So much had slipped away already ...

Taeros whirled from his beloved books and made for the door. He hit the stairs like a racing gale, cloak streaming behind him, and was out the front doors before the doorguards could do more than gape.

Once through the front gates, he *really* started to hurry.

No less than three Watch patrols hailed Taeros Hawkwinter during his sprint down Whaelgond Way, for a lone running man in North Ward is unlikely to be anyone other than a thief. Yet it seemed his bright amber cloak was becoming known by sight; a senior officer striding out of a side-street curtly ordered off their heavy-booted pursuit—allowing Taeros to fetch up, panting and red-faced, at the Helmfast gates.

Thankfully, the splendidly armored guards there knew him, too, and let him stagger inside without a word . . . which was good, because Taeros was damned if he could find breath enough to produce one.

In similar manner he gained entrance through the front doors, where his ruffled state and limp—his knee was afire again, despite all the healing potions he'd swallowed—goaded a servant into scurrying ahead, as Taeros discovered when Korvaun came down the stairs at a frowning trot to meet him.

The hard-panting flower of the Hawkwinters pointed up the stairs in the direction of Korvaun's rooms, and Korvaun took that arm and helped Taeros ascend.

Broad steps tiled in swirling sea-waves of blue and green seemed to rush past, and then they were in the upper hall. Edwind Helmfast, Korvaun's eldest brother, strolled out of the gilded doors of the Great Solar, a chart in one hand and a large goblet in the other, and greeted them with a disapproving sneer.

Too winded to speak, Taeros managed to give the Helmfast heir a pitying look and was rewarded by utter bafflement dawning on the Young Captain's face.

Korvaun saw that and turned his head away to favor a marble bust of old Lathaland Helmfast with a grin. The founder of the house had been sculpted with a grim, lopsided smile, and that did not change as the two friends swept past together, and into Korvaun's rooms.

Korvaun slammed shut his door and whirled around. "What news? War? Castle Waterdeep's fallen over? The Lords've all been unmasked as Mother Amaltha's pleasure-girls? What?"

The winded Hawkwinter swallowed hard and gasped, "They're saying Piergeiron's dead!"

Korvaun nodded. "Every tenday, it seems. Is this talk gaining ground?"

Taeros nodded, still fighting for breath, and sank into a chair. "Half the city's saying so!"

The youngest Lord Helmfast headed for the decanters on his sideboard. "That's bad. Is anyone speaking out against these rumors?"

Taeros waved his hands in a "who knows?" gesture. "Probably, but against truth, rumor spreads faster, dies harder, and is usually far more interesting."

Korvaun turned with a frown, decanter in hand. "And reminds us of the obvious: Piergeiron will not outlive every rumor. Some dark day, that rumor *will* be true."

"Yes!" Taeros gasped. "Wherefore I ran here! If enough citizens can be made to think about such things, we've the best chance we'll ever have to change things in Waterdeep! Make the Lords unmask, at least."

"How are we going to manage that, without violence? I can't imagine they'll *want* to reveal themselves, or that, if we try to force change with shouts and crowds and fists in the streets, the drunks and thieves and troublemakers won't swiftly make sure the whole city explodes into swords and blood. We'll have shops smashed, folk murdered, and the Watch and the Guard called out. Jails and blood and *very* hard feelings, fences broken that might not be mended for lifetimes . . ."

Taeros stared back at his friend, his red face going white to the lips, and eagerly took and drained an offered goblet. Korvaun calmly filled it again.

Taeros stared down into it. "So for the good of the city," he asked it bitterly, "we should just sit and do *nothing* as the Lords choose someone else to sit in the Palace, and everything goes on as before?"

Korvaun shook his head. "No, I didn't say that. I pointed out peril right before us and wondered why unmasking the Lords matters so much. Convince me."

"Who proclaims our laws?"

"Piergeiron, of course."

"Right. Who writes and decides them?"

"The Lords of Waterdeep, Piergeiron and . . ."

"And the gods alone know how many masked Lords, yes. And who chooses *them?*"

Korvaun chuckled. "I know not—no one does. That is, the Masked Lords choose their own, ah, reinforcements."

"Aha, and who administers the laws?"

"The Watch, and the Magisters decide guilt."

Taeros waved his goblet. "Who does the Watch report to? How are the Magisters chosen?"

"They report to Piergeiron, ultimately, and I believe he appoints the Black Robes, too."

"Just so. How's the Open Lord chosen?"

Korvaun frowned. "Strangely enough, I've no idea."

"Precisely!" snapped Taeros, slamming his fist down on a sidetable. "The most powerful man in Waterdeep, and no one knows just who gave him that power or who else decides things for this city. Piergeiron's worthy and just—few dispute that—but who's to say the one who follows him will be anything of the kind? He'll be the choice of the Lords, of course, but *who are they?* Why're we so willing to trust in what's kept secret from us? Who's to say we're not obeying the whims of liches? Or the very hissing sahuagin we *thought* we hurled back from our walls? Why—"

There was a commotion outside Korvaun's closed door: Booted feet coming swiftly closer. Then the door opened precipitously and one of the house doorjacks thrust his head in and blurted, "Pray pardon the interruption, Lords, but you have a visi—"

A long arm jerked the man back out of sight, trailing a startled "Eeeep!"

The owner of that arm swept into the room, face set in dark anger.

Beldar Roaringhorn sported an impressive bruise on his jaw, and there was fire in his eyes as he kicked the door shut, causing a muffled groan and thump from its far side. Taeros swallowed anxiously as Beldar strode forward.

To meet Korvaun's gaze squarely, and snap, "Pray accept my apologies for ... last night. The fault was mine; I shouldn't run around disparaging servants, no matter what foolishness they offer me. What I said darkened the memory of poor Malark. Your anger was just. Pray, let it be forgotten between us."

"Let it be forgotten," Korvaun agreed, stepping forward to offer Beldar a goblet.

The youngest Lord Roaringhorn took and drained it. "Fine stuff, and sorely needed!" He set it down with a *thunk*. "Now, to business."

Korvaun poured himself a goblet. "Taeros came to me a-fire, and now you. What fuels your flame? All this talk of Piergeiron's death?"

"That and more. The city's roused worse than I've ever seen it. Even when scaly things were slithering up out of the harbor and folk were trembling in their beds, Waterdeep stood *together.* Now the city feels like ... like an alley-full of roughblades spoiling for a fight, eyeing you just before the first of them pulls his knife."

"And Malark's dead," Taeros said softly, seeing what lay beneath his friend's anger.

A ruby-red cloak swirled glimmeringly as Beldar whirled around. "*Yes,* hrast it," he snarled. "Dead, just like that! Gone from us when—when it should *never* have happened! He had *years* left to joke and prance and—*years!*"

Korvaun deftly replaced Beldar's empty goblet with a full one. "Tell us more."

"More?" Beldar snapped. "This isn't *enough?*"

"Humor me," Korvaun replied, his voice mild but firm.

Beldar stared at him, breathing hard, then sipped from his goblet, swallowed, and growled, "The old Open Lord may just be gone at last, so Malark's passing is forgotten in an instant . . . and the shopkeepers and dockers are snarling at *us* as both the cause and all that's bad and wrong about Waterdeep . . . and blast me if I can find the words to refute them, with my own mother, Mratchetta bloody Roaringhorn, sitting there in her pearl-and-gold bedchamber *right now* shouting at her maidservants and *everyone* else within reach, to get out and scour every last jeweler in the city—just so she can find out how many sapphires Alys Jardeth has had fitted into her new upcomb, so *she* can have *more!*"

The rivalry between Alys Jardeth and Mratchetta Roaringhorn was well known, and a traditional source of sardonic amusement among the Gemcloaks, but it took few wits to see Beldar was deeply upset —and not about upcombs.

"That would be those tiara-trellis things the ladies use to make their hair stand up like a rooster's comb, yes?" Taeros asked quietly, to fill the furious silence.

Beldar nodded as he drained his goblet again, somehow managing not to choke in doing so.

"Beldar," Korvaun said quietly, "be fair to your mother. She's grown up knowing she's but a cousin of the Lords Roaringhorn, and that even if neither of them marry and produce heirs, they've a younger brother who probably will. Moreover, with nigh a dozen strong, capable male Roaringhorns striding the halls of your High House, and—forgive me—her neither the most beautiful nor the most capable noble lady in Waterdeep, with no head for business nor easy hostess graces, what does life offer her but frivolous pursuits?"

Beldar Roaringhorn looked up with murder in his eye, and for a moment Taeros wondered if he was going to lose one friend to a burial crypt or perhaps his own life through getting between the two of them . . . but then the leader of the Gemcloaks set down his empty goblet on the nearest bright-polished sidetable with exaggerated care, drew a deep breath, and whispered, "You . . . see clearly and speak truly, Korvaun. I thank you for that. As you say, how could my mother be otherwise?"

He strode to Korvaun's windows and asked the city outside grimly, "How can *any* of Waterdeep's nobility be otherwise? So all of us *fine* nobles stand blind to the anger in the streets or dismiss it as the usual grumblings of the underclasses."

He made a fist and drew his arm sharply up as if to smash his hand down on a handy table that wasn't there, and then burst out, "Why can't folk just *know their place?*"

Taeros and Korvaun exchanged glances. It was the youngest Lord Helmfast who ventured to say quietly, "So we stand here concerned but uncertain of how to proceed. I suggest we go see Mirt the Moneylender and ask his advice. After all, he's a merchant of Dock Ward, and—"

"As everyone knows," Beldar said wearily, "he's a Lord of Waterdeep. But come now, Korvaun—*advice?* Even assuming the truth of that old rumor, what wisdom can fall from the mouth of that puffing, strutting old pirate?"

"You might be surprised," Korvaun said quietly. "I was."

For a long moment his two friends stared at him. Taeros found his voice first. "*You* have much to tell us."

"On the way to Mirt's Mansion," Beldar added, striding to the door. Taeros and Korvaun hurried in his wake, cloaks swirling.

⚓ ⚓ ⚓ ⚓ ⚓

They found Starragar Jardeth in his favorite gambling house. The Eagleshield brothers, both still bearing evidence of their recent battle on Starragar's behalf, threw down their cards and urged him to join his fellow Gemcloaks. A carriage ride and a brisk walk later, Taeros was beginning to understand why.

Starragar was besmitten. Every woman they passed gave him fresh reason to praise his lady's charms. This lass had a form almost as lithe as Phandelopae Melshimber, and that one's face, though lovely enough, wasn't half so fair. Yonder spill of dark hair echoed hers, but wasn't near so long and lustrous...

Taeros would never have thought it possible, but it was almost a relief when they entered Dock Ward, and Starragar's rhapsodies gave way to his usual litany of complaints.

Beldar strode on ahead, oblivious to his friend's grumbling, leaving Taeros and Korvaun to keep Starragar's incendiary comments from sending sparks into all-too-ready tinder.

"Gods above!" Starragar snarled as the Gemcloaks dodged around another pair of apparently abandoned handcarts. "Don't these lowlife idiots know this is supposed to be a *street?*"

They were still a lane or three away from Mirt's Mansion, on a busy street that reeked of fish guts. It was all cobbles and puddles and hurrying folk, most of whom were carrying crates or kegs or wheeling creaking carts.

Right in front of them, a fat, puffing little man tipped his delivery handcart upright, kicked its axle-prop down, and pulled free a wheel-pin and the wheel it held in one smooth, expert movement. Unlocking the iron cage that held the goods on his cart, he took one wooden delivery box from among a dozen, hung wheel and pin on their hooks, slammed and locked the cage down over everything and trotted into a shop to make a delivery, all as swiftly as an angry nobleman might draw his sword.

Starragar stared at this deft dance in astonishment, then started to look as if he might just *be* that proverbial angry nobleman. Taeros and Korvaun hissed "Come *on!*" in urgent unison and hustled him past, around a larger cart piled high with wet, noisome crates of eels, and between another pair of handcarts.

"This is how coins flow in our city," Korvaun murmured. "Deliver fast, yes? When you call for fresh wine, you expect it at your door before next dining, right?"

"Well, yes, but—"

"But nothing. The man locks his goods and wheel. That strut on the cage makes sure the prop can't be kicked over by some prankster. The only way he can suffer theft while he's gone is if enough beefy lads together lift and carry the thing, which would hardly be worth the effort."

"All right," Starragar snapped, pointing at a large conveyance pulled by sweating men, that was just drawing to a halt, "but what's *that?*"

"Rental carriage. Shuttered, so it's someone who doesn't want the whole city to know they're coming down here—see? Lady Sultlue!"

Starragar whistled. "So it's true, she *does*—"

His attention was caught by a clumsily painted signboard, nailed askew over a door.

"Gamelder's Quaffhouse?" he asked incredulously, peering at the barred-window, ramshackle warehouse beside him. "*This* is what passes for a tavern in Dock Ward?"

He surveyed sagging roof and blackened boards with an open sneer. "I wouldn't deign to spew my guts in a place like this! Fancy downing a drink that's been poured in such squalor! Why, there're prob—"

"We're almost at the moneylender's," Taeros said loudly, taking Starragar's arm and peering through gaps in the broken window-boards behind the bars, at unfriendly faces—with bad teeth—glaring out at them. "If we hurry—"

"It looks like a fire-damaged warehouse," Korvaun put in hastily, taking Starragar's other elbow and steering him away, "because it *is* a fire-damaged warehouse. If rented out as a tavern, the rent just might make coin enough to pay for a new warehouse, see? There're many such taverns this end of the city. Now—"

Starragar growled, shook off their hands, and strode on down the littered street, muttering.

Too late.

The quaffhouse door banged open, and a dozen sailors charged out, fists and bottles flying. Korvaun had to dive desperately over the nearest handcart to avoid losing his life right there and then.

Taeros sprang away, trying to draw his sword and shouting a warning. Beldar whirled around, saw the onrushing sailors, and grinned with what Taeros, stumbling on the cobbles as women and barefoot boys shrieked all around him in excitement, could only describe as "savage glee."

Starragar, too, seemed pleased, and drew his blade with a flourish. "For honor, for glory, for *Phandelopae!*" he howled.

In the time it took Taeros to roll his eyes, his view of Lords

Jardeth and Roaringhorn was lost behind dozens of burly, dirty sailors. Right behind them came some calloused laborers whose grinning faces were familiar.

Taeros Hawkwinter had last seen them in a worksite on Redcloak Lane, dodging among boards and scaffolding.

"Oh, Lady Luck, kiss all Gemcloaks *now*," he whispered fervently.

⚓ ⚓ ⚓ ⚓ ⚓

"Aye, Marlus is better'n most," a trustyhand growled, thumping his chipped mug down on the windowsill to join his elbows. "I know crews as *never* gets a day off and don't see coin enough to drink even in a place like this!"

"*Hey*, now!" one of the burly, hard-faced men behind the bar called angrily. "You want fancy lasses, you go up the street and pay three nibs for brew with a lot more water in it than this!"

"Aye," a sailor called back, from beside the trustyhands who worked for Marlus the carpenter, "but there, they don't use the water ye've scaled the fish into."

The man behind the bar scowled and drew back an empty mug threateningly, as if to hurl it. Then he took quick measure of the six or seven sailors turning to face him with the grim grins of men spoiling for a fight, despite a collection of scars that would have impressed any priestess of Loviatar or priest of Ilmater, and turned away.

The sailors had barely started to jeer when another of their number, the foremastman of the *Glorious Goblet* out of Athkatla and the owner of the fastest fists in the crew, pointed out through the broken window-slats and barked, "Hey! Coupla fancynoses coming, see?"

"No!" the steersman beside him corrected. "*Four* strutting codpieces, unbearded lads all, a-holding their noses and sneering at the likes of us. *Well* now—"

Others peered, and chuckled eagerly.

"Let's be rearranging those noses for 'em—and whatever else we can reach of 'em, besides!" someone called.

Whereupon the trustyhand who'd worked for Marlus the longest let out a sudden roar. "'Tis *them*, lads! The ones as put swords to us at Dyre's site an' had our rig down! *Get them!*"

This became a general chorus, and the window-counter emptied in an instant, wooden mugs bouncing off walls, floors, and nearby patrons.

"Loins of the Lion!" a Calishite sailor growled, clutching his bruised head.

"S'why we make 'em of wood, sealord," one of the barmen told him laconically, retrieving the mug that had done the damage. "Else ye'd be picking glass shards out of yer brain right now by way of your nose, eh?"

One of the drunkards down in the darkest end corner roused enough to ask, "Awha? Whut's befalling, hey?"

"Some nobles've lost their ways and come prancing past, and the hammerhands an' the sealegs of the Goblet have gone out to teach the young highnoses a thing or two."

A gap-toothed old sailor elbowed his friend awake, and made for the door. "This oughta be good. Got anything left to bet with, Suldyn?"

★ ★ ★ ★ ★

The tingling warning behind Mrelder's eyes became a red throbbing. He sprang up excitedly. Piergeiron was heading right toward them!

His father's door stood open. Golskyn had just returned from another mysterious errand, and was standing behind his desk still wearing his overcloak.

"I've ordered the chains," Lord Unity was telling Hoth, "but they tell me it'll be at least a tenday before the first links are ready. For all the talk of coin and competition ruling Waterdeep, they don't seem to work all that fast."

Hoth nodded. "Should I buy the cages?"

Golskyn nodded. "Ironbar, and large enough to hold two horses, nose to tail. We'll be wanting *large* beasts, not treecats."

"Any preferences?"

"Thuldaar, but only if he has some in stock. Buy from anyone who has ready stock—in the barns nigh South Gate, nowhere else. Take Daethur's wagon, and store them in the north warehouse. Don't have them delivered here; this street has far too many curious eyes as it is."

Hoth bowed deeply, turned, and strode out, ignoring Mrelder.

Golskyn did, too, until his son said insistently, "My spells tell me Piergeiron's very close by and heading right toward us."

Lord Unity looked up sharply. "You're sure?"

As Mrelder nodded, sudden shouts, crashes, and the ring of swords striking swords erupted in the street below.

Father and son rushed to the windows together and peered down at a chaos of yelling, brawling men, overturned handcarts, and running Watch officers. Folk were peering out of windows up and down the street, and spilling out of doorways to watch and cheer.

At the heart of the fray, four well-dressed young men sporting glittering cloaks were beset by seemingly dozens of ragged sailors—and were plying their war-steel like desperate men, which is just what they were. If the Watch didn't arrive quickly, that gaudy quartet was doomed.

CHAPTER TWELVE

Swords flashed and clanged, men shouted and screamed, and Watch officers converged from all directions. Beyond them, far down the street, a small knot of armored men were striding purposefully toward the fray.

"There!" Mrelder said excitedly, pointing. A head taller than those around him, magnificent in bright helm and armor, the Open Lord of Waterdeep paused for a moment to peer ahead and frown, trying to see just who was fighting whom and why.

"I see him," Golskyn replied. "This can only work to our benefit."

As he spoke, one of the bright-cloaked men struck aside a sailor's cutlass and ran the man through. A breath later, another of the fancy-cloaks vanished under a swarm of punching, kicking laborers.

Watchmen blew horns, shouted, and waded into the fighting, taking blows from fists and improvised clubs. Piergeiron snapped an order and trotted forward, pulling gauntlets from his belt and drawing them on as he plunged into the battle.

Mrelder cursed softly. He had the right spell ready; he should have used it when Piergeiron stopped to survey the fight! Now, he might never—

A sailor took the red-cloaked man's slender steel through his gut and reeled, his scream fading into wet coughing as he sank to the cobbles to die. Another sailor punched someone else right back through the curtained window of a rental carriage whose runners had long since fled, then jerked open the door and dived in at his victim. The carriage swayed, received the enthusiastic charges of several more sailors anxious to join in the fun, rocked violently . . . and slowly crashed over onto its side amid screams and splinterings.

Piergeiron had to leap for his life as the falling coach loomed over him. He slammed right into a handcart. It crashed over onto a wounded sailor with the Open Lord riding it. The paladin wallowed atop the cart-cage, trying to get his balance, his bodyguard still far behind him . . .

Now! Mrelder spread his hands, vaguely aware that his father was no longer watching at the windows beside him. He hissed out his spell, gaze intent on Piergeiron. A sailor was charging the armored Lord, whose best route away would be—

The Open Lord found his footing and met the sailor with a raised arm that blocked the man's wild swing and an uppercut that started near his knees and ended up over his head, with the sailor flung away senseless.

So great was the force of Piergeiron's blow that the paladin staggered sideways on the slippery cobbles toward a nearby shopfront.

Just as Mrelder had hoped.

Pointing at the shop's signboard —"Ye Happy Harlot" it proclaimed to the world, in shabby, peeling paint on wood carved into the shape of a buxom reclining woman—he carefully said the last, triggering word of his spell.

Rusted chains flew apart. The faded Harlot happily plummeted to the street below, crashing down on Piergeiron's helmed head and shoulders, driving the Open Lord of Waterdeep to the cobbles in a crumpled instant.

Golskyn was suddenly back at the window, a lit candle in his hand. "Hold this," he ordered.

As Mrelder took the little candle-lamp, the Lord of the Amalgamation raised the first of three egg-shaped bundles of clay he'd fetched. It bristled with wicks, sprouting in all directions like a potato gone to seed. Golskyn held these into the flame, one after another, until wisps of thick smoke curled up. Then he opened the window, tossed out the egg, and calmly drew the sash down against the sudden billowing of smoke.

Without pause the priest moved to the next window, lit his second smoke-egg, and hurled it. He did the same for the third before pinching out the candle and waving Mrelder impatiently toward the door.

"But Father, how'll we see?"

Golskyn tapped his eyepatch. "*I* will see for us both. You will listen for my orders."

They hastened out and down to the street together.

🐞 🐞 🐞 🐞 🐞

Mirt's old, flopping seaboots flapped as he strode along, humming to himself. Sune and Sharess, if he wasn't but a few indolent days away from turning entirely to jelly! If 'twasn't for these little sallies forth to see Durnan about which warehouse to buy and what cargo to sell, he'd have *long* ago—

Been felled by his own failing heart and some unlooked-for tumble, thanks to the unpredictable cruelty of Faerûn, which was whirling around his head now, smashing wind out of him and dashing him to the hard cobbles in a bewildering instant—

Mirt rolled over and up, blinking. He'd just been literally run over by a trio of running, battling men. Their swords sang and struck sparks from each other and the nearby walls as they fought on, faces twisted with anger and effort.

Well, Blood of the Whale, if young sailors and Dock Ward louts thought they could trample and ignore the Old Wolf himself—

Mirt rose like an enraged and puffing walrus, drew his curved saber and favorite dagger, and lumbered after the trio, who were reeling back out of the alley into the street they'd evidently come from ... which seemed rather noisy and crowded, come to think of it.

Mirt frowned. The cobbles were crowded with dying, groaning, hacking-at-each-other men—and billowing smoke, too! Through those spreading clouds, the street seemed to be a veritable *slaughterhouse* of a battlefield! Ye gods and little fishes!

He thrust his head out of the alley, peering through the thickening haze at a fallen signboard and a magnificently armored, somehow *familiar* leg protruding from under it.

Someone charged at him out of the smoke, shouting in anger and swinging a glittering sword. Mirt knew the man at a glance: one of Piergeiron's bodyguards. So *that* must be old Steelhead himself, lying there like—

The glittering sword slashed open one of Mirt's sleeves, and the wheezing moneylender ducked away and forward, to rise suddenly *behind* the guard's backswing.

He clouted a helm solidly with his saber hilt, snarling, "Young puppy! More fancy armor than a dancer doing the Lady Knight Surrenders, and *this* is the best you can do?"

The man fell untidily and did not get up.

Someone else came sprinting out of the alley, and Mirt lurched around to face this new foe, puffing and blowing through his mustache, just in time to have a Dock Ward roughblade—stormhowl it all, someone *else* he recognized!—slam into his capacious gut and send him staggering.

Whereupon a handsome man in fine clothes and a swirling ruby-red cloak lunged out of the smoke to slash open the man's throat, neck, and shoulder with one vicious cut of his blade.

The Dock Warder fell, gurgling, and the nearest of Piergeiron's still-living bodyguards turned in time to entirely misread the situation and leap at Beldar Roaringhorn with a shout of anger and a wildly thrusting sword.

Suddenly sailors and Watch officers and everyone else afoot in all Dock Ward, it seemed, were converging on the fallen paladin and swinging steel as they came.

This being Dock Ward, windows had already flown open to let folk peer down through the rising smoke. Some hurled insults, and others preferred to toss small, expendable objects or the contents of chamberpots. Bets were shouted from window to window as sailors and Watch officers groaned, thrust, parried . . . and died.

The last and most drunken of the *Glorious Goblet*'s crew came staggering out to join the battle, roaring and swinging their blades wildly. One of them promptly reeled into a handcart and sent it crashing over. Its owner erupted out of the shop he'd been delivering to with a rising scream of fury, spitting out insults and curses as he smashed the sailor to the cobbles with a three-legged stool the shop owner had just rejected.

The sailors all around the stool-seller growled in menacing unison—and the bustling little man growled right back at them, drew his belt-knife, and flung himself at the nearest one, wielding knife and stool with deadly ruthlessness.

🏰 🏰 🏰 🏰 🏰

Overhead, in an attic not far above the tumult, the smoke and noise had awakened two elderly, dozing sisters: Rethilda, who called the bat-infested rooms home, and Undaera, from the farm crossroads of Windy Hill nigh Secomber, who was visiting her sister in the big city for the first time.

She'd been horrified at the filth, noise, and dangers of Dock Ward and had said so, colorfully and at length, almost causing a rift between them.

So it was with a certain satisfaction that Rethilda surveyed the brawl now filling the street and turned triumphantly to the gaping, trembling Undaera to ask, "Well, sister? Does Windy Hill offer *this* sort of free entertainment? Hey?"

🏰 🏰 🏰 🏰 🏰

"Too many people are watching from above," Golskyn snapped, as swearing, snarling sailors clawed at the ruby-cloaked man and the splendidly armored bodyguard. "Far too many blades here, too!"

Mrelder nodded. "There'll be no dragging Piergeiron through our front door—not unless we want half the Watch, and the Guard, too, coming in after him!"

"We don't need *him*," Golskyn said sharply, "just the Gorget—but folk must not notice us taking it!"

A dying bodyguard reeled back, with three burly sailors stabbing him so swiftly and repeatedly with their daggers that it looked like they were drumming their fists on his armor, leaving Golskyn's path to the paladin clear.

Two bodyguards who now lay sprawled and very dead in their own spreading blood had earlier dragged the signboard off the Open Lord. Piergeiron lay on his back, eyes shut and mouth open, dead or unconscious; the Lord of the Amalgamation didn't care which. Just now, all he cared about was that Piergeiron was so cursed *big* that he didn't think he could drag the man anywhere.

"Mrelder!"

"Here, Father!" Mrelder gasped, fighting his way free of the heavy body of the Watchman who'd been trying to throttle him. He'd spell-frozen the lawman long enough to slice open the Waterdhavian's throat with his dagger.

"Stop amusing yourself and *help* me, here!"

Mrelder leaped to obey, and the paladin's armor struck sparks from the cobbles as they dragged him, limp limbs bouncing and rattling, into a doorway.

More bodyguards were bearing down on them, but Golskyn could bark orders as grandly as a king when he wanted to. He drew himself up to block their view of Mrelder tearing at the Gorget and commanded, "The Open Lord lives! See that you keep him safe!"

The foremost bodyguard promptly burst past the priest—and saw what Mrelder was doing.

He raised his blade with a yell, but Golskyn whirled and drove his own dagger into the man's throat from behind, dragging it viciously crosswise and spraying Mrelder with more blood.

Without slowing the priest whirled around again to face the second bodyguard, who stood horrified, and told the man sternly, "Fear not! We've nothing against you—or Lord Piergeiron, either! This is a personal matter involving *his* villainy!"

Golskyn pointed grandly at the bodyguard he'd just murdered with his dripping dagger—and so did Mrelder, who was clutching the Gorget behind his back with his other hand.

The bodyguard raised his sword and bellowed, "Blayskar a villain? He's me cousin, you murdering *bastards!*"

Mrelder whirled and fled, and the bodyguard plunged after him. Golskyn coolly swept his overcloak off and over the man's head, then throat-punched him as he stumbled.

The stumble became a topple, and Golskyn swept his cloak away again as he plucked up the bodyguard's sword, dragged the man's helm off, and brained him with the hilt. Tossing the blade down, he ran after Mrelder.

The smoke was thick enough above them now to set people to coughing and prevent anyone at a window from clearly seeing where they went. It was high time to retire from this field of victory.

* * * * *

A new crowd was wading through the smoke now, almost all of them Watchmen. Mirt knew them—and more to the point, they knew him, even through all the blood and heaped sailors' bodies.

"Old Wolf, let's be having you on your feet," one grunted, heaving and dragging. Mirt let out a roar of pain that ended in a sob.

Gods, he *was* hurt . . . hurt bad!

"Get me," Mirt gasped raggedly, as Watchmen rolled dead sailors aside, "back to my house: There's healing there!"

They raised him to their shoulders almost tenderly, but the Old Wolf nearly fell out of their grasp in his eagerness to point across more bodies at a gleam of armor, and gasp, "Grab Piergeiron there, too! Bring him to my place! If that damned squarejaws goes down, some fools'll start a war in the city to get onto his throne, sure's sure!"

Watchmen rushed to do just that, the Open Lord's helm and one gauntlet rolling away forgotten as they hoisted him and began the swift trot to Mirt's Mansion.

The street was empty of both moneylenders and Open Lords even before a father and a son finished groping their way through their own doorway with a stolen gorget and got the door safely bolted and barred in their wake.

☗ ☗ ☗ ☗ ☗

"Perhaps the tunnel repairer moved away," Naoni sighed, "or died; dwarves are long-lived, not immortal."

"*Perhaps*," Faendra sniffed, "the folk at the rooming house were lying to us!"

Lark chuckled at the girl's indignant tone. "Of course they were, but that might have nothing at all to do with Buckblade. Some people lie for no better reason than to keep in practice."

"Mayhap we were given the wrong address in the first place," Naoni said—and then stopped abruptly and threw up her hand in warning.

The others looked along her pointing finger, down the street ahead, where men were spilling out of doorways and rushing at each other. There were shouts and the flash of swords. There were far more familiar flashes, too: bright gemweave cloaks!

Lark rolled her eyes. "Watching Gods above, are those men *everywhere*?"

"Perhaps they're following you, sister," Faendra teased, staring in fascination at toppling handcarts and clattering blades.

Lark laid firm hands on Dyre elbows. "We don't want to be here, mistresses," she warned, even as loud crashings erupted behind them.

The three whirled around and found themselves staring at more Watchmen than they'd ever seen together before. Forty or more hard-faced lawmen were hastily dragging handcarts and carriages together to form a barrier.

"*Excuse* me," Lark called, dragging Naoni and Faendra forward, "but—"

"Sit you down out the way and keep silent, lasses!" a Watch armar barked back. "There'll be no getting past us this way!"

Watchmen were hurriedly scaling the barrier and taking up positions in front of it, as others came trotting out of alley mouths, drawing blades as they came.

The street fight swirled closer, and Lark sat down. Faendra swiftly followed, leaving Naoni standing uncertainly, turning this way and that as she sought escape.

"We can't flee," she concluded reluctantly, and crouched down just as a Watchman sprinted past.

"Why do these things always have to happen on *my* watch?" he growled. "Why can't they have their brawls..."

His voice was lost in the rising clangs and cries of men trying to butcher other men, as the three crouching women watched the battle come reeling to meet them.

A man whose face was a mask of blood hurried toward them out of the fray, ruby-red cloak billowing behind him. He'd been cut across the forehead and was running blindly, cursing fervently yet slowly, as if amazed.

♜ ♜ ♜ ♜ ♜

So much blood... so much blood...

His wounds didn't hurt all that much, but Lord Beldar Roaringhorn felt empty and betrayed, as if—as if the gods had been lying to him all along, and the world was very different from how he'd thought it worked.

Scores—nay, hundreds—of fights he'd been in, his blade sending men reeling, and he'd never been cut before. Never. Wasn't he invulnerable to such things, at least until his promised destiny was achieved?

His wounding had been so hideously swift and *easy.* Just like Malark, under those falling beams...

♜ ♜ ♜ ♜ ♜

Watchmen were moving to intercept the young noble, snapping, "*You*, goodsir! You! *Stop!* Stand! The Watch commands you! Halt where you are!"

The youngest Lord Roaringhorn wiped at his streaming forehead with the back of his hand and stumbled onward as the three women gawked up at him.

He reeled on the littered cobbles as a Watchman came at

him—and was suddenly looming above the three lasses.

Lark made a sudden, wordless sound and rose to flee, and Beldar slashed out blindly at the sound, cutting only empty air as Faendra shrieked. He lunged, slipped, and came crashing into Lark.

They fell heavily to the cobbles together, Beldar a sagging, dead weight. Two Watchmen sprinted over, blades reaching down.

"Away!" Lark shouted at them, as fiercely as any warrior. "Get your steel *away!*"

As the two officers stared down at her uncertainly, she waved down her blood-streaked front at the man whose surprisingly heavy body was sprawled across her lap, and snapped, "Can't you see he offers no threat?"

"Some sort of lord," one Watchman said to the other. They traded quick, satisfied smiles.

"So dawns the New Day," Naoni whispered to Faendra, her gray eyes wide with horror. "Gods above, what has Father started?"

🏰 🏰 🏰 🏰 🏰

Mrelder leaned back against the bolted door and stared down at what gleamed in his grasp: The Guardian's Gorget. This small metal plate enabled the First Lord of Waterdeep to command the Walking Statues. Little was publicly known about it—few thought it more than mere "show" armor—but Mrelder's life-long fascination with Waterdeep had led him to many of her secrets. He'd sought out and memorized every scrap of Waterdhavian lore in all Candlekeep.

"What wait you for?" snapped Golskyn.

"I'm holding history in my hands," the sorcerer murmured, eyes fixed almost reverently on the Open Lord's crest. "This touched royalty, as surely as has any king's crown or warsword."

"You're holding the future in your hands," his father snarled, "and it's time you realized your role in shaping it. What is a king but an accident of birth and blood? True men *become*, powerful tyrants *take*. All your life you've yearned for this city—if you're my true son, you'll stretch out your hands and take what you desire!"

Mrelder nodded and put the surprisingly heavy gorget around his neck. Closing his eyes, he sought for the calm that would let him attune himself to it.

Instantly vivid fire flashed through his mind: a path of golden light. He was swept along it at incredible speed, through thick woods. Suddenly a smoothly rounded black tower loomed up before him, and a spectral voice demanded the password.

Of course. No man, not even Piergeiron, would wield such power without safeguards. The Open Lord and Khelben Arunsun were fast friends; of course the archmage watched Piergeiron's back.

The archmage watched . . .

With dawning horror, Mrelder realized there was a burning in the back of his mind, the shadow of a strong—and growing—presence. An alien will blossomed in his head, like a glowing web of power. A small, bright tendril twisted from it, questing deeper, closer . . .

Gods above! He'd drawn the attention of the Lord Mage of Waterdeep!

And he was *mind-linked to the Blackstaff!*

Mrelder tore the metal off with desperate hands and flung it away. It was still in the air when he hurled the most powerful detachment spell he knew at it, a magic crafted to break the hold of a scrying device and turn its power back upon the seeker.

The gorget flared into brilliant red flame an instant before it crashed into the wall, searing right through a tapestry and biting into the stone beyond. Then it rebounded and fell, leaving dusty wool smoking in its wake.

Golskyn pounced on the smoldering tapestry, tore it down, and emptied two ewers of water over it. The stench of wet, burnt wool filled the room.

His son paid little heed. Mrelder crouched over the fallen gorget. It seemed whole and unharmed, its flame gone.

He touched it with a cautious fingertip. It was already cool.

Warily he picked it up. There was no lingering sense of the seeking magic.

Strong hands seized his collar and dragged him to his feet.

Before he could draw breath, Golskyn slammed him against the wall so hard that Mrelder's vision swam. The gorget fell from his numbed fingers.

His father leaned close, hands at Mrelder's throat and face contorted with rage. "Fool!" he snarled. "I should have let this wretched city burn and you with it!"

🏰 🏰 🏰 🏰 🏰

Strong spellglows flickered around a bare spellchamber in Blackstaff Tower, lighting the awed faces of Khelben's apprentices. They'd been working for hours now, building a web of glowing, humming lines of magical force without really knowing what they were doing.

The Blackstaff was directing them as gracefully as any dancer, crooking a finger here and silently beckoning there to call forth their castings in precise places, as the spellweb grew to fill the room. The apprentices were accustomed to Laeral's encouraging murmurs and directions, but Khelben Arunsun worked in silence, black robes swirling, and the web was brighter and had risen faster than anything Laeral had ever guided them through. Only he knew what he was striving for, and he—

Was reeling, suddenly, clutching at his head with both hands and *screaming*.

As the apprentices stared at him in rising terror, Khelben swayed as the lines of force plunged *into* him, converging with terrifying speed.

There was a soundless crash that rocked the room, rippling waves of magic raced out past their ankles to slam into the wall and strike clattering shards of stone free ... and the great spellweb was gone, leaving only a faint, fitful glow around the rigidly upright body of the Lord Mage of Waterdeep, whose eyes were wide, staring wildly and unseeingly in different directions and whose mouth was slack and drooling, even before he started to topple.

CHAPTER THIRTEEN

'Tammert!" the wild-eyed apprentice sobbed, long hair still crackling about her shoulders in the swirling chaos of magic that was eddying around them like so many tugging waves of sparks. "Is he *dead?*"

Tammert Landral had once, several rooms below this one, tried to put a sword through Qilué of the Chosen and been scorched by silver fire for his pains—and he was the closest of them all to the fallen Lord Mage of Waterdeep. He swallowed, stretched out a hand that he snatched back hurriedly when magic rose up from the Blackstaff's apparently intact body to shock into him with a burning, menacing snarl, and replied, "I—I don't think so. Get Maresta! And Araeralee! *Hurry!*"

The apprentices of Blackstaff Tower being what they were, his order would have ordinarily evoked not obedience but a flurry of dispute and loftily offered opinions, but just now almost everyone in the room wanted desperately to be somewhere else. Aside from Tammert and Callashantra, who stood uncertainly right where she'd been when she'd shouted to him, the room emptied in a few frantic moments.

While Tammert hoped desperately that Maresta Rhanbuck, motherly whirlwind that she was, and Araeralee Summerstar, of whom the Lady Laeral was so fond, would know what to do.

"Mother Mystra, guide us," he prayed fervently, going to his knees and sacrificing a spell from his mind to make his prayer flame up and hopefully be heard. "Oh, that Laeral was here!"

However, it was the impish and beautiful little seductress Jalarra who next appeared in a doorway, to say brightly, "Everyone just came tearing past me like all the devils in the Nine Hells have come visiting! What'm I missing? I—oh."

Eyes going very wide, she stopped, feeling the magic still roiling around the room wash over her, and peered across its fading, flickering glows at the sprawled body of Khelben Arunsun.

"What happened? Is he—?"

"I don't know," Tammert told her grimly, not turning to take his eyes off the fallen archmage for a moment. "Go get Maresta, will you?"

Surprisingly, Jalarra whirled around to do just that—and let out a little shriek of alarm as Maresta and Araeralee almost flattened her in their own hasty arrivals.

"We've sent a calling-spell to the Lady Laeral," Maresta panted, looking more flustered than any of them had ever seen her before, "and we can only hope—"

There was a soundless flash, and the room suddenly held one more person. Jalarra shrieked again.

"Have we trained you that badly?" the Lady Mage of Waterdeep demanded, from where she stood towering over Tammert. "That 'hope' is the only thing you can think of to do?"

She whirled around, saw Khelben, and hurled herself at him. Tammert almost gratefully flung himself out of the way.

The apprentices watched Laeral crawl atop the Blackstaff, eyes closing as if she was trying to *feel* something. Then she turned her head, gave them a grim nod, and announced, "Backlash—and a bad one."

The apprentices kept silent, not knowing what to say.

"Maresta," Laeral added briskly, "you're in charge. Waterdeep must believe the Lord Arunsun is still here and at work. All of you: if anyone asks, we're both here but we're busy, right? If anyone gets insistent, tell them we're busy *with Mystra.*"

There was another soundless flash, and all of the glowing, swirling magic in the room was gone. The stones where the Lord and Lady Mages of Waterdeep had lain were bare and empty.

Tammert Landral trembled, then, and started to sob in awe. A vast smile was unfolding in his mind amid silver fire . . . fire that swept over him in wordless reassurance.

"Tammert!" Maresta snapped. "What befalls?"

"Mystra," he managed to gasp. "She heard my prayer!"

▲ ▲ ▲ ▲ ▲

White motes of light danced in Mrelder's darkening vision. His father's hand tightened on his throat . . . the winking lights swirled faster, flashing like tiny stars and clustering ever-brighter.

"Fool!" thundered Golskyn, giving the sorcerer a shake that let Mrelder sob in a breath but brought pain bursting through his head like a stabbing lance. "I waste my time chasing a magical trinket, only to have you lose your nerve and *destroy* it?"

"No," Mrelder managed to croak. "Not . . . destroyed."

The cruel grip loosened. "Then why did you cast it aside? Why hurl spells at it?"

Mrelder cautiously backed away, shoulders scraping along the wall. "My knowledge of the gorget was incomplete," he husked, head pounding. "Didn't realize . . . trying to use it . . . would mind-link me to Khelben Arunsun."

He waited for his father's explosion.

To his surprise, the ghost of a smile flitted over Golskyn's face. "Ah. And how fared Waterdeep's archmage, when you left him?"

"How fared?" Mrelder echoed, not understanding what his father was asking. "I . . . took no time to inquire after his health. My only thought was to sever the link: through it, he could find me. Find *us*."

"Indeed," Golskyn agreed, that odd smile still lingering on his face. "I find myself reluctantly impressed by this archmage of yours and his sensible precautions. After all, it would not do to let just *anyone* command a stone golem as tall as fifteen men—to say nothing of eight such golems. If such control was easily mastered, it would not take long for the mustered Walking Statues to smash down this entire city, every last building of it."

"Yes," Mrelder gasped. "Most magics this powerful bear many safeguards and wards."

"You could not be expected to know them all," the priest said soothingly. "In time you'll discover them. Now put on the gorget again, that we may learn more."

Dread shimmered icily down Mrelder's spine. He wasn't sure what terrified him more: the thought of donning the gorget or his father's silkily mild tone, the searing promise of silver fire or the calm before the tempest.

"I am ... no match for Khelben Arunsun," he said at last. "He could take over my mind as easily as you could assimilate a giant rat's tail."

"An unfortunate comparison, but one we'll leave unexplored for the nonce," Golskyn replied, sounding calm, even amused. "Are you afraid of this archmage?"

Fear was something Lord Unity of the Amalgamation scorned, but dishonesty he simply would not tolerate. Knowing this, his son nodded reluctantly.

"Then consider this: Whatever doom Khelben Arunsun might visit on you is a mere possibility, whereas what I, Golskyn, will do here and now if you do *not* try to master the gorget is a cold and final certainty."

The priest strolled away, then turned back to face Mrelder, still wearing that faint smile. "Perhaps," he added, his tone still disconcertingly reasonable, "that serves to put matters into proper balance?"

Because he had no choice, Mrelder lifted the Guardian's Gorget with quaking hands and placed it around his neck. He sensed

. . .

Nothing.

The tendril of magic connecting him to the silver fire of the great wizard's mind was gone.

Mrelder breathed an intense sigh of relief. The shields he'd unintentionally raised fell away. With their passing, a faint glow of magic filled his thoughts.

The link was not quite gone, but it was changed. No longer a road that ran two ways, it was fading fast but sending Mrelder an image such as he might have seen in a scrying bowl—one whose powers were swiftly dimming.

Khelben Arunsun lay in slumber, beard singed and hands and face blackened as if by fire. What seemed to be deep green woods surrounded him, and a woman with long silver hair knelt over him, her eyes closed and her lips moving like someone praying.

The vision receded, dwindling behind him as if Mrelder was riding away from it, until dark mists closed over all. Then the faint glow of magic faded entirely, and Mrelder opened his eyes and gave his father a jubilant smile.

"The archmage," he announced, trying to sound victorious rather than relieved, "won't trouble us for some time."

Golskyn nodded as if he'd expected Mrelder's triumph. "And the gorget?"

"Nothing more," Mrelder admitted. "Yet."

Golskyn nodded, very slowly. "If Piergeiron lives, we will find him. In time, he'll tell us what we wish to know."

The likelihood of this struck Mrelder as slight indeed, but he knew better than to do anything but nod agreement. He cast the spell that allowed him to sense the little copper badge Piergeiron wore.

"He still lies below," he announced, frowning in surprise.

The angry din from the street was diminishing, which meant order was being restored. Surely tending the fallen First Lord would be paramount in the minds of the Watch!

The two men hastened back down into the smoke-filled street. Mrelder promptly pulled Golskyn aside to let several frantic Watchmen rush past, carrying on their shoulders a fat, ragged-mustached man wearing floppy sea-boots, seaman's breeches, and a blood-stained tunic.

Then the sorcerer led the way through bodies and wreckage and suspiciously frowning Watchmen to the alley where they'd dragged Piergeiron.

There they stopped in dismayed silence. The signboard that

had felled the Open Lord had been tossed aside. Piergeiron was gone.

"Well?" the priest demanded coldly.

A glint of metal caught Mrelder's eye. Kicking aside the twisted splinters of a wooden crate, he plucked up the Open Lord's helm. The copper badge was still affixed to it; the spell of binding he'd placed to keep it there had done its job. This was, alas, cold comfort.

He turned the helm so his father could see the badge. "The spells worked as intended," he said haltingly.

Golskyn regarded him with disgust. "Better you should have fed him the copper piece in his morningfeast sausages. Then your 'spell of binding' could have been put to better use!"

"We were set upon, officer," Korvaun Helmfast repeated for perhaps the tenth time, feeling the cold stares of the Watchmen who stood in a tight circle all around, "as I told you. We were simply walking past that quaffhouse, and they all came charging out at us."

"And you had no blades drawn? Made no gestures? Said nothing?"

"No swords and no gestures," Taeros put in. "As I recall, we were explaining what a quaffhouse was to Lord Jardeth at the time."

That earned him a sneer of disbelief from the grizzled old Watch rorden. "Come now, milord! You seriously expect me to believe that your friend here—" He waved at Starragar, who, with his glittering black cloak and blood-smeared face, looked like a large carrion bird—"is unfamiliar with alehouses?"

A chorus of sarcastic chuckles arose from the surrounding Watchmen.

Taeros felt unaccustomed anger rising in him. "What my friend *meant*," he said rather sharply, "is that the Lord Jardeth expected a drinking establishment to present a more inviting face to the world or lack for clients, just as *I* expect the Watch to keep the streets safe or at least stand aside to allow us to procure healing for our friend."

The Watch officer regarded him rather coolly. "Part of keeping the streets safe, *Lord* Hawkwinter, is ascertaining who's to blame for bloodshed—and I note that two young lords stand before me unhurt, whereas over a dozen outlanders and citizens lie hurt or dead, many by wounds almost certainly made by your swords. If for some reason you feel it beneath yourself to answer a few questions . . ."

"I feel nothing of the sort," Taeros snapped, truly angry now, "yet as we seem to be *noting* things here, *I* note that you've not assisted these ladies to rise, nor asked after their health—or asked them anything at all, for that matter."

Another Watch officer snorted. "Ah, yes, shift eyes to your doxies; *that'll* prove an effective distraction. D'you think we're all dunderheads?"

Surprisingly, it was Naoni who erupted from the cobbles like a leaping flame. "Doxies? *DOXIES?*"

She flew at the man, heedless of his drawn sword, and delivered a slap that spun his head sideways and brought roars of laughter from other Watchmen.

"We're crafters," she shouted at him. "Honest women doing an honest day's work, *not* the playpretties of titled men!"

By then, several Watchmen had tugged her arms down, and the swordcaptain she'd attacked had staggered back out of reach, more startled than angry.

"Naoni," Faendra cried desperately, afraid she'd see her sister stabbed right in front of her. "Have done!"

Her sister heard and fell silent but didn't stop struggling against the hands that held her.

"Well, we seem to have touched some nerves here," the grizzled rorden observed. "Not had your share of battle yet, m'dear?"

That "dear" and the patronizing tone it was delivered in brought Faendra to her feet. She flounced over to put herself between Naoni and the graying officer, hands on her hips and blue eyes ablaze.

"Surely *Mistress* Dyre, the daughter of a guildmaster, is worthy of more respectful address!"

The officers exchanged glances, and the men holding Naoni released her and stepped back.

"See now, young mistress, no harm was meant."

"Oh? Perhaps if *your* daughters and sisters were penned into a battlefield, left to fend for themselves, then mocked as dockside trulls," raged Faendra, "less rust would have collected on your weapons! Speaking of which, my sister's 'battles' are her own business, but no graybeard with 'rusted weapons' need apply as sparring partner."

A few uneasy chuckles arose. Faendra, however, was not quite finished. She turned and pointed at Naoni dramatically.

"And know this: my sister is a sorceress, goddess-gifted with the ability to spin anything into thread! She could conjure *every* sword you carry into scraps of fishing line."

She cast a scathing glance over the gathered Watch and added, "Not that most of you would perceive the change."

A young Watchman stepped forward, eyes narrowing. "Threatening the Watch with sorcery, are you?"

"Thellus," an older swordcaptain hastily interrupted, "I think we'd better take these lasses in for some proper questioning. Separately. I'll take—"

"No, goodsir," Korvaun announced then, his sword out and his voice even colder than his drawn blade, "you'll *not*. These women are now under my protection, and I'll fight any man who tries to—"

"Oh, gods drown *all*," the grizzled rorden said feelingly, "put up your steel, lordling! You, too, Lord Hawkwinter. There'll be no taking anyone anywhere—by us, anyway. Stand back, men."

He looked down at Lark. "I can see by their, ah, liveliness that your friends here are unharmed. How fare you?"

"Covered with the blood of a man whose weight prevents me from rising," she replied, "but otherwise unharmed." She turned her head to regard Taeros and added coldly, "Yet uncertain of what value lies in the protection of men who inherited titles rather than wits—and whose solution to all impediments seems to be drawing a sword."

A few Watchmen chuckled, at least one whistled in anticipation of fireworks to come, and everyone watched the face of Lord Taeros Hawkwinter redden.

In that expectant silence, Taeros sheathed his sword, inclined his head to Lark, and replied politely, "I bow to the wishes of a lady whenever possible, and as the good officer here has promised you'll not be imprisoned or interrogated, I'm content to let matters run their lawful course."

He turned to the rorden. "I assume you'll wish to interview other witnesses to ascertain the true cause of this disturbance. If you've further need of me or my friends, kindly send word and we'll happily answer any questions put to us."

"Prettily said," the old Watchman replied. "Down blades, men. I think our work here is done—unless, milords, you'd like us to carry Lord Roaringhorn somewhere?"

"I—I can carry myself," a quiet answer startled him, from the bloodstained form at their feet. "I think."

Taeros peered down. "Beldar, how badly are you—?"

"I'll live," was the curt reply, followed by a groan as Starragar hauled the Gemcloaks' leader to his feet.

"I'll see him safe home," Lord Jardeth announced.

Korvaun Helmfast turned to Naoni. "If you'd not think it an imposition, we should serve you three likewise."

A Watch officer who stood safely behind his fellows chuckled. "Ah, now—who'll be protecting who, hey?"

Amid the mirth that followed, Naoni Dyre drew herself up and said with quiet dignity, "We accept your kind offer, Lord Helmfast. Courtesy and duty, it seems, aren't always strangers to men of Waterdeep."

Taking the cue, Taeros extended a hand to Lark.

"Help yon stormcrow take your friend to a healer," she told him coolly, ignoring his outstretched hand to rise unaided. "Lord Helmfast's protection will be quite enough for us. We helpless lasses might not be able to keep *two* of you from inciting bloodshed."

Beldar shrugged off Starragar's helping hand and took a few tottering steps. The street blurred and tilted precariously, and he leaned on the nearest wall until his vision deigned to sort itself out.

"The lass was right," Taeros said, materializing out of the haze. "Let me call a carriage and take you to a healer."

Beldar lifted tentative fingers to his forehead. To his surprise, his wound was shallow, little more than a scratch.

"It's not serious," he said, something of his surprise creeping into his voice.

Starragar regarded him skeptically. "There's a lot of blood. You were knocked senseless. Either alone, much less both, justifies a healer's fee."

"Head wounds bleed freely," the Roaringhorn responded shortly.

It was hard to admit that most likely he'd simply fainted, like a swooning maiden in one of those foolish chapbooks his sisters were always reading. With an effort, he straightened and stepped boldly away from the wall.

"I'll have the wound tended," he told Taeros. "If it's all the same to you, I'd prefer to be alone."

There was understanding on his friend's face. "I feel much the same way," the Hawkwinter admitted quietly. "Never before have I taken a man's life. It's a grim and serious thing, not to be lightly regarded or easily forgotten."

Beldar stared at Taeros. What the Hawkwinter had just said was truth, of course—but it hadn't even occurred to him. And what did that lack reveal of Beldar Roaringhorn?

Still, the mask offered him was preferable to revealing his humiliation. He clapped the shoulders of both friends gently. "Thanks. Get you home, and we'll talk later."

The Hawkwinter nodded and reached for the strings of his readycoin purse. "No arguments," he said firmly, pressing the bag into Beldar's hands. "The women of Waterdeep would never forgive me if I withheld the means needed to keep a scar from marring that face."

The Roaringhorn managed a smile. "You'll have it back, to the last nib."

Black eyebrows arched in feigned amazement. "That knock on your head must have been harder than we thought!"

Beldar chuckled, because it was expected, and waved Taeros and Starragar on their way.

After the last swirl and glimmer of black and amber gemweave had disappeared around a corner, Beldar removed his own cloak and turned it so only the dark lining was showing. His task ahead would be harder if eyes marked him and wagging tongues repeated his name.

He made his way purposefully along now bustling streets. Ducking down a particularly noisome alley, he picked his way through litter and offal to where it ended against the stout stone wall of a warehouse, adorned with crude graffiti and fading blazon-bills of events long past.

Finding the stone that was lighter in hue than the rest, Beldar ran his fingers around its edges, widdershins. A stone door swung open reluctantly on silent hinges, letting him slip into a narrow, low-ceilinged passage beyond.

The stairs at its far end glowed faintly. Beldar drew the door closed and proceeded cautiously; the glow came from a spongy lichen that made the steps slippery. The last time he'd traversed them, it had been in a bone-bruising tumble that his older brother had found highly amusing—yet Beldar smiled in grim satisfaction, remembering how he'd wiped the smirk off his brother's face.

Or rather, the necromancer's prophecy had stolen that smile and put a swagger into Beldar's step that hadn't yet deserted him.

Until today.

His first real battle had been an utter disaster. He was destined to be a leader of men, a hero who could rise from seeming death. That was the prediction his brother's coins had bought, yet to his utter mortification, he'd let some lout get a fish-gutting knife past his guard, then *swooned* at the sight of his own not-quite-blue-enough blood!

He'd atone for this. He *would* win his next battle, which was why he was here again. It would be a simple matter for the necromancer to seek out the man who'd cut him and the names of those who'd caused the fray in the first place. Thus armed, Beldar Roaringhorn would seek vengeance on them all.

The stairs ended in a small, dark stone hall. Its far wall was carved into the likeness of an enormous skull, a faint greenish glow emanating from the empty eyesockets.

Beldar strode forward to put the purse Taeros had given him on the ledge of the skull's nose.

"I seek names. Their fates have already been decided."

A moment of silence greeted his boast. Then a dry chuckle came from behind the skull-wall, and a voice he knew. A crone's voice. "Welcome, young Roaringhorn. Come in, and learn those you wish to slay."

The front four "teeth" swung inward, and Beldar ducked and climbed through that opening—and a tingling moment of warding magics and spells of darkness—into a surprisingly lavish room.

Fabulous tapestries softened its stone walls, and a warm red glow came from a marble hearth. A winged imp, the necromancer's familiar, was curled up before the brimstone-scented fire like a somnolent cat.

A shapeless pile of black rags rose haltingly from a deep-cushioned chair. Beldar went to one knee—not out of respect, but from memory of the pain the old woman had inflicted at his last visit, when as a lad he'd been too proud to bend a knee.

The old crone nodded approvingly and raised a wizened hand to remove the black mask concealing her face. Bright blue eyes gazed out of a maze of wrinkles. "So you've come to Dathran again."

He bit back a retort about stating the obvious, for the old woman's calling was more a title than a name. Dathrans were rogue witches cast out of Rashemen for doing evil or using magic in a way proscribed by her sisterhood—in her case, death magics of Thay.

Those dark spells and her second sight had earned "Dathran" a place in Waterdeep's underground. Like many nobles, Beldar had more of an acquaintance with the dark underbelly of city life than he would admit to in polite society.

"I want the man who did this," Beldar said, touching the wound on his forehead, "and those who started the battle in which I received it."

Dathran nodded again and hobbled to a shallow scrying-bowl. "Blood," she said, looking at him expectantly.

The Lord Roaringhorn swallowed a grimace and came over to the basin. The necromancer mumbled a brief incantation as she reached up to touch his forehead, her fingers as dry and brittle as bird's feet. They traced the wound, calling forth the memory of its making, and with it, a swift new flow of blood.

Beldar leaned over the basin, letting the dark drops fall into the water. Light promptly began to rise toward the surface, like a glowfish rising from the depths of a cave pool. The water roiled briefly, then smoothed, a vivid picture forming: a roadside smithy, the South Gate of Waterdeep rising close behind it, where a leather-aproned man was tapping a new shoe onto a carthorse hoof. The man's face was familiar, and the sign over his forge-wagon read "The Lucky Horseshoe."

All of Tymora's luck, Beldar thought grimly, would not be enough to keep him alive. "And the instigators?"

The necromancer bowed her head, spread her hands over the bowl, and rocked gently back and forth. Dreading what he might see, Beldar dropped his gaze to the bowl again.

In the scene now floating in those depths, an elderly man was lowering himself into a vast tub of steaming water, a tiled indoor pool that already held several other men. This was common enough in a city of public baths, but there was nothing common about the bathers.

Judging by their scales, clumps of fur, and odd limbs—talons, scales, claws and the like—most of them were mongrelmen.

A few of the bathers, including the old man, seemed different. They looked to be pureblood humans who'd been deliberately mutilated to acquire monstrous limbs and features.

The old man was quite possibly the strangest creature Beldar had ever seen. One of his eyes had been replaced with a glowing red orb. A pair of tentacles grew from his torso, which was armored with many-colored scales. A snake coiled around his forearm, seeming to grow directly out of his wrist.

There were other oddities, too, but Beldar's stunned mind could not make sense of them all, much less catalogue them.

He looked at the other bathers who'd probably been born human. Even the most normal-seeming, a youngish man with dust-colored hair, had an odd-colored glass orb where one of his eyes should have been.

A servant came into the room, bearing a tray. His words, not passed on by the scrying magic, seemed to displease the old man.

A thin bolt of crimson light flashed from his glowing eye. The servant staggered back, staring stupidly at a black-edged, smoking hole that had suddenly appeared in—or rather, through—his forearm. The other bathers glanced at the wounded man but made no comment, as if this was no unusual occurrence.

"Eye of the beholder," murmured the necromancer, awe adding richness to her papery voice. "Skin of the yuan-ti, poison of the adder . . ."

She went on at some length, but Beldar was no longer listening to anything but his own tumbling thoughts.

He'd sworn vengeance against a villain who, through some fell magic, had augmented himself with the powers of monsters. Beldar had heard of monster cults, and both sorcerers and clerics who worshiped strange gods, but he'd never heard of people *becoming* monsters, piece by living piece.

Such foes were beyond him, and Beldar Roaringhorn knew it.

His despair was short-lived, for another of the Dathran's prophecies came vividly to mind: His path to greatness would begin when he *mingled with monsters.*

Beldar had tried to forget those words since that night in the

Luskan tavern, tried to consign them to the crypt of lost opportunities. Now they sang through his mind as he gripped the scrying bowl with white-knuckled hands, studying the fading image as if it was a missive from the gods.

Never once had he contemplated such a path, or seen this possibility in the old witch's words.

Mingling with monsters . . . *yes.*

⚓ ⚓ ⚓ ⚓ ⚓

As twilight stole across the city, the harbor horns rang out, telling all that the massive harbormouth chains were being raised. Lamplighters hastened along the streets to fill and trim lamps, and three Gemcloaks strode the streets of Sea Ward, cloaks of amber, blue and black glimmering behind them.

"You've inquired at all the houses of healing?" Starragar demanded. "All the temples?"

Korvaun nodded grimly. "Not even the Roaringhorns have seen Beldar since you two parted from him. He's *not* sought healing."

"Which probably means he *can't.* He's too vain to want a scar." Starragar sighed thoughtfully. "Have you checked the jails?"

Taeros snorted. "While you're listing rosy options, why not the corpse haulers?"

The youngest Lord Jardeth grimaced, as if chiding himself for this oversight. "Most likely he went seeking revenge; that's why I suggested the lockups, yet—"

"Such thoughts occurred to me, too," said Korvaun, "and I inquired. No, he wasn't arrested."

"Which brings us back to scouring taverns, clubs, and festhalls. For what remedy remains to him, but to get harbor-spewing drunk?"

Taeros sighed. Even the finest boots start to chafe when one pounds the cobbles all night.

Right ahead stood The Gelded Griffon, a new festhall popular with rising-coin dandies who had the wealth but not the cachet of the nobility. Ordinarily the Gemcloaks would never deign to step inside, which was precisely why Taeros had thought it should be their twenty-third place to search. They nodded to the doorkeeper, who was already bowing low, and swept inside.

Korvaun dropped a few coins into obviously delighted hands, received the news they'd all been hoping for, and the trio of Gemcloaks traded grins and headed for the indicated row of curtained booths along the back of the dimly lit hall.

A burly, stern-faced man in a Griffon-badge tunic was standing guard to ensure privacy, but when Korvaun dropped a dragon into his palm, the guard pointedly strolled away. Still watching him go with a cynical grin, Taeros gently parted the curtains of the first booth.

There sat Beldar ... or what was left of him.

Bloodshot Roaringhorn eyes looked up. "Sit down," their owner ordered thickly, "before you fall down. You're weaving like saplings in a storm, all four of you."

The three sober Gemcloaks exchanged glances, and slid into the booth. "We've been looking everywhere for you," Taeros told him. "What in the Nine bloody Hells have you been doing?"

Beldar raised a tankard as large as his own head. "Seeking ovlib ... libbynon ..."

"Oblivion?" Starragar offered helpfully.

An emphatic, slightly wobbling Roaringhorn finger pointed at his dark-cloaked friend, as if celebrating a correct response. "And looking for the man who cut me," he added with sudden, grim clarity.

Korvaun leaned forward. "Beldar, I understand your desire to even scores, but please reconsider any hasty vengeance. This morning's trouble was no fault of ours, but if reprisals follow, the Magisters *will* blame us and won't be lenient in their judgments."

A sputtering snort was Beldar's only response.

Starragar rolled his eyes and refilled their friend's monstrous tankard from a tall, moisture cloaked metal ale jug. Beldar's third, judging by its two toppled companions.

"He can barely hold his eyes open," Starragar murmured,

meeting Korvaun's incredulous stare. "Let him drink himself into slumber, and the night will pass without bloodshed."

After a moment, Korvaun nodded reluctantly.

The three sober Gemcloaks sat with their friend, quietly trading jests they'd heard many times before, until Beldar's sagging head dropped onto the seat-cushion Taeros had thoughtfully placed on the table. When the gentle snores began, they eased out of the booth and gave another coin to the guard with instructions that henceforth *no one* was to disturb the Lord Roaringhorn's privacy.

🏰　🏰　🏰　🏰　🏰

When his friends' quiet footfalls had faded, Beldar hauled himself more-or-less upright. His usual impulse was to scoffingly dismiss Korvaun's cautions, but those last words had set Beldar to thinking.

Dimly he clung to one phrase, as if it was a flaming sword in his hand on a dark night, a lone lifeline on a storm-drenched deck, a . . . the Hells with it! He *must* not forget it: *hasty vengeance.*

Korvaun was quite right. He, Beldar, had come to that same conclusion, right? Hadn't he spurned vengeance immediately at hand and resolved to undertake long years' work . . . to make real the possibilities glimpsed in the necromancer's scrying bowl?

The scrying bowl.

Memories flooded back and with them the grim path he'd seen, whereupon Beldar remembered why he'd come here to drink.

Much pain lay ahead of him: pain, and shunning from kin and the Watch and . . . mere shopkeepers and beggars in the street.

Yet why not walk that road, when he could gain so much?

He would never be *The* Roaringhorn, patriarch of the clan. If the street battle was anything to go by, he'd never even be much of a warrior. His friends no longer looked to him as their leader; their devoted gazes were shifting from him to Taeros or Korvaun. Soon he'd have nothing. *Be* nothing.

Unless.

Unless he found a way to be stronger—and seize his destiny.

Beldar used the table to find balance enough to stagger out of the booth.

"Call me a coach," he growled, pressing yet another coin into the delighted booth-guard's hand. "I need to be at a certain bath-house in Dock Ward. *Now.*"

CHAPTER FOURTEEN

Mrelder studied the gleaming helm on the table. In his imagination, its empty eyes were watching Golskyn's pacing with faintly amused curiosity. He wished he could regard his father with the same shining detachment.

Suddenly Golskyn stopped. Mrelder tried not to shrink back as the priest leaned in close and snapped, "Again your sorcery fails us! It doesn't seem good for much—not that the mages I've known fare much better. I'd cast you aside as worthless, right now, if I hadn't made a grave error myself."

Mrelder knew just what *casting aside* meant. His life was balanced on the proverbial sword edge—and it was a very sharp sword. He hardly dared ask about this "grave error," but his father obviously expected him to. No matter, as long as the man who so grandly called himself Lord Unity didn't conclude his son would never be able to use the Gorget.

Mrelder thought he saw another way, a mere glimmer thus far ... but there was no time to think now, not with his father glaring at him.

"Error, Father? We have the Gorget, with no Watch yet pounding on our door ..."

"And *that* was my mistake," Golskyn said almost triumphantly. "Magical baubles can be traced and in the end are but tools, usable in only a few set ways. More reliable than weak and treacherous men, yes, but I know how to move men to my bidding. We should have grabbed Piergeiron, not this scrap of metal!"

"But Father, they'd have torn Dock Ward apart trying to find him!"

"Torn Dock Ward apart! *Exactly!* With a few Walking Statues, perhaps? Hah! Why control this or that stone man when you can control the one who commands them and the entire *CITY?*"

Golskyn's shout echoed around the room, and Mrelder winced.

"We could barely drag him; we'd never have got him in here without fighting off a dozen Watchmen! He's out of our reach, now, carried away—"

"Aye, carried off *dead*. Or possibly dead. More than possibly, if you send the right spell after him, and Waterdeep thinks him dead already! With sufficient strife in the streets, and if our magic from afar can keep him drooling or maimed long enough, no matter what healings are cast, the other Lords will be forced to choose and present his successor."

Golskyn drew lips back from teeth in an unlovely smile. "Such a man, chosen in haste, is hardly likely to be one so strong in faith. He's far more likely to be everyone's 'second choice,' in other words, a ready tool."

This was a very long chain of hopes and suppositions, but Mrelder knew better than to say so. When his father was like this, 'twas best—

"You," Golskyn hissed, leaning in again until his nose was almost touching Mrelder's, "will find this man for me. You can redeem yourself by identifying him and delivering him into my power. *Bring me the next Open Lord of Waterdeep!*"

Mrelder felt Piergeiron's helm being slapped into his hands. He'd not even noticed Golskyn snatching it up.

He stared into the fiery eye so close to his, swallowed, and managed to say, "I'll set to work. Right now."

Whirling around, he almost fled from the room.

He had just time to put a soft, cruel smile on his face before he flung open the door—and met the inevitable measuring gazes of several Amalgamation believers who'd been listening. By the misshapen gods! Why didn't Golskyn graft dogs' ears onto the lot of them? At least then they could eavesdrop at a distance!

Hurrying down the stairs, Mrelder made for the rear door. The back alley was far less likely to be full of bodies and Watch officers looking for handy persons to blame for them. He hefted Piergeiron's helm, and shook his head.

His father was getting worse.

All his life he'd been awed by Golskyn's shrewd eye for truths and seeing how things *really* worked, and how the priest could move men to his bidding. Even if there'd been no gods his father could call on and no Amalgamation, Golskyn could go far and rise high on wits and judgment alone. No, strike that: on his ruthlessness, too. But somewhere along the line, the priest's single-mindedness had become obsession.

Finally Mrelder faced a truth he had long known: He was never going to win Golskyn's respect. And strangely enough, he no longer craved it. A small part of Mrelder still ached for his father's approval, but he was ready to move on.

There were things to be learned from Golskyn. The deft cleaving between and through foes. The knowing what was going on behind the masks, the sneering at laws and conventions that bound others ... that *was* the way to power and achievement.

It would be his way, and this grasping, brawling, coin-rich city of Waterdeep would be his home, this city he was coming to know so well. Before he was done, Mrelder would end up covertly controlling Lords and laws from the shadows.

But his father had stepped over the parapets of prudence long ago and just now clearly flung himself off the battlements of sanity. There'd be nothing safe and subtle about Golskyn of the Gods from now on. Mrelder had mastered enough Waterdhavian history to know that men who were boldly ambitious but neither safe nor subtle seldom lasted long.

And Mrelder intended to last a long time indeed.

Ordinarily, Korvaun Helmfast would have been hugely enjoying himself. After all, 'twas no accident all the assistants in The Right Foot were stunningly beautiful, dressed in elegantly revealing garb, and obviously *enjoyed* flirting.

What strange madness had prompted him to enter this place? Malark was dead, Beldar off drinking himself blind, and his own sword still warm with the blood of the men who'd died on it. He had set himself to discovering why buildings were collapsing. But it was one thing to fervently promise action, and quite another to think of some way to successfully start going about it! The buildings were rubble now, and it wasn't as if their stones were going to talk ... or was it? Could the right spell ...

Tasleena pouted at his frown and ran teasing hands up his thigh. "My Lord Helmfast," she breathed, "do I displease you that much? Should you ... punish me, perhaps?"

The fop next to Korvaun, a wealthy merchant who could only dream of nobility, given that his wreck of a face and grasping ways would bar him from ever successfully wooing any noble lass Korvaun could think of, grinned at Tasleena's sally.

So did the amply bosomed young lass who knelt at the man's feet, assisting him into mauve, lace-trimmed thigh boots that would've looked overdone on a lady dancer.

The Right Foot deliberately employed beautiful female assistants to entice male purchasers to pay inflated prices for showy footwear. Moreover, Korvaun *liked* Tasleena. She was fun, liked jests, and in days past had enjoyed a little skindance now and then without expecting marriage or wanting to cling. The boots she was proffering now were splendid supple black thigh-high affairs, too. It was just that ...

All of this could be smashed if Waterdeep went the wrong way, and he'd never forgive himself if he did nothing about it.

Korvaun managed to smile down at Tasleena—she winked, of course—and then was further distracted when the foppish merchant lost his balance and hopped awkwardly, almost putting one mauve spike-heel into the magnificent cleavage, glowing with moonstone dust, on display below him.

Ondeema—*that* was her name—captured his foot expertly and leaned forward, moondust and all, to force the man back against the leaning-bar and restore his balance, murmuring, "They *are* a trifle high, aren't they? Perhaps something more . . . substantial. To match you, milord . . ."

The merchant agreed breathlessly. Watching the man's hungrily bulging eyes, as he stared down his leg to where Ondeema was pressed against him, Korvaun judged that he'd agree to just about anything, right now. Tasleena's sly smile told all Waterdeep she thought so too.

Ondeema suddenly stiffened, frowned, and then nodded as if in answer to something unheard. Letting fall the man's foot abruptly, she rose in a whirl of high-slit skirts and leaned over as if to kiss Korvaun's ear.

A moment later, Lord Helmfast was stunned to hear her softly murmur a lone word to him: "Stormbird."

He stared at her for a moment, gaping like a fish—and then stepped right out of the fashionable footwear Tasleena was sliding up his leg, yanked on his own boot, and strode out of the shop.

Those left behind in The Right Foot saw him grab protective hold of his stylish sword and break into a run the moment he'd cleared the shop door.

Tasleena and the merchant stared after the departed Lord Helmfast in utter astonishment. When he'd vanished, they had no one left to stare at except Ondeema, who merely gave them a serene smile and silence.

"Wha-what did you say to him?" the merchant demanded at last.

"I merely reminded him of what my four brothers said would happen next time he followed me home from the shop, milord," Ondeema replied sweetly, fixing the fop with large and twinkling eyes. "Now, where were we?"

▲   ▲   ▲   ▲   ▲

Find and control Piergeiron's successor. An order delivered as off-handedly as one might say, "Bring me a plate of herring and eggs."

Mrelder shook his head in disbelief. As if Waterdeep lacked a Khelben Arunsun, or a Laeral, or an entire gods-cursed Watchful Order, to say nothing of priests high and mighty who'd be able to detect a magically controlled Open Lord or a spell-disguised impostor in his place. They'd know, all right.

Hefting Piergeiron's war-helm, Mrelder halted in mid-stride. *They* would know, yes, but if he crafted a light sorcery of false half-memories of masked Lords meeting and Palace passages by night in the mind of the nearest carter or dungsweeper and presented the result to his father as the next Open Lord, how would a certain overconfident Golskyn know?

He resumed his swift walk to the Palace. The sooner this helm was out of his hands and the risk of being traced through it gone, save as the maker of its little copper badge—something Piergeiron's pet wizard knew already—the better.

The Palace guards knew Mrelder by sight this time and recognized the helm too. He thrust it at them. "Here. I trust my *good friend* the Lord Piergeiron is well enough to be needing this? I managed to keep him alive after he was struck down in the fighting, but departed when the Watch ordered me to; 'twould seem they left this behind when they carried him away. He took a fearsome blow; how fares he?"

The guards traded glances and drew back in frowning uncertainty, one clutching the helm. Behind them, a tall, unfamiliar woman in the full gleaming armor of the City Guard hastened down the Palace steps.

"We thank you for this," she told Mrelder crisply. "The Lord Piergeiron's well but in private conference." Her nod was both thanks and dismissal.

Mrelder nodded back, very slowly, and was rewarded for his tarrying by what happened next.

One of the many doors at the head of the stairs opened, and two Guard commanders hastened out, helms under their arms, with a trio of grim, grandly garbed Palace officials behind them.

"Get word to him right away," one official was ordering the Guard officers. "Mirt's Mansion."

⛫ ⛫ ⛫ ⛫ ⛫

The tall Guard commander watched Mrelder turn away, her face thoughtful. Then she hurried back up the steps, yanked open another door, and snapped, "See that man?"

She pointed at Mrelder's back, dwindling into the usual crowds of people striding importantly to and fro across the great open cobbled expanse in front of the Palace. "I want him followed. See where he goes and what he gets up to. *Don't* let him spot you, and report back soon. Two of you, so one can return and the other keep watch."

The door opened wider and two men strode out. They looked like dusty, none-too-well-paid merchants' carters, or veteran dockhands, and carried a large, heavy crate between them.

Or at least they walked as if it was heavy. In truth, it held only cloaks and hats they could use as disguises, but they saw no need to let all watching Waterdeep know that.

⛫ ⛫ ⛫ ⛫ ⛫

Did Mirt's lady always wear dark, skintight leathers? Roldo Thongolir was swallowing and staring openly, and Korvaun knew just how his friend felt. Asper drew the eye with every lithe movement, that mare's-tail of ash-blonde hair dancing behind her, and a slender sword bouncing at her hip. When she was in the room, it was difficult to look elsewhere ...

Knowing eyes met his, and Lord Korvaun Helmfast felt himself blushing.

"Lords," Asper said firmly, "stare all you want, and help yourselves to yon decanters, but *pay attention.* Waterdeep has need of you."

Korvaun and Roldo found themselves nodding and mumbling in hasty unison. They traded glances, and with one accord, reached for decanters.

Asper grinned, rolled her eyes, and waited for glass stoppers to rattle back into place. *Nobles.* They seemed to need oiling even more often than dockworkers ...

When they were both staring at her again, Asper handed a small silver device to Roldo.

"Don't lose or drop those, or all our strivings are wasted."

The two nobles looked down at their slipshields. The device Mirt had given Korvaun was a tiny shield of dull metal, but Roldo's was a fanciful pendant of a hawk soaring across a large and intricate snowflake.

"Winterhawk," Roldo murmured, recalling a tale he'd read in an old and rare book his bride had acquired in Silverymoon. For resale, of course.

Asper nodded. "An old tale, not often told," she said quietly, eyeing Roldo with something that might have been respect in her eyes.

Then she went on as briskly as before, "Now at the Gentle, you'll follow Laneetha—dark purple robe, eyes gray as a harbor mist—to her curtained chamber, where you can make the switch unseen. She'll identify herself. I'm telling you this in case anything happens to me in the tunnel. Come."

"Tunnel?" Roldo asked, face tightening.

"It'll get us behind Laneetha's curtain rather more quickly than the carriage could take us there, through underways neither of you will ever remember and have never seen nor heard of—and if you don't follow my instructions *precisely* as we proceed, will never be able to forget."

Roldo frowned. "Is that a threat?"

The smile fell from Asper's face so suddenly that Roldo half expected to hear it shatter on the floor. "No, it's a promise, on the part of the traps awaiting there. They're *very* good at keeping promises, believe me. Now, Lords, answer me this: do you swear to serve Waterdeep in utter secrecy, upon pain of death?"

"Lady," Roldo told her a little stiffly, "we *are* nobles."

"That's why I'm asking," she said quietly, as their eyes locked.

After a long moment, Roldo sighed and shrugged. "I swear. Of course." Korvaun echoed him, without the shrug.

"Good. Thank you." Turning to the nearest wall, Asper thrust aside a curtain.

Both Roldo and Korvaun knew the battered figure standing in the dimly lit room beyond leaning on a crutch—wherefore they both swallowed hard and rose to their feet in hasty unison.

This earned them a smile and the dry words, uttered in a strangely slow and thickened voice: "Well met, loyal lords."

♠ ♠ ♠ ♠ ♠

Mrelder had never before seen so many people just lounging around an alley in bustling Dock Ward. Laborers were casually draped over barrels, fishmongers tallied catch-crates with chalk on a handy wall instead of inside whatever warehouse held those catches, and three burly men were fixing the axle-pins of a wagon even a sorcerer could see wasn't really broken.

Even if he stood boldly in the center of the cobbles like a man awaiting a duel, there wasn't much space left. Wherefore Mrelder went into a handy net mender's shop, pointed up its stairs, and offered the toothless old man behind the counter two gold dragons for "the use of yon upper window."

The old man grinned. "Three dragons. Chair's extra."

Mrelder rolled his eyes, dropped a third coin into the man's palm, and ascended. He was only half-surprised to discover a dusky-skinned, scowling titan of a sailor and a pale, thin girl who seemed to be clad entirely in scabbarded daggers there already, seated in chairs at the lone open window. It seemed there was a deep daily local interest in the comings and goings at Mirt's Mansion.

Either that or half the city already knew Lord Piergeiron was inside the stylish fortress. Mrelder settled himself in the last chair—a crack-seated, wobbly wreck, of course—just in time to see a very drunken young man in splendid but disheveled garb carried down the mansion steps by Mirt's doorguards and loaded into the moneylender's carriage. The glittering blue cloak marked the drunk as one of those who'd sworded sailors in a recent brawl.

"Lord Korvaun Helmfast," the dagger-lass chuckled. "My, he must drink fast?"

The sailor's dirty laugh broke off in a grunt as the guards

went inside and a sudden singing shimmering sprang from rune-pillar to rune-pillar. "They've set the night-wards," he growled in surprise. "That's it, then. No one'll be leaving 'til morn."

The girl spat thoughtfully out the window as Mirt's carriage rumbled past, and Mrelder sat frowning and thinking.

Then he sprang to his feet and hurried down and out, following the carriage. About half the watchers who'd been loitering in Tarnished Silver Alley had suddenly found good cause to be elsewhere; Mrelder saw only two others oh-so-casually strolling from shop to shop along the route he was taking.

"This window's the best," a hoarse voice came down to him, as he passed under the open windows above one ramshackle shop, "and a good arrow's a small price to pay for a new Open Lord who's not quite so firm and upstanding, *if* ye take my meaning."

Mrelder hurried on. Best to pretend he'd heard nothing and keep in close under awnings and downspouts, where no arrow might find *him*. Of course there'd be folk in Dock Ward who'd want Piergeiron dead and welcome all the accompanying tumult. Why—

He stopped. Ahead, Mirt's carriage had halted outside a large, new-looking building. Mrelder vaguely recalled that an old rooming-house, its roof sagging into collapse, had stood there as sahuagin had raged down the streets. Newly rebuilt, it now sported steps up to elegant double doors flanked by formidable-looking doorguards, beneath a truly splendid signboard.

"The Gentle Moment," he read, then deciphered the more fanciful script below: "Skilled hands to tend all your hurts and needs."

The horses, their heads tossing, were already unhitched and being led around to the near end of Mirt's carriage, to draw it right back down the street to the moneylender's stables.

Mrelder frowned. His purse was now slender enough to make the prospect of following some drunken noble blade—whose connection to the Lords of Waterdeep was probably nonexistent—into a brand-new and surely overpriced house of healing and pleasure rather less than appealing.

A woman who wore little more than a collar adorned with long strips of glittering cut-glass "gems" suddenly burst out of the doors, planted herself on the steps in a pose that showed Mrelder and everyone else on the street all the charms the gods had given her, and blew a horn.

A Watch horn.

Before Mrelder's jaw could even drop, she'd vanished back up the steps in a flashing of false gems and a bouncing of trim flesh, and voices could be heard shouting inside the Gentle Moment— angry male voices.

A brawl must be brewing. Mrelder strolled away from the house of healing to somewhere he could lean casually against on the far side of the street. Mirt's carriage rumbled away, and from the east came the hasty jingling of scabbard-chains and the bobbing of torches.

The doorguards stood motionless, staring coldly at Mrelder and several other curious Dock Warders who'd heard the horn and come to see the trouble—or being as this *was* Dock Ward—the fun.

They stared back and forth, the guards on the steps and Mrelder and the others across the street, both casually ignoring the Watch patrol who rushed up the steps into the Gentle Moment, then sent out two Watchmen to blow another horn-call.

The Watch wagon that responded to that summons was rather less elegant than Mirt's carriage and sported enough window-bars and firequench-glowing metal plates to seem part of a fortress rather than a conveyance.

The doors of the Gentle Moment opened again and *another* unconscious young noble—this one wearing a gem-bright cloak of a soft rose hue—was carried out, unconscious, and stuffed through a hastily slammed hatch into the armored wagon.

"Where's he off to, I wonder?" Mrelder murmured aloud.

An old salt standing near threw him a sharp look, spat on the cobbles while deciding to humor a visiting outlander, and growled, "Palace dungeons, o' course. Watch wagons go nowhere else—unless they're carrying deaders to be burned at the Castle."

"Ah," Mrelder said, nodding his thanks. Then he froze, staring. Lord Korvaun Helmfast, smiling and nodding to the Watch officers in a manner that could only be described as stone cold sober, was descending the steps of the Gentle Moment, and thanking one of them for letting him "borrow" some men to see him "safely closer to home."

Mrelder frowned. An instant sobriety spell? Well, that just might account for the amount of revelry the nobles of Waterdeep were famous for, and where better to acquire one than a house of healing?

Or was it all part of something more sinister?

♜   ♜   ♜   ♜   ♜

Roldo Thongolir batted aside a veil of cobwebs and wondered why the tunnel didn't seem quite so terrifying on this return trip.

The underground walk from Mirt's Mansion to the Gentle Moment had been a nightmare. The traps Asper had warned about were plentiful and dangerously imaginative, but far worse were the close walls, low ceiling, and suffocating knowledge that crushing tons of rock and soil loomed just overhead.

On this trip the ceiling was even lower, thanks to his borrowed form, but somehow it bothered him less that his hair frequently swept the ceiling-stones. Perchance something of Lord Piergeiron's famed courage came with the tall, broad, hard-muscled frame.

It was strangely exhilarating, striding about in the shape of Waterdeep's greatest living hero. Roldo was still not entirely certain why he, Korvaun, and Piergeiron had just traded shapes. Answers would surely be his soon; wasn't that glow ahead the end of the tunnel? And wasn't his lovely guide turning to him, stepping so close that she could—

Kiss him, full on the mouth.

She had to stand on tiptoe to do it, thanks to his new height. Only the grace of Lathander—and perhaps Piergeiron's armor— kept Roldo from staggering back in stunned surprise. 'Twasn't every day fair ladies expressed their thanks so delightfully to him. His own new Lady Thongolir, alas, was . . . reticent in such matters.

"Now, can you feel this?" Asper asked softly.

"This" was a small, cold, and very sharp blade held at Roldo's throat. He started to nod, swiftly thought better, and murmured, "Y-yes."

Asper stepped back. "Good. 'Twill set to work on you—*very* slowly—if you ever reveal what you've done and seen this night, until I give you permission to speak of such things."

"Lady," Roldo replied stiffly, "there's no need for your blade. My honor binds my tongue. *This I swear.*"

Asper stepped back, eyes steady on his. "Then please accept my apologies," she said softly, "and come and take wine. You'll have to stay in Piergeiron's shape until we hear the signal."

Roldo frowned. They were back in Mirt's Mansion, and he was thoroughly confused by what he'd just taken part in. "Certainly and gladly, Lady, if you'll *please* explain what we just did."

Asper nodded and led him up a curving stair to a room with a high northeast window, where lamps glimmered and warm covered platters waited. Waving at him to help himself, she said, "The Lord Piergeiron's badly wounded. Due to his age and the longevity magics that sustain him, he isn't . . . healing well. Half the city knows it, including many who see gain in slaying the Open Lord."

"So Sunderstone and Piergeiron's pet wizard want him somewhere secure. The Castle."

Asper smiled. "You grasp the basics. Problem: Piergeiron can't be teleported safely through the Castle or Palace wards because he can't speak the trigger words properly just now."

Roldo nodded. "His mouth was hurt. Swollen."

"Yes. Moreover, his wounds make it unlikely he'd avoid the tunnel's traps. Korvaun swore an oath to serve Waterdeep, so we called on him. A slipshield let him trade his likeness with the Lord. As drunken Korvaun Helmfast, Piergeiron could be taken to the Gentle in our carriage."

"While you took us through the tunnel, and when was *that* dug?"

"Centuries ago. It's why my Mirt had the Gentle Moment built."

"So you gave me this slipshield so Korvaun could take his own form and be seen leaving, and Lord Piergeiron could be taken away in yet another man's likeness. That whole brawl was staged, wasn't it?"

Asper grinned. "We can't hope to fool true brawlers such as yourselves."

Roldo reddened. "Lady, do you hate nobles so much?"

"No, Lord Thongolir. My tongue makes sport of everyone. Please forgive me."

Roldo swallowed. Women didn't stir him much, but when Asper looked at him like that . . . "So in my shape and feigning drunk, Lord Piergeiron was arrested."

Asper nodded. "And conveyed safely to the Castle in a prison-wagon."

"All this just to fool watching eyes?"

She nodded again. "I saw scores of them, just glancing out the windows here."

Roldo caught sight of himself, still in the Open Lord's form, in the light-reflecting window. He grimaced at the unseemly disarray and peeled another cobweb from his hair. It was uncanny, seeing Piergeiron's hands obeying *his* thoughts!

"We'll arrange for the payment of your fine. I apologize for any blot this might leave on your good name."

"A night in the Castle for drunken brawling in a house of healing and pleasure? That can only enhance my reputation," Roldo said dryly.

"With your noble friends, but there remains your wife. I can explain matters to her, if you will—not everything, but enough to ease her mind."

Roldo managed a smile. "Your offer's both kind and appreciated, but I suspect the sight of you would more unsettle my lady wife than thoughts of an entire festhall of hired beauties."

236 · The City of Splendors

"Gallantly said, milord! If you didn't resemble Piergeiron so closely, I'd suspect you of flirtation!"

They shared a chuckle as a high horn-call rang out, echoing off Mount Waterdeep in a triumphant ascending flourish.

Asper smiled. "He's safe inside," she announced, drawing him away from the windows into another room, where she reached for the hawk-and-snowflake pendant resting on the breastplate of Piergeiron's armor.

As she lifted the charm, a strange tingling swept through Roldo, and the armor felt suddenly heavy and cumbersome. Looking down, he saw that his hands were his own once more.

Asper helped him out of the too-large armor, and handed the slipshield back. "A small reward. In case you ever need it."

Roldo regarded the device with unease. Magic was something he preferred to regard from a distance . . . and there was something deeper and disturbing about the slipshield, something personal. To one who hides from the world behind a mask, this little thing was ultimate power . . . and temptation.

"I'll not deny the worth of this gift or the honor you do me in giving it," he said slowly, "but I'm not the man to carry it. Pretending to be someone you're not is a great burden."

Mirt's lady eyed him shrewdly. "One you know something about."

He raised his eyes to hers. "I've never pretended to be other than I am. But I have responsibilities, obligations . . ."

"And the slipshield might tempt you from those?"

"Lady, you may think me a coward, but that's something I'd rather not learn about myself."

Asper kissed his cheek. "Courage comes in many forms, as do those who possess it. You came without question when your friend called."

"Korvaun's a good man. If he says a thing must be done, I trust his reasons."

"You're right to trust him." Her hand closed his fingers around the slipshield. "Then find another you judge able to bear this little burden. Dawn breaks; we'll see you safely home."

Roldo lifted her fingers to his lips. "I'll strive to be worthy of your trust."

He bowed, strode back to the room of windows, and then turned with a frown. " 'We'?"

Asper smiled and drew aside another curtain, and Roldo found himself staring at three scarred, monstrously large sharpswords whose very looks made him shudder. Two of them tried to smile, and that made it even worse.

"Some of Mirt's friends," Asper said sweetly. "They'll see you safely out of Dock Ward—to whatever front gates you'd like."

Gods, if this dangerously capable woman ever crossed wills with his Sarintha . . . Roldo stowed the slipshield carefully in his pouch. Taeros would wear it well. Moreover, it would settle his gambling debt to the Hawkwinter, avoiding Sarintha's wrath at coins wasted. And what is life but deftly dealing with little debts and unpleasantnesses?

Giving Asper the deepest, most courtly bow he could manage, he turned, nodded to the sharpswords, and strode away with them.

Mirt's lady watched him go thoughtfully, and suspected the burden young Lord Thongolir had taken upon himself was far greater than the one he'd declined.

As sages said, courage and honor took many forms.

CHAPTER FIFTEEN

A high horn-call rang out from the magnificent turrets and spires of Piergeiron's Palace. Lark listened as the short, ascending melody echoed off Mount Waterdeep once, twice . . . and thrice.

Folk in Waterdeep thought nothing of those echoes, but people familiar with mountains found it strange that echoes could bounce from a single small peak. She'd said as much on the long-ago day when she'd ridden into the city with Texter. The paladin had told her magic aided the echoes to amplify signal horn-calls.

Lark quickened her pace, striding briskly through the familiar bustle of Trades Ward. Arriving early for her shift, and working hard before her expected time, would win approval.

The carvers at the Maelstrom's Notch were deft at butter-seared seafood, and their superb table was making the inn very popular. Extra hands were needed to serve the later evening meals, after most lodgers had eaten and set off in search of fiery drink and festhalls, and a weary army of hungry guildsmen arrived to dine after a long day's work.

She was fortunate to have found a place; ill repute had a habit of clinging to a girl like a damp cloak, and her rare moment of temper had cost Lark her last position and several days' wages: the cost of the tray she'd dented over Beldar Roaringhorn's hard head.

Bah. Swaggering Lord Redcloak was worth not another thought. Those horncalls, now . . . everyone knew they were messages for those who knew how to read them. Who sent those notes soaring out into the evening, and to whom? Had she just heard gladsome tidings or a warning?

Once it would never have occurred to her to wonder. She cared little about what great folk did or whose backside warmed which throne. What mattered was honest work and the quiet, respectable life it could earn. Master Dyre's fair wage, bolstered by the coins this serving work brought, would in time buy a small shop with a few rooms above it she could call her own. To be her own mistress ... her one desire. Her dream.

That dream burned as bright as ever, but Texter, the man who'd put her on a path toward it, had also opened her eyes to other things. In this city, those who listened could hear secrets in tavern tunes, vendors' calls, even twilight hornsong. Lark absently hummed the horncall as she walked.

"Larksong in the evening," murmured a melodious voice, so close to her ear that she could feel warm breath. "To whom are you preparing to sing, my little brown bird?"

Lark whirled, as startled as if her own shadow had tapped her shoulder and asked her the time of day.

Elaith Craulnober gave her a faintly amused smile and glided forward a step to reclaim the distance she'd hastily put between them. "If I wasn't aware of your sterling character, I'd suspect you of being troubled by a guilty conscience." His voice was gently mocking.

Lark swallowed. "You—startled me."

"You *did* seem rather lost in thought. Care to unburden yourself to a sympathetic listener?"

She gave him a glare. "Why? Know you of one?"

Silver brows rose. "The kitten has claws. How very ... tiresome."

The Serpent's dark reputation tempered Lark's next words. "A lord as important as yourself has many demands on his time," she murmured, careful not to sound mocking. "Pray tell me how I can serve you."

Craulnober nodded at the nearest shop: Andemar the Apothecary, who greeted passing Waterdeep with a fancifully carved arch-topped door flanked by large windows set with many small, diamond-shaped panes.

Lark opened that door and stepped into a pleasant-smelling room crowded with gleaming vials and fragrant hanging bunches of drying herbs. Andemar's welcoming smile froze as he recognized Lark's companion.

Elaith waved a dismissal, and the shopkeeper's head bobbed in frantic assent as he scuttled into his back room, closing its door firmly behind him.

The elf swiveled open the domed top of a silver stud on a dagger-sheath that adorned his inner left wrist. In the revealed hollow was a tiny blue bead, which he tipped into his palm. He passed his other hand over it, fingers flashing in a swift, complex pattern.

The bead promptly expanded into a soft blue haze that drifted smoothly around them both, surrounding them like mist glowing about a lantern.

"Speak freely; none can now hear. The message you delivered was extremely interesting. I desire to know everything you can tell me about the activities of the New Day."

"Activities?" Lark sniffed. "Precious little, thus far. Just grand scheming and bluster."

"The battle in Dock Ward was mere 'bluster?' Dyre's men started it."

Lark's eyes widened. "I— I know nothing of that."

"No? Three young women were seen there, one of them a little brown bird with a green ribbon on her arm."

Lark frowned. "Yes, I was there, but by happenstance! I was with my mistresses, who had cause to pass one of their father's worksites."

Elaith's eyes were bright with disbelief, and he seemed somehow to glide nearer without actually moving at all.

"Wait," Lark blurted, cold fear rising. "I—I think I see how the brawl began! Some of Master Dyre's trustyhands frequent a quaffhouse just where the fighting broke out, and they hold a grudge against several young lords."

"Helmfast, Hawkwinter, Jardeth, and Roaringhorn," Elaith

murmured. "What inspired that particular flock of peacocks to strut through oh-so-common Dock Ward?"

"They'd a debt to settle with my Master Dyre, and they seem taken with his daughters. Both are young and pretty."

"So this settling of grievances befell when blind chance met young love?"

"I believe so, though 'love' is putting it a bit high. Lord Helmfast's skirt-sniffing around Mistress Naoni, much luck may he enjoy."

"And it just so happened that Lord Piergeiron chose that moment, of all the unfolding season, to wander along that particular street of Dock Ward?"

Lark drew a long, shuddering breath. "I know nothing of the Open Lord's doings, beyond brisk tavern-talk of his death—and *that's* nothing new."

"He was wounded, and carried to Mirt's Mansion. No more is known."

"Not even by the Lords?"

Elaith smiled thinly. "The Masked Lords must, of necessity, keep many secrets."

True that might be, but Lark's interest lay in matters closer to home. "From what I've seen and heard, I can't believe Master Dyre had any part in what befell Lord Piergeiron. He only desires the Lords to renounce secrecy and be accountable to all."

"Varandros Dyre is not so lacking in initiative as you claim, but on this particular matter I'm inclined to agree. These young noblemen, however, warrant closer scrutiny."

Lark was too astonished to quell her burst of scornful laughter.

"Scoff less quickly," Elaith murmured, sniffing some herbs approvingly. "The skill exhibited by the most foolish of our nobles when it comes to keeping secrets would astonish you."

⛪ ⛪ ⛪ ⛪ ⛪

"A remarkable young man," Mrelder said, concluding his recital of Korvaun Helmfast's virtues—all of them boldly invented for this occasion.

Mrelder had arbitrarily chosen the youngest Lord Helmfast as Lord Piergeiron's successor. With so little time to accomplish his impossible task, he'd been forced to consider the most familiar candidates. A few discreet questions had won him the names of the young noblemen in this morning's brawl, and he'd spent the afternoon finding and observing three of the four. Lord Helmfast's visit to Mirt's Mansion had sealed the matter.

He'd never be able to persuade his father that the scribbler Taeros Hawkwinter could be anybody's choice for the next Open Lord, and Starragar Jardeth was the sort of blustering, haughty, hot-headed noble the minstrels lampooned. The Helmfast lordling's golden good looks, his skill with a blade—Mrelder recalled the swirl of glittering blue as Korvaun cut his way through the fray, and his calm, considered speech: these echoed qualities of the Lord Piergeiron. When Mrelder was done with the Helmfast heir, he'd wield some of Piergeiron's powers, too—enough, hopefully, to convince Golskyn.

Thus far, his father seemed far from convinced. "So this paragon of virtue—whom I've not failed to notice you've yet to name—was seen coming from a moneylender? Is being short of coin, in your eyes, a mark of lordliness?"

"This Mirt wields much power in Waterdeep," Mrelder insisted. "Recall the fat bearded man the Watchmen were carrying with such haste they nearly ran us down? That was Mirt. When talk turns to the hidden Lords, Mirt's name is always spoken: everyone in the city 'knows' he's a Lord. Why *else* would Lord Piergeiron be carried to his mansion?"

"Mansion?" Golskyn's manner brightened. "He's wealthy, this Mirt?"

Mrelder knew well his father's preoccupation with wealth. The priest had amassed a fortune, and considered accumulated wealth one mark of a leader.

"Mirt's Mansion is a city landmark. They say he captained a mercenary company in his youth, and some insist he owned a pirate fleet! His pillaging obviously proved highly profitable."

His father nodded approvingly. A good part of Golskyn's fortune had been acquired the same way.

"So your young noble was summoned to Mirt's Mansion shortly after the wounded First Lord was taken there . . . yes, things may well stand as you say. Fighting prowess, his fellow lordlings look to him . . . and he has money."

Heavy footfalls echoed down the hall, approaching in cadence. Golskyn frowned at the open door.

"He wears a cloak woven from gemstones magically spun into thread," Mrelder added hastily, concerned he might lose his father's attention.

Golskyn turned to his son, grunting, "As to that, he'd be better off putting his coins to less vain uses. A wise man, in a city such as this, would put his coins into investments."

"That, good sir, is my intention," announced a cultured male voice.

The priest turned slowly back to face the doorway, every inch a holy patriarch.

In the doorway stood two mongrelmen, flanking a richly dressed young man. One made a swift gesture that made Golskyn's eyes widen.

"Gemweave cloak," the priest murmured. "Tall, fit, handsome, well-spoken—yes, he's much as you said, and he desires to join the Amalgamation! You failed to mention he'd been wounded in the fray outside our doors, but then, so was Lord Piergeiron, who's said to be a peerless fighter. You've done well, my son. Very well indeed."

Mrelder shut his gaping jaw with an audible click.

Later, he'd worry about how this young noble had so swiftly discovered what and where the Amalgamation was. Yes, he'd worry very much indeed, but just now . . .

"Lord Unity," he said grandly, "may I present Beldar Roaringhorn, a Lord of Waterdeep."

Lord Roaringhorn inclined his head to Golskyn in a small but adequately respectful bow. "I'm honored to meet so great a necromancer."

"I'm only a sorcerer, and a minor one at that," Mrelder said hastily, seeing his father's face turn stormy. Nothing angered Golskyn of the Gods more than being mistaken for a wizard of any sort. "Yet I'm often mistaken for a necromancer because folk misunderstand the natures of those with whom I associate. My father, Lord Unity of the Amalgamation Temple, is a great and holy man, a priest who speaks for gods whose names cannot be shaped by human tongues. The mongrelmen and those granted monstrous enhancements through the grace of these gods revere and follow Lord Unity."

Beldar Roaringhorn bowed again. "An honor. I hope you'll not think me irreverent when I say I'm willing to pay a small fortune to receive a graft similar to the one beneath Lord Unity's eyepatch."

Golskyn greeted these words with a dry, grating chuckle that might have held derision, admiration, genuine humor, or all three.

"Incorporating any graft is difficult," Mrelder warned, "and if your first graft is a beholder's eye, you'll have little chance of surviving."

Golskyn raised a hand. "Let us not judge hastily. The request is not unreasonable. A great lord's heir should prove himself strong."

"Then let me prove myself indeed," Beldar replied, saying nothing of his distance from ever becoming *the* Lord Roaringhorn. "Am I correct in assuming a graft must come from a living creature?"

"You are," said Golskyn, acquiring a small and approving smile.

"I'll bring you a living beholder. Let it be both proof and payment."

"Agreed."

Beldar Roaringhorn bowed again, more deeply, and then turned and strode from the room.

"Capturing a beholder alive's no easy thing," Golskyn murmured, staring at the empty-of-noble doorway. "If he succeeds, we'll know Lord Piergeiron chose well."

"And if he fails," Mrelder added hastily, "I know who the second successor is!"

It would seem Korvaun Helmfast was destined for greatness after all!

🏰 🏰 🏰 🏰 🏰

"Lord Roaringhorn!" Old Dandalus was as jovial as ever. "It's been some time, aye? Be welcome!"

Beldar gave the shopkeeper a wry smile. All noble lads flirted with disgusting monstrous trophies—taloned this and tentacled that—at a certain age, if only to make young noble lasses shriek at revels, wherefore Beldar Roaringhorn had been to the Old Xoblob Shop many times before. At every visit Dandalus greeted him with the same words, even if his previous visit had been but a tenday earlier.

Dandalus 'Fire-Eye' Ruell was bearded, balding, big-nosed, and bigger-bellied. He looked no different than he had the first time Beldar had wandered into this shop as a boy, eyes shining with the wonder of the Dathran's vision.

Beldar's gaze wandered around the shop, which was both familiar and ever-changing. The shelves were crammed with greenish jars of pickled, staring eyes and less identifiable remains, and hung with a scaly forest of tentacles and serpentine bodies spell-treated to keep them supple. All around Beldar were thousands upon thousands of strange "monster bits." Twenty men could be hiding in all this carrion-tangle and him none the wiser.

No. Dandalus had his smallest finger raised in the signal that meant "We are alone." Beldar glanced quickly up at the shop's infamous beholder, looming over him like a watchful shadow, and then looked away, managing not to shudder.

"Thanks for your good cheer, Dandalus," he said, choosing his words carefully, "and your *discretion.*"

The proprietor of the Old Xoblob Shop leaned forward over his glass countertop, ignoring the tray of jutting fangs just beneath it, and murmured, "In that, Lord Beldar, you can trust absolutely. I hold my tongue, and not even the Blackstaff himself can pry secrets from me. As for why he can't, well, that's one of the very secrets I guard. There's no profit in this line of business if I flap my jaws, nor much of a personal future, if you take my meaning."

Beldar nodded. "Straight to it, then: I need directions to the nearest beholders' den you know of and advice on how to enter it without swiftly greeting my own death." He tapped his chest to let Dandalus hear the stony jostling of gems in his innermost purse, to signify that he could pay well.

"A moonstone for my words," the shopkeeper murmured, "and two more for *this*."

Reaching several layers down under the counter, he drew forth something that almost fit his palm: a brooch of smooth-polished hemispheres of unfamiliar gemstone, each cut to display a staring-eye image: a large central orb surrounded by ten smaller ones. This signified a beholder, obviously, but—

"A safe passage token," Dandalus explained. "Worn at throat or brow, it tells eye tyrants you're a willing minion of one of their kind—an agent of proven loyalty."

"Ah. Wear it or die?"

"Indeed. Beholders, plural, you said; is this what you truly meant? A 'wild' den, or the lair of just one?"

Beldar swallowed, nightmarish images flooding his mind, and then pulled firmly on the fine chain that brought his gem-purse into view and started shaking out moonstones. "A wild den shared by several beholders. Is it far?"

"In the Rat Hills," Dandalus said merrily, waving southwards. "Now heed: Despite what the sages and all their books tell you, the powers of their eyes vary from beholder to beholder—you'll not always be facing the same magics. That goes double for beholder-kin, and that's what this particular lair is full of: there're gauth and some of the little floating ones about as big as our heads, too. You'll not be finding many pureblood eye tyrants sharing lairs—and none at all that I know the way to, no matter how many moonstones you throw at me."

Beldar looked up and saw the glint in the old shopkeeper's eyes.

Clearly the thought of a ruby-cloaked noble tramping about the Rat Hills—small peaks made up of centuries of Waterdhavian garbage—was vastly amusing to him. Likewise the vision of a lone swordsman in a den of beholder-kin.

Well, perhaps there was some grim humor in it, but didn't most adventures have far more to do with grime than glory? Even a paladin in shining armor betimes must dash into bushes and hastily unbuckle to answer needs of the body; did that make his quest any less noble?

This was *his* quest, a firm stride closer to seizing his destiny. If it took him into the Rat Hills, then by the gods, to the Rat Hills he'd go.

"Problems, lad?"

"This is all one huge jest for you, isn't it?"

Dandalus leaned close. "Beldar, my lad," he replied, as if he was a god or a king or the Lord of the oldest, haughtiest noble house of Waterdeep, "*life* is one huge jest."

Beldar smiled in reply. 'Twould be the act of a fool to dispute with Dandalus. Rumor insisted the beast parts filling the shop around him would, upon the old man's command, animate and combine into horrors hitherto unknown to Faerûn. The Roaring-horn might be preparing to walk into a beholders' den, but he wasn't *entirely* moon-mad!

⛰ ⛰ ⛰ ⛰ ⛰

Golskyn reached for a decanter. "Will you scry young Lord Roaringhorn to learn where he finds his eye tyrant—or how he knows of one?"

"Certainly, if I can do so without drawing the attention of the Palace wizards who often scry *him*," Mrelder lied. Roaringhorn was doomed; his time would be far better spent learning all about Korvaun Helmfast.

"Should we then be arming for the fight of our lives on the heels of these mages watching him, when they come here to treat with us?" Golskyn asked silkily, suddenly looming over his son.

"No, Father. Your wards stand undisturbed—as you're well

aware—and I've been very careful to cloak myself from them. *Very* careful."

Of course, there was the small matter of the two spies who'd been following him, but Golskyn needn't know about that. They were dead, and the mongrelman who'd slain them would take full responsibility, thanks to Mrelder's first attempt at controlling an Amalgamation minion by casting a spell he'd crafted at another creature's monstrous grafts. Successfully, *at last!* After all, he didn't want his first victim to be "Lord Piergeiron's heir!"

"You answer well," his father replied, pouring himself a much larger drink than usual. "You're learning at last. Whenever possible, stand firm when pushed."

· · · · ·

Beldar crept cautiously through the tunnel, moving by the soft glows of fungi on the walls and some vivid green radiances rising from small pools of slime that seemed to be creeping along the rocks ever so slowly. Despite such . . . plants? . . . the air was as damply unpleasant as a wet cloak, but its mustiness was vastly better than the choking reek of the Rat Hills. Better even than the foul stench of the deadwagon that had brought him here, bouncing along with the carcasses of an ancient mule and several one-eyed dogs, and now stood awaiting his return at the fading end of a trail.

Trails amid soaring mountains of trash! Who—or what—might find reason to visit this desolate place often enough to make a trail?

The glows were growing few, and the soft darkness deeper. Target or not, 'twas time to unshutter his lantern.

"That's far enough, doomed meat," a soft, liquid voice said almost tenderly, from very close by Beldar's left ear.

Beldar clapped his swordhilt, but resisted the urge to whirl around. He was a dead man if they wanted him so, despite all the little Roaringhorn family magics he was wearing and no matter which direction he faced.

The inky darkness all around him seemed to shrink and

dwindle, receding with the suddenness of powerful magic to reveal some sort of ancient, long-abandoned cellar, its walls furred with mold he'd been smelling for some time now, and its floor visibly damp.

For all Beldar cared, it could have been walled and roofed entirely with nude, imploringly beckoning noble lasses; he could only stare in mute terror at dozens—*dozens!*—of beholders. He did not need to turn to know they were floating all around him. A swarm of miniature eye tyrants drifted like lazy fish amid the larger dooms.

The largest beholder-kin was floating right in front of him. It had a gaping, skull-like socket where its central eye should have been and was surrounded by floating, slowly orbiting glowing gems, and what looked like ornate scepters that winked and glowed softly. Its great jaws, bristling with jagged fangs, were twisted into a grotesque parody of a smile.

Flanking this beholder mage was another horrific creature, of the sort sages called a "death kiss." Around its baleful red eye writhed not eyestalks but ten eyeless tentacles like taloned fingers that lazily opened long slit-like jaws from time to time.

Several of the surrounding beholders were smaller and had only six eyestalks each. Dandalus had said beholder eye-magics varied from one eye tyrant to another in nature as well as strength, and some eye tyrants weren't nearly as powerful as the fearsome reputation legend gave them, but standing alone gazing upon so many gently writhing eyestalks and so many malicious stares, Beldar Roaringhorn knew better.

The smallest one here can slay me at will.

"I come not to harm," he rasped, finding his mouth and throat suddenly dry, "but to warn and seek advice."

"Are you alone?" the beholder mage demanded, "Do you know spells?"

A sudden crushing force blossomed inside Beldar's head, leaving him gasping and numbed, barely able to think or move. He struggled, thick-tongued, to answer ... and then, as suddenly as it had come, the awful invasion ended.

"You stagger under the weight of magics you know not how to use," the beholder hissed contemptuously. "Speak now, ere we slay you. You offer poor sport."

Beldar took a deep breath, reminding himself of the Dathran's prophecy, and said, "I come from the city of Waterdeep, where a man now dwells who seeks to 'improve' himself by grafting claws and tails and other body parts of wild beasts—monsters—to himself. He's done so successfully at least a tencount of times, winning new limbs and organs that live and thrive, obeying him as if they were his own. They now *are* his own."

"And this concerns us how?" the eye tyrant mage sneered, though the glows encircling it brightened and its surviving eyes flashed in evident excitement.

"This man keeps one of his eyes hidden behind a cloth patch," Beldar replied, "to keep other humans from seeing it's been replaced with . . . an eye from a beholder."

A hiss went up all around Beldar that was almost a roar, drool-wet and furious. Eyes flashed, eyestalks writhed like angry snakes, and a dozen beams and bolts of deadliness stabbed at the quaking human from all sides.

All of them vanished in amber glows that brightened until Beldar could see a soft aura all around him. His skin tingled painfully, and he bit back a moan of fear.

"Soil yourself not, human," the beholder mage said coldly. "That was but a simple truth-test. I'd not have believed your tale, else. You spoke truth and so live yet, but this blasphemer, this human who *dares* to butcher our kind, must *die*—swiftly and knowing one of *us* is his slayer!"

Eager babble filled the cellar in an instant—and ceased, knife-sudden, as amber radiance blazed anew about the beholder mage.

One of its eyestalks curled to tap thoughtfully at its fanged mouth in an oddly human gesture. "Dealing death to this blasphemer would be a pleasure to everyone here, but one of us has a prior claim. Who sent you here, human, to tell us this?"

"No one." Beldar tapped the badge Dandalus had sold him, the device that marked him as a man in thrall to a beholder. "There is no one *now*," he added meaningfully.

"I see. Your master was slain by this human."

That hissing voice was not quite questioning. In case a truth-magic remained in the soft amber glow, Beldar said, "I decided to come here—alone—and parted with valuable gemstones to learn the way."

"You earn my protection already," the great beholder said, turning to face him fully, almost as if its blind, empty eyesocket could still see. "Are you willing to do more?"

"I am your servant," Beldar replied with dignity, knowing no other sane answer.

"Then one of us shall accompany you back to Waterdeep."

Though Beldar saw no gesture nor word pass among the floating horrors, one of the gauths—if he remembered the Roaringhorn library bestiary correctly—drifted forward to hang just above and in front of him. Before he could look at it properly, it began to circle him as if surveying a roast boar for a tasty-looking place to start devouring.

"You shall lead Alanxan without delay to this man, that his death may be accomplished without arousing the city's defenders, attracting undue attention, or leading this arm of our vengeance into any traps. Failure to do this, Beldar Roaringhorn—oh, yes, human, I read all I want of your mind in our brief contact—and not only will you die in long torment, but so shall all your friends and kin. Perhaps every so-called noble house of Waterdeep needs one of us commanding it."

"I thought you loathed . . ." Beldar stopped, realizing nothing he might say could be well received.

"We do. Save as cowering slaves to fetch, enact our wills, and provide us with entertainment. Yet with your ridiculous airs, you prancing humans entertain and even amuse—some of the time."

"A—a deathwagon waits to carry me back into Waterdeep," Beldar almost gabbled. "It has, uh, grim cause to travel every street of the city, so Alanxan can be safely brought to the back door of the, ah, blasphemer's abode, if, of course, this meets with your approval!"

"It will serve. Go."

Beldar bowed, turned, and strode hastily back out of the lair, eagerly seeking the stomach-churning reek of rotten garbage. The gauth drifted behind him, its largest eye half-closed but its others trained on him, as if anticipating betrayal at any moment.

The Roaringhorn allowed himself a grim smile. As the creature was expecting treachery, it would be ill-bred of him to disappoint it!

CHAPTER SIXTEEN

Taeros stood on the Westgate ramparts, the siege of Waterdeep raging all around him.

Far below his boots, a host of sahuagin pounded at the gate, using great waterlogged timbers from sunken ships as rams. Wizards hurled down magical fire at them, and City Guard archers loosed wave after wave of flaming arrows. Scores of fish-men fell, until the wet sands were hidden by heaps of blackened, smoking scaled corpses.

Suddenly a gigantic squid rose from the dark, roiling sea, towering higher than Mount Waterdeep. An enormous tentacle lashed out, impossibly long, dashing a screaming line of Waterdeep's defenders off the battlements, leaving Taeros standing alone, armed with only a quill and a fistful of parchments. The tentacle curled back slowly, arching menacingly on high . . . and then descended at him, vast and dark and terrible . . .

He was blinking blindly into the bright morning sun, bolt upright in bed and gasping hard. It took some time before Taeros realized the thudding in his ears wasn't just the pounding of his heart. Someone was insistently striking the knockplate of his bedchamber door.

Mumbling curses, Taeros swung out of bed. The shirt and breeches he'd worn the night before were conveniently right on the floor where he'd left them. He yanked them on, strode barefoot to the door, and flung it open.

Onarlum stood with his staff of office raised to strike again, mute apology on his face. Behind his shoulder Taeros could see a young woman—tall, blonde, formidable, and all too familiar.

His irritation fled before the bright wrath burning in her blue eyes.

"Sarintha," Taeros murmured, staring with growing concern at Roldo Thongolir's bride. "Is anything amiss?"

"My *husband* is amiss," she snapped, pushing past him into the room. Over one shapely shoulder she sent Onarlum a white-hot glare of dismissal. The steward hastily bowed and scuttled gratefully away. "Or rather, missing."

"Missing?"

Sarintha's look of scorn might have melted glass. "Lord Hawkwinter, even in infancy, I was neither stupid nor naive."

Taeros blinked. "I—I've never suggested you were. If I knew where Roldo was, I'd surely—"

"Invent some story to cover his tracks," Sarintha said sharply, "but as it happens, I know all: he went to a moneylender, and lacked even the decency to lie about it!"

Taeros blinked again. Roldo was careful with his coins, as nobles went. He owed Taeros a small gambling debt, true, but 'twas nothing pressing, certainly nothing to send him a-borrowing . . .

Sarintha gathered volume. "Do you know what he did with these borrowed coins?"

Taeros shook his head, feeling like a particularly stupid student being tonguelashed by a supercilious tutor.

"He went straight to the Gentle Moment—for 'healing'— and got into a drunken brawl. They carted him to the Castle *dungeons* like a common sailor!"

Taeros frowned. "That . . . doesn't sound like Roldo."

"Nevertheless, that's the tale his manservant *dares* to tell me! Take this!"

Sarintha thrust a coin-heavy purse into his hands. "Now go and pay his Watch-fines *and* his debt, whatever it may be. I would be *grateful* if you handled this with as much discretion as possible."

She glanced pointedly at the amber cloak lying in a glittering puddle on the floor.

It was little surprise that Sarintha mistrusted the Thongolir steward's tongue. She'd want no word of Roldo's indiscretions to reach his parents' ears, lest they conclude Sarintha couldn't manage her husband, much less family business.

"I'll see to it at once," Taeros promised. "You'll have Roldo back before highsun." *Whether you want him or not*, he thought.

Sarintha was already nodding curtly, and Taeros was left bowing at a swirling of skirts as she turned and strode from the room.

Taeros didn't know whether to glare at the open doorway or sigh. After a moment he shrugged instead, dressed quickly, and strode out, leaving his telltale cloak behind.

Hurrying to the carriage house, he bade the groom harness the unmarked coach, a workaday carriage with curtained windows of the sort used by many slimcoin travelers and merchants.

The hostler knew his work. Without prompting he passed over the stalls of sleek, highbred horses to choose a pair of cart nags, and brought out unadorned harness. The drover stripped off his Hawkwinter livery and turned the tabard inside out, so its plain dark lining showed. The same routine was well-rehearsed among most noble house servants in Waterdeep, for many masters frequently ordered errands best done quietly.

After a seemingly interminable ride through bustling morning streets—ye gods, didn't anyone in this city *sleep*?—the coach rumbled to a halt before the Castle entrance known as the Dungeon Doors. A panel in the heavy iron gate slid open, and a gray-bearded man looked out expectantly.

Taeros jerked the coach-curtain aside. "I've come for Roldo Thongolir. Brought in last night for drunken brawling."

The gateguard shook his head. "Here no longer; fine's paid."

"*What?* By whom?"

The guard's steel-gray gaze sharpened. "And who might be asking?"

Taeros thunked Sarintha's purse down on the coach's door-ledge. "A friend to Lord Thongolir, acting on behalf of his lady wife."

The graybeard eyed the purse—or rather, the Thongolir crest worked into its soft leather. "Guess there's no harm in telling you to take Lady Thongolir's coins to Mirt. The moneylender sent word last night pledging payment."

Gritting his teeth, Taeros gave the man a curt nod of thanks. Calling the new destination to his drover, he flung himself back in his seat, not bothering to close the curtain.

They were nearly at Mirt's Mansion when Taeros caught a glimpse of glittering rose hue and rapped hastily on the coach wall. Even before the drover had quite pulled the horses to a stop, Taeros was out and down into the street.

Striding through the street crowd, he clapped Roldo on the arm. His friend spun around, hand on sword.

"Save that for Sarintha," Taeros said sourly. "She sent me to settle your fines and debts."

Roldo grimaced. "My lady's well informed."

"Better than your friends." Taeros slapped the purse into Roldo's hand. "If you'd need of coin, why not come to me?"

"All's settled with the moneylender—and if you're willing, I'd like to settle the debt between us with something more handsome than coins. I've received a gift more suited to your name and tastes than mine: A charm wrought in white gold."

Cradled in his hand was bright, silvery fancywork: a pendant of a smooth, stylized hawk soaring across a beautifully carved, intricate snowflake, on a fine chain. Roldo put it into his friend's palm with great care.

"*Very* fine," Taeros murmured, peering at it with dawning pleasure. "I think I've won the better part of this bargain."

Roldo glanced around, and then took his friend's arm and pulled him into the angle formed by two mismatched shop walls.

"Perhaps, and perhaps not," he muttered. "This is a magical thing; it lets you trade shapes with another man . . . and it comes with two solemn oaths: to never tell anyone about its powers and to use them only for the good of Waterdeep."

Taeros stared at his friend. "Who—"

"The moneylender's lady gave it to me. Korvaun has one too.

We did Lord Mirt some small service."

"Then why not keep it your—"

"I'm not the one—the right one—to hold such power." Roldo's stare was like fire. "You know heroes and their great deeds, Taeros. I've seen pages of your gift to the child king; Thongolir scribes are embellishing them now. If a time comes when this is needed, who'd know what had to be done better than you?"

Who, indeed? Taeros saw himself again as he'd been in his dream, standing alone on Waterdeep's ramparts with only quill and parchment in hand. Poor weapons . . . but perhaps Roldo was right!

After all, his Hawkwinter head and heart were full of wondrous stories. Surely one might yield a plan when the city stood in need, so he could tell Korvaun what to do!

Korvaun, not Beldar . . . now that was unexpected, yet felt oddly right.

Taeros put the pendant around his neck. "I accept with honor, and I swear to so serve Waterdeep," he said solemnly.

Roldo managed a wavering smile. "Thank you. I'd consider it a courtesy if we spoke no more of this."

"As you wish." Taeros cleared his throat. "So, where were you heading in such haste?"

"Korvaun wants all of us to meet this morn. Didn't you—? I guess his messenger came after you were up and about."

"At the clubhouse? I've a coach!"

Roldo grinned. "And I've the sloth to take it!"

⚔ ⚔ ⚔ ⚔ ⚔

Korvaun and Starragar were waiting in the club, tankards ready.

"None of my messages seems to have reached Beldar," Korvaun told Taeros, serving forth ale, "so we might as well start."

Starragar frowned. "Shouldn't we find him?"

"I don't believe he wants to be found," Korvaun said quietly. "If we hear nothing for, say, another two days, we should search, but right now it's probably best to leave him his privacy."

Roldo shook his head. "This isn't like Beldar."

"No," Taeros agreed dryly, "usually *he'd* be the one starting brawls at a house of healing and pleasure." Waving away
Starragar's quizzical glance, he asked, "So why are we here,
exactly?"

Korvaun leaned forward. "I've been looking into all of these
fallen buildings."

"'All of these'?" Taeros asked sharply. "There's another?"

"A tallhouse in North Ward, fortunately empty at the time.
However, hear this: both it and the Slow Cheese were owned by
Elaith Craulnober."

Taeros whistled. "Interesting. There was some unpleasantness
three or four years back, talk of a band of elves from the forests
come to the city and fighting here under Craulnober's command.
He left for Tethyr soon after and presumably took his elves with
him. Now, not long after his return to our streets, two of his properties are destroyed. Some sort of retribution, d'you suppose?"

Korvaun shrugged. "Possibly, but I've come across a remarkable
amount of property owned by the Serpent—and I don't think I've
found half of it. That two out of all these collapsed is not quite
the coincidence it might at first seem."

Starragar frowned. "What else?"

"Varandros Dyre is insisting to anyone who'll listen that the
Lords are digging new tunnels to spy on citizens."

"Well, the Lords couldn't do that without hiring Dyre or rivals
he'd know about," Roldo pointed out, "but the Serpent, now . . . if
there's anyone in Waterdeep who warrants watching right now,
'tis him."

As the friends exchanged grim nods, Taeros said slowly, "The
Lords may not be the only ones watching Elaith. Now that I think
of it, Dyre's maidservant was at Craulnober's party the night
Malark died, not to serve but gowned as a guest."

"You're certain?"

Taeros nodded. "I *thought* she looked familiar at the time but
couldn't place her. Yes, I'm quite sure."

Korvaun ran a hand through his hair, sighing. "This is truly troubling. Is she watching Elaith Craulnober or watching *for* him?"

"The latter seems more likely," Starragar put in darkly, "but if we put a man to watching her, we'll know soon enough."

"'Twould be better to send a woman," Taeros mused, "A sellsword who can pose as a serving wench and go where Lark goes. Hiring blades is Hawkwinter business, so I'll see to it."

Korvaun frowned. "If Lark's working for Elaith Craulnober, anyone you send will be at risk."

"I'll make sure she's pretty," Taeros replied with a wink, "and if my father has any sword-wielding she-elves for hire, so much the better. If rumors tell truth, Elaith Craulnober collects more than real estate."

🏰 🏰 🏰 🏰 🏰

Varandros strode through South Ward, his heavy coin bag thumping at his hip. It would be lighter on the return trip, more's the pity.

The brawl in Dock Ward was costing him dearly. Four of his trustyhands had died in the fighting, all workers on the Redcloak Lane raising. The sorcerer who'd bought the building would be less than pleased by further delays, so men would have to be pulled from other jobs, and skilled hands came dear in these busy days, with every jack across the city rebuilding . . . and then there were the burial costs and widows' fees.

He couldn't recall exactly where on Telshambra's Street his man had lived, but the place wasn't hard to find. A small, somber group was gathered outside a narrow stone building, ale cups in hand.

Varandros made his way over. The mourners—many of them his men—moved aside to let him pass. He strode inside.

The small front room was almost filled by a trestle table draped in dark cloth. Rowder had been laid out on it in his best clothes, a chisel in his folded hands.

Dyre managed not to scowl. A needless extravagance; it was customary for great folk to be buried with some sign of their house or station, but he doubted practical Rowder would have appreciated the waste of a good tool.

He nodded to the woman behind the table, face composed but eyes rimmed with red. She bobbed a curtsey.

"We're honored you've come, Master Dyre. Please have a cup of my Rowder's funeral ale."

"I'll drink to him gladly, Mistress," Dyre said gruffly. "A fine man, a good worker. He'll be missed."

"Aye," she said softly. "That he will."

He put the bag in her hands. "This is his portion. If you've further needs, the guild will see to them. I'll make sure of it."

She nodded gratefully, eyes like empty holes, and Varandros found himself standing awkwardly with nothing more to say. He did as he'd promised, raising a cup of ale to Rowder's memory, and then turned and set out for home.

Children playing in the street fell silent when they saw his face, and got out of his way. One of them made a warding sign, but the stonemason said nothing. Something like dark fire burned behind his eyes.

⚔ ⚔ ⚔ ⚔ ⚔

He found his daughters in the kitchen around a trestle table very like the one Rowder had been lying on. To his astonishment, the Dyre kitchen table had a dead man on it, too—pale, naked, and middle-aged, loins draped with a towel for modesty. Naoni, face serene despite the grim work, was sponging dried blood from the body.

Varandros gaped at her—and even more at his dainty little Faendra, who was handily stitching up a gash along the corpse's ribs and not looking the least bit squeamish. His younger apprentice, Jivin, hovered in the buttery doorway all but wringing his hands.

"What *is* this?" Dyre growled.

The three looked up. "I-I had to bring him here, Master," Jivin said hastily. "There was nowhere else for him."

"He'd no family, poor man," Naoni added. Dipping her cloth in a fresh basin, she gently wiped blood from the battered, staring face.

As the gore came away, Varandros recognized Cael, one of the masons who'd been setting the foundation on Redcloak Lane.

"You did right, lad," he said heavily. Every man in his employ was entitled to a fair wage and a decent burial. Yet this was not a task he'd wish on his daughters. "What of Lark? Where's the wench?"

Naoni's reply was quiet but firm. "She comes early and gives an honest day's work, Father, and in the evenings, she serves at an inn or a revel in one of the great houses. She said she'd be working late last night and would take a bed at the inn. She'll be here in time for the churning and the cheese."

Dyre nodded approvingly. "A hardworking lass."

Nor was Lark the only one. Almost for the first time, Dyre noticed how capable Naoni was, how warm and welcoming she made their home. She had her own craft, too, the spinning of fancy threads. Several skeins of pale, glittering green hung behind her on a neat row of hooks. Her mother would have loved them. Aye, Ilyndeira had been fond of pretty needlework . . .

Rare nostalgia swept through Varandros. He seldom thought of his wife, despite the living reminders before him. Faendra had her mother's pink-and-gold beauty, and Naoni, though plain and pale, had Ilyndeira's long, slender fingers. His gaze fell to Naoni's hands—and his brow darkened.

Around each wrist was a ring of dark bruises.

"What happened to your arms?"

Faendra looked up from her work, eyes blazing in sudden wrath. "She was rough-handled during the fight in Dock Ward yesterday."

"You were there?" Dyre demanded, aghast.

"Aye," Naoni said. She met his gaze with calm gray eyes. "No lasting harm was done, Father. Lord Helmfast saw us safely home."

"Again, that insolent *pup!*" Dyre's shout rang around the room, and Jivin fled. "I told him to stay *away* from me and mine! Was it he who marked you?"

"No, 'twas the Watch!" Faendra said indignantly. "They called us noblemens' doxies, and Naoni gave one of them a clout to remember her by!"

"Good for you, lass," he said gruffly, pride rising through his anger. "What part did Helmfast have in this?"

"It was a chance meeting in the street, Father. He and Lord Hawkwinter drew their swords to defend us against the Watch."

"Did they, now? Well, that's something," he said grimly, "but never forget this: They're still the same worthless, unthinking louts who nearly brought down all our work on Redcloak Lane!"

Naoni looked up. "They intended no harm."

"Bah! What of *intentions?* They'd not *intend* to drag a woman's good name into the dust either! To them it's all fun and frolic, but the damage done is the same!"

The look Naoni gave him was surprisingly steely. "I'm not such a child, Father, that I know nothing of the ways of men. Nor am I a fool who simpers and swoons whenever a man looks at me. Neither's Faendra. You needn't fear for us."

"That's simple truth, Father." Faendra narrowed her eyes in a parody of menace. "'Tis the men who should tremble before *us.*"

That teased a faint smile from Dyre.

Seeing it, Naoni considered the matter resolved and said briskly, "I've called the coffinmaker and the carter and sent word to the keepers of the City of the Dead. Cael can be buried six bells after highsun, after down-tools, so those honoring him need miss no work. Perhaps they can return here, after, for the cakes and ale?"

Varandros nodded. "Of course. You've handled it well, lass."

Naoni looked up at him, and her faintly puzzled expression smote Dyre's heart. Was he so sparing with praise, that his daughters were *this* unaccustomed to it?

"I'm for work," he said abruptly. Turning, he strode from the house, thinking thoughts that were both new and disturbing.

Men of the Watch had laid rough hands on his daughter. A message, perhaps, from those in power? If so, who knows what more might have happened, if not for those silly sword-swinging nobles?

In his desire for a New Day, he'd never considered the consequences for his family, never thought his daughters might be endangered. More fool he!

Aye, *this* striding fool.

His wordless growl was as bitter as peacebound warsteel—trapped in its scabbard, denied a foe it knew too well.

After all, who knew better how the great folk treated common-born women of Waterdeep than a man whose wife had died from the grief they'd caused?

⁂

"I trust Hoth instructed you correctly?" Golskyn's cold words were barely a question.

Mrelder looked up from the tiny golden ring balanced atop scorched stones on the table before him—the Guardian's Gorget, shrunken small enough to incorporate into the graft. The spell-glows playing around it promptly flickered and started to fade. "I believe so, Father, and my follow-all spell definitely captured the effects of the graft-chantings. That's proven by our successfully giving Narlend a lamprey-mouth in his palm—and that lamprey was none too fresh."

Ending his spell, he added, "Unless Roaringhorn bears magics that interfere with our work, or fails physically—much as I've done, thus far—the graft should work. I know how to craft new ocular muscles now."

"So you should. Eight blinded dogs are quite enough, even in Dock Ward. Had we needed more and been foolish enough to take them from North or Sea Wards, the Watch *would* have come calling."

Mrelder nodded. "No doubt, yet everything's neatly disposed of. The first few went out on the deathwagon, and as for the rest, well, the mongrelmen said they made a quite tasty stew."

"It was; I had a bowl myself. Will your little toy be ready in time?"

"It's ready now, not that I expect our ambitious noble to return quite so swiftly. Capturing a beholder—"

"Yes, yes, may cost him his life," Golskyn snapped, tiring of the conversation. Turning on his heel, he strode out of the spell-chamber.

Mrelder wore a little smile as he took up the little stone that had been the focus of the spell he'd just quelled. No probing questions about it, or just what magics he'd perfected, or precisely what he'd done with them. Sometimes his father's scorn of sorcery came in quite useful.

Golskyn's door slammed, and Mrelder heard something unexpected: the front door warning gong. He frowned. Beldar Roaringhorn had found his way here out of the blue; *now* who—?

Hoth rushed up the stairs wearing a wintry smile, heading for Golskyn's chamber without a word to Mrelder.

"Hoth!" the sorcerer snapped. "Who is it? Who's at the door?"

Hoth made no reply, and Mrelder barked his question again, making his voice as cold and authoritative as his father's.

Hoth turned, his hand already on Golskyn's door-handle. "The Roaringhorn lordling's returned, and is asking to speak with Lord Unity. Alone."

Mrelder frowned. "Is he—?"

The rest of his words were swept away in the shattering roar of his father's door—with Hoth still holding it—being hurled into a splintering meeting with the far wall.

"Father?" Mrelder shouted, breaking into a run. "*Father?*"

Hoth was moving feebly under the wreckage as Mrelder pounded past into smoke and two ruby-red beams of magic, flashing at each other in the gloom like thrust swords.

One came from Golskyn's beholder-eye, of course ... and the other was identical, which could only mean ...

Mrelder had to *see*. He dare not—

He cast a swift and simple clarity spell that should sweep away the smoke and banish both shadows and darkness.

There were shouts and pounding feet from behind Mrelder. He

stepped aside swiftly so he'd not be in the way of angry Amalgamation believers rushing into the room with ready weapons.

Wards were flickering in Golskyn's chamber as strong magics lashed out and rebounded, and the feeble clarity spell struggled to expand like mist swirling in a gale. Through it, Mrelder caught a glimpse of his father standing fearlessly, hair singed and his tentacles holding his desk—its top scorched and smoldering—in front of him like a shield.

Golskyn was murmuring spell-prayers as fast as his lips could move, gesturing to bring down the wrath of the gods on something across the chamber. A foe that was, yes, high up near the ceiling: Spherical, and with—

Something flashed through the thinning smoke, and Mrelder felt himself stiffening. He fought to turn and lift his arm, panic flaring like a flame, but . . . he was caught . . . and frozen.

His hand slowed to a drifting thing, then stopped altogether, and Mrelder turned what was left of his will to breathing and turning his eyes, trying to see—

Wall and floor, rushing up to meet him swiftly as mongrelmen burst into the room and struck him aside.

Mrelder slammed into unyielding hardness and bounced, hearing a mongrelman grunt in pain behind him. Then there came a heavy crash as another blundered into a chair and fell through it to the floor.

Then came more bright red flashes, somewhere above him, and more groans. Weapons were dropped with heavy clangs and clatters, someone shouted in pain, and someone else shrieked in agony, cries that receded swiftly back out the door and ended in an abrupt wail that could only mark a plunge down the stairwell.

Golskyn said something cold and crisp and triumphant, and Mrelder felt that horrible *shifting* in his mind that could only mean one thing: his father was collapsing most of the wards laid on his chamber into a mighty spell to make it even stronger.

Mrelder's skin tingled, and a sudden, high singing began, so thin and high-pitched that it felt almost like a needle driven into his ears . . . and it went on and on.

All other sounds ceased, but for a few distant groans and the imperious tread of his father's boots, crossing the chamber to thrust bruisingly into Mrelder's ribs and roll him over.

"Well, *you* exhibited your usual scant usefulness," Golskyn of the Gods commented, staring scornfully down at the paralyzed sorcerer. Mrelder gazed helplessly back at him.

One side of the priest's head was scorched, his bared torso was a mass of sickening yellow-and-blue bruises, blistered burns, and blackened tatters of clothing largely burned away down to his belt. The little snake graft that sprouted from his wrist was thrashing about convulsively, biting the air in agony . . . but the priest's own surviving eye was its usual cold, confident self. The other one—the beholder orb—stared with deadly promise down at Mrelder, the eyepatch that customarily concealed it dangling around Golskyn's neck.

Beyond him, shrouded in flickering magics, a beholder—a small one, little larger than a round shield, and with only six eyestalks, but yes, *a beholder!*—hung motionless.

His father's head turned. "Well, Hoth?"

"Four dead. Ortarn here, Danuth and Velp yonder, and Skeln's face was burnt off, even before he fell over the rail and broke his neck. The rest of us will live until we can heal each other. Shall I show the noble up?"

Golskyn started to chuckle, a harsh, mirthless sound that went on for some time. Mrelder tried again to move his hand and found that it responded now, but slowly, drifting in dreamlike torpor despite the fiercest exertion of his will.

Hoth ignored the sorcerer at his feet entirely, his eyes fixed on Golskyn as the priest's chuckle ran down. Gazing at the frozen beholder, the leader of the Amalgamation replied, "Of course. Tell him—"

"I found my own way up, as it happens," Beldar Roaringhorn said calmly from the doorway.

Hoth whirled around, but Golskyn snapped out a tentacle to coil around the man's arm and ordered, "Leave us, Hoth. Peacefully. The Lord Roaringhorn stands very much in our favor, just now."

Mrelder's paralysis was falling away very quickly now. He rolled over and got to his feet.

Beldar Roaringhorn was strolling forward, one hand on sword-hilt and the other at his belt. Heedless of the strong likelihood that the noble was clutching his two strongest battle-magics, Mrelder stepped into his path and snarled, "You sent that horror in here to kill us!"

Lord Roaringhorn lifted one brow. "That was obviously the beholder's intent, yes, but how would that serve *my* purpose?"

Golskyn eyed him keenly. "A test, perchance, to see if we of the Amalgamation were powerful enough to grant you what you seek."

The young noble nodded.

"And now that you know?" the priest demanded.

Beldar met his gaze squarely. "Now that I know, I'd like to proceed immediately."

CHAPTER SEVENTEEN

Mrelder glared at Beldar Roaringhorn, reaching for the dagger Piergeiron had given him a lifetime ago.

Golskyn's scaly hand closed around his son's wrist before that fang could be drawn.

"Enough," Lord Unity of the Amalgamation said coldly. "You found the right man, and I'll look *very* darkly on any attempt to harm him now."

Mrelder opened his mouth and then shut it again, swallowing his fury behind set teeth. If this fool of a noble had managed Golskyn's slaying, that would have been a delight, but now ...

He'd never expected the man to return, and had laid his plans with Korvaun Helmfast in mind. This Beldar showed a disturbing boldness and wits, too. Could it be he'd actually stumbled on a worthy heir to Lord Piergeiron? Did the Watching Gods laugh that much?

"Your son's right to be suspicious of me," Beldar was telling the priest, "for even as I arrive at your door, this beholder—the sort known as a 'gauth,' I believe—enters your house forcibly, by another way."

He glanced at the charred ruin of Golskyn's back room beyond the office-chamber. What had been a window was now a ragged hole opening onto a high view down over the alley behind.

"I must assure you I'm guilty only of overconfidence. I thought the spells I'd purchased—I dared not specify too closely what I wanted them for, you'll appreciate—were sufficient to keep it securely captive until you could assume control of them, and, ah . . . of it."

Golskyn waved a dismissive hand. "Irrelevant. We all make mistakes. So long as you don't make a habit of doing so or betray the slightest hint of any malice toward the Amalgamation or our goals, I care not if you bought, borrowed, stole, or personally gave birth to this beholder or overcame it by strength, guile, or beguiling minstrelsy. What matters are *results*."

"Father," Mrelder said quietly, "there's a matter of magic I must speak with you about privately, *right now*. I need only a few breaths of your time and mean no disrespect to you or to Lord Roaringhorn, but magic has already done much damage here, and we may yet have the Watch pounding at our doors as to why. We'll certainly have them doing so if there are further . . . eruptions."

"I've had my own dealings with the Watch," Beldar put in quickly, "and will be glad to withdraw for as long as you need. Magic can be dangerous, and the Watch all too vigilant."

Golskyn nodded. "You speak truth. Stand you then by the head of the stair while I speak with Mrelder."

The moment Beldar had bowed and withdrawn, the priest rounded on his son, and his whisper was fierce. "*Well?*"

Mrelder kept his voice low. "I'm alarmed at how swiftly we've embraced this noble—and how quickly he's brought us a beholder! Father, if he's been chosen as Piergeiron's successor, don't you think a dozen wizards have scoured his thoughts scores of times, and taken full measure of his motives? Hasn't he been trained, probably for years, to put Waterdeep first, and ruthlessly put down all threats to—"

Golskyn swung up his hand like a cook hefting a cleaver. Mrelder knew what *that* meant and fell abruptly silent.

"I meant what I said," the priest muttered. "You found us the right man: this must be the next Open Lord of the city. I think you speak sound prudence now: yes, of *course* he's formidable, swift-witted and loyal to Waterdeep, yet he's never crossed swords with Golskyn of the Gods before, to say nothing of those I serve! Do you think so little of my own abilities to subvert *anyone?* Have you forgotten Braeldra so soon? And Aummaduth of Calimport? Both wanted my head before I bent them to the true faith, and you know the eternal price they both paid in the end. *Willingly,* I might add."

"True," Mrelder muttered, not wanting to voice his own suspicions that proud Braeldra had undertaken her last, foolhardy mission purely to escape Golskyn's bed, once she'd seen she could do nothing against his magic. "Forgive my doubts, Father. If you'll just let me make sure there're no tracing spells on him right now, that might let others in Waterdeep—"

"See through my wards? Impossible, unless he's bearing focus items—and those we'll have off him, 'for his own protection,' of course, before we start." Golskyn's beholder eye seemed to glow, just for an instant. "After we do the graft, he'll either be dead or ours, won't he?"

Father and son stared into each other's eyes for a moment, then nodded in curt unison.

Together they turned to face Beldar Roaringhorn.

"My son is concerned with the magic that has been expended in this room and the state of the warding-spells around it," Golskyn announced. "Do you still want to forever lose one of your eyes—at some small risk to your life—and gain a beholder's eye in its place?"

Beldar raised an eyebrow. "After willingly walking into a beholders' den to get it? Of course."

"Then I am willing to do it. Here and now. Are you also ready?"

The youngest Lord Roaringhorn nodded, folding his arms across his chest to hide his nervousness. "I am."

"Mrelder," Golskyn murmured, "fetch what we'll need."

Beckoning the noble with two of his tentacles, he pointed at the floor. "Remove every item you wear or carry that bears the slightest magic," he ordered, "and leave them outside the doorway before you lie down here. *Everything.* If you're not sure about something, remove it: The intrusions of stray spells can be disastrous."

Beldar stared at him then began disrobing. He was down to little more than a silken clout before he was done.

By then, Mrelder had cleared ruined furniture out of the way and laid a clean cloth on the floor, carefully keeping his distance from the silent, motionless beholder all the while. A silent crowd of Amalgamation believers had gathered at the doorway. Golskyn held up a hand to keep them there.

Beldar settled himself on the cloth as the priest and his son peered at the immobile gauth.

"That one, that, and this are sufficiently extended," Golskyn murmured. "I believe I recall what those two hurled my way; what do you recall?"

"That one wounds by spell, not fire," the sorcerer replied, pointing.

"Then that's the one we want," Golskyn decided. He glanced at Mrelder, who held up the delicate ring. Bound into the graft—practically *in* Beldar Roaringhorn's brain—the Guardian's Gorget would give him control over the Walking Statures, and spells would give the priest control over *him*. If Mrelder's spells were laid deftly enough, Roaringhorn need not know that until it became necessary to violently force him to do something—or refrain from doing something.

Stepping back, Golskyn ordered, "Begin."

Mrelder carefully set the ring on what was left of a table behind him, spread his hands, and muttered the incantation that would attune him to the least of the many wards in this chamber—the only one Golskyn had allowed him to cast.

It responded, the air itself seeming to shift in silent, ponderous solidity in a far corner of the room. Sweat suddenly glistened on Mrelder's face as he turned the unseen ward with slow, deliberate care, bringing it toward the trapped gauth at just the right angle.

Wards crafted in a certain way, with sharp edges rather than a fading, clinging field, could cut like the sharpest sword—if, that is, a sword could shear through anything: stone, metal . . . beholder eyestalks . . .

Golskyn held out his hands, palms up, and muttered the prayer that would cause one of the other wards to gently catch and hold the severed eye.

Beldar Roaringhorn lay on his back, waiting, the air cold on his skin, wondering how much this was going to hurt and if it was his first step toward glory or if he was making the worst—perhaps the last—mistake of his life.

Mrelder drew in a loud, shuddering breath. Sweat was almost blinding him, now, dripping off his nose in a steady stream. He blinked furiously; until that ward was back in place, bonded once more to its neighbors, he dared not flinch or falter—unless he wanted to bring the house down in a deadly heap of falling stones that would kill everyone in it and probably open a new shaft down into deepest Undermountain, too . . .

A tiny chip of stone Golskyn knew nothing about was ready in Mrelder's belt, the putty that would hold it inside the oval of the ring already stuck to it—and one of his father's hairs was thoroughly tamped into that putty.

He'd cast seven spells on that lone hair, trusting in something he'd read at Candlekeep. Each magic captured his father's hand, or reflection, or some deed or property of Golskyn of the Gods as if from Golskyn's own viewpoint. If Watchful Order magists, or Mystra forefend, the Lord and Lady Mage of Waterdeep, probed the ring in time to come, Mrelder wanted them to see nothing at all of a certain young sorcerer and a lot about a man who called himself Lord Unity.

That time of reckoning might not be all that far off. From what little he'd seen of the high and mighty of Waterdeep—not the strutting nobles, but those who held real power at the Palace and over magic and the defenses of the City of Splendors—Mrelder was stone cold certain of one thing: any attempt to control a Walking Statue would instantly awaken the full awareness and wrath of the Lords, the City Guard, and the Lord and Lady Mage of Waterdeep.

When that happened, the son of Lord Unity wanted his father and his fellow ambitious fools of Amalgamation to face the spell-storm—not Mrelder the sorcerer.

Golskyn was on his knees, hands spread like reaching claws over Roaringhorn's face. He allowed only himself to do the deft spell-surgery that would cost the noble his right eye, and bind the beholder orb floating bloodily at hand into its place.

Magic flared up bright and white, the priest murmured, "Close your left eye and keep it closed," and blood fountained.

Everyone standing in the doorway drew in a breath at the same moment in what was almost a gasp.

Then a trembling, sweating Beldar Roaringhorn strained suddenly against the knees—Mrelder's—that were pinning down his wrists. As the grafting began, he gasped out a ragged curse.

⚔ ⚔ ⚔ ⚔ ⚔

The sound of distant temple bells drifted in through the open windows of the Dyres' front room, the sixth chiming since highsun. Lark polished the silver candlesticks one last time and stepped back to survey the funeral spread critically.

Neat rows of mugs stood ready beside a barrel of ale, and heaped plates of almond cakes were arranged down the polished table. Naoni and Faendra stood ready to serve the traditional fare, clad in softly flowing gray gowns, the traditional family mourning hue.

That was Naoni's idea, and Lark thought it clever. When Master Dyre's workmen came from the City of the Dead, they'd see how Cael was being honored and hear the silent message that they, too, were regarded as family. Given such encouragement, they should linger long and drink freely.

Lark turned to her mistresses. "You're certain you don't want me to stay?"

Naoni shook her head. "Things are well in hand." Leaning close, she whispered, "Faen'll serve the men warmly; she knows how fine she looks in that gown."

They traded grins. "Off with you, then," Naoni added more loudly. "'Twon't do to be late on your second night at the Notch."

Lark undid her apron and put it in Naoni's hand. "There's something you should know," she said softly. "All day someone's been following us."

Naoni smiled gently. "My halfling guardians."

"Not so." Faendra's hearing was very keen when she wanted it to be. "I glimpsed him, too—never a really good look, but 'twas a man, not a halfling."

"I see," Naoni murmured, looking at her bruised wrists. "Perhaps we shouldn't tell Father. You saw him when he heard about the street battle; I don't want to worry him."

Lark frowned. "Mayhap you *should* worry him. If he minded his own family more, he might have less time to poke about in the Lords' business." Remembering Elaith Craulnober's demands, she asked, "Speaking of which, where's he steering the New Day now? He's not one to take deaths of his men lightly."

Naoni sighed. "Father's been all too quiet since the battle. I wish I knew what to think of that."

Faendra's eyes danced. "Perhaps *he* put a guard to watch us. If so, one of the men will know." Her smile became a purr. "And they'll tell me *everything* I want them to."

Where once they might have rolled their eyes, Naoni and Lark now nodded approval.

"Tell me all about it in the morning," the maid told her mistresses. "I'm off to the Notch."

⚜ ⚜ ⚜ ⚜ ⚜

The steward's pantry at the Notch was already bustling. An unfamiliar voice, humming nigh her elbow, made Lark look up from the scrawled table assignments, her fingers still tugging at the knot of her apron.

A tall elf maiden she'd never seen before stood beside her tying on another server's apron. Lark tried not to stare at her striking good looks: Moon-pale skin and night-black hair framing a narrow, angular face dominated by eyes the color of new leaves.

Lark blinked, hoping the aristocratic features didn't mean haughtiness to match, but the new server smiled, asked Lark's name, and laughed in delight at the answer.

"How perfect! I'm Ezriel: 'song bird.' It's well we're working together. As the old saying runs, *L'hoira doutrel mana soutrel.*"

"Birds of a feather fly together?" guessed Lark.

Green eyes widened. "You speak Elvish?"

"No, but if one serves drink to men long enough, one hears a lot of old sayings," she said dryly, "most of them more along the lines of, 'If I said you had a beautiful body, would you hold it against me?'"

Ezriel chuckled. "Surely not!"

"A wager: A copper to you if the night passes without some drunken guildsman trotting *that* offering out, but a nib to me each time you hear it."

"Done!" A shadow passed briefly across the narrow face. "Though if I lose, you may have to dig your winnings out from under the speakers' thumbnails, for *that's* the coin I'll be tempted to pay for such compliments."

Lark winced. "That's . . . inventive."

A sour look from the steward sent them scurrying to tend tables, and there was little time for more talk. Yet as the night wore on, Lark found her gaze turning Ezriel's way more often than was strictly polite. In fact, she found it hard not to stare.

Not many elves served tables in Waterdeep, and there'd been even fewer in Luskan. Lark had little experience of the Fair Folk, and this willow-slim beauty seemed woefully out of place in a South Ward dining-den. She looked as if she should be wearing fine gowns and reclining on silken pillows idly strumming a lyre with a peacock quill.

Lark grimaced at that fancy. Such thoughts were for idle lords and their fancy ladies, not a practical worker like herself!

The elf emerged from the kitchen bearing a large, steaming platter of sea harake, and Lark found herself hurrying over to help.

"Let me carry that," she said firmly, taking its handles. "'Tis hot; there's no sense in you spoiling your hands."

Ezriel gave her a keen look, as if she suspected mockery. Seeing none, she extended her hands, palms up.

"That's kind of you, but as you can see, I'm no delicate flower." She ran her thumb proudly over the calluses on the fingertips of her left hand then the hard ridge on her upper palm.

Lark's smile froze. Both of her own hands were similarly marked from years of handwork. She glanced quickly at the elf's right palm.

Its pale skin was as smooth as a courtesan's, and the elf's left forearm, though slender, was slightly more muscled than the right. Lark knew of only one kind of work that left such signs, and it didn't involve serving tables.

The smile she gave Ezriel was wry. "Forgive me my misjudgment. I'll serve this fish to the hearthside table if you'll get their drinks."

The elf nodded and glided over to the bar. Lark watched her from the corner of her eye as she served the harake.

At a table near the bar, a trio of master tailors was laughing uproariously over their fourth round of mead. One pinched Ezriel as she walked past.

She whirled, left hand darting to her hip, and the flat warrior's stare she leveled at the tailor made her eyes look as cold as green ice.

Lark looked away quickly, laughing perhaps a bit too heartily at whatever cleverness the nearest harake-loving Calishite merchant had just said to her. She dodged deftly away from his groping hand—and froze as she saw Elaith Craulnober, sitting alone at a small table near the door.

He lifted one elegant hand in an imperious beckoning. Drawing a deep breath, Lark threaded her way to him, snatching up one of the small dishes of salt-smoked mussels that served as this night's thirst-starter.

"Evening, milord," she said brightly, setting the dish before him. "What may I bring you to drink with this?"

The moon elf eyed the grayish blobs with distaste. "The only fitting choice would be a large flagon of hemlock. Take this excrement away and bring me some deep-ocean fish, prepared as simply as possible. A bottle of elverquisst if you have it. If not, a pale wine, unwatered."

"Of course. Anything else?"

"What do you have?" he asked softly, his look making it clear he meant information, not seafood.

"Very little," she murmured, bending low to take up the spurned mussels. "Several workmen were killed or injured in the brawl, and Dyre's had time for little else, but someone followed his daughters—and me, of course—wherever we went today."

"Don't you find it of passing interest that the proprietor of Maelstrom's Notch has taken to hiring warrior-elves to befriend the help?"

"How did you—" She broke off abruptly, not wanting to offend him.

Elaith looked faintly amused. "She's as out of place here as a unicorn among cow rothé. No offense intended."

Lark bit back a retort. After all, hadn't she thought much the same?

"Give your shadow no more thought," the Serpent murmured. "I'll see to that matter. In return, I need you to relieve young Lord Hawkwinter of the silver-hued charm he wears about his neck."

As Lark nodded, it occurred to her that they'd been talking for longer than she could readily explain away. She glanced toward the steward—and met his hard, unfriendly stare.

Turning back to Elaith, she blurted, "Begging your pardon, milord, but perhaps you should pinch my backside, or . . . something."

Silvery eyebrows rose.

"To explain why I've been here so long," she explained hastily. "They expect serving wenches to parry men's advances. If there are none, some will wonder what else might have passed between us."

"I see."

His hand shot out as swift as any striking serpent. A quick tug at her wrist brought her tumbling into his lap. Before Lark could even draw startled breath, his lips claimed hers.

For a moment all she could think of was the shock of staring into those descending amber eyes. Now she knew precisely how a hare must feel as a hawk glided in . . .

There came a light caress down her back, as if the elf was writing on her with his fingertips.

And the world dissolved into darkness, in an overwhelming wave of *something*—something wonderful and terrifying at the same time—that swept over her like a sudden storm, and left her weak, shuddering, and bewildered. Blinking up at Elaith's dark smile, Lark fought her way free of . . . whatever it was and leaped to her feet, heart pounding.

"You used magic on me!"

The elf gave her an unreadable smile. "Or . . . something," he replied, his voice managing perfect mimicry of her own.

⚔ ⚔ ⚔ ⚔ ⚔

Elaith watched as Lark flounced to the bar, offended dignity in every stride. She held a low-voiced but heated conversation with the steward, during which his gaze shifted more than once between his mountainous brawl-queller and Elaith, as if measuring the bouncer's chances against the elf. Finally he shook his head. Lark pointed at one of the other serving girls, there was more talk, and the steward nodded.

All of this meant: No, he wouldn't have Elaith Craulnober thrown out, but he would allow Lark to send another lass to serve Elaith's meal.

The Serpent smiled approvingly. Yes, the wench was clever and quick-witted. Now if she proved light-fingered enough to get the slipshield from Taeros Hawkwinter without drawing attention, he'd be truly impressed.

The Gemcloaks were proving entertaining indeed. Young Korvaun Helmfast was unearthing information about Elaith's properties with impressive speed, digging into the Serpent's business with a determination usually managed only by dwarf miners. By now he undoubtedly knew Elaith held title to both the Slow Cheese and the tallhouse formerly owned by Danilo Thann—or to be more precise, those two piles of rubble. It would be interesting to see what young Lord Helmfast did with that information.

More interesting still was a slipshield right here in Waterdeep.

Did Taeros Hawkwinter know what sort of treasure he wore? Most likely not; its magic was nigh-impossible to detect.

Elaith twisted the small, silver ring that had first warned him of a slipshield at work, prompting him to seek out its bearer and confirm with his own eyes that a noble pup still wet behind the ears had the audacity to wear the winterhawk badge, the slipshield that had once protected King Zaor himself. The boy's family name, Hawkwinter, made a bad jest of one of Evermeet's great secrets.

Slipshields had never been plentiful. Borne only by royal guards of Evermeet who might have to act as a decoy for one of the royal family, they were so secret that, supposedly, only the ruling Moonflowers and their guards knew what a slipshield was. No one in Waterdeep—*no one*—should have been able to perceive the true nature of what the Hawkwinter carried.

Elaith knew it all too well. The silver ring on the smallest finger of his left hand allowed him to perceive slipshield spells. He'd left a similar ring behind when he'd fled the island kingdom all those seasons ago—it wouldn't have occurred to him, even in disgrace, to do otherwise—but Amnestria, his princess, his lost love, had brought him hers when she followed him across the seas, in hopes that it would help him remember what he'd once been.

Elaith thrust such thoughts from his mind to return to the puzzle of the slipshield. How had this so-secret creation of elves found its way to Waterdeep?

He lifted the goblet a nervous servant placed before him and sipped absently. So rare a magic; almost as rare as the humans of Waterdeep who might have dealings with fair Evermeet . . .

Laeral. Laeral Silverhand, the Lord Archmage's lady. She was a friend to Amlaruil of Evermeet. Perhaps the elf queen had granted this magic after the sahuagin attack to aid in the city's protection. It was unlikely anyone on Evermeet or in Waterdeep knew that a certain Serpent could detect slipshields.

Abruptly Elaith rose from his table and stalked out into the night. Its shadows swallowed him even before the angry steward emerged to send men rushing after the patron who'd paid not a nib.

They found no sign of the notorious elf, but the steward would have shivered to learn how close to him Elaith lounged, watching unseen as he waited with elven patience for the Notch to empty.

It was a long time later when Lark emerged alone, heading north with her light, quick stride. One of the Notch's better brawl-quellers stepped out of a doorway to trail behind her. Elaith was not at all surprised to see the green-eyed elf server emerge from the night to follow them both.

The Serpent joined the tail of this silent procession, a discreet distance behind the elf. When it became clear Lark was going straight to her dismal rooming house, Elaith took a parallel street, gliding along swiftly. Choosing a side way overlooked by no eyes he knew of, he stepped out right in front of the elf warrior.

For a moment she stared at him, her green eyes wide with wonder. Then, to Elaith's astonishment and chagrin, she went down on one knee, fisting her sword hand and touching it to her heart—clan—and then her forehead—a warrior's salute. Archaic tribute not seen at court in Evermeet for many summers, but Elaith knew it well. Old ways died hard among the dark green fastnesses of Evermeet's northern wilderlands.

"Who are you?" he demanded. "Do I know you?"

"Ezriel Seawind, my lord," she replied respectfully, "and no, we've never met."

Elaith stood absolutely still. He knew that name. The Seawinds were one of the clans of fisherfolk who lived on his ancestral lands, in the shadow of the scorched shell of Castle Craulnober.

How inconvenient. He'd told Lark he'd deal with those following her. Human liege lords slaughtered their peasants from time to time, but such things were considered bad manners on Evermeet. However . . .

"We're not on Evermeet," he said quietly.

The young warrior rose, obviously assuming that he was dispensing with elven formalities.

"I started training the year before you resigned as captain of the king's guard, but I heard all the tales about you," she said, hero worship bright in her eyes, "so I came to the mainland to seek adventure, as you did."

Her words both pained and amused him. So *that* was the tale told to explain away his sudden departure! It was, he supposed, as good as any.

"Yet I've heard many troubling things about you since I came to this city," Ezriel added softly. Her eyes searched his, almost pleading with him to deny them.

"Humans say many strange things," he replied lightly. "I'll give you my hand on that."

Ezriel Seawind read the answer she sought in his words, and took his offered hand eagerly.

Elaith's grip tightened. Ezriel's face went slack . . . and she slid to the street like a prance-puppet whose strings had been cut.

He held up his hand, palm out, to show her the small pin protruding from one of his rings. A tiny, glistening drop fell from its hollow point as it slid back, disappearing into the thick band.

"Statha. The Bane of Elves. A poison no rarer than it should be," he told her matter-of-factly.

Those trembling lips couldn't reply, of course, but her eyes, oh, her eyes . . .

He wasn't prepared for the hurt he saw there or his own reaction to it. He'd been betraying allies for decades, but for some reason this doomed young warrior's silent accusation struck him like a blow to the heart.

He could see her tremendous struggle against muscles that could no longer obey her. Green eyes darted this way and that, their flicker slowing as the statha halted even that last fading freedom.

Suddenly Elaith understood what she wanted, what she was fighting to say. Her gaze went repeatedly to the sword on his hip, then back to herself, and then to the sword again.

Of course. This painless, bloodless death was no fitting end for a warrior of Evermeet. She had lived by the sword and wished to die the same way.

She lived as *he* once had lived and desired the death he no longer deserved.

Elaith thrust his half-drawn weapon back into its scabbard and made a sharp, impatient gesture over a bag at his belt. Its strings flew open, and a small vial soared up into his waiting hand.

Serpent-swift, he unstoppered it and dropped to one knee beside the dying elf. Taking her hand, he poured a few drops of shimmering fluid onto the tiny wound.

Faint motes of light seemed to dance under her pale skin, racing away through her. After a moment she twitched once then sat up, face uncertain but leaving her hand in his.

"What's said of me is true," Elaith said quietly. "Having heard the tales, you were a fool to trust me."

"And yet I live," she breathed, waiting for his explanation.

"Things in Waterdeep are seldom what they seem."

At this, Ezriel did tug her hand free. She rose to her feet, and he rose with her.

"So by poisoning me, you were cautioning me to walk with care?" Her voice was low but incredulous. "Forgive me, Lord Craulnober, but that was a stern lesson. I am neither child nor fool, incapable of learning through the hearing of words."

"Then hear these: An elf lord of Evermeet might rule nothing more than a sprawling, complex, and largely unsavory business empire."

Ezriel regarded him. "Yet you rule it, do you not? At the heart, is this not much the same?"

"Hardly!"

"Whyever not?"

Her quiet question left Elaith blinking. Why indeed? He'd been wont to regard the City of Splendors—*such* ignorant arrogance in these human names—as a rich treasure chest to plunder, its folk mere minions and victims-in-waiting. He followed city laws when it was convenient to do so and protected Waterdeep only when his interests were at stake.

Why, then, did his absence from Waterdeep during the sahuagin attack grate at him so?

If Evermeet were attacked, he'd empty his vast caches of wealth and magic to aid her. He'd gladly die in her defense, as befitted a former captain of King Zaor's guard, but Waterdeep wasn't Evermeet. He had dwellings here—more than a few—but it was not, and never would be, home.

But then, how congenial had he ever found his family holdings? The Craulnober lands held little charm for him. He'd never bothered to rebuild the ancestral keep, firestruck when he was a babe in arms. Queen Amlaruil had taken him in as a ward of the court, raising him among her own children. Where Amlaruil was, where Amnestria once had been—that was the only home Elaith's heart knew, and he looked to find no other.

Yet he *ruled* the Craulnober lands, did he not? To this day, he met with his steward each solstice to discuss matters of import to the simple folk who farmed and hunted northernmost Evermeet, and fished the waters about the outer isles. He did these things not from any deep love of those wild places, but because he owed a duty to his ancestral lands and the folk who dwelt there. *His* folk.

How was Waterdeep any different? He'd inherited here no lands or titles but was widely acknowledged as a crime lord of considerable power and influence. Could this human cesspool rightfully expect him to assume a lord's responsibilities and obligations to the city he'd plundered for so long?

"Lord Craulnober?" Ezriel's voice shattered his thinking.

"To whom to you report?" he asked briskly.

"I'm now a Hawkwinter hiresword."

"No fitting position for a swordmaiden of Evermeet. I'll settle things with Lord Hawkwinter and see you more suitably employed—in one of my legitimate enterprises."

Green eyes glowed with excitement. "Yes, I would see my agreement with the Hawkwinters concluded with honor. Beyond that, I care little for human laws."

"Lack of regard for human laws? Shocking!" Elaith took her hand again and tucked it companionably under his arm. "Walk with me, and tell me more."

Morning sun was stealing into the kitchen as Naoni wiped the last mug dry, and Faendra danced merrily into the room, sparkling-fresh despite her sleepless night.

She rolled her eyes. "Gennior finally left. I'm not entirely certain, but he might think we're betrothed."

"If so, Father will beat the notion out of him before highsun," Naoni said calmly. "What've you learned?"

Faendra sat on a crate and smoothed her grey skirt. "Father hired no guards. I doubt he had one of his men watch us, either, as none of them gossiped or bragged about it."

"So you spent the better part of the night charming a glue-maker's apprentice for nothing?"

"Not exactly," Faendra said, examining her fingernails with a smug little smile. "Gennior's cousin serves at Hawkwinter Hall. It seems Lord Taeros hired a guard on behalf of his friend Korvaun Helmfast, who put up the coin for it."

Naoni felt the blood drain from her face, leaving her light-headed and dizzy. "He's paying to have me . . . *us* watched?"

"Protected, more likely."

"I've no desire for his money, nor need of his protection," Naoni whispered, so enraged she was scarcely aware she was clenching her fists, "and I shall tell him so . . . as soon as I change into something more suitable for an audience with nobility."

She stalked off, pretending she didn't hear Faen calling teasingly after her, "Or to cleave closer to the truth: As soon as you change into *a more fetching gown!*"

CHAPTER EIGHTEEN

The scream shattered Lark's dreams into bright shards.

As they fell past, forgotten, she found herself awake, bolt upright in bed, heart pounding.

A second shriek brought remembrance, fury, and her wits, all at once. Her landlady's new rooster, a large, handsome bird with pure white feathers and a keening crow piercing enough to make a banshee rise up and applaud, was an early riser with no respect for hard-working lasses who'd fallen into bed only two or three bells ago.

"Blast it all to the Abyss and back!" Lark swore, pounding the bed with both fists. "Bugger that wretched fowl on a leeward run!"

She went on in this vein for some time, until thumping on the wall told her she'd awakened—and possibly offended—the sailor next door.

Muttering dire threats of chicken stew, Lark tossed aside her covers and stumbled to the window. If the sun had risen, its rays had yet to reach the small fenced yard behind her rooming house. A streetlamp, visible over the low roof of the stable next door, sparked and guttered as the last of the night's oil burned dry.

No sense burrowing back into the warmth; she was needed at the Dyres' by sunrise. Slamming and bolting her shutters, Lark fumbled for the flint to light her current candle-stub.

Its feeble circle of light reached all of her walls; Lark's room was barely large enough for its narrow cot and tiny table. A chest under the bed held her smallclothes and ribbons, and her two changes of clothing hung from hooks on the wall. Her carefully hoarded coins were in the vault in the Warrens, and they'd stay there until she'd earned enough to buy free of this place. This life.

Pouring water into her chipped washbasin, Lark dipped in a scrap of linen to wash. Out of long habit, she lingered over the mark of indenture on her upper arm, scrubbing it vigorously though she'd learned as a child that nothing she could do would make it go away. Someday she'd have coin enough for magic to remove the brand, but first must come her own shop and her own rooms . . . and before that, this day's work ahead.

She dressed swiftly, as the cock crowed several times more. She sent dark thoughts its way as she set off through the swiftly awakening streets.

To her surprise, Faendra met her at the kitchen door, still wearing her gray mourning gown. In silence she tilted her head meaningfully in the direction of her sister.

Naoni was sitting on the high kitchen stool, lacing her best slippers with sharp, impatient movements. Despite the early hour, she wore a fine pale green gown.

She looked up, her eyes bright as angry stars. "I'm glad you're early. If you'll help Faendra press the cheese, we'll change the mattress straw when I return."

Lark glanced at the younger Dyre sister, eyebrow crooked quizzically. Faendra rolled her eyes and towed Lark into the buttery. "It's about the man who's following us," she whispered.

"There's no need to do aught," Lark murmured, seeing again Elaith Craulnober speaking his promise. "He'll bother us no more."

"Good, but 'tis only one side of the coin. 'Twas Lord Helmfast hired the guard!"

"Ah." Lark's smile was less than nice. "Such a *generous* gift, and given with no thought of repayment."

"Generous indeed," Faen agreed, ignoring Lark's biting tone, "but like you, Naoni always thinks the worst of wealthy men. She assumes he's buying, not giving, and she's determined to let him know she's not for sale at this price or any other."

"Good for her. Better yet, I'll carry that message and save her the wear on her fine shoes and good name."

Faendra whispered in Lark's ear, "And take away her excuse to visit Korvaun Helmfast?"

Lark blinked. "Ye gods! *Thus* blows the wind?"

"Aye. She'll deny it, of course. Yet I've—"

"Faen!" Naoni called.

Her sister stepped back into the kitchen, her smile so open and guileless that none might guess she'd been gossiping.

None but Naoni, who sent her a narrow, knowing look.

Lark smiled. Her elder mistress was no fool—save, perhaps, when it came to her taste in men.

"Jivin's lurking in the herb garden," Naoni told her, "doubtless come early in hopes of a morning mug of ale. Take him some, then send him to summon a carriage."

Faendra's blue eyes grew round. "A carriage?"

"I'm certainly not going to *walk* to Helmfast Hall! I've far too much work waiting to waste a half a day or more on this foolishness."

Faen's eyes misted at the grand image of an ornate conveyance, all gilded upswept ornamentations and tossing-headed matched horses . . . Oh, yes. "A carriage . . . I'm coming with you."

"As am I," Lark put in, her voice every bit as firm as Naoni's. "If you want no word of this to get back to your father, you must make sure no servant gossips. I know the man who keeps the Helmfast gate by day; his wife's a laundress, and they both serve tables at the Black Flagon of an evening, when they've need for extra coin. He's a decent sort, and our best chance of departing Helmfast Hall without rumor racing like wildfire behind us."

Naoni's unsmiling lips pressed together in a thin line as if to hold back an argument she knew she could not defend. When they opened, it was to tell Faendra, "Have Jivin hire a conveyance large enough to carry three in comfort."

"Of that," her sister replied with relish, "you can rest assured."

The carriage that rolled up to the Dyres' doors proved to be almost as large as Lark's rented room and far more comfortable. Its velvet seats were somewhat the worse for wear, but the padding was only slightly lumpy and the cloth had been brushed clean.

Faendra settled back into a corner with a deeply contented smile. "Life hands me far too few excuses to visit North Ward. 'Tis *so* beautiful; as I gawp at all the finery, I'll dream of living there someday!"

As they rolled through ever-widening streets, Lark had to agree with that judgment of North Ward, even if she didn't share Faendra's ambitions.

Here the city's wealthiest new-coin citizens traveled streets of cobbles so smooth the carriage seemed to glide. The glittering folk dwelt behind ornate iron gates, in grand homes fashioned from gleaming marble, white-stone, and fine woods. Stately trees shaded all, and the gardens surrounding the homes displayed flowing plants in frames of sculpted hedges, rather than the practical herbs and vegetables crowding the Dyre's tiny backyard plot.

Helmfast Hall was a grand affair, with a sweeping iron arch soaring above its gate. Flanking the arch stood two small forehouses, of the same pale-gold stone as the mansion beyond. One was little more than a covered bridge, and in it stood a coach, liveried staff gentling the harnessed horses, awaiting Helmfast whims. The other was the gatehouse, and Lark was relieved to see the black-bearded man seated within was her friend from the Black Flagon.

As the carriage rumbled to a stop, Lark hastened out and down. "Good morn, Stroamyn."

"And to you." The guard glanced at the hired carriage. "You've not come to serve, not in that rolling ship. Are you a ladies' maid, now?"

"In a manner of speaking," Lark replied. "My mistresses wish to speak with Lord Korvaun. Know you one of the staff who can be trusted to carry that message to his master and no other?"

Stroamyn snorted. "In this house? *You* know grand folk can buy everything but discretion, yet by the luck-fall of Tymora's dice, it happens Lord Korvaun's not in residence."

"Can you tell me where he is?"

The guard gave her a considering look. "I'm not one to tell tales."

"Nor am I," Lark said firmly. "For that matter, I doubt anyone'll think to ask how I came by the information. Lord Korvaun carries so many magical trinkets he's probably come to think of them as commonplace. He'll no doubt assume my mistresses found him through a seeking spell or some such foolishness. His sort never think others can't drop coins as freely as they do."

Stroamyn nodded ruefully and tugged at the neck of his tabard, revealing a green tunic beneath. "One of Lord Korvaun's brothers asked me why I wear this several times a tenday, as if all men could cast coin away on ten tunics of every hue in a rainbow!"

Thus bonded by common disdain, they leaned heads together and talked. Stroamyn imparted the address of Lord Korvaun's new and *very* exclusive club, as well as the password Helmfast servants gave that establishment's doorguards. Lark thanked him, left best wishes for Rosie and the children, and hurried to give Stroamyn's directions to their hired coachman.

"We're off to Dock Ward," she told the Dyre girls as she climbed back into the carriage. "It seems Lord Korvaun's an early riser."

Faendra winced. "Father'll be livid when he gets the bill for this."

"I've my own money," Naoni said firmly, the first words she'd spoken since they'd left home.

The other two joined her in silence until the carriage stopped outside a ramshackle warehouse not far from Redcloak Lane. As Stroamyn had warned, a heavily armed guard stood grimly at its open door—a tough old sailor who kept his hands on ready weapons. The tattoo of the *Ice Dancer* stood out clearly on one brawny forearm.

Lark knew that mark well; sailors from the *Dancer* had frequented the dockside tavern where she'd been born and raised.

Perhaps her mother had entertained this man. Perhaps . . .

Cheeks flaming, she forced herself to look away from the man's impassive face as she followed her mistresses through the doorway and up the stairs.

Four men were lounging in the open-to-the-rafters room at the head of the stair: Korvaun Helmfast, Taeros Hawkwinter, and two others. The one who wore a glittering black cloak was exceedingly pale, his long, narrow face framed by lank black hair. The other was a small man with neatly shorn brown hair, mild blue eyes, and well-cut but simple brown garments. Lark assumed his cloak was the fall of rose-hued gemweave hanging on a peg beside more familiar cloaks of blue and amber.

They all looked up, and then rose, as the three women stepped into the room.

"Mistress Naoni," Korvaun said slowly, his eyes only for the red-haired woman at the fore. "This is a most unexpected pleasure."

"Perhaps you should hear me out before saying so," she replied quietly. Lifting her chin, she added, "You hired a man to follow us. I insist on knowing why."

Korvaun frowned and took two quick steps toward her, hands rising, before he caught himself and halted. "A man's been following you?"

Naoni frowned. "You pretend to know nothing of this?"

"'Tis no pretense, Mistress," Korvaun replied grimly. "I hired no man to follow you. Unless . . ." He glanced at Taeros.

The Hawkwinter lord shook his head. "No. I followed our plan."

Naoni's face darkened as she looked from one man to the other. "Plan? Tell me."

Korvaun nodded to Taeros.

The Hawkwinter lordling sighed. "Actually, it was Lark we wanted followed." His gaze went to the maidservant's face then swiftly away again. "I didn't hire a man. We thought an alternative might be . . . less conspicuous."

"Ezriel," Lark murmured. "The elf at the Notch." She stared at him incredulously. "You thought an *elf* would be less conspicuous serving in a South Ward inn?"

Taeros shifted uneasily from one foot to another. "I had other reasons for my choice."

Lark stared at him for a moment. When the answer came to her, she burst out laughing. This fool thought to distract Elaith Craulnober with a pretty elf female! Ye gods, did all men keep their brains in their codpieces?

"I fail to understand your amusement," Taeros said stiffly.

"Really! What a large surprise!"

"Lark," murmured Naoni in gentle admonition.

The servant nodded to her mistress and put away her grin. Indeed, now that her first mirth was spent, she found this more troubling than humorous. If she was correct about Hawkwinter's motive for hiring Ezriel, it meant he'd seen a link between her and Elaith Craulnober.

Naoni shot Taeros and Korvaun both pointed looks. "Right, then, why were you watching Lark?"

Korvaun gave her a small bow of apology. "This requires more than a little explanation. Won't you sit? Perhaps take refreshment?"

"I'd be grateful for some ale," Faendra announced. "I'm as dry as Anauroch."

As the brown-clad man drew a tankard for Faen, Lark took her mistresses' half-cloaks and hung them on the empty pegs beside the glittering nobles' gemweave. Her gaze lingered on Lord Hawkwinter's cloak. Its amber gleam was as cold and bright as a certain pair of mocking elven eyes.

Staring at it, Lark suddenly knew how she'd fulfill her bargain with Elaith. If Taeros was wearing his silver charm, she'd have it off him before she left this room. Schooling her face to a servant's expressionless calm, Lark took a seat beside Naoni.

"Ere we continue," Korvaun was saying, "allow me to present my friends Lord Roldo Thongolir and Lord Starragar Jardeth. Gentlesirs, I give you Mistresses Naoni and Faendra Dyre, and Mistress-Lass Lark."

Roldo and Starragar stood, bowed to the three common-born women with no hint of mockery, and resumed their seats.

"As you know, we lost a friend when the Slow Cheese came down."

"Lord Malark Kothont," Faendra murmured, almost wistfully.

"Yes. Had he been slain by a blade or mage's spell, we'd have avenged him forthwith, but how does one take vengeance on a building? The only satisfaction left to us is to ferret out why the collapse befell."

Naoni leaned forward. "When you learn the cause, you'll avenge your friend?"

Lark wondered at the excitement in Naoni's voice. When had her elder mistress developed an interest in vengeance?

Perhaps she was thinking of Master Dyre's mutterings about the Lords digging new tunnels to spy on dissenters. If she could win these lordlings to her father's cause, that would certainly cast aside shields between Naoni Dyre and Lord Korvaun Helmfast.

"Yes, we *will* avenge our friend," the black-clad Lord Jardeth said suddenly, his voice as dark as his garb. There was a faint ripping sound as he shifted forward in his seat. Lark saw that the trailing hem of his black cloak was uneven, as if pieces of gemweave had simply fallen away.

Korvaun gave Starragar a swift, quelling glance. "For now, we seek only answers. A second building fell, a fine townhouse in North Ward. So far as we know, these buildings were unrelated except for their owner, an elf of considerable means and power: Elaith Craulnober."

"Again, what has this to do with Lark?" Naoni demanded.

"She was at Craulnober's recent revel," Taeros said quietly.

Lark met his eyes. "I'm surprised you recognized me, milord. Most men of wealth don't look closely at a servant until she unlaces her bodice."

Before Lord Hawkwinter could respond in kind, Naoni said, "Lark attended that function at our request!" Then she stopped, mouth still open but indecision clear on her face. Dared she...?

Korvaun gave her a nod of encouragement. Keeping her eyes

on his, Naoni took a deep breath and then said slowly, "You've tasted my father's anger, lords. Sharp and bitter, yes? Well, he's taken it into his head to bring about a New Day: To demand the Lords of Waterdeep unmask and henceforth be accountable to all citizens."

"Reasonable enough," Taeros Hawkwinter agreed, astonishing everyone in the room but his friend Korvaun. Shrugging away incredulous stares, he waved at Naoni to continue.

"My sister and I fear for our father," Naoni Dyre said carefully, seeking the right words, "but know not where to turn. Lark knew how to get word to a wise and good man, seeking his counsel."

"And what did this wise and good man advise?"

"We've not yet received his reply."

"I see. How's the elf entangled in this?"

Lark frowned. How indeed? She remembered the plans strewn across Elaith's desk and suddenly realized what they were: maps of the sewers under the city. If he was one of Waterdeep's secret Lords, could things be as Master Dyre claimed? Were the Lords spying? If so, who better to do so than the Serpent, rumored to command half the ruffians in the city?

All of this fit all too well, except for one thing: the fallen buildings had belonged to Elaith; surely he'd not toss away his own valuable properties!

Faendra elbowed Lark sharply, letting her know everyone was awaiting her answer.

Well, what answer could she give?

"He has many resources," Lark said at last, "and is readily able to convey messages."

"And *that's* why you've been seen with the notorious Serpent? You trust him to carry messages betwixt you and your advisor? Reliably and sharing them with no one else?"

"For a price," Lark replied, truthfully enough. Her eyes slid to the glint of silver at the Hawkwinter throat.

Korvaun's frown was grave. "A dangerous risk. Tales of Elaith Craulnober's treachery abound."

"Lark's very resourceful," Naoni said firmly. "You need not

fear for her and certainly need have no fear *of* her!"

Three of the nobles inclined their heads in acceptance, but Taeros Hawkwinter's face suggested he was reserving judgment on this matter.

Korvaun lifted his tankard. "May I ask what Master Dyre says of these building downfalls?"

"He thinks the Lords control the sewers and dig new tunnels as desired to keep a close watch on citizens—tunnels that caused the collapses."

Taeros nodded. "All too likely. If anyone bears watching, 'tis the elf."

Lark frowned. "You believe as Master Dyre does?"

The Hawkwinter shrugged. "I'm willing to entertain any reasonable explanation."

"*I* believe it," dark-cloaked Starragar said grimly, "and if unmasking the Lords is needful to force someone to account for Malark's death, I'll tear off every last one of those masks with these hands!"

"Hear, hear," murmured Lord Thongolir. "It seems we have common cause with these ladies. Perhaps we should work together?"

"We've given our word to Master Dyre that we'd not seek the company of his daughters," Korvaun reminded him. "We're honor-bound to obtain release from this promise."

Faendra gave her sister a sly glance ere she told Lord Helmfast, "If you can sway Father, you can do *anything*. Let's go to him at once!"

"Hear, hear," Roldo said heartily, looking to Korvaun.

Lark needed no lord's approval. She rose and retrieved her mistresses' wraps, then took up the glittering amber cloak and held it out to Taeros, her gaze challenging. When he reached to take it, she snatched it away.

"I'm a servant, Lord Hawkwinter. One of my duties is to help people on with their cloaks."

He made a futile grab for the gemweave. "You're not *my* servant, blast it!"

"Nevertheless," she said firmly.

With an impatient hiss, Taeros turned his back and let her drape his cloak over his shoulders. She smoothed its glittering folds with swift, practiced hands . . .

And when they came away, the silver chain and the magical device it bore were hidden in one palm.

With it, she could repay her debt to Craulnober. The sooner she could get shed of that one, the better.

But . . . was she making a mistake handing a magic of unknown power to the Serpent? There were spells that could reveal the true nature of magics, but a wizard's fee was well beyond her means, even if she spent her every last, laboriously hoarded nib.

A sudden thunder of boots on the stairs drew every eye. Beldar Roaringhorn paused in the doorway, ruby cloak a-swirl, gazing bemused at the three women standing in what was perhaps the last place in Waterdeep he might have expected to find them.

Lord Beldar looked considerably the worse for wear. He was richly dressed, a-gleam with jewels and fine weapons, his mustache freshly trimmed, but grayness lurked on his sun-browned face, and his right eye was covered with a black patch.

"What in the Nine bloody Hells happened to you?" Starragar pointed at his own right eye to show what he meant.

Beldar waved airy dismissal. "Nothing of great consequence. My eye was scratched during the Dock Ward brawl, and a healer bade me rest it."

Lark recalled the bloodied face of the man who'd fainted in her lap. Beldar's wounds had been slight, and nowhere near his eye. Here was a man who kept secrets from his friends. A small, humorless smile touched her lips as she realized that wizard's fee was all but in her hands.

"I'm gratified to hear so, Lord Roaringhorn," she said demurely. "For a moment I feared you might have met with some lawless, murdering rogue—say, a half-ogre—and suffered thereby."

The consternation that arose on Beldar's face made Lark think a bit more highly of him. Perhaps he hadn't knowingly sold her to the half-ogre, after all.

"We're off to speak with Master Dyre," Korvaun told Beldar uncertainly. "Will you accompany us?"

Beldar, into whom healing potions had been poured not once but many times throughout a long and agonizing night, found no appeal whatsoever in this prospect. "I'll pass."

"As will I," Lark echoed quickly. She turned to Naoni. "Someone should press the new cheese and get it into the buttery before it spoils in this heat. I need to start highsunfeast, or Master Dyre will have to forage for himself—and make do with the bony ends of the salt herring and yestereve's rabbit stew. I'm not even sure he'll touch the stew; it's sure to have a top-skin of fat by now. None of which will please him."

"Very well," Naoni agreed absently, her eyes on Korvaun Helmfast. "At this time of day, Father's likely to be in his office meeting with tradesmen. We've a carriage outside that's large enough to take the rest of us there."

She turned toward the door, then looked back over her shoulder at Lord Helmfast. "And I," she added, in a tone that brooked no argument, "am paying for its hire."

🏰　🏰　🏰　🏰　🏰

Varandros Dyre was not in his office. He was standing in a narrow, stinking Dock Ward alley, gazing down at what was left of his youngest apprentice.

Jivin Tranter lay on his back, staring endlessly up at a sky that would never change for him, now. His mouth was agape. His eyes, which Dyre remembered as too clever by half, were covered with dust, yet still held dawning pain, fear, and the realization that something was very, very wrong.

Dyre wondered if the lad had found time and wits enough to know he was dying. Likely yes; by the amount of blood pooling under Jivin's head, the apprentice's heart had still been beating when that symbol was carved into his forehead.

"A necromantic rune," one of the Watchmen muttered. "No priest or mage'll get the killer's name from this one."

That explained the mutilation—the lad's corpse was shielded

from spells that allowed speech with the dead, and the other magic some priests practiced that recalled the last thing a dead person had gazed upon. The rest Dyre could read for himself.

The blade that had taken Jivin's life had been rapier-thin, piercing the apprentice's heart like a needle. His shirt had been slashed and peeled aside, so four words could be carved into his hairless chest. Dyre was no scholar, but after a few moments of study he made out these chilling words: *"The Wages of Curiosity."*

"Guildmaster Dyre?"

The swordcaptain's grim voice was still respectful, but growing sharper. Dyre realized the Watchman had been repeating his name for some time now.

"Aye?" he growled, blinking, as he tore his gaze from Jivin's forever frozen face to the swordcaptain's weathered frown. "What?"

"Goodman Dyre, I asked: D'you have any idea who might have done this?"

The stonemason's face hardened into a bleak, stone-like mask, a mask adorned with a mirthless, unlovely grin that made the Watchman draw back a step and reach for his sword out of long habit.

"No. I have no idea at all. Not one," Varandros Dyre said, biting off his words as if each was a stone dropped over a parapet, one at a time.

He pushed past the Watch officer without a backward glance, lifting one hand in a circular gesture his employees knew well.

The little group of mute, pale-faced stonecutters hastened forward to take up Jivin's body, and bear it along in the guildmaster's wake. They knew better than to say even a lone word to any of the Watch, who in turn agreed on one thing to a man, without need for any words: Varandros Dyre had a very good idea who might have ordered the apprentice's death and was seething with rage at being thus warned, or threatened . . . or goaded.

CHAPTER NINETEEN

Beldar Roaringhorn's friends and the three women vacated the club in swift tumult, leaving him alone in blessed silence.

For long breaths he simply stood and enjoyed the stillness, his back to the door so he could gaze the length of the room and just relax, letting his thoughts wander and his innards start to settle.

After a calming pause, he strolled across the room and poured himself some ale. Sniffing it appreciatively, he took a small sip, not trusting his roiling stomach to welcome more.

"You didn't hurt your eye in that brawl," a cool voice commented, from behind him.

Beldar froze. Then he made himself turn slowly. He knew that tone—one usually used by someone holding a weapon, who was exceedingly pleased that the person being addressed was *not*.

The servant girl was alone, and her hands were empty. By the look on her face, she didn't consider that one dented serving tray had settled the score between them.

Swallowing rising unease, Beldar mustered his most supercilious smile. "Weren't you off to mount a gallant defense of cheese or some such?"

The lass didn't rise to his bait. "You didn't hurt your eye in that brawl," she repeated.

Beldar set down his tankard. "Oh? And how could you possibly know?"

Lark smiled thinly. "After you fainted and fell on me, I passed much time with your head on my lap, while your friends argued with the Watch. Your wounds were right under my nose, and as I don't happen to own wardrobes full of gowns, just where you were bleeding was of some importance to me. You had a cut on your head above the hairline, but nothing more."

Beldar stared at her. He remembered few details of that humiliating episode, but—blast it!—she was probably speaking simple truth. The reason for her candor was appallingly clear. She'd been witness to his least shining moments, and with the instinctive cunning of the coin-poor lowborn, understood that he did not want his falsehood—or the events of that night in Luskan —to reach the ears of his friends.

"I assume your silence has a price?"

She nodded. "I need the services of a wizard who can truly tell the nature of magical things."

This was hardly what he'd been expecting. "Why?"

After a moment's hesitation, the lass half-turned away from him and then swung back, with a small silver charm in her hand that hadn't been there before. "I came across this and want to know what it can do. Find a wizard for me and pay his fee, and your friends need never know their gallant, noble friend sold an unwilling woman to a murderous half-ogre."

He couldn't quite suppress a wince. "I didn't know his intention."

"Not at first, perchance, but then you did—yet stood like a post as he dragged me away."

Beldar stared at Lark, seeking some defense for his behavior. The best he could muster was, "I broke no law in Luskan, and in all fairness, I should advise you that the magisters of this city have recently begun punishing extortion rather severely."

"I'm unsurprised," Lark replied softly. "Why else would you not parry my request with threats to reveal . . ."

She let silence fall between then until he gently finished her sentence: "Your circumstances when last we met."

"Aye. My *circumstances,*" she said with soft, searing bitterness.

Beldar drew himself up. "Because, Mistress Lark, that would be as unworthy of me as it is of you."

A flush rose into her cheeks. "So you'll not help me?"

"I'll *help* you," Beldar replied, "but such aid is *not* to be construed as payment for your silence on this matter or any other."

Lark's smirk told him she saw his carefully worded parry for what it was: cowardice, dressed up in a magister's fine black robes, but cowardice all the same. And why should she think otherwise, when laws written to prompt men to own their words and actions were so often used to shrug off responsibility?

That was a question for another day. The wench was obviously determined to view any aid he might offer as silence-coin, and it was a reasonably cheap road to her immediate silence. Of course, those who wore black mail invariably made additional demands, but she was, after all, a woman, and common born at that. He could charm her into compliance long before her wits took her that far.

And if you can't charm her, a ghostly voice hissed deep in Beldar's mind, *you can always kill her.*

That notion was so absurd Beldar was able to brush it aside as absently as he might wave away a stingfly.

"It so happens," he told the unsmiling lass, "I know a wizard who just might serve our purpose . . ."

🏰   🏰   🏰   🏰   🏰

As the carriage pulled away from the offices of Dyre's Fine Walls and Dwellings, Naoni silently reckoned the cost of her impulsive extravagance. In her rush to leave the house, she'd snatched up the coinsack holding the entire profits of her latest delivery of gem thread. The fare for their hither-and-yon travels, plus gratuity for the patient carriageman, would devour nearly every coin.

Faendra was also reconsidering the morning's adventure, shifting uncomfortably in her seat as the carriage bounced and rumbled. At Naoni's look, she smiled ruefully. "I never thought I'd say this, but I'd rather walk. The novelty's worn thinner than the padding under these seats."

"Novelty's like silk and passion," observed Starragar Jardeth in the disgruntled way Naoni now knew to be his usual manner. "All three wear out quickly."

Taeros, who'd proclaimed himself in need of a nap, lifted one eyelid. "Speaking from sad experience?" he asked archly. "The fair Phandelopae, perchance, has turned love's silken embrace into threadbare rags? Take heart, man. I know an herb . . ."

"Most amusing," snapped his dour friend. "Save your herbs to impress the Dyres' prickly maid. You'll need all you can muster to win past the thorns on *that* rose!"

The Hawkwinter's eyes opened wide, and for a moment he looked ready to dispute Starragar's words. Then a puzzled expression crossed his face. He closed his mouth without saying a word and settled back into his seat. Though his eyes closed again, Naoni doubted very much he sought slumber.

She pushed aside sudden dismay. Lark was a sensible girl, too proud to dally with the likes of Lord Taeros. On the other hand, the man's tart wit was like enough to hers that they might . . .

No, surely not. Even if Lark were interested, Korvaun would remind his friend to observe propriety. If ever a man could be trusted in such matters, Naoni mused, 'twas he.

Or could he?

A small sigh escaped her. She'd been reared believing *no* man raised with a noble's sense of entitlement could be trusted in such matters. It was a conviction too deeply and painfully engraved to lightly abandon.

The carriage stopped by the Dyres' door. Naoni accepted Korvaun's hand to alight then counted out coins to the carriageman. It seemed she'd reckoned fare and gratuity correctly; he tipped his cap in thanks before shaking the reins and rumbling away.

The front door opened before Naoni reached its latch, to reveal Varandros Dyre wearing an expression that brought to mind a gathering storm.

"Where've you been? I was about to call the Watch and report you missing!"

"Just tending to errands, Father," Naoni replied soothingly.

She waved at the men behind her. "Lord Helmfast's here to speak with you . . . to ask you to release him, and his friends, from their promise to keep clear of the women of your household."

"*Why?*"

Varandros Dyre launched that word like a war-arrow, leaving Naoni blinking in sudden realization that she had no words to answer him.

These men have offered to help us spy on your New Day activities, Father, was fairly accurate, but hardly likely to sway him. *These young nobles desire to make common cause with you, in working to unmask the Lords . . .* No. The first, approving reaction of Taeros Hawkwinter to this notion was too flimsy a foundation for that—and her father would never believe it.

Help came from a most unexpected quarter. "It's been pointed out to me," Taeros Hawkwinter said dryly, casting a glance at Starragar, "that I may have some interest in your maidservant."

Dyre glared. "The girl suits us fine and is not for hire!"

Faendra giggled. "Father, you're not *that* old, to have forgotten how matters of the h . . . ah, such things go."

The guildmaster flushed, redness swiftly darkening to the deep, mottled blood-red of fury. "If you're even *thinking* of debauching my servant—"

"I assure you, goodsir, I'd not insult that woman if I were in full plate and defended by the City Guard's griffonback lancers!" Taeros declared fervently.

Puzzlement chased ire from the guildmaster's face, and he passed a hand over his forehead. "I'm in no mind for puzzles just now, young lord."

The deep weariness in his voice smote Naoni's heart. "What is it, Father?" she asked softly.

He turned tired eyes on her. "We've another death, lass. Jivin was found in an alley with a warning carved into his hide." He looked at Taeros with more worry than anger on his face. "You might have need of armor and lancers if you plan to keep company with my lasses."

Korvaun said quietly, "Some might hear a threat in those

words, sir, but I doubt that's your intent."

"No," Dyre said simply, ere turning back to Naoni. "I bade Jivin watch over you lasses, as he was quick on his feet and knew the streets. They killed him to warn me off, that's plain enough, but 'twas me who sent him to his doom."

Naoni heard Faendra's quick gasp and whirled around. Faen's eyes were wide, and the hand she held over her mouth trembled. Naoni reached for her sister's other hand. The small, suddenly cold fingers curled tightly around hers.

Starragar Jardeth lifted a hand. "The warning: What was it, exactly?"

Every face turned to him, incredulously.

"I mean no disrespect," the dark-cloaked lordling told them, "but if I'd seen someone in my employ so served, I'd not be of a mind to see past the outrage. One who stands apart may see clearly, and the precise wording may shed light on the intent—and the murderer."

Varandros Dyre stared at the young noble in silence for an uncomfortably long time before muttering, "Well said."

It was even longer ere he added, "Thorass, 'twas: 'The Wages of Curiosity.' I've been asking questions of late—never mind what about. Someone's warning me off."

"Perhaps we're not so far removed from this matter as Lord Jardeth suggests," Korvaun said slowly. "You should know, Master Dyre, that we've been seeking answers about the fallen buildings. A friend of ours died in the collapse of the festhall, he whose dagger you found. A good man, who shouldn't be judged by that one day's mischief at Redcloak Lane."

"So say you," observed Dyre, something also like sympathy in his tone, "and so you *should* say. Even if that foolishness told young Kothort's true measure, men should stand by their friends."

"We are agreed on that, and perhaps in other matters, as well," Korvaun said carefully. "These mysteriously fallen buildings may touch on matters that concern us both. If this is so, release us from our promise, and our swords are yours to command."

The stonemason blinked, staring at the young noblemen as if he'd never seen them before.

"I . . . I'll think on it," he said curtly. Giving them an abrupt nod, he pointed at his daughters and then imperiously at his open door, and strode off down the street.

Faendra whirled to face Naoni. "*Jivin* was following us!"

"Yes, Father just said so," Naoni agreed, puzzled by the fear in her sister's eyes.

"Lark . . . Lark told me not to worry about the man following us. She said he was being dealt with. *Being dealt with!* I never thought—"

"Nor should you," Naoni said firmly, ignoring the sick, sinking feeling in her own stomach. "We've known Lark nearly a year, and she's as reliable as the tides."

"Perhaps Mistress Faendra has cause for concern," said Starragar gravely, his eyes on Taeros. "You were wearing a silver medallion this morn, were you not?"

Taeros's hand flew to his throat. "It's gone! Blast it!"

"I saw you wearing it when you got up to leave the club—before the lass so tartly insisted on helping you with your cloak. I just noticed its absence now."

Naoni frowned. "That could be mere happenstance. Perhaps it fell off in the carriage?"

Starragar shook his head. "I was last to alight, and I *always* look about for items that might have been left behind. As for happenstance, is it also *happenstance* that your servant's been seen with Elaith Craulnober, the owner of those two fallen buildings?"

"Nine happy Hells," Taeros murmured softly. "The elf I hired to watch Lark hasn't reported back. I wonder if she's . . ."

"We'll look into it," Korvaun said briskly. "Mistress Naoni, where might Lark be now?"

"She implied she was returning here to tend to chores, but Father's worry rather gives the lie to that."

"Lark stayed behind to talk to Beldar," Faendra said confidently. "I looked back as our carriage pulled away, and neither had come down the stairs."

The nobles exchanged worried glances.

Naoni peered from one to another. "What? What is it?"

"Beldar hasn't . . . been himself of late," Korvaun told her. "I'd put it down to grief about Malark. Much as I hate to admit it, we may have *another* worry in common."

🏰 🏰 🏰 🏰 🏰

Beldar glanced back at Lark. "Take care. The steps are damp and slippery."

She put her hand on the mossy wall, her face ghostly green in the faint lichen-glow. Beldar took some satisfaction in her tense expression. Clearly, the wench had no fondness for tunnels and close places, or perhaps she was reconsidering the wisdom of blackmail, though she should hardly have expected a sordid transaction to be free of discomfort.

The look on her face when they stopped before the Dathran's skullgate was all Beldar could have desired. It turned to open fear when the front four "teeth" swung inward to reveal the way on.

"Well met again, Lord Roaringhorn," the dry and familiar voice came from the darkness beyond. "I see you are something more than you were . . . and something less. Come in, the maid first."

Beldar waved Lark forward. She clenched her teeth, climbed through the opening—and promptly squeaked in surprise at the touch of the warding magics.

Beldar joined her. The old witch was standing with her black Rashemaar mask in her hand and her keen blue eyes bent on Lark. "Welcome, child. I sense in you a great longing to know. Tell Dathran what you seek."

Lark handed over the charm. The Dathran passed it from one wizened hand to the other.

"Stolen," she announced, her voice devoid of judgment. "More than that, I cannot tell."

Lark swallowed. "Is there . . . magic about it?"

Dathran closed her eyes, and her face took on the expression of one who listens to distant voices. "None," she said slowly.

"So you can tell me nothing about it."

"Only that you fear the use that might be made of it and need not, yet. Perhaps I can tell something of its history, if that would ease your mind."

When Lark nodded, the woman began to chant. A soft, humming haze gathered around the charm but faded at the end of the incantation.

Dathran handed it back. "I learned one word, nothing more: *slipshield*. Holds that any meaning for you?"

Lark shook her head and slipped the charm into the bag at her belt. "No, but I thank you for trying."

A high-pitched chuckle came from the gargoyle-like figure perched on the mantel. Lark caught her breath as the small gray form she'd thought a mere carving flapped batlike wings and showed its fangs in a leer.

"You needn't thank her," the imp mocked. "You have to *pay* her."

Beldar handed over a palmful of coins and ushered Lark out of the Dathran's lair. When they emerged from the skullgate, he seized her arm and spun her around to face him.

"What's this about? From whom did you steal this, and why did you think it might be magic?"

Lark tugged free and stepped back, lifting her chin defiantly. "You keep your secrets, Lord Roaringhorn, and I'll keep mine."

Beldar's first inclination was to let the matter go; after all, what cared he about a silver trinket? Yet a dark, hissing murmur in the back of his mind wanted the charm.

Without another thought he seized the bag at her belt and tugged sharply. Its strings broke, Lark lunged for it—and he backhanded her across the face.

She reeled, face showing none of the astonishment Beldar himself felt. Before he could offer a word of apology, she hauled up her skirts in obvious preparation for a groin-high kick.

He sidestepped into a crouch to shield the Roaringhorn family jewels—and astonishingly, the lass punched his face, hard.

Blast! He dropped the bag to clutch his bleeding nose. Lark snatched up her property and raced away up the stairs, as nimble as a sewer rat.

Two high-pitched, evil chuckles arose behind the skull-wall, but for once Beldar's thoughts were not of his own humiliation.

He, a noble of Waterdeep, had robbed a commoner. He'd struck a woman. By any lights, these were not the deeds of a man destined to be a death-defying hero!

You are something more than you were ... and something less.

The Dathran's words haunted Beldar as he trudged up the steps into a future that had never looked so uncertain.

⚜ ⚜ ⚜ ⚜ ⚜

"Ah ... Master Dyre?"

Varandros Dyre glanced up sharply. "I'm starting to dread news unlooked-for," he growled, letting fall a sheaf of building plans onto his littered desk. "What is it *this* time?"

The man at his office door was a senior framer who'd been with Dyre's Fine Walls and Dwellings from the early days. A calm, capable worker, Jaerovan was first hand of his own crew for nigh a decade and well worthy of that trust, a man of prudence and few words. It took much to bring any expression at all onto Jaerovan's old boot-leather face, a face that, just now, looked very grim.

Varandros lifted an eyebrow. "Well? Out with it, man!"

"Another building's down. One of ours."

Dyre's mouth dropped open.

"On Redcloak Lane," Jaerovan added, before the guildmaster could snap the inevitable question. "The one Marlus was—"

Varandros Dyre went as white as winter snow. His fist crashed down onto his desk so hard that the massive piece of furniture shook, with just a hint of splintering lacing the thunderous boom of his blow.

Then Dyre was moving, snatching up the swordcane Jaerovan had only seen him carry twice before and striding for the door like a storm wind. The framer hastily got out of the way.

As he strode past, Dyre snapped, "Have your men spread word to all my workers: Be sharp of eye and fleet of foot, for this may not be the last message the Lords of Waterdeep send this day!"

Jaerovan gaped at the Shark's swiftly departing back. "The Lords—?"

"This is a blade meant for my guts," Varandros Dyre muttered to himself as he hastened down the street, leaving his doors standing wide open in his wake and servants scuttling to close them.

"They'll have my house down next! My lasses to an inn . . . my oddcoin chest removed to safety . . . then muster the New Day. And buy a good sword!"

    🏰   🏰   🏰   🏰   🏰

A dozen dockworkers, stripped to the waist and deeply browned by long labors under the suns of many summers, tossed bales of Moonshae linen and wool into waiting carts, swinging the heavy bundles as easily as a street juggler tosses matched balls. With every bale, they sent rumors flying though the air with the same practiced ease.

"Crashed right down into the street, it did! Took old Amphalus *and* his oxcart, beasts and all, and left 'em bloody paste on the cobbles! They're hawking pieces of what's left in the Redcloak Rest and the taverns all down Gut Alley!"

"Can't Dyre's men lay two blocks together straight? Or is he crooked enough to skimp on stones or deep pilings?"

"Neither, they're saying! 'Tis the Lords, setting their men to work with picks—and conjured gnawing things, too!—to dig out the pilings and bring everything down! For daring to say we should all know who's behind every mask and how they vote! They're going to ruin him!"

"Aye, and crush the rest of us! Stupid dolt, can't he see they wear masks for a reason? The gods don't *make* enough gold to let us pay the bribes we'd all have to, once everyone knew who every Lord was, to get 'em all to rule our way—and outbid every *other* jack in Waterdeep, who'd be payin' just as hard to buy votes into fallin' their way! Serves him right, *I* say!"

"Oh, does it now? What of the rest of us, who happen to be trading inside a building he worked on a dozen summers back or just passing it by on the street below when the Lords decide to work a little justice on him? What did *we* do to be smashed down alongside him?"

"Grew up in Waterdeep, 'swhat! Got on with earning coins like greedy little packrats, an' never looked up to challenge those ruling the roost! So now the Lords hold it their right to go on doing just as they please, an' slapping down anyone who dares to question! *We've* done it, jacks, all of us! So have we the spine, I wonder, to stand up now an' *un*do it?"

"How?"

"By standing forth an' dragging down a few men in masks, that's how! Or stringing up Old Lord Fancyboots, the only Lord we all know!"

"I thought he was already dead!"

"So 'tis said, time and again, but have we ever seen a corpse, hey? That strutting paladinspawn has more lives than a troll! My sister Hermienka works the laundry in the Castle, an' she seen him yestermorn, stalking about bigger than life."

"You've the right of it, Smedge: A corpse is what's needed! If we can't find the Hidden Lords, get the one we know. *That* ought to lure the rest of 'em out!"

There was an uncomfortable little silence.

"That's ... that's lawless talk, that is. You *sure* you're Waterdeep born?"

"So my mother says, an' I doubt she'd've reared me on Ship Street if she'd been able to claw up coin enough for us to get out the gates an' live anywhere else! So don't be trying to wave my words away as some dark outlander plot 'gainst the Deep!"

"Why talk of stringing up poor Piergeiron's corpse, then, if you love Old Stinkingstreets so much?"

"Use your *head*, man! If they can take down Varandros Dyre—a *guildmaster*, mind—while we stand and stare and do naught, what's to stop them coming for you next? Or you—or *you?* Or me? When the walking fish came, we fought! When the orcs came, years back, we fought! Well, these're just as bad—*and they're inside the walls with us!*"

The chorus of curses that followed was heartfelt, and the hearts were not happy.

♦ ♦ ♦ ♦ ♦

Sunset was a bell away as Naoni left the cool green shade of the City of the Dead behind and stepped into the Coinscoffin. Merchants' Rest, more properly, but only haughty folk ever called it that. Down its tiled, high-vaulted, echoing forehall she walked, not looking at the statues of the mighty, and stepped through the everglowing arch she'd hated for years.

Her next step was bone-chilling, as always, and then she was shivering in a wooded garden, on a path somewhere far from the sound and bustle of the city, heading for a familiar glade.

All around, flanking the ribbons of winding paths, was a rough pavement of small, flat stones set into the ground, so numerous that the open space between the trees looked very much like a huge cobbled courtyard. Naoni was in the Guildbones.

Every stone was a life gone, and every grave was covered with a row of them, for guildworkers and their families were buried in layers. Some guildmasters were wealthy—and arrogant—enough to buy grand, statue-guarded vaults in the forehall before their passing, but Naoni's father had been a long way from guildmaster when his wife died.

More than that, Naoni knew he'd have to resign the mastership the moment Master Blund recovered from brain-fever. He'd been chosen as acting guildmaster purely because guild rules prevented anyone with standing in another guild—and Varandros Dyre was a member of the Stonecutters and Masons as well as the Carpenters and Roofers—from permanently warming the master's chair, so no one had to fear he'd try to keep it when the Hammer returned.

So like the stillbirths of the lowliest apprentices' wives, Naoni's mother "rested" in a simple wooden box with two sailors below her, a carter and a wool-carder above, and layers of dirt and lime

Greenwood and Cunningham · 315

between them all. Years from now, this glade would be dug up to make space for the newly dead, and any bones left put into a common vault. The markers would be given to descendants, unclaimed ones to the stoneworkers.

Playing in her father's workshop, Naoni had spent much childhood time wondering about the forgotten lives graven into such stones. Few folk knew nearly every building in Waterdeep contained at least one of them. Small wonder tales of ghosts abounded in the city!

Naoni knelt, placed a small spray of blueburst on the marker that read "Ilyndeira Dyre," and then sat back on her heels to wait for memories of her mother to ease her heart.

Or, perhaps, firm her resolve.

Ilyndeira Dyre had loved a noble and come to grief because of it. Naoni had known this since her twelfth summer, after her mother's death, when she'd found Ilyndeira's hidden journal, letters, and a few sad little keepsakes. Her mother had never forgotten, and Naoni had sworn she'd never forget, either. Yet when she looked into Korvaun Helmfast's steady blue eyes, she found herself in danger of breaking the oath she'd sworn over her mother's grave.

He seemed a good man, and growing into his own before her eyes. Quiet ways and all, Korvaun was fast becoming a leader of men; she'd seen his friends' faces when they looked to him, and she was only a guildsmaster's daughter and housekeeper, a simple spinner of threads. He was courteous to commonborn women, and had honored a servant girl at the funeral, before many nobles. None of that swept away the fact that he was a noble of Waterdeep.

Everything was happening so *fast*. Father had come roaring home, bellowing orders and all but dragging them from the house! She'd barely had time enough to seize her spinning tools before he hustled them to an inn. Faendra, of course, had been pleased at the novelty and the prospect of some leisure, but Naoni wanted silence and solitude, the solace of soft shadows, in green places like this one. Grand folk had their private gardens and arbors, but this garden of the dead was the only haven available to the likes of Naoni Dyre.

So she sat in silence, waiting for the quiet green peace to find its way into her heart.

🏰 🏰 🏰 🏰 🏰

"Another building's down! The Lords did it!"

Heads turned as the shout rang back off magnificently carved tomb walls.

The City of the Dead was crowded with folk escaping the stink of Dock Ward fish-boilings and a harbor dredging. There had been many mutters of "The New Day, they call themselves!" and "Piergeiron's *dead*, and they've shoved someone else into his armor to fool us! He crossed some Hidden Lord or other, and they killed him for it!" and even darker sentiments as peddlers and stroll-cooks moved through the throngs.

There was a restless mood in the parklike cemetery. The Watch patrols, walking their usual patrols, felt it. As angry talk swelled around them, they kept their mouths shut and pretended not to hear, where at other times they'd have stepped forward to warn and remonstrate.

Nor were they the only ones treading lightly in the cemetery. Highcoin folk who might on other occasions have loudly called on the Watch to chastise and more, kept their peace and walked warily, listening instead of airily voicing opinions.

"The Lords are driving Dyre down, building by building!"

Heads turned.

"What's that? *What* building?" a merchant bellowed, in a voice that rang out like a warhorn.

"The Lords are smashing the New Day!" someone else shouted, bringing inevitable calls of, "What's the New Day?"

Folk were gathering quickly, striding frown-faced from bowers behind more distant burial halls. In the darker shadows of the tombs, half-seen ghostly shapes stirred restlessly, called forth into the sunlight by the sudden anger and fear riding the air.

"The Lords are against us all!" a man roared, waving his belt-knife.

A woman standing near shrieked, "They can blast down *all* our homes, and take our coins from among our bones, and build anew!"

"They're hunting Varandros Dyre in the streets right now," a breathless cap-merchant gasped, trotting up the cobbled path from the nearest cemetery gate. Others, standing near, took up that cry.

"They'll kill us all, if they think we're of the New Day!"

"What's this 'New Day'?"

"Get home and get your coins before they bring the walls down on your children! Fetch your swords! *This is it!*"

"The Lords are hunting the New Day! The Lords are after us all!"

"What by all the blazing Hells *is* the New Day?"

That exasperated outlander's shout was lost in the rising roar of angry Waterdhavians drawing belt-knives and gathering nose-to-nose to shout rumors into dark truths, and dark truths into war-cries.

A Watch horn rang out—then another—and suddenly the crowd knew its foe.

Heads turned, eyes peered, pointing arms shot out—and in an instant the Watch became the hunted.

"This—this is *not right!*" an old noble growled, reaching for his sword. "*Give* me that, man!"

And he plucked a Watch-horn out of the hands of a paling, stammering officer and blew it as hard as he could, in the old, frantic dah-DAH, da-DAH blast that meant *Aid! Aid here! All aid here NOW!* That call was echoed in the streets around the City of the Dead, and helmed heads turned, peering down from the towers of the city wall along the east side of the cemetery.

"They're coming for us!" a cobbler shouted, waving a stool around his head like a club. "They'll hunt us down! Fight for your necks! Fight for your freedom! *Fight for Waterdeep!*"

"*For Waterdeep!*" the roar went up, as furious as any beast's howl, and all Watchmen within reach died in a few panting moments of furious hacking.

Watch-horns were sounding closer, now—and the high, clear song of a City Guard muster-horn rang out from a wall-tower.

Some folk cowered, but others bawled defiance and fury, and ran at all who stood against them. The old noble's blade bought the whimpering young Watchman a few moments more of fearful life ere they were both hacked down. Then everyone was running, racing amid the tombs as Watchmen and armored Guardsmen with drawn swords burst into the cemetery at every gate. Women and children screamed and wept and ran wildly across the sward, men snatched up cobblestones and funeral urns and turned to fling and overwhelm anyone in uniform—and swords were snatched from failing hands to be swung against the law-keepers.

"The New Day!" someone shouted. "For the New Day! Down with the Lords!"

"They killed Piergeiron! *For Piergeiron!*"

A fat man swung a captured Watch blade so hard that it burst apart in shards and sparks around him as it bent the sword it struck and drove a tall Guardsman head-over-booted-heels down a short stone stair into bushes, where shrieking women, clawing and kicking, overwhelmed him.

Guard-horns sang out over the tumult as astonished commanders stared open-mouthed over the sea of angry citizenry.

"'Tis a bloody *war!* A war within our gates!" one snarled, and blew the horncall that would summon the Watchful Order. Surely this fury must be spell-driven . . .

A few frantic breaths later, he blew his horn again, this time the call for his men to rally around. It was soon accomplished, for anyone who'd dared stray too far from his fellows had already been slain.

"This is madness!" he shouted, to those who were left. "If we try to stand, we'll be butchering fellow citizens until it's too dark to see! So: Sword-ring, blades out, and walk steadily back to the gate we came in by! We'll form a shield-wall outside the Deadrest!"

With his horn he told Guardsmen elsewhere what they was doing as screaming, curse-spitting citizens crowded close around his men again, striking with bench-slats, lamplighting poles, and anything else long enough to outreach a Guard's blade.

Hardened Watch and Guard officers cursed in amazement as they fought their way back to the gates.

"They've gone mad! *Mad!*" one snarled, and others nodded grimly, their eyes wide in sweating faces.

"That's it," a white-haired Guard officer snapped from his saddle, as blood-drenched Guardsmen staggered out through the gate in front of him. "Form two shield-walls, funneling back *that* way! Arrest all who leave, and at sunset, *close this gate!*"

The woman sitting cold-faced on the horse behind his lifted her hand in a swift gesture, and a sudden blue glow swirled around the officer's mouth. Abruptly, the sounds of other men shouting came out of it, and another cold order, from unseen lips: "Spread the word. I, Marimmon of the Guard, do so order: round up all who flee the City of the Dead before sunset—and close the gates at that time on those who don't. Fell magic's at work among the tombs! Ghosts or no ghosts, I'm not having this butchery spill out into the streets!"

CHAPTER TWENTY

Something—she never knew what—brought Naoni out of her reverie and abruptly to her feet with a small cry of dismay. The shadows had deepened alarmingly while she'd been lost in thought; the sky was already the soft purple of coming twilight. She gathered her skirts and ran down the path, plunging through the cold magic of the portal.

A strange din—*battle?*—grew louder as she hurried from the Rest toward the grander tombs, but Naoni never slowed. Better to dash through a scuffle than cower in the shadows and be locked in when the gates were closed at nightfall.

A flung cobblestone flew past her shoulder. She ducked hastily into the nearest tomb, spun around, and peered back out.

Ahead, men and women were throttling each other, punching and thrusting daggers into whoever was nearest, clubbing people bloodily to the ground with walking-sticks and bench-slats. More than once Naoni winced and turned away, feeling her gorge rise.

Only to turn back again, not daring to look away too long, lest someone come charging her way with murder in their eyes.

She felt sick. So many shouts of "New Day" and "Down with the Lords" . . . and now, so much blood.

Half the shopkeepers and crafters in Waterdeep seemed to be out there on the grass and now-trampled gardens of the City of the Dead, angrily trying to slay each other. Soon it would be dark, and the Watch patrols were nowhere to be seen. Were they just going to let people kill each other here all night?

Here, in with the restless dead?

Something cold touched her spine, sliding down to her hips in what was almost a caress, and Naoni whirled around, unable to stifle a little shriek of alarm.

There was no one there—nothing but a hint of movement in the gathering darkness of the tomb.

Naoni swallowed hard. The dead walked the City of the Dead after dark, 'twas said. She'd always thought that a scare-tale, put about to keep honest folk out of the walled cemetery by night, to cut down on carousing and trysting and knifings—but now she could see something *grinning* at her. Something not quite seen, not quite there ... something with teeth that glinted as it came toward her, a shifting darkness in the darkness.

She couldn't stay here!

Naoni whirled and ran out of the tomb. She shrieked as a thrown dagger flashed over her arm and past her, almost catching on her bodice.

Its owner was a tall, burly man, stinking of fear and of badly cured hides. He struck out wildly with his fists, catching Naoni on the forehead and sending her reeling. The target of his fury, however, was a crawling, stumbling scents-seller Naoni had seen in Ship Street a time or two.

"*Now* you're caught, you dirty Lords' spy!" the big man snarled, pouncing.

A hooked hide-knife flashed across the perfumer's throat. Dark blood sprayed, and the doomed man's cry of protest came out as a despairing, sobbing gurgle.

The murderer let go of a fistful of hair, and the dying man's face thumped onto the turf at a sickening angle. The leatherworker turned, wearing a bloodthirsty grin.

He caught sight of Naoni, who'd fetched up against the tomb wall to wait for the world to stop spinning—and his smile changed.

"Well now," he said hungrily, gazing at the swift, frightened rise and fall of her chest. "I never much favored skinny, flame-haired wenches . . . but here we are."

Oh, *gods*. Naoni scrabbled for the tiny shears in her belt-sheath. Waving them like a dagger, she backed away along the roughness of the wall and all too soon felt it end, and that cold, bone-chilling caress come again. On her leg, this time, and—

She whirled with a despairing sob, knowing she couldn't hope to outrun the leatherworker, and launched herself across the grass with ghostly fingers tugging at her and the leatherworker's eager chuckling right behind her.

Then another man came around the corner of the tomb with a bloody sword in his hand, heading right at her with stern murder in his eyes: Korvaun Helmfast!

The wave of relief and pure, incongruous joy that flooded Naoni left her weak-kneed. "Korvaun!" she cried.

He raced up to her, eyes blazing, and thrust his blade right past her as an angry shout rose right behind her—a hout that twisted into a startled shriek of pain, dying swiftly into a gurgling howl . . . and trailing away.

Korvaun turned from the leatherworker's body, blue eyes still afire. "Are you hurt, Mistress Naoni?"

Naoni shook her head, gasping, and managed to say, "N-no. Thanks to you, my lord."

Korvaun winced as if the word 'Lord' had been a blow across his face. "You'll not mind if I accompany you until we can get out through the gates?"

Naoni managed a tremulous smile. The ghostly clawings seemed to be gone, but the doorless arch of the tomb yawned like a dark and hungry mouth just a few paces away.

"No, I'd not mind that at all," she said gratefully.

Korvaun cast a swift, searching glance all around to ensure no one was approaching with drawn steel, then gave Naoni a smile. His long hair was tousled and spattered with someone else's blood, and there was a lot more of it all over his splendid clothes. His cloak—

Naoni put a hand to her mouth. "Where's your cloak?"

Strangely, its absence troubled as much as all the bloodshed. There'd been something reassuring about seeing her handiwork swirling grandly about his shoulders.

"I left it with a servant before I came in here; I didn't want to be so brightly marked as a noble in *this* crowd."

Naoni stared at him. "Is it your custom to come strolling through the Deadrest before dusk? When it's full of an angry mob killing each other?"

"'Tis my custom to go seeking friends who may need aid and stand with them," Korvaun replied quietly. "Born with coins enough to do as I please, in a city that has more well-to-do wastrels than any great kingdom might need, 'tis almost the only deed of worth I *can* do."

Naoni swallowed. There'd been clear bitterness in his voice, but . . . "Friend? You came seeking *me?*"

"Yes," Korvaun said simply.

Then his gaze went past her, and his face changed.

"Into the tomb," he snapped, reaching out a long arm to gather her in. "I can defend—"

"*No!*" Naoni almost shouted. "There's a ghost—"

"Well of *course* there is," Korvaun replied, plucking her up like a bundle of cloth. "Every tomb in the City's crawling with them."

"No, no, *no!*" Naoni cried, struggling to get free. "It was *clawing* at me!"

Korvaun swung around to look behind him, whirling her like a rag doll to do so. "Inside," he said urgently. "There're six—no, *seven*—men running right at us, with swords out! I wear a talisman that can ward spirits away!"

"Well, *give* it to me!" Naoni said, finding her feet at last. "I'm not going in there withou—"

"Naoni, I've no time to—'tis my belt buckle! I can't fight with my breeches half down—get *in*, woman!"

With a roar the foremost man arrived, a giant of a dockworker in a tattered black-buckle jerkin swinging a wicked, blood-smeared scythe.

Korvaun shoved Naoni back at the darkness—where three pale, watching faces now floated, with no bodies beneath them at all—and raised his slender sword in a desperate, ducking parry. He dare not let steel meet steel squarely, or his blade might snap off like—

There was a ringing clang, sparks danced, and the docker was snarling into Korvaun's face as his scythe rebounded. Two more dockers were coming up fast; Korvaun knew he had to down the man quickly. He spun up out of his crouch dagger-first, driving it in under the man's ribs and ripping up and out.

Blood spouted, and the wounded man wailed. Letting go scythe and his last meal in untidy unison, he staggered away, clutching his gut. His stagger took him right in front of one of his fellows, giving Korvaun time to slash at the face of the other man. When that docker threw up his knife to parry, Korvaun hooked the man's feet out from under him and landed on him, knees first, to stab once and spring back up.

Then the rest were arriving in an untidy, shouting knot, and Korvaun was sprinting back to the tomb, where a white-faced Naoni stood trembling, tiny shears held up before her like a dagger. Korvaun scooped her up like a babe, despite her wail of fear, and plunged right at the three—no, four, now—glowing ghostly faces.

The ghostlight promptly winked out. Korvaun lost his footing in the sudden darkness, and they landed hard on the cold stone floor. Naoni rolled away and promptly screamed. Korvaun cursed his way up to his feet and whirled to face the first charge.

Two of the men who'd come to slay him skidded to frantic halts, wide-eyed, and started to shout in fear.

Ghosts were all around them, half-seen and chilling, all skull-faces and wasted limbs and horrible battle-wounds gaping. Naoni was sobbing on her knees with long-fingered phantoms clawing at her. Korvaun ran to her, waving his sword.

A horrible boneless thing—the phantom of someone who'd been crushed by something heavy—reared up before him, mouth working horribly. It melted away into tatters as Korvaun and his talisman rushed right through it.

He fell again and skidded to a halt on his knees, his arms around a weeping, quivering Naoni Dyre. The ghosts melted away from them.

"Easy, love," he murmured awkwardly. "All will be well, I swear!"

She turned and sobbed into his chest but then went stiff and silent, pulled herself away, and looked toward the tomb-mouth, eyes wide and wild.

Korvaun followed her gaze. It was almost night outside the tomb now, and he could see distant figures running frantically and hear a great chorus of iron clangings, followed by terrified howls of "The gates! They've closed the gates on us!"

In the deeper, closer darkness of the tomb, a silent host was gathering in a pale ring close around Korvaun and Naoni. Not all the ghosts tarried: phantom after phantom slid out through the arch into the falling night, but ever more were seeping out of burial runes and rising up from the flagstones to join the silently staring throng.

Korvaun stared at them, and they stared back, their eyes so many cruel, patient points of light. Coldly menacing. Waiting.

He shivered despite himself, as Naoni whispered, "They've closed the gates. We're shut in here until morning, aren't we?"

"It seems so."

The lass in his arms hadn't yet seen the ghosts gathered all around them, but she was trying to turn around now, pushing firmly against him. "Are those men gone?"

"They are," Korvaun replied nervously, watching the ghosts drift a little closer. One got too close and melted into tatters, its darkly furious eyes vanishing last of all. They were testing the strength of his talisman, seeking to wear it down or find some weakness . . .

"Lord Helmfast," Naoni said more calmly, "I thank you for your timely aid, but if you don't mind, I'd like to get up now, and—"

"Keep still," Korvaun hissed. "Please."

She froze, and peered up sharply. "Why?"

Korvaun drew a deep breath. "The ghosts are all around us,

lass. My—all my talisman does is keep them a little at bay. If you stand away from me, I can't stop them from ... from ..."

Naoni shuddered. "So cold," she whispered, remembering. "Like searing frost."

There was a sudden commotion outside, the thudding footfalls of a large, booted man running as fast as he could. He panted past, then someone else screamed suddenly, "No! Noooo! *Take them away!*"

"Are—" Naoni started to ask, voice rising in fear, and Korvaun held her tightly, wincing. Outside, something pale glowed and flashed—and the screaming man fell silent and toppled, staring forever at nothing.

The ghost whirled away from its victim, giving Lord Helmfast a grin of coldly savage glee. Lifting skeletal hands, it moved bony digits in a brief, complicated dance.

Korvaun was no wizard, but he knew a spell when he saw one. So, apparently, did the watchful ghosts. They drifted closer, well within the range of the talisman's power.

He glanced down at his belt buckle. The faint, silvery glow of its holy power was fading away.

Korvaun's heart started to pound. This shouldn't be possible! The talisman was no wizard's charm but a blessed object. No ghost—not even that of a great wizard—could undo a holy blessing.

Or could it?

Torm preserve us ... what if the ghostly spell had been cast on *him*, not the talisman? A magic to make him afraid ...

"The presence of fear does not mean the absence of faith," he said fiercely, his voice almost steady. "I believe. Torm's blessing *will* protect us from the angry dead."

The ghosts did not retreat. "Protect *you*," came a hollow, mocking voice from deep in the tomb-shadows. "*You.*"

That fell meaning was not lost on Korvaun, and his heart sank. A glance at the swiftly fading buckle confirmed his grim suspicions.

"Naoni?" he asked suddenly, voice quavering.

"Yes?"

"The talisman's power was meant for one. It protects us both, but overtaxed as it is, it will not last the night."

"And then the ghosts . . ."

"Yes," Korvaun said, gritting his teeth as the phantoms all around them began to move, whirling up into an eerie dance wherein they *leaned* at him, one after another, to reach for him with arms ending in dangling, almost-severed hands, leer with jaws that hung half-off, and glare at him from severed heads floating well below the bleeding stumps of necks that had once supported them.

Naoni lifted her head, saw, shivered, and quickly ducked back against him. "Your buckle keeps us safe for now, but is neither large nor powerful enough to see us safe to morning," she whispered, eyes large.

"I fear so," Korvaun replied. Unclasping his belt, he used his dagger to slice the silver buckle free.

"This will protect one person until daylight," he said, pressing it into Naoni's hand. "I want you to have it."

Her slender fingers closed around the faint silver glow, and Korvaun eased away from her. As long as Naoni was safe, he could die content. Like a true Helmfast, he—

But Naoni seized the front of his tunic and pulled him back. "I'm going to stand," she told him briskly. "Rise with me, and hold me close, but stand behind me with your arms about my waist, leaving my hands free."

He obeyed the firm purpose in her voice, encircling Naoni Dyre's waist with his arms, and despite the danger was struck by how *right* it felt.

Korvaun drew in a deep breath and stared into the dark, cold eyes of the ghosts. For a moment Naoni rested her head against his shoulder, then straightened, once more brisk and swift, and dug purposefully into her largest belt-pouch.

"I can spin anything into thread," she announced, taking something small and wooden from her bag and beginning a mysteriously complex twisting and turning. "Anything. And what I

328 · The City of Splendors

spin increases in the spinning. A single sweet can yield enough sugared-string to satisfy Faendra's sweet tooth for a tenday. A handful of gems becomes skeins and skeins of shining thread. The sugar-string retains its flavor, the gem-thread its luster. They're the same, only *more*."

Korvaun blinked. "You can do that to something *magic?*"

"We're about to find out. Quiet, and let me work."

Korvaun watched in wonder as shining, silvery thread spilled from Naoni's twisting fingers and fell to the odd wooden spindle whirling just above the stone floor. As the thread accumulated, the light grew.

"Take up the spindle," Naoni ordered, "and turn with me as I spin."

Lord Helmfast carefully cradled the whirling thing, and found himself moving with her in a slow, peculiar dance. Thread continued to stream from her busy fingers but now wound loosely about them, cocooning them together in a soft, shining web. With each turn, the ghosts retreated deeper into the darkest corners of the tomb.

Finally Naoni held up empty hands. "We can sit down side by side. 'Twill be easier waiting out the night than standing."

They shuffled carefully to the nearest wall and sank to the stones together. "This is as soft as fine linen," Korvaun marveled, lifting a handful of shining threads in his spread fingers. "How strong is it? Will I be able to cut us free, if someone charges in here with a blade?"

"Spidersilk's stronger than most metal," Naoni told him, "but you can brush it aside with a broom. Nearly anything, spun so fine, can be easily cut."

"Extraordinary," he murmured. "You can be sure the Watchful Order will be calling on you very soon. Such power can hardly be kept secret for long."

Naoni shrugged. "I'm a very minor sorceress. Speaking of the Watchful Order, why don't they drive down and bind these ghosts?" Her voice trembled as a phantom loomed up and caught her gaze.

"They do, but as more and more dead are laid here, and more and more spells cast, things have started, ah, *leaking*. A Palace wizard told me all about it at a revel. Usually they're not bad—vigils keep them back, and they don't leave the tombs, so the gardens and bowers are safe—but death, especially murder, draws them. And there's some dark magic at work here, this night."

Naoni shivered.

"Tell me of your spinning," Korvaun said hastily, not wanting her to dwell on the butchery she'd seen. "You're marvelously skilled at it, all magic aside. Who taught you?"

Naoni tensed. Though she didn't move, she suddenly seemed farther away.

"I taught myself," she murmured. "I taught myself many things. My mother died when I was twelve."

Korvaun knew old pain when he heard it. "What did she die of?" he asked gently.

"Lack of coins," Naoni said in a strangely lifeless voice.

Silence fell, and Korvaun carefully said nothing, waiting.

"Not something any noble would know about," she added bitterly, turning around in his arms until her back was against him. "You with your rich clothes and carefree carousing and days so full of whim and idleness."

Korvaun decided not to even try to defend himself or the other proud Houses. Instead he asked, as gently as before, "How can one die of poverty when married to a guildmaster?"

"Father wasn't guildmaster then, and commanded just a building crew. He did the work of six, but couldn't earn coins enough. Not nearly enough."

"For?"

"For cure-potions and temple-healings to banish Mother's fever. We barely had enough for her funeral."

"So you had to become mother to the Dyres."

"Yes," Naoni said, and added in a voice as soft and steely as the thread she'd spun, "and *I* will die before any Dyre lacks for coin again!"

"Well, the cloaks you made for us should soon have you set up in a grand house—in North Ward, say—with all you could want. We've been asked about them scores of times already, by many of Waterdeep's finest."

"*Finest*," Naoni echoed scornfully. "Finest thieves, finest swindlers, finest—gahh!"

Korvaun held silent, seeking the right words. A great wound begat Naoni's pain, but 'twas an old one. It seemed she'd spent a lifetime rubbing salt into it. If there was any chance of a life for them together, they had to be done with this.

"I wasn't aware that the gods gave any noble child the slightest choice as to the station it was born to, any more than they offer that choice to a babe born to a tavern dancer in some Dock Ward alley. That's a lot of venom to be born of mere envy," he said, picking words likely to goad her into wrath.

The woman in his arms almost exploded. Naoni Dyre managed to sit bolt upright and twist herself around to face him all in one movement. She glared at him with more fire than all the ghosts in all Waterdeep could manage.

"Envy? *ENVY?* Let me tell you something, Lord High and Mighty Helmfast! I don't *envy* nobles, I pity them—but I pity far more the folk who must live with them and suffer the hurts of their thoughtless or malicious caprices!"

"Caprices?"

"Hah, think you a mere stonemason's daughter can't know a fancy word or two, do you?"

Naoni was literally trembling with anger. Korvaun held her very gently, wondering what to do.

Nose to nose with him, she hissed fiercely, "Do you truly want to know why I despise nobles?"

Korvaun swallowed. "Yes."

He remembered what he'd seen in the Warrens vault: Varrencia Cassalanter's wedding invitation, adorned with an etching of the happy couple. He'd seen at a glance what he'd never noticed until that moment: Varrencia and Faendra Dyre looked startlingly alike.

"Once, not so long ago," Naoni hissed, "there was a young and beautiful lass, a commoner who loved a young noble. Loved and was loved, or so she believed, until the day she knew she was with child, and shared that joy with her lord—and had his gates slammed shut in her face. Her *kind* and *faithful* lord promptly took a wife of as high station as his own."

Naoni's face was wet, now; in the light of the web Korvaun could see tears on her cheeks.

"When she was large with child, he sent masked men to snatch her away to a country estate. The ride was hard, and her time came early. Lying there broken on a fine bed in a strange house, she was told her babe had died. Then she was bundled back into her clothes, still dusty from the ride that had brought her, taken back to the street she'd been seized from—and tossed to the cobbles."

Naoni's voice broke, and they sat together in silence for several moments. Even the ghosts had left off their eerie moans. Still and silent, they seemed to be listening.

Drawing a deep, shuddering breath, Naoni added, "While recovering, she heard the triumphant news that her lord and his hitherto-barren wife had been blessed by the gods, who'd miraculously given them a daughter. In those safer days, great lords still threw open their gates to let the unwashed view their future masters, and my—and the lass went, and knew the babe was hers, with her red-gold hair and eyes like midsummer blueburst."

Some of the fire seemed to go out of Naoni's voice, and she sank down a little in his arms. "Servants drew her out into the back gardens and threatened her with the law if she so much as touched or spoke to the lord's daughter—ever. Then she was marched to *another* corner of the gardens, where her Lord Faithful's wife was waiting with a threat of her own. She told the lass that the gods *had* bestowed a blessing: she was now pregnant with her lord's child. If the lass did or said anything to make the merest hint of scandal touch her husband, her little girl would disappear. Forever."

Korvaun winced. This was not the tale he'd expected. It was far worse. "You're telling me dark truth. How'd you learn it?"

"I found ... love letters, and a journal, with a portrait—a

miniature, something my ... no tradesman's family could have afforded. All hidden in a coffer. Some of the letters were pleading. Desperate." Naoni shivered.

"I believe it. I believe it all," Korvaun told her. "Many take anything they can grasp, caring nothing for others, yet not all nobles are like that. *I* am not like that."

"I know," Naoni whispered, "yet you can't undo what was done. No one can. It's marked me forever."

"A smith hammers and hammers a blade, then quenches it in oil and reheats it to hammer it more," Korvaun said gently, "and not all blades break in such forging. Some emerge strong and true. You've no reason to be ashamed by what happened."

"*I am not ashamed!* I have done nothing to be ashamed *of!*"

"Yet you've never told anyone your mother's story until now, have you?"

Naoni was silent for a long time before she sobbed, "No. My mother said nothing, and I didn't—and *don't*—want to hurt Father. My mother's family were successful merchants, with a good house and coins to spare, the sort of folk who fear scandal more than anything else. They married her off to the first man who asked. An ambitious day laborer. Father."

"I doubt he was as deaf and blind at the time as that telling suggests," Korvaun said gently. And waited.

"You're ... perceptive, Lord Helmfast. No doubt Father knows all. I most fear Faendra learning of this and preening to all that she's almost nobility, or should be. No good can come of that, only heartbreak for her and unpleasantness for us all."

Korvaun nodded grimly. Some nobles would sport with such a lass with glee ...

He laid his dagger in her hand and closed her fingers over it. "Take this. If you feel the need to protect your honor and your good name—even from me—use it with my blessing."

She stared at his calm face through fresh tears. "You make it hard for me to despise you."

Korvaun's mouth traced the wry beginnings of a smile. "I suppose that's a beginning."

"A beginning?" she asked suspiciously. "A beginning of what?"

"Friendship, at first. In due time, love and marriage—if you'll have me. And after marriage, gods willing, children."

Naoni stared at him, mouth agape. He added quickly, "I know things can only happily befall if they're also your desire, and we come to know each other well and trust each other fully. Don't fear that I'll take the one without offering the other. Nobles are good at vows, and I make one to you here and now: if I get you with child, it will only be as my Lady Helmfast."

She shook her head incredulously, tearstained face bone-pale. "Marriage ... children ... *Lady Helmfast!* You're crazed!"

"Quite possibly. Nevertheless ... the words are said and I mean them."

Naoni stared into his eyes, breathing fast. "I believe you'll stand by your vow, Lord Helmfast, and I give you one of my own: I'll no longer be ridden by the ghost of my mother's pain. I'll not judge you by he who wronged her. *And I'll no longer pretend I don't love you.*"

Her lips found his, and they were warm and sweet and willing.

When at last they broke apart, breathless, Naoni murmured, "Now, *that*, my lord, is a beginning!"

Korvaun chuckled and stroked her cheek. "Nay, love, let it be an ending—for this night. Let the priests chant their prayers first, so you never have reason to fear dishonor or scandal."

"Haven't I vowed an end to such fears?" she replied. "Morning's not far off, and the ghosts fade. There are none to see the promises we make, or judge how we seal our vows to each other."

Korvaun shook his head. "You need prove nothing to me."

"Have I reason to fear dishonor or scandal?"

"No. Not while I live." As this was simple truth, and because she gazed at him with such shining trust, Korvaun took a ring from the smallest finger of his right hand and slid it onto her finger.

"You have my pledge and my heart—and I'll give you my name as soon as the ceremony can be arranged."

Naoni's smile was dazzling. "Give me your love, and I'll be content."

Echoing sighs faded at the back of the tomb as the last wan ghostlight winked out—and there were indeed no witnesses to the promises made in the last hours of that night.

Yet when bright morning came, neither lord nor lass doubted that the whispered promises between them would be well kept.

CHAPTER TWENTY-ONE

For the first time in his life, Taeros Hawkwinter held vigil for dawn. All night he'd paced the mooncast shadows outside the City of the Dead, praying to every god he knew to hasten the coming of morning, and dreading what dawn might reveal. The stern line of Guardsmen had been unmoved by his pleadings and use of the Hawkwinter name. Scores of times he'd cursed himself for noticing Varandros Dyre striding out of that inn. If they hadn't found Faendra to ask her where her sister had gone, Korvaun would never have gone sprinting off to find his Naoni, and—

Enough. 'Twas done, as surely as Malark's entombment, the gods save us all.

Taeros wasn't alone in his fearful restlessness. A throng had gathered outside every gate of the cemetery, anxious to learn the fates of friends and loved ones locked within—or to reclaim the dead and dying who were only too visible through the high iron gates. A veritable army of Guardsmen, Watchmen, and Watchful Order magists grimly barred passage, unmoved by threats, brandished blades, and sobbing pleadings alike.

Throughout the night several frantic folk had tried to scale the walls, only to be hurled off by warding magics. Others had wept helplessly as they recognized a familiar voice, inside the walls, raised in terror or pain. The cries soon died away, leaving only ominous silence, and still the citizens waited, shivering in the chill grey damp of the night-mists.

At last the darkness started to lighten, and men started to call, "In! In!"

Others took up the cry, and it quickly rose into a chant. Taeros stood nose to nose with the Guardsman who'd firmly denied him several times and saw the man's eyes change as someone spoke inside his head.

The officer turned and said curtly, "Open the gates."

Binding spells wavered and sighed away, locks were undone and great bars hurled aside, and the great iron gates swept silently open. With a collective sigh, the waiting throng streamed inside.

Taeros jostled with dozens of robed priests and heard the rattling progress of many haulcarts behind him. The carters would convey the known dead to their grieving families and haul the unclaimed to The Last Bath in South Ward, the grim house where unknown dead were laid out in hopes someone would miss them and come looking. Taeros prayed silently that this day wouldn't include a trip there to seek Korvaun Helmfast among those ever-quiet faces.

He pushed his way through the growing thunder-rumble of carts, looking this way and that for some sign of his friend. Heartsick, he saw nothing, nothing . . . no gleam of blue gemweave amid the sprawled bodies.

And then, in the far tree- and tomb-studded distance, above the heads of the milling crowd of searchers, he caught sight of disheveled fair hair. Korvaun was taller than most—it could be . . .

Taeros broke into a run, dodging and darting.

Yes! Korvaun *alive*, by all the Watching Gods! And beside him, both clinging to and supporting the rather bedraggled Lord Helmfast, was a slender, flame-haired lass who could only be Naoni Dyre.

Relief flooded the Hawkwinter. Laughter welling out of him, he raced forward and threw his arms around them, and the three clung together, laughing and crying, as carts rumbled by and others wept.

Finally, starving for air, Taeros pulled away. "Thanks be to Torm for friends too bloody stubborn to die!"

A shadow passed over Korvaun's face, and Taeros winced. For what were the ghosts that so swarmingly haunted the Deadrest, but folk too stubborn to die?

"Do you count me among your friends, then, Lord Taeros?" Naoni Dyre asked quietly. "On such short acquaintance, and me a common-born lass?"

Her stare told the Hawkwinter that his answer really mattered to her. Glib phrases rose readily to his tongue—and there stopped. Taeros blinked, realizing that what he was about to say was simple truth.

"Strangely enough, I do," he marveled.

Before he could chastise himself for *that* slip of the tongue, both of his friends, the old and the new, burst into laughter.

Taeros heard the high, wild edge to Naoni's mirth and told her quickly, "Let's begone from here. I saw not your father nor sister outside the gates, but in all candor, I wasn't looking for them."

"Nor would you have found them. Father told us not to expect him in at all last night—New Day work, I've no doubt—and I took his room, so I could sleep while Faen slipped out to a revel. She's probably not back even yet, and neither of them knows I came here. But they'll soon find me missing, and worry."

"I've a coach waiting, if you can walk four streets west."

Relief and gratitude shone on Naoni's face, making her look like a lamp lit from within, and Taeros wondered why he'd ever thought her plain.

The three lost no time in departing the City of the Dead. Handcarts laden with corpses were already rumbling past. Naoni winced as an arm slid off its chest to sway and dangle, but Taeros gazed at smeared lip-paint on the dead man's face and said softly, "I'll wager that one never thought, hurrying to an afternoon tryst, that he was rushing to his grave."

"Few think of their own deaths until they lie dying," Korvaun replied. He looked down at Naoni with the future in his eyes and added, "Much less what comes after. I'd never had reason to do so myself, ere last night."

Taeros stiffened in enlightenment. First Roldo, now Korvaun! With Malark gone and Beldar so troublingly preoccupied, he'd soon be reduced to drinking and wenching with just Starragar. And Lord Starragar Jardeth was certain to wed young, for what better way to maintain his customary ill spirits?

Leaving him alone, with his books and inkpots.

Another handcart rumbled past, bearing a lone dead man. It was followed by a sobbing, staggering woman. Taeros winced. Well, there was alone and then there was *alone*.

♦ ♦ ♦ ♦ ♦

"Nao! *Naoni!*" The frantic whisper resumed, and so did the rattling of the heavy bolt.

Striding through cheering merchants to take his place at the gleaming table where citizens could confer publicly with the Lords of Waterdeep—all of them unmasked and rising to applaud his entrance—Varandros Dyre frowned. That sounded like Faendra, and what would she be doing *here*, whispering for her sister in all this tumult?

"Naoni Dyre, *wake up!* If you don't get up and out of here soon, Father'll be back, and *then* what—"

Varandros Dyre was suddenly receiving applause from no one, and the glossy carved chair under his hands was . . . the smooth-worn lip of the inn bed, and he was blinking at the door as its bolt rattled again.

"*Naoni!*"

Not bothering with his breeches—the knee-length inn night-shirt would do—Dyre rolled out of bed, shot the bolt, and pawed the bolt open.

Faendra staggered back, wide-eyed. "*Father!*"

"*What,* lass?"

His youngest daughter peered past him frantically. "She's not here!"

"Naoni? Why would she be *here? Out* with it! *Where is she?*"

"I . . . I *don't know!*" Faendra looked ready to cry. "I thought she was in *here!* S-she—"

Fear closed iron fingers around Dyre's throat. There'd been some sort of brawl in the City of the Dead last night, with the Watch and half the *Guard* called out! What if Naoni'd been there? She went betimes to put flowers on . . .

Gods, what if she'd somehow still been inside when they closed the gates at nightfall?

"No!" he growled fiercely, "She's a stubborn lass, and house-proud to a fault. Most likely she went back to the house for some of her spinning and stayed to work, trusting she could keep it standing if the Lords came a-calling by . . . well, by sheer pride."

The trembling beginnings of a smile touched Faendra's worried face. "Yes, that sounds like Naoni. We must go and make sure!"

"Aye." Varandros Dyre looked at his younger daughter, so pale, dark hollows hooding her eyes. Her mother had looked just so, when the fever'd begun . . . "I'll hire a carriage."

She winced. "If it's all the same to you, Father, I'd rather walk."

🏰　🏰　🏰　🏰　🏰

It was past full dawn as Lark hurried down the street. She was late for work two days running, and Master Dyre wasn't one to dismiss that.

Her misadventure with Beldar Roaringhorn had kept her from her duties for too long, yesterday; by the time she'd reached the Dyres' it was locked and empty. Her employers must have been making their worksite rounds, and with the fire out and no food ready to hand, they'd likely take their evening meal out, perhaps even at the Notch.

So she'd gone to serve there at her appointed time, planning to arrive at the Dyres' very early the next morn, but her cheek was so bruised from Lord Roaringhorn's blow that she looked frightful. She'd lingered too long at her mirror trying to cover the damage with tinted unguent lent by a sympathetic highcoin lass at the rooming house.

Her face felt stiff and strange under the unfamiliar paint, but she strode through the Dyres' kitchen garden with her usual swift step. To her surprise, the buttery door was still locked. The kitchen door, the front entrance: locked tight, all. No smoke rose from the chimney, and no sounds came from within.

A strong hand descended on her shoulder and spun her around to face—

Her grim-faced master, with tearful Faendra at his side, her gaze fixed on the chimney.

Lark's heart sank. Every morning, Naoni rose before dawn to stoke the kitchen fire. By now she'd have a pot of broth or spiced cider simmering, and morningfeast would be bubbling and sizzling. The cold chimney proclaimed all too loudly that the mistress of hearth was absent.

Master Dyre's eyes were flint-hard. "Where's Naoni?"

Lark shook her head, swallowing. "I know not. The house's locked up tighter than a Calishite harem."

The rattle of an approaching coach rose behind them, and the hooves of its horses were slowing. Everyone turned.

They were in time to see Lord Korvaun Helmfast leap out, even before the coach had quite stopped.

Varandros Dyre stared in disbelief. The noble's blue gemcloak was gone, and his fine clothes were stiff with dried blood. As the horses snorted and pawed, Korvaun reached up to help someone alight from the coach—and Naoni Dyre's slender form and bright head suddenly filled its door.

Varandros Dyre growled something wordless and took a step forward, but by then Faendra had flung herself past him with a cry and thrown her arms around her sister, bursting into tears.

Naoni soothed her, murmuring reassurances and stroking her sister's hair as they rocked together in Faendra's tight embrace.

As Lord Taeros Hawkwinter emerged from the coach, Korvaun bowed to the glowering guildmaster. "Your daughter's unharmed, Master Dyre. I apologize for my rough appearance. We shared the misfortune of being locked inside the City of the Dead at nightfall, along with scores of others."

Varandros Dyre swallowed, swayed, went pale, and then blazed crimson again, all in a single breath. "She was locked in the Dead-rest all *night?* With the likes of *you?*"

Korvaun's lips thinned, but his voice stayed calm, even respectful. "Something turned the usual crowd of mourners into a slaying mob; so fierce was the fighting that it threatened to spill out into the streets. Even the Guard and Watch together lacked time and swords enough to quell the fray before nightfall and . . . were forced into a hard decision. Many folk didn't survive; we're among the fortunate few."

Naoni gently slipped out of Faendra's arms and went to her father, who was now staring at her as if *she* were one of the Dead-rest ghosts.

"Lord Helmfast came to my rescue," she told him, "saving me first from a man who tried to . . ." Her voice failed, but she drew in a deep breath and went on. "Then he fought for me against a band of armed men who attacked us in their madness. We . . . took refuge in one of the tombs. Korv—Lord Helmfast had a blessed talisman that kept the roaming spirits safely from us throughout the night. And he gave me this."

She pulled a fine dagger from her belt and held it up. Its sharp, clean blade glinted in the morning light.

"Lord Helmfast bade me use it if I felt he in any way threatened my honor. As you can see, I had no cause."

Varandros Dyre looked at Naoni's fierce face, at the bright-bladed dagger, and then back at the young noble. "It would seem," he said slowly, "I must again thank you for protecting my daughter."

Korvaun bowed again. "It was my pleasure as well as my duty, goodsir," he said quietly. "If it please you, might your daughters and I have a few private words with your maidservant? We're concerned about a friend of mine and believe she may know something helpful."

"Aye, that's always the way of it when trouble befalls. All the day long, folk'll be seeking each other out." Dyre seemed to shake himself and added briskly, "I should be off to see how many workmen remain to me."

Faendra caught at his sleeve. "Should we stay here, Father? Or go back to the inn?"

The guildmaster sighed heavily. "There's no truly safe place in this world, lass, and I'd rather have you both home than tossed about by mobs and spirits. I'll have some of my men bring your things back here." He started to stride off down the street, and then turned and gave Korvaun a nod that was almost a bow.

Leaving Lark facing several cool, measuring gazes.

She turned to Korvaun. "If your friend's named Roaringhorn, I'm not the one to guide you."

"Who better?" Faendra snapped. "Yestermorn, you and Lord Roaringhorn lingered in the club after we left. Since you didn't return here to see to highsunfeast and the cheesemaking, as you'd said you would, I'm thinking you might indeed have some notion of what befell him."

"None whatsoever. We exchanged words, yes, and that delayed me. When I got here, you'd all left already—for an inn, apparently."

Naoni frowned. "We should have left a note, but Father was in such a hurry . . ."

"Another building fell," Faendra explained. "The worksite on Redcloak Lane."

Lark winced, seeing quite well why Master Dyre had hauled away his daughters with such haste.

"You know nothing of Beldar?" pressed Taeros Hawkwinter. "We've not seen him since we departed the club."

Lark didn't have to feign anger. "I know not where he is, nor do I care!"

Plucking forth her ready-cloth from its belt pouch, she swiped most of the unguent from her cheek. Lifting her chin, she stared defiantly at Taeros and let him read what he would from her bruised face.

His expression grew grim. "Beldar?"

Lark nodded.

"Are you . . . otherwise unharmed?"

"I am, though I think you'll find your friend somewhat the worse for wear."

Korvaun sighed. "Beldar's not been himself of late. We're all grieving over Malark, but ..."

"When it seemed you went off with him ... " Naoni murmured.

"After all that talk about Elaith Craulnober," Faendra added tearfully, and then threw her arms around the maid. "Oh, Lark, I'm so sorry!"

"It ... matters not," Lark replied, patting her younger mistress awkwardly on the back before disentangling herself from the embrace. "You were right to be cautious. I take no offense, and only hope your minds are at ease."

Faendra nodded happily, but Naoni ... *glowed.*

Lark looked at that smiling face. Then her elder mistress moved her hand, and Lark saw the glint of gold on one finger.

Gods above! No good can come of this. She glanced at Korvaun, and what she saw there did not put her mind at ease.

"One matter remains unresolved," Korvaun said carefully. "It appears Lord Hawkwinter here has lost a silver charm on a neck-chain. Lark, know you anything of this?"

Lark's heart beat a little faster, but she knew nothing showed on her face. No lass raised on the Luskan docks escaped accusations, and when death or maiming could reward a guilty face, one learned fast.

Looking at all of the watchful faces, she decided to cleave close to the truth. There was no knowing what magic trinkets the lords might carry, and if she was caught in a lie ...

"After you all left in such haste, I found such a thing, fallen on the stair—snowflake and hawk." Then she told them rueful truth. "It didn't occur to me until now that the design meant 'Hawkwinter.'"

"Where is it now?" Taeros demanded, with far more interest than one might expect from a wealthy nobleman over a simple silver charm.

Lark faced him squarely. "Lord Roaringhorn had lingered in the room, so I asked him to help me learn more about the charm. He took me to an old woman, a mage or priestess of some sort who tried to read its secrets. If you're concerned about losing valuable magic, Lord Hawkwinter, be at ease. The charm has none that she could find."

Taeros sighed in exasperation. "Did it not occur to you to simply *ask* who among us might have dropped the charm?"

Lark risked a lie. "Of course. I asked Lord Roaringhorn."

The nobles exchanged frowns. "He'd not know," Taeros mused, "but why'd he take it to some witch-woman or other, rather than simply follow us and ask?"

"That was my idea," Lark said. "Serving in taverns, I've seen such charms before. Some men give them as gifts—to girls whose virtue might otherwise be unassailable."

Everyone stared at her.

Lark shrugged. "Such things happen."

"Not among the Gemcloaks, I assure you," Korvaun said firmly.

"What became of the charm?" Taeros asked.

"Lord Roaringhorn was ... acting strangely. He talked of The Serpent liking such things. We struggled, and he seized my belt-bag. I got it back from him and fled. What became of him after, I cannot say, but the charm's no longer in my belt-bag."

That was true enough. The charm now rode in a small cloth bag sewn firmly to her shift and hidden beneath her kirtle. If the two lordlings concluded the charm was in Lord Roaringhorn's possession, all the better. He'd deny it, but the frowns on their faces suggested they might now be as disinclined to believe his words as those of a maidservant.

Still, there was little sense courting discovery. Touching a finger to her bruised cheek, Lark turned to Naoni. "By your leave, Mistress, I'd like to use this morn to tend to personal matters."

Naoni promptly proffered her smallcoin-purse. "Take this and see a healer."

Lark backed away, putting her hands behind her. "I can't take your coins for so trifling a hurt! I need rest, nothing more."

Her mistress's smile was weary. "As do we all. Take the day, or two if you see fit."

"This is all fine and well," Taeros murmured in a tone that suggested it was anything but, "yet it serves nothing in retrieving the charm."

"Perhaps," said Korvaun slowly, "there's a way it could be traced ..."

Lark bobbed a curtsey and hurried off, Lord Helmfast's words speeding her step.

If magic could track the charm, better the hunt end at Elaith Craulnober's door than at her own!

⚜ ⚜ ⚜ ⚜ ⚜

Varandros Dyre set aside another many-times-amended chart of the sewers and rubbed his eyes wearily. His daughters sporting with wastrel nobles—sneering emptyheads who knew best how to insult people and break things—buildings crashing down and taking good men to their deaths, and now he'd drawn the baleful eye of the Lords of Waterdeep.

Laughing at him behind their masks, preening as they plotted to reach out and smash down one more man who'd been fool enough to stand up to them.

Yet how was a man to make honest coin—in Waterdeep, too, gods cry all? This wasn't Thay or Calimshan or Zhentil Keep! Here the guilds were a man's shield against tyrannical clerks or spiteful Lords—weren't they?

Or was it all a game, and every hard-working merchant of Waterdeep a dupe left to scramble like an ant, as his "betters" sneered down at him?

If they reached out to crush him, as a man swats a stinging fly, what would befall Naoni and Faendra? Who'd stand with them, against ... oh, *gods*.

Who but those nobles: Helmfast, Hawkwinter and the rest? Men who wanted but two things from his daughters, their charms and their coins—and would be gone the moment they'd snatched both.

"Tymora keep me *alive*," Varandros muttered under his breath.

"Father?" Naoni's voice was sharp with concern.

Dyre's head jerked up. How'd she opened the door without him hearing?

Both of his daughters were standing before him, Faendra bearing a tray holding three tankards of steaming mulled cider. Aye, three, not just his own.

Varandros frowned. "Yes?"

"Are you . . . well?"

"Well enough." He glanced at the tankards. "You've something to discuss with me?"

"Yes," Faendra told him firmly. Dyre snatched away a pile of building plans as she lowered the tray. Naoni was already moving two chairs to face him across his desk.

"Father, Faendra and I have eyes and ears," Naoni began. "We can't help but notice when things go awry."

"I'm doing well enough," Dyre said gruffly. "When was the last time either of you lacked for anything you needed, or the little fripperies you fancy?"

Naoni grimaced. "This isn't about pretty gowns and trinkets, Father. We're not children. I haven't been a child since my twelfth winter."

The double-edged truth of that struck deep. "Sit then," Dyre growled, "and speak."

The girls sat in smooth unison, gray eyes and blue regarding him gravely.

"You're worried about the Lords of Waterdeep," Naoni said bluntly, "and thinking they're behind the building collapses. You think they're targeting you and your friends in the New Day."

His eyes narrowed. "What know you of the New Day?"

"I heard it shouted like a battle cry as the City of the Dead went mad," she told him. "I saw people die with 'New Day' on their lips. By highsun, not more than a handful of folk in Waterdeep *won't* have heard of the New Day."

"And these worries are eating at you, Father," Faendra put in, lifting a tankard. "Time and again you stare at yon cellar and sewer maps, thinking the Lords are tunneling under—"

"Yes, *yes*," Varandros snapped. "So I do! And what affair—"

"Is it of ours?" Naoni broke in. The cold ring of sudden steel in her voice cut through her father's bluster, leaving him gaping at her in silence. "Faendra and I might not actually put mallet to stone, but we manage your home and offices, offer hospitality to your guild friends, run your errands, visit your worksites—and bury your workmen. Why don't you ever confide in us, when there's so little we don't already know? *Speak* to us."

"And hear our advice," Faendra put in, the quaver in her voice betraying her nervousness. Varandros rounded on her out of long habit; pounce on any weakness in negotiations, and press it—

"You always told us a prudent man enters no tunnel alone," Naoni declared. She tapped the sewer plans. "Yet that's what you're planning, yes? If you're right about the Lords, they'll be waiting . . . and you'll die."

"And if you take a crew down without a city contract," Faendra added, looking at the ceiling as if trying to remember her lines and say them precisely, "they'll know, and others will notice—and one way or the other, the Lords will have to move against you."

Varandros Dyre drew in a deep breath and reached for his tankard with a hand that was not quite steady. Then he set it down again, untouched.

"So, now," he said heavily, "you lay out my choices as clearly as I see them myself. Yes, I see those same roads before me. So, now, your advice?"

Naoni stared straight into his eyes and said softly, "You need men to go down into the tunnels with you, men whose status will be your armor and shield. Noblemen."

"Not your—"

He bit off his own snarl to stare at both of his daughters. Mayhap there was something to that notion . . .

"The Lords Helmfast, Hawkwinter, Jardeth, and Thongolir," said Faendra, "men of *proven* honor, Father."

"Men of powerful houses," Naoni pressed. "The Lords would have to want you very badly indeed to risk angering so many nobles."

"One of those young lords is the heir of his house," Varandros mused. "Two more aren't far behind. The Lords would hesitate to spill blood so blue." He frowned again. "But what if they're the very Lords who're after me? Or are working for them?"

Faendra hissed in exasperation, but Naoni made a slashing gesture to cut her off. A familiar gesture. His own. Varandros blinked as sudden affection rose in him. Suddenly his serene, quiet elder daughter was not so unknowable as she'd always seemed.

"If they're what you fear, then you're right where you are now, Father, except that they'll be standing within your reach, if you ... dare to try that way."

"You were going to say if I was foolish enough to try that way, weren't you?" he asked quietly.

She nodded, meeting his gaze squarely, then raised her chin and said, "Yes, because you would be."

Varandros gave her a crooked smile. He sat back, his tankard warm in his hands, and told the ceiling huskily, "Thank you, gods, for giving me two daughters such as these."

He sipped soothing cider and then asked, "Can you bring your young nobles here? Or would it better if I went to meet them?"

The Dyre girls exchanged surprised glances.

"Well, ah . . ." Naoni began.

"We hadn't reckoned on getting this far so swiftly, Father," Faendra said sheepishly. "We'd expected to be wearing that cider by now."

Varandros Dyre stared at her for a moment and then bellowed with laughter. His roars of mirth echoed back to him off the ceiling, louder than he'd laughed in many a year.

After a moment, with a hesitation and uncertainty that made him suddenly want to weep—gods, were they *that* afraid of him?—Naoni and Faendra Dyre started to laugh, too.

🏰 🏰 🏰 🏰 🏰

Elaith Craulnober stalked through the tunnel, his mood darkening with every stride. It boasted a dry floor, fine stonework, and an arched stone ceiling high enough to allow his little band to walk upright, but it was still a sewer. Worse, it was a *new* sewer, so new that it wasn't on the most recent maps.

He turned to face the two roughblades dragging the dwarf. Their captive's just-broken legs trailed limply, and his gray beard was matted with dried blood, none of which had dimmed the defiance in his rheumy old eyes. Nor did the dagger Elaith drew from a wrist sheath.

"Who ordered this work?" the Serpent demanded, waving his fang in a sweeping circle at the tunnel all around.

Battered and swollen lips cracked into a sneer. "Bunch of stinkin' drow. Said they knew yer mother real well."

"Very amusing." The elf looked at his men. "Kill him."

Knives flashed, and the dwarf who'd for years been Waterdeep's most knowledgeable tunnel builder thudded unceremoniously to the stones.

"Heavy bastard," one of the slayers observed, cleaning his knife on his victim's tunic. "Not much for talking, though."

"Indeed," Elaith agreed. The dwarf had been his "guest" for some days now, and in all that time had adamantly refused to say a useful word about recent activities beneath the city streets.

No matter. Living or dead, they all talked in time. Elaith nodded to the pale woman in black and purple at the rear of their small procession. The symbol of the god of the dead, the Bonehand clutching golden scales, was emblazoned on her tabard in glittering thread—perhaps the gem-spun thread now creating an uproar in Waterdhavian fashion, and clear proof he was paying this priestess far too much.

This whole affair was becoming damnably expensive. His recent adventures in Tethyr had strained his coffers, and he'd lost two valuable properties this tenday. There must be an end to this, and soon.

Elaith watched intently as the Kelemvorite knelt by the body, held out her hands, palms-down, and chanted an eerily tuneful prayer.

A faintly shimmering cloud rose from the corpse, swiftly taking on the shape of the dwarf—but whole, showing no signs of the injuries inflicted on him over the last few days.

The apparition stared at the priestess with contempt and then glared at Elaith impatiently. "Well? Get on with it. I got places to go, friends to meet, tankards to drain."

"Three questions," the Skullsister intoned, as if she hadn't heard the spirit. "The Lord of the Dead grants me the power to hold you until three questions are answered *fully* and truthfully."

The ghostly dwarf snorted. "Ask away."

The priestess looked to her employer.

"Who laid this stonework?" Elaith snapped. The priestess echoed his words exactly.

The spirit sneered at that.

"I *told* you I knew not. Use truth more often, Slyboots, an' you might know the sound of it." The apparition seemed to grow a little fainter. "Stones well-trimmed and tight-fitted, not half-bad work. It'll hold a good long time. Not up to dwarf standards, of course, but close as Tall Folk are likely to get. Done by either folk new-come to Waterdeep—stoneworkers I never heard of—or Varandros Dyre. One or 'tother."

Elaith bit back a curse. Witless humans, endangering their own properties—and infinitely worse, his as well! "If the tunnel's sound, what brought the building down?"

The dwarven spirit's reply was swift and firm. "This digging's too close to one of Ahghairon's old wards. There's a warren of sewers under this city, and under *that* levels upon levels of caverns and dungeons and what-have-you. D'you think Waterdeep stands on *that* anthill thanks to human 'stonecraft'? Bah!" The ghostly form was noticeably fainter now.

It was Elaith's turn to sneer. Stonecraft? Hardly. Ahghairon? Well, perhaps the human had renewed or augmented the high magic he'd found, left behind from Aelinthaldaar. *That* was what kept half of Waterdeep from tumbling into the depths . . .

A remembrance of his long-ago fosterage rose unbidden to mind. A particularly creative nurse once brought to the royal nursery a wonderfully complex toy made of hard-spun sugar in rainbow hues. As she told a tale about a powerful human wizard whose spells bored through the depths beneath his city seeking gold, the children had taken turns breaking off and eating bits of candy, until the toy collapsed into fragments—a lesson, of course, about the fragility of magic and the dangers inherent in hasty greed.

That game had fixed the tale in his memory so firmly that Elaith still saw it clearly, all these years later. He'd known enough to break off small bits, not pieces that were part of the supports, but little Amnestria, her sapphire hair a curly halo around a face sticky from the treat, had known less restraint. Her sweet tooth, impatient nature, and grasping little hands had brought the sweet wonder down in short order.

Firmly banishing that memory, Elaith spread out the map of Waterdeep's underground passages on the tunnel floor. Taking quill and ink from a belt-pouch, he addressed the dwarven spirit for the third and final time.

"Where are the wards of the wizard Ahghairon? Fully describe the locations and natures of all that are known to you."

CHAPTER TWENTY-TWO

The High House of Roaringhorn was even noisier than usual that morn. Fortunately, Beldar's stout bedchamber door muffled sounds, reducing the tumult to a steady murmur spiked with occasional incoherent outbursts.

Lying in bed staring at his familiar sculpted and painted ceiling, Beldar pondered the probable cause. Perhaps Thann ships had brought a score of fine black stallions from Amn, resulting in a sudden drop in stud fees for prize Roaringhorn racers; or mayhap his elder brother's betrothed—a pretty, flighty thing whose affections seemed to wax and wane more frequently than the moon—had undergone yet another change of heart. Quite likely it was something as trivial as his mother's twittering dismay over a rival's gown, worn yestermorn and too similar to one she'd intended to don on the morrow. In short, the usual nonsense.

It was mid-morning when Beldar checked his reflection in a gilt-edged mirror taller than he was, grimacing at the effect of eyepatch, thin black mustache, and plumed, broad-brimmed hat—not to mention the assortment of bruises and scrapes he'd incurred the last few days. Ye gods, he looked like a villainous pirate from some two-copper chapbook!

Tilting his hat to a more rakish angle, Beldar gave his image a self-mocking salute, touching fingertips to forehead and then tracing a pair of circling flourishes. Scaling the hat to the floor in disgust, he snatched up his gemweave cloak.

Lacking all desire to explain his eyepatch to the family just yet, he took the back stairs, departing the High House of Roaringhorn by the servants' entrance. The usually bustling courtyard was quiet, but the din from the streets seemed more appropriate to the bustle and strife of the southerly wards than to the quiet, tree-shaded Roaringhorn gardens and the similarly luxurious estates beyond its walls.

The stable doors stood open, and Beldar hastened to them. "A coach, quickly! I'm bound for Hawkwinter Hall," he called.

The stableboy's head arose from a stall and shook denial. "Can't be done, lord. The streets 'twixt here and there be still crowded with folk coming from the City of the Dead."

Beldar frowned. Were the rumors of Lord Piergeiron's death true, after all? "From the *Deadrest?* What befell?"

The tow-headed lad blinked. "You've not heard? A brawl broke out yestereve, inside the Deadrest walls—a terrible fray, 'twas! At nightfall, with it still raging, the Watch shut the gates."

"With people *inside?*"

"Aye, so! Many died, and a lot more sore-hurt. Some came out screaming and scramble-witted. They say carts by the score took the wounded to Hawkwinter Hall for healing. All manner of mounts and carriages still be going hither and yon—streets're full."

"Well, *that'll* put a crimp in Taeros's morning!"

"Oh, he weren't at Hawkwinter Hall come dawn," the boy said loftily, obviously delighted to know so much more than dashing Lord Beldar. "Ne'er came home last night, the servants're saying. Yer friend Lord Helmfast, neither."

Beldar's heart plunged. For once, he wasn't furious servants always seeming to know so much about noble business. Plucking a silver coin from his purse, he waved it at the wide-eyed lad.

"Tell me all, and this is yours."

⚜ ⚜ ⚜ ⚜ ⚜

The temple bells were chiming their last time before highsun as Beldar swung down from his swiftest horse, lathered from its gallop out and around the city, and in again by the South Gate.

He raced up the clubhouse stairs, calling for Taeros as he ran. Of all the Gemcloaks, the Hawkwinter seemed to treasure this haven most highly.

And if not Taeros, well, gathering here for a late—and for some, second—morningfeast was fast becoming a daily ritual.

The door, however, was closed and locked. A note addressed to Roldo Thongolir was pinned to it with a small silver knife.

A Hawkwinter table knife. Beldar pulled it free, spirits lifting at recognizing the firm, neat hand of Taeros on the parchment.

I hope you've already eaten, the note read, *for instead of the usual bellyfilling, we'll be meeting at Master Dyre's worksite on Redcloak Lane. Seek chaos and ruin—of late, our shared banner. If you're not there by five bells past dawn, we'll proceed without you.*

Taeros had signed it with his usual rune. Beldar frowned at that mark. Redcloak? The site of their mock battle? What business could await there? And why was this addressed solely to Roldo, when it concerned them all?

Five bells past dawn had come and gone, but not by much. If he hurried, he might be able to catch his friends, or learn whither they were bound, and follow.

He gave the parchment a wry smile. Didn't every leader go about his business much the same way?

A few workmen were hauling rubble out into carts standing in Redcloak Lane and morosely probing what was left of the stone foundations. Their work had exposed the cause of the collapse: a new tunnel connecting with the old, damp wellhouse underway Dyre had walled off.

The guildmaster shoved at the ladder they'd put down into the new tunnel, making sure it was steady. Nodding, he took up a lantern and led the way down into the gloom, sure-footed as a cat.

His daughters followed ably enough with their own lamps, closely followed by their trio of lordlings: the fair-haired Helmfast lad, as protective of Naoni as any wood-nymph her tree; the smart-tongued Hawkwinter; and the sour-faced one in the black cloak whose name Dyre kept forgetting.

Then they were in the tunnel, turning their backs to where the collapse had blocked it and striding beyond reach of daylight—where Dyre all but forgot the others, barely noticing when one of his daughters slipped past.

"Not dwarf work," he mused, lantern held high to study the fitted stones of the passage where they arched overhead, with nary a crude lintel-slab in sight, "but close to it."

"Korvaun . . ."

Naoni's voice was soft and steady, yet it held a note that lifted the hairs on the back of Dyre's neck. He charged toward whatever danger threatened his daughter; may young Helmfast be fleeter of foot or be damned!

Arriving first, he pulled up short alongside Naoni, and after a stunned moment, slid a steadying arm around her waist.

A burly, battered body lay sprawled on the stones—a dwarf. More than that Dyre couldn't say, for the dead face had been battered beyond recognition . . . but there was an all too familiar rune carved bloodily into the corpse's forehead.

♠ ♠ ♠ ♠ ♠

Beldar found it surprisingly easy to win past the workmen. One looked up, saw his glittering red cloak, and pointed with his hammer at a ladder sticking up out of a pit.

Beldar nodded thanks, took a torch from a sand-bucket bristling with them, lit it from the lantern sitting hard by, and climbed down into the darkness.

After his last and exceedingly unpleasant underground experience, he was relieved to find himself in a stone-lined tunnel: well-built, dry, and smelling of not much more than damp earth. He started to walk briskly, hoping to catch up with his friends.

Very soon he saw the glimmerings of several distant lanterns, and quickened his pace.

Just as he was about to call out a greeting, he passed the mouth of a side-passage. A dark shape exploded out of it.

Beldar grabbed for his sword, but—

The world whirled around him. He fought for balance, and somewhere in his flailings lost hold of his torch. It whup-whupped into the wall and exploded into sparks at about the same moment Beldar's back slammed bruisingly onto flagstones, smashing the wind out of him.

He gasped for breath in the sudden darkness and then went very, very still. There was no doubt at all about the nature of the cold sharpness pressed against his throat.

"I've got him!" a familiar voice called from just above him. "Bring a lantern!"

"Korvaun?" Beldar gasped in disbelief. "Helmfast, is that you?"

There was a long silence, during which two lights approached.

"Aye," Korvaun said at last, and the steel was gone from Beldar's throat as Taeros and Starragar, lanterns held high, stopped and stared down at him.

"How'd you know where to find us?" Starragar snapped.

Beldar frowned. Did they think he couldn't read? Surely they hadn't planned to undertake some sort of adventure without him!

"You left a note on the clubhouse door," he replied, not bothering to hide his exasperation.

His fellow Gemcloaks exchanged dark glances. Their manner was beginning to grate on Beldar's nerves, already frayed over the last few days. He struggled to his feet unaided, and gave Korvaun Helmfast his best glare. "You ambushed me. Why?"

Korvaun slid his dagger into its sheath. "My apologies." His voice was flat and cool. "We heard footsteps and decided to lie in wait for whoever—or whatever—was following us."

Beldar lifted an eyebrow. "Admirably cautious."

"We've good reason," Taeros said bluntly. "The Dyre girls are with us—and Master Dyre's apprentice was murdered while following them."

Beldar frowned in bewilderment. "And you thought to find his killer *here?*"

"There's little chance of finding him at all," Starragar said. "Some sort of necromantic rune carved into his forehead blocks magical inquiry. A popular spell, it seems; there's another corpse in the tunnel yonder sporting the same rune."

A little chill wandered down Beldar's back. The mad priest Golskyn, his burning-eyed sorcerer son, the Dathran . . .

"Magic's nearly endless in form and variety," he murmured. "I know an outlander mage well versed in dark arts."

Again his friends shot looks at each other. Starragar thrust his head forward. "Oh? And how came you by this . . . acquaintance?"

"My brother took me to her as a prank, years ago," Beldar explained impatiently. "She mumbled the usual dire prophecies and grand promises. What of it, if she knows a way around those runes? I'll take something personal from this body you've found; it might help her find the killer."

"Worth trying," Korvaun admitted. He looked at Taeros, who handed Beldar an intricately worked iron medallion.

"We'd planned to take it to the Warrens in hopes someone could name the owner," the Hawkwinter explained.

"Your corpse is a halfling?"

"Dwarf."

Beldar waited for Taeros to elaborate, but his friend merely regarded him. With unfriendly eyes.

Suddenly he understood; Lark must have already reneged on their deal.

"What did she tell you?" he demanded.

His friends gave him only silence. After it had lasted long enough to become uncomfortable, Taeros asked, "Just when did you take up beating unarmed women?"

Shame and relief swept over Beldar together. If this was the sum of their complaints, a simple half-truth should set them at ease. "She bore a stolen charm: Silver, on a silver chain. I tried to take it from her. Though I'd no intention of striking her, my hand . . . connected, ere she fled. I deeply regret this mishap and will tell her so at first opportunity."

Taeros absently reached for his chest, at just the place where a charm might hang, and Beldar knew his words had hit their mark.

"And where's this charm now?"

Beldar shrugged. "Find the wench, and you'll find your property."

Starragar scowled. "She said much the same of you."

For a long moment Beldar regarded his boyhood friends, realizing they'd become strangers all. With all the dignity he could muster, he said, "If you think me a liar and thief, put me to the test. Surely at least one of you has a truth-seeker."

Starragar stripped a ring from his hand and all but threw it at Beldar. "Put it on. You'll be compelled to answer three questions truthfully."

Beldar donned the ring and waved at the other Gemcloaks to proceed.

Korvaun winced. "Blast it, this isn't right! Never once has Beldar Roaringhorn given any of us cause to doubt his word! Never once has he forgotten a debt or failed to stand beside his friends!"

He turned to Beldar. "Take off the thrice-damned ring and tell me straight out you don't possess the charm or know its whereabouts—and I'll believe you."

Beldar regarded Korvaun, held up his hand so the ring was prominently displayed, and said flatly, "I don't have it, I don't know where it is, and this ring is far too garish and made of *brass*, which is utterly, unforgivably common. Is that truth enough for you?"

"Please accept our apologies," Korvaun said. "There should be no talk of truth-spells among us."

"It's forgotten." The Roaringhorn tossed the ring back to Starragar. "I'm off, then. What say we meet at the club come sundown?"

"Agreed," Korvaun replied.

The other Gemcloaks just nodded, content to let Korvaun speak for them. At that moment, a truth hit Beldar hard. The

Gemcloaks now looked to Korvaun—steady, decent, honorable Korvaun—rather than to him.

Loss—almost grief—stabbed at Beldar. Forcing a smile onto his face, he gave the dwarf's medallion a jaunty swing, wheeled around, and started the long walk to the Dathran's lair.

♦ ♦ ♦ ♦ ♦

The Dathran handed back the dwarf's medallion, shaking her head.

"Nothing." Surprise laced her voice. "Not a face, not a name. Again, naught. What sort of magic have you been bringing Dathran?"

"I was hoping," Beldar replied grimly, "you could tell me."

♦ ♦ ♦ ♦ ♦

"It's elven magic, you ignorant hag," murmured Elaith Craulnober, answering the question floating up from one of his gently glowing scrying bowls.

Strictly speaking, the rune was Netherese, but the long-ago mage who'd crafted it had based his Art on elven lore. Of course, few elves these days knew such ancient magics, and fewer still would use them.

Elaith had no such scruples. Moreover, he'd added a twist to the rune, binding a rebounding spell to it so any attempt to magically seek the killer would be turned back against the seeker, revealing *his* identity.

Yet another incantation had empowered the rune still more. Elaith uncorked a tiny vial and tapped a pinch of its glittering powder into the scrying bowl. The ripples took the noble and the witch away, replacing them with a miniature map of the city, lit by a lone red spark.

Its radiance marked just where their conversation had taken place. The area around it began to expand, bringing to mind the way the ground loomed up at one riding a giant eagle to the ground. In moments Elaith was regarding a close, clear view of the witch's lair. Softly glowing footprints marked a path from her rooms up a stair to a hidden door and out into an alley Elaith's henchmen knew well.

With a small silver ladle the Serpent dipped some fluid from the bowl into a crystal goblet. Dipping a finger into that liquid, he traced circles around the goblet's edge, coaxing an eerie note from it.

All of his agents wore rings adorned with flat silver ovals that sang in unison with the crystal, awakening a magic that sent anyone wearing them a mind-vision of the telltale map. It would only loom large and clear enough to read in the minds of those close to the site.

The water in the goblet began to boil, without heat or steam—the signal that his message had been received and understood. Elaith poured the contents of the goblet back into the scrying-bowl and waited to see which agents' faces took shape in the swirling water.

When three faces became clear, a smile touched a corner of his lips.

Lord Beldar Roaringhorn was said to be an excellent swordsman. The coming battle would sorely test his skills. It should, therefore, be most amusing to observe.

Or very, very short.

🏰　🏰　🏰　🏰　🏰

Beldar Roaringhorn plodded up the dark stone steps, the Dathran's words ringing in his ears. Nursery tales and hedge-wizards' claims notwithstanding, magic wasn't going to answer all secrets and banish all troubles in a trice and a twinkling of stars. "What a large surprise," he murmured mockingly, as he came to the tiny chink of light around the door out into the alley. Slipping out into the familiar refuse, Beldar wondered where, in this city of myriad secrets, he should go now to lay bare this latest mystery.

The route to the Dathran's lair was a blind alley, with no other way out other than a warehouse door somewhere to his right that had long ago been buried in a huge heap of shattered stone and rotting wooden shards tossed down in a clumsy rebuilding.

So it was hardly likely that the three figures advancing purposefully down the alley with blades drawn and hard faces fixed smilingly on him were here for trading purposes—or to consult the Dathran, for that matter.

They were here for him.

Beldar's hand wavered between swordhilt and eyepatch as he watched the foremost flex long and slender arms. Both held long, hooked swords that had been tarred to quell their shine. The movement pushed back the hood of his foe's half-cloak, revealing a face that was far from human.

A silver beard tufted the chin of a long, narrow face topped with a crest or shock of stiff hair or . . . or something. Eyes as gold as a sun elf's bore slitted vertical pupils. It seemed as if a proud elf had tumbled into bed with a dragon and in time had somehow borne—this.

His gold-eyed foe also boasted things no elf had ever possessed: massive shoulders and faint silvery scales. The two bullyblades flanking him a respectful—cautious?—step behind looked human enough, but hardly more welcoming.

Oh, *naed.* Beldar gave them a bright smile and an airy wave—and spun around to sprint back to the hidden door.

He was through it in moments and racing back the way he'd come. There were crashings of shifting rubble under hurrying boots behind him.

Beldar half-ran and half-fell down the slippery stairs, shoulders and knees bouncing bruisingly off stone, and lurched to the waiting skull.

"Dathran," he gasped, scooping a handful of bloodstones onto the nose-ledge from his smaller purse, "I must consult with you—urgently!"

"So soon? Years steal memories and leave grayer men forgetting things and having to return. To see this in one so young and bold . . ."

Fortunately, the teeth-stones were moving during these mocking words. Beldar flung himself into the widening way and tumbled onto the rune-bedecked rugs of the witch's hearth-chamber. "Close the portal!"

The Dathran, imp alert on her shoulder, was staring past Beldar at his three onrushing pursuers.

"You bring these?" the crone snapped.

"Not by invitation," Beldar gasped. "I—"

As the three slayers dived into the room, rolling up into fighters' crouches, the Dathran calmly turned to touch a tapestry with a single murmured word. It promptly melted away into nothingness, revealing a shelf of human skulls.

Beldar snatched off his eyepatch and backed away as the three slayers advanced menacingly. The half-dragon thrust one of its swords through a belt loop and fumbled something small out of a belt-pouch, reaching back as if to slap it against the skull-wall.

The Dathran turned a cold smile upon the half-wyrm and folded her arms across her breast. Three skulls soared off the shelf behind her and raced across the room at the intruders. Flinching back, the dragonblood threw whatever it held at them.

Beldar dropped to the ground just before three bright, ear-splitting blasts rocked the room and flung him upright again, stumbling unsteadily amid swirling dust.

There were hoarse shouts of pain, a shriek, and the imp's shrill laughter. Then warmer light was blossoming somewhere in front of him, as the Dathran called, "Follow the light, Lord Roaringhorn. That way lies your safety. Go!"

Beldar staggered forward into fresh dustfalls, small stones stinging him as they plunged and bounced all around. He could see nothing but glowing dust, tapestries, and . . . a door.

Opening it, he stepped into quieter, damper darkness, and the faint privy-reek and stronger mold-stench that proclaimed "sewer" to any Waterdhavian.

An eerie chiming rose behind him, and with it came a blue-green radiance that swirled, clung to Beldar numbingly, and thrust him forward in a fell tide, shoving him along dark stone walls.

It released him suddenly, retreating to hang in a singing, seething cloud. Beldar whirled around to behold a blue-green mist that seemed studded with half-seen, gently drifting spikes and chains. A narrow face began to form in its roilings.

The half-dragon. Beldar drew his sword and thrust hard between those golden eyes, hoping to slay the dragonblood before it could fully regain solidity.

Frigid pain slammed up his arm into his chest, so sharp and searing that he fell. Beldar rolled away, fighting for breath—gods, the *cold!*—but his collapse had thankfully torn him free of the killing frost.

The strange mist drifted nearer. Floating in the glowing blue-green haze were three skulls, empty eyesockets glimmering in warning as their bony jaws moved in unison, and the Dathran's voice hissed, "Go fight your battles elsewhere, Lord Roaringhorn. When next you come, come alone!"

Beldar groaned at his own stupidity. No attack by the half-dragon, this, but one of the Dathran's wardspells.

He staggered to his feet and stumbled away into deeper darkness. Fumbling for his eyepatch, he found with relief that it still hung about his neck, but he didn't don it, for only his beholder eye could see in this gloom.

To its gaze, the pulsing ward was almost blinding, but even as he fought to clear his sight, Beldar saw something moving beyond its bright curve—something silver and scaled.

When the half-dragon came into clear view, one of its hands was empty. At least one dark bulk was bobbing along behind it. Beldar hissed a curse and turned away, seeking—

The first bright flash and roar almost lifted him off his feet, but he got turned around again in time to see the snarling half-wyrm swing the smoking, twisted stub of its sword at the second hurtling skull.

Steel shards clanged and sang off stone in all directions in the roiling heart of the blast that followed, and Beldar winced and shrank away as the third skull came flying out of the mist. The half-dragon hurled a dagger at it and flung itself back, crashing into the bladesman behind it. Beldar found himself seeking the floor, too, as—

The skull exploded.

The roar of its rending echoed strangely, making his ears ring, but nothing tore at Beldar this time, and he heard no cries of pain.

When he turned back to face the ward, it was pulsing as if nothing had befallen, and the portal behind it was gone. The Dathran had thrown them all out into the sewers to settle this on their own.

The half-dragon was already struggling to its—his?—feet, and Beldar strode forward and glared at the creature, closing his left eye in case this would help the beholder graft unleash its full power.

Beldar felt a strange warmth in his head, a dark stirring that flared into excitement, even hunger . . .

🏰 🏰 🏰 🏰 🏰

Elven magic was not alone in seeking Beldar Roaringhorn. Mrelder, Golskyn, and Hoth bent over a large scrying bowl, watching Beldar's attempt to use his beholder eye.

"He's a bold one, to hurl magic so soon after the graft," the priest said approvingly.

Stupid, more like. Mrelder knew better than to say those words aloud.

"Look at that magnificent creature," Golskyn breathed, his lone remaining human eye shining as he gazed at the half-dragon. "What a marvel. A natural melding of man and monster."

The epitome of your insane aspirations, his son thought silently.

"A good sign," the priest continued. "Waterdeep's future ruler has the sense to consort with superior beings. Very good."

And with those words Golskyn ambled away, not seeming to notice that the "magnificent creature" and "Waterdeep's future ruler" seemed bent upon mutual destruction.

His father, Mrelder concluded grimly, was utterly insane.

Glancing up from the bowl, he found himself looking into the eyes of Hoth and saw his own opinion of Golskyn mirrored there.

Hoth held his gaze, not in challenge but inquiry. He seemed to be waiting for something.

A moment later, Mrelder realized Golskyn's many-armed second-in-command was awaiting instructions. From *him!*

This had possibilities!

"This place isn't far," Mrelder said calmly, pointing into the bowl. "Take two men in all haste to help Lord Roaringhorn. If possible, retrieve the half-dragon alive. If we can't convert him, I'm sure we can find another use for him."

Hoth offered neither scorn nor argument. His nod was curt but respectful, and he turned and left the room at a run. The young sorcerer watched him go, feeling a smile slowly spreading across his own face.

♦ ♦ ♦ ♦ ♦

The half-dragon was on its feet with another blade in its grasp now, eyes glaring angry gold at Beldar as it strode to meet him.

Roaringhorn's new eye quivered, and the beast rocked back on its booted heels, grunting in pain. It had short, backswept silver horns instead of ears, Beldar saw, as it staggered under whatever wounding magic his eye had visited upon it.

Then it opened its jaws and spat at him—a white, frostlike roaring that sprang out, spreading swift and wide in a deadly racing chill that told Beldar all too painfully that he wasn't the only one able to unleash magic.

He flung himself back, ducking into a side-passage that reeked chokingly of human waste. Biting cold settled over him. A warding talisman an aunt had given him long ago crumbled to worthless powder all down his chest, and a gem adorning his belt shivered into fragments with what sounded eerily like a whimper. Cold gnawed at him like a small beast with many teeth as the half-wyrm and the other two bullyblades advanced again, blades out.

Slowly and warily they came on as Beldar winced at the chill still clinging to him and retreated reluctantly into the choking stench behind. He'd rather attack and meet his death with sword in hand, but wasn't certain his numbed fingers could hold a blade.

He was going to die here in the darkness, somewhere beneath the hurrying boots and rumbling cartwheels of unwitting, uncaring Waterdhavians. He'd go down, hacked and stabbed, destiny unfulfilled, not even knowing who'd ordered his death.

This was no chance encounter. Three slayers wouldn't simply find the alley leading to the Dathran's lair by chance. These were assassins sent for *him*.

Beldar smiled grimly. It was the first indication that his graft had resulted in a rise in his status. Cold comfort indeed!

His three pursuers were in the mouth of the passage now, crouching against the walls to shield themselves against any attack from him. They knew about his wounding eye, so there'd be no more surprises.

A door swung open almost beside his nose, startling him almost into heart-stop. Beldar sprang back, giving way to a tall and very wide man with shoulders almost as broad as the doorframe—and a familiar face.

Hoth of the Amalgamation was coming through the door with a hot shuttered dark-lantern in one hand and an iron staff bristling with vicious-looking spikes in the other. Judging from the sound of hurrying boots, he'd brought others with him.

Hoth looked at Beldar with something in his eyes that just might have been respect, and growled, "Stand aside, Lord Roaringhorn, and leave the vermin to us."

Beldar stumbled back to let the burly man stride past. Two men in leathers followed at his back, swords out. One of them had a wrist encircled by half a dozen coiling eels that held daggers ready in their jaws for the human hand to pluck and throw. The other had a forearm that bristled with a row of long, sharp fangs that lengthened as Beldar stared at them, sliding forward out of sheathing flesh in preparation for battle. The hand at the end of that wrist was no longer human, but a head-sized knob of bone studded with well-worn bony spurs, like a great mace.

The half-dragon stepped away from the passage wall and strode to meet Hoth, one of its hands reaching to pluck daggers from hidden sheaths as it came. The two humans moved, too, spreading wide to gain sword-room.

"Kill the humans," Hoth told the two Amalgamation believers. A thrown dagger flashed from the half-dragon's hand, and a swift movement of Hoth's dark-lantern sent it clanging aside.

Then Hoth tossed his lantern behind him. Beldar's jaw dropped in astonishment as it halted to hover in midair, casting its light over suddenly rushing men. Steel rang on steel, men snarled and grunted, and the sewer-passage was alive with blood and men seeking to spill it.

Beldar glared at the half-dragon again, seeking to harm it with his eye as he snatched out his sword, leaping high to avoid two rolling, struggling men—

Too high. Something cold and very, very hard slammed into his head, or he slammed into it, and all Faerûn went away into darkness amid a sudden, fading roar . . .

🏰 🏰 🏰 🏰 🏰

Beldar's neck ached, and there was a fire in his head that made him wince and groan whenever his boots came down just a trifle too hard on uneven cobbles. He had vague memories of finding a rusting ladder, shoving aside a rotting trapdoor that had spilled squeaking rats in all directions, and staggering through a warehouse that sported more of the same, to find himself in the lamplit darkness of last twilight.

Shortly after sunset, which meant his fellow Gemcloaks would be at the clubhouse.

Well, this wasn't going to be one of his more triumphal entries, to be sure. Setting his teeth against the pain, Beldar stumbled to the nearest street-moot and peered around, seeking landmarks. The city wall yonder meant that way was east, so the waulking-vat reek was coming from the north—which meant his destination couldn't be more than about three streets *that* way.

Not even Watchmen bothered him during his painful plod to the familiar guard and stair, so Beldar supposed he looked dirty and drunken enough to be mistaken for a true Dock Warder. He was well past caring. There'd be cold ale in the clubhouse, and if Korvaun was true to form, fresh cheese and meats, too.

He almost fell on the stairs but fetched up with a relieved sigh—

And froze, staring at the unexpected tableau.

His friends were at ease in the cozy lamplight, tankards in hand and platters of food in their laps, talking earnestly to two sisters who were becoming all too familiar.

"We *saw* nothing untoward," Starragar was saying with his usual sourness, "but that means little. For all we know, some of the rats might be spies for the Lords. We may all be marked right now! 'Tis not every day nobles take pleasure excursions into Dock Ward sewers!"

Which was when Naoni Dyre caught sight of Beldar, and her widening stare made every head in the room turn. Silence fell in an instant.

Naoni and her sister were cradling tankards and dining on lap-platters of cheese and fancy pickles, feet up on the footstools just like Beldar's fellow Gemcloaks. They were co-conspirators and trusted friends now, not awkward common lasses, all prim and glaring and scandalized. Well, at least they'd left their black-mailing servant-wench behind!

"Ale for a thirsty warrior," Beldar croaked, managing a smile and thanking Tymora to the depths of his heart that he'd remembered to put his eyepatch back on.

"Where've you been?" Starragar snapped.

Beldar's heart sank. Korvaun might still trust him, but the same could not be said of the others. Starragar and Roldo were regarding him grimly, and even the face of Taeros betrayed wariness.

"I've been strolling through sewers, not far from here," he replied lightly. "Can't you smell?"

"*You* certainly do," murmured Taeros.

"There you have it," Beldar said lightly, heartened by the familiarity of an acerbic Hawkwinter comment. "I took the dwarf's medallion to my spellhurler—to no avail, I might add—and ran into a bit of trouble on the way out: Three slayers after my head, one of them half a dragon by the looks of him. Others came, swords clashed, spells were hurled." He shrugged to indicate that it had all been a minor annoyance.

"So how," Starragar asked his tankard, "did the valiant but lone Lord Roaringhorn escape?"

Beldar grimaced. "In truth, I know not. At some point in the battle I hit my head. I was alone in the dark when I . . . woke up. I blundered around until I found a way up to the streets and got myself here as fast as I could. Not my finest foray, but there 'tis."

"Did any of the Watch see you?" Korvaun asked. "Or anyone who might be inclined to report this fray to them?" The Watch wouldn't look kindly on Gemcloaks sword-brawling, so soon after the street fight wherein Piergeiron had been wounded.

"I don't think so," Beldar replied, going to the ale-keg. "I didn't seek battle this night, and I doubt those who did are likely to air their business before magisters."

Korvaun frowned. "Why d'you think they came after you?"

"I don't know," the Roaringhorn replied wearily, discovering some cheese and his own great hunger in the same instant. "Truly." He munched, reached for the spigot, and asked, "So what befell, and what do we do next?"

The only reply he got was an uneasy silence.

"Friends," Beldar said grimly, hefting his tankard, "you were talking of such matters when I arrived. What god's stolen your tongues now?"

"We . . ." Taeros began, then fell silent again.

"We were down in the sewers, too," Starragar said. "Great spell-blasts, you said?"

"I did."

"We heard and felt nothing like that," Taeros said quietly.

A short, uncomfortable silence fell.

"There was a time," Beldar said softly, "when my friends the Gemcloaks would have unhesitatingly taken my word, a time not so long ago. Starragar, hand me your ring and let's be done with this."

"No," Korvaun said firmly. "Your word is good enough."

But the other three nobles neither nodded nor smiled.

The silence returned, and this time its weight was crushing.

CHAPTER TWENTY-THREE

Taeros sighed. "The slipshield's gone." Asper stiffened. He added hastily, "We think we know who has it."

Shapely eyebrows rose. "So get it back."

Korvaun winced. "That may be difficult. We believe it's now in the hands of Elaith Craulnober."

It was Asper's turn to wince. "I see. I quite see."

Her tone was dry and light, but her smile was wry, and concern stood in her eyes. "By and large, we leave the Serpent be. He conducts himself carefully, with an eye to not threatening governance of the city overmuch—and were we to eliminate him, the struggle to take his place would inevitably cause much bloodshed."

"We didn't come here to beg aid," Korvaun said quietly. "We consider this matter our responsibility, but if Taeros and I are to have any hopes of recovering the slipshield, we'll need help. To get it, I need you to relax my vow of silence, so I may share this secret with my lady. Naoni Dyre's a sorceress whose gift is to spin anything into thread. She does business with a gnome weaver in the Warrens, spinning precious stones into this." He patted his glittering cloak.

"A young woman carrying such treasures needs guarding. The halflings of the Warrens are as good as watchblades come, and have some swift fingers among them. The best hands to recover the slipshield are those of a thief. Am I right?"

"About most things, I'd wager," Korvaun murmured.

Her grin was impish. "Been talking to Mirt, have you? Lord Helmfast, you may tell your lady about the slipshield, swearing her first to the same oaths that bind you. I leave its recovery to you. Send swift word if the Serpent does anything . . . significant."

"Lady, we shall," Taeros replied. "Assuming, of course, we're still alive to do so."

☖ ☖ ☖ ☖ ☖

Korvaun and Naoni stood together in the moonlight, gazing up into the Moon Sphere with unseeing eyes.

At least a score of laughing, chattering revelers floated in its softly glowing haze. On the balcony overhanging it, a pair of well-oiled young tradesmen were playing tickle-slap with an equally inebriated lass. She bubbled false protests and delighted giggles as they tipped her over the rail, skirts flashing, into the globe. She plunged into the iridescent haze like a sea-diver, righted herself, and joined an ongoing, languorous midair dance.

"I can't *believe* this," Naoni murmured. "Never once has Lark stolen from us—not so much as a honey cake! Why would she lie about Lord Hawkwinter's charm?"

"She spoke truth, just not the whole truth. Betimes what's left unsaid means more than what's uttered."

Naoni gnawed on her lip. "I know of some suitable halflings. If you've coin enough, let's go hire them right now—one to follow Lark, the other Beldar."

"I do, and thank you. 'Tis vital we retrieve the slipshield before anyone learns its secrets."

Naoni set off at a brisk pace, and Korvaun fell into step beside her. After a few strides, she said wistfully, "I hope you're wrong about Lark."

"So do I," he replied.

And while we're hoping, he thought grimly, *let's hope all of Waterdeep's wrong about Elaith Craulnober.*

☖ ☖ ☖ ☖ ☖

Returning to The High House of Roaringhorn in his dirty, bloodied state had been surprisingly easy, once Beldar decided to swagger along with his sword half-drawn and his hand on its hilt. He'd greeted the curious stares of Watchmen and Roaringhorn servants alike with nods and grimly satisfied smiles, and passed on his way leaving them whispering and wondering.

In fact, *life* was surprisingly easy, he concluded grimly, when expectations were low. Men like him were a source of gossip and inconvenience. Fortunately, it was the nature of humankind that folk enjoyed the former sufficiently to consider the latter a fair price for their entertainment. The Watch would make inquiries into duels fought that night, and the House servants would inform the steward that some sort of financial amends would likely need to be made on the morrow. In short, business as bloody usual.

By the time Beldar reached his room, his head was throbbing, and the burning in his new eye made him long to tear it from his head. He ached all over, and no wonder. Each garment he shed revealed new bruises.

Gazing regretfully at his ever-handy decanters, Beldar went to one end of the sideboard, unlocked the hidden compartment there, and downed a healing potion.

It snatched away his headache in the time it took him to pad to his waiting bath. Ah, a long, warm soak! Sorbras was worth every last shiny dragon the Roaringhorns paid him . . .

The waters did nothing to ease his mind nor banish his restlessness, and Beldar lingered only long enough to scrub himself clean. Dripping his way back to his bedchamber, he found his bed far less inviting than he'd expected.

Bone-deep exhausted he might be, but something within him was driving him on; he *had* to be out there again, in the night.

Seeking . . . danger, perhaps. Well, hadn't Roaringhorns been famous battle-lions of old, and was he not a Roaringhorn? No battle was ever won, and no lands ruled, by a man languidly counting his bruises in a scented bath.

He'd need boots on his feet for the streets and something above them more suitable than an open-fronted, swirling chamber-robe.

Beldar padded barefoot to his robing-rooms.

He had no spell-spurning talisman to replace the one the half-dragon had destroyed, but he refilled his gem-pouch and selected his grandest "dashing yet refined bladesman of action" garb. Crimson shirt, breeches fashioned of red and black, black tunic ... the eyepatches he'd ordered had been delivered, and Beldar selected one that bore a stylized lightning bolt across its darkness. Dashingly overbold, but it suited his mood.

His gemcloak was as bright and unwrinkled as if he'd never worn it. Beldar settled it around his shoulders in all its ruby splendor. Folk were beginning to know him in the streets by its striking hue; the notoriety he'd long sought was his at last.

Yet notoriety was a poor substitute for destiny. Small wonder he'd snatched so eagerly at the first chance at fulfilling the Dathran's prophecy. He touched his eyepatch lightly; yes, he'd quite literally 'mingled himself with monsters.' The Dathran had promised such a mingling would be the beginning of his path to greatness. She'd also said he'd be a deathless warrior and a leader of men.

Beldar smiled grimly at his reflection in the tall robing room mirrors—a smile that froze when a grim thought smote him: The Dathran had said nothing about the *sort* of men he'd lead nor the nature of his great and unknown destiny. Did not scoundrels require leaders more than honest men? Had he taken his first step to lordship over rogues and villains?

Frowning, he swept down the back stairs and out into the street. He knew not what he sought, aside from trouble. He'd welcome another chance at that half-dragon—or Hoth, for that matter. And this time, he'd fight his own battle!

"I am Beldar Roaringhorn," he proclaimed in a self-mocking murmur as he turned a corner, hand on hilt, "and 'twere best, m'lord, if you feared me."

A Watchman lounging in the lee of a greathouse gate-pillar waiting for a certain personage to obligingly step out of that gate to be arrested, overheard that murmur, and rolled his eyes before carefully not smiling. Young idiot.

He would have been more than surprised to know that for all his grandly carefree air, Beldar Roaringhorn agreed with his assessment.

Not knowing this, the Watchman had to settle for being surprised to notice a halfling in leathers the hue of mottled gray stone—and with hair to match—stroll along the street after Beldar, pausing briefly here and there to admire carved faces on pillars and grand ornaments on iron gates, but glancing repeatedly at the young noble.

A bit old and small for a cudgel-thief. Ah, but perhaps the elder Roaringhorns had hired a "vigilant eye" to see where their young lance went and what he got up to . . . yes, that must be it.

It must be pleasant to have coins to waste on such matters. Heh, if *he* came into gold, he'd find better uses for it! Fine horses, hunting hounds, perhaps a lodge on the verges of Ardeepforest where he'd guest friends for days a-hunt and nights of loud, laughing revelry. Warm fires, games of dice and cards, plenty of sizzling roasts and cold ale to wash them down with—and pretty lasses to serve it all, aye!

He went on thinking such thoughts long after his memories of Beldar Roaringhorn's passage faded.

⚜ ⚜ ⚜ ⚜ ⚜

Sun or starlight, Waterdeep never slept. Beldar's aimless stroll had taken him into Castle Ward and past the Palace, where the hurrying throngs were always thickest. The streets were busier than usual, but as he turned into Sea Ward, he looked back, as was his wont, to admire the lamplit Palace, standing forth proudly from the rocky flank of Mount Waterdeep.

Descending its magnificent stone, his gaze fell upon a small, gray-clad figure. Nothing unusual about an aging halfling walking a street in Waterdeep; as Taeros never failed to observe, they were scarcely in *short supply*.

Ha ha. Yet when he turned a corner nigh Myarvan the Minstrel's gaudy mansion, glanced idly back again, and saw the same halfling, Beldar grew thoughtful.

He knew no hin personally—not beyond nodding and handing coins to those who worked in shops he frequented. Beldar was obviously armed and just as obviously young and strong, so no skulk-thief would think him easy prey.

Easily spotted, yes, and thus easily known. Moreover, known to the gossips of Waterdeep as an idle young blade, not the Roaringhorn heir, and hence worth no ransom, nor likely to be carrying *serious* coin. So this was a spy rather than a thief . . . but for whom? Who had reason to follow Beldar Roaringhorn?

Who but Golskyn of the Gods and his surly son?

Hmmm. The most likely culprits, yes, but they'd hire no halfling. Their sneak-eyes would be a human with some beast claw or tail hidden under-cloak.

Well, he'd take an unusual route and so make certain this was a spy.

Beldar turned onto one of the paths—stairs, actually—cut into the flank of the mountain, ascending to the City wall. Too narrow and windswept to be used by the Guard, who had their own tunnels inside the mountain, safe from winter sleet and summer storms, this sparsely lamplit way was mostly used by folk desiring to hold long conversations in relative privacy, such as shady traders and lovers. Thankfully, there seemed to be a shortage of both at the moment.

Perhaps a hundred steps up, Beldar stopped and looked back. The small gray figure was right behind him, hurrying now that concealment was impossible.

Beldar came back down the steps to meet his shadow. "You have business with me?"

The halfling's reply was to hurl a small cloth bag at Beldar's face—a bag that flew open as it came, spilling sand in a flurry intended to blind. Beldar leaped up and back, catching his heel on the next step and almost falling as he came down hard.

A second bag was already bursting blindingly across his gaze, its onrushing hurler behind it.

Beldar raced a few steps higher, whirled as he snatched down his eyepatch—and *glared* at the hin.

The running halfling faltered. Beldar drew his sword from its scabbard and took another careful step up and back, his eyes never leaving the halfling's face.

That face wore a deepening horror now, staring back at him with eyes going wild. Suddenly, the hin whirled to flee.

Beldar flung his sword under the blur of gray boots, and the little spy crashed to the steps, bouncing with a loud gasp.

Beldar sprang down the stair like a hungry wind. Before the hin could roll to its feet, the Roaringhorn seized a gray shoulder, clawed the winded spy over, and glared into the sharp-nosed, paling face.

A small hand tried to snatch at a belt-dagger, but Beldar was ready for that and slapped it away, hard.

Winds rose around them as the man and the halfling stared into each other's eyes—Beldar smiling grimly as the hungry warmth arose in him . . . and the halfling sagging into slack-jawed darkness as Beldar's beholder eye worked its wounding magic.

"Who are you working for?" Beldar snarled, pinning the spy against the steps and thrusting his head forward until their noses were almost touching. "What were you after? My life?"

"N-nay," the dying halfling whispered. "Something you stole, high and mighty lorrrr . . ."

That last word became a gurgling rattle, and the flickering light in those doomed eyes faded.

Leaving Beldar Roaringhorn holding a dead halfling on the side of Mount Waterdeep in a cold, rising breeze—and uncomfortably aware of the City Guard lookouts somewhere above and behind him and the watching city spread out below.

Stunned, Beldar cradled the body of the hin as if comforting a chilled friend.

He'd just murdered someone. In the space of a few breaths. A stranger, who didn't seem to be carrying anything more than two daggers—just small knives, for all their wicked sharpness. Someone trying to recover something he, Beldar, had stolen?

That made no sense. The gauth whose eye he now possessed was dead, sliced into dozens of bloody cantels to yield up eyes and innards to the Amalgamation. Beyond that, Beldar couldn't think of anything he'd taken, beyond a few kisses at the Slow Cheese, before . . .

Before everything had fallen, and Malark had died.

Beldar shivered and thrust the halfling away from him. Head lolling, the body started to topple. In sudden horror Beldar caught hold of it and arranged it hastily in a lounging position on the steps. The head lolled over again.

He put it back in a reasonably lifelike pose, and it slowly lolled to one side. Again.

Sickened, Beldar stood up, fetched his fallen sword, and hurried on up the steps, trembling in revulsion. He'd just done murder.

So swiftly, so *easily.*

"Gods," he whispered aloud to the wind, "what have I become?"

Behind and below him was a city full of mages and priests who could snatch secrets from the newly dead, Watchmen who arrested murdering young lords, and black-robed Magisters who pronounced sentence with the full force of Waterdeep's laws . . .

As he came up onto the City wall—deserted here, with no guardpost near—Beldar realized he'd been whispering his question over and over.

He clapped a hand to his beholder eye. It was magical—and all too powerful: Its wounding magic could slay. An appendage of *his*, now, and not the other way around.

Right?

It felt warm, and—though he knew this was impossible—*larger* than his entire head. Hastily Beldar slipped his eyepatch up into place.

The world seemed to shift slightly, some of the color going out of it. Beldar stumbled, reeled, and muttered, "What in the name of all the Watching Gods is *happening* to me?"

He strode a few paces, passing a dark dome beyond the battlements: the top of the great stone head of one of the Walking Statues of Waterdeep. It stood in its niche below the wall-walk, staring blindly out to sea.

Staring blindly. Beldar almost envied it.

Something warm and dangerous stirred behind his eyepatch. The dead hin would soon be found; he must get down off this wall in all haste.

No, that was craven ... unworthy. He'd done what he'd done, and must face the consequences.

But a fierce voice rose within him, filling his head and spilling out of his mouth. "Move," Beldar muttered. "Get you gone, idiot! *Move!*"

Just ahead, the next Walking Statue stirred.

Beldar's heart jumped. The Guard had seen his crime! They were causing the Statue to turn and smash him, right here!

"Turn around, blast it all!" he snarled. Must *run* ...

The Statue turned and settled back into its niche.

Beldar gaped.

Staring at it in bewilderment, he found himself wondering just what it was that looked *different* about this Statue.

Oh. This was the Sahuagin Statue.

He'd see its cruel, monstrous stone face more clearly if it turned a bit *that* way ...

Obediently, with a few grating sounds as it brushed against the mountainside, the titanic stone sahuagin turned to show him its profile.

For a long time Beldar Roaringhorn stood as still as the Statues along the wall he stood on, as the wind whistled past and chilled him thoroughly.

He'd become someone important, after all. The voice commanding the Walking Statues of Waterdeep was coming *from his own mind.*

CHAPTER TWENTY-FOUR

The sky was fading from black to sapphire as Elaith Craulnober strode up the mountainside, his mood as foul as the cold, damp seawind blowing into his face.

He was in *Waterdeep*, gods cry all! Not Evermeet, not even Suldanessellar. He should have no lord's duties here, not in this noisy, stinking pile of humans and their coins!

Yes, he'd been born noble and raised as a royal ward. Yes, he'd honed skills bright enough to merit command in the royal guard. *Yes*, he'd been betrothed to a princess of Evermeet—and yes, he was heir to the Craulnober moonblade.

There it all ended. Hadn't he done enough dark work by now to break with all of that?

It must be bred into his bones, this sense of duty. Why else would the slipshields trouble him? Amnestria's ring told him when and where they were used, and slipshield magic—*elven* magic—had recently been flitting about Waterdeep like starving will o' the wisps rushing to mass drowning.

Though it irked, a *few* humans could be trusted with such power: oh-so-noble Piergeiron, and even that fat blusterer Mirt. The moneylender might resemble a walrus and outmass a boar, but his wits were almost elder-elf shrewd. Almost.

But now the latest litter of untrained noble whelps held not one, but *two* slipshields. This was *intolerable*.

It was also dangerous. They were empty-wits, a flock of bright-feathered, squawking *goslings*, prancing about blithely and brainlessly unaware that one among them was running with foxes.

How such a reckless fool as Beldar Roaringhorn had managed to acquire a beholder's eye of wounding was bewildering, but whoever was behind that transformation had sent slayers to defend the witless Roaringhorn against the fangs of the Serpent.

That was *more* than intolerable. Tincheron had gone missing in that battle in Elaith's service, and half-dragons grew not on trees.

Some Craulnobers had been dragon-riders. Matings of dragon and rider brought instant shame, and any offspring were outcast. Elaith had only ever heard of one during his lifetime—the one he'd sought out and befriended, Tincheron. Their long seasons of working together had built Elaith's greatest treasure: trust.

Tincheron would be found, or avenged.

🏰　🏰　🏰　🏰　🏰

The young noble stood on the city wall gawking down at the Walking Statues like a raw country dullard seeing something larger than his own barn for the very first time.

Marvelous. Not only was young Roaringhorn a fool and a careless waster of magic—*really*, dispatching an aging halfling with wounding magic when a knife-thrust would do—but, judging by his slack-jawed stupor, he was also a drunkard.

"Lord Beldar," he snapped.

The human spun around. His uncovered left eye—the remaining human one—stared at Elaith alertly enough.

Good. Not drunk, and judging by his expression, sober enough to be insulted by anyone not a close friend using his title and his first name together.

"I am Lord Beldar Roaringhorn," the lordling replied with dignity, putting hand to hilt.

Another insult, but at least the lad had sense enough to know when he faced a foe. Elaith smiled. "Men of your birth are, in Waterdeep, necessarily men of business. I've a shared venture to propose."

Roaringhorn's visible eye narrowed. "I think not," he replied flatly. "Roaringhorn interests couldn't possibly coincide with *your* affairs."

"Words a trifle grand for one five generations removed from reavers and horse thieves, but let it pass. You've a problem, Beldar Roaringhorn, and I a solution. In exchange for it, there's a small service you could do me."

Remarkably, the noble was managing to school his face into unreadable calm. "What problem might that be?"

"Dead halflings litter the streets so, don't they?"

Beldar Roaringhorn smiled bitterly. "And for a price, you'd make one particular corpse disappear?"

Elaith had already made it vanish, but saw no need to say so. "In return, I ask only for information that might lead to the recovery of a servant of mine you recently met. A half-dragon."

"*You* set that ready-slayer on me? To what purpose?"

"Obviously not your demise." Elaith inspected his nails. "If I wanted you dead, I'd hardly be standing here enduring this fine weather and the pleasure of your company."

"I asked you a question!"

"I'd noticed as much," Elaith said smoothly, "but you've won time enough to consider my proposal. Have we a bargain?"

"We do not." Beldar gave Elaith a hard stare, proving he was either braver than most men or far more foolish. "What's done is done. I'll take responsibility for my deeds, but I'll make no further alliance with evil."

Elaith didn't bother to hide his amusement. It was rather gratifying to be so clearly and swiftly understood. Mildly entertaining, even, if not quite worth climbing all those steps.

"I did not fail to notice, young Lord Roaringhorn, that you spoke of '*further* alliance.' If you should find yourself too deeply mired in whatever evil you now enjoy, do not hesitate to call on me."

Beldar's mouth set in a thin line. "I thank you for your offer, Lord Craulnober, but I must decline."

The Serpent's reply was a small, slightly mocking bow followed by smooth departure.

The wind was rising as he hurried down the mountain. He might yet have use for young Roaringhorn, who seemed to be growing into the sort of human destined for great things—provided, of course, he didn't get himself killed first.

The boy had surprised him. He'd expected insults, and heard none. Nor had Roaringhorn tried to turn aside blame, seeming determined to face the consequences of slaying the halfling. The bleak determination to "do the right thing" was written across his face. Yes, Beldar Roaringhorn was that annoying collision of nobility and stupidity Elaith knew all too well.

Waterdeep held so human-gods-be-damned much of it.

☖ ☖ ☖ ☖ ☖

The Dyres' old red rooster was still lustily greeting the dawn as Lark hurried into the garden. His feathered harem fluttered to greet her, eager for their morningfeast.

Lark frowned as she flapped her skirts to chase them off. Naoni should have fed them and gathered the eggs by now. What had befallen *this* time?

She hastened into the kitchen to find Naoni on the floor, face in her hands and slender shoulders shaking. Faendra knelt beside her, arms wrapped comfortingly around her weeping sister, and a somber-faced halfling stood over them cradling a tankard of ale. Even in distress, Naoni was ever the hostess.

Faendra looked up at Lark, her blue eyes sharp, almost accusing. "One of Naoni's hin guards has gone missing. He'd been ... following someone. Beldar Roaringhorn."

"Mother of all gods," Lark murmured feelingly, going to her knees to clasp Naoni's hands. "Much as I dislike the man, I didn't think him the sort to do murder! I'm sorry, Mistress, truly. However this unfolds, 'twill be hard on Lord Korvaun."

"Harder still if Beldar's killed." Naoni's eyes filled again. "He shouldn't have struck you, Lark, but surely he doesn't deserve to *die* for it!"

Lark gaped at both sisters, stunned. "You think this is *my* doing?"

Naoni bit her lip. "I hardly know what to think. Jivin was following us. You told Faen our shadow would be seen to, and he was slain. Taeros hired an elf-maid to follow you, and she disappeared. Now this halfling."

"You're linking Lord Roaringhorn to me. Why?"

"Because of the charm belonging to Lord Taeros—the *missing* charm." Naoni sighed heavily. "You and Beldar saw it last, and each of you accuses the other of having it. We hired Warrens-folk to follow you both and recover it."

Lark turned sharply to the halfling. "The one following me—how fares he?"

"She's not yet attempted to retrieve the charm," the halfling told her, his voice surprisingly deep. "As of this foredawn, she's unhurt."

"Call her off," Lark said wildly. "For her life's sake, tell her to stay far from me!"

The halfling looked at Naoni, who nodded. He bowed his head, drained his tankard in one long gulp, and left without another word, hurrying.

Naoni reached for Lark's hand. "I think you've much to tell us."

Lark nodded unhappily, and began the story she'd hoped never to have to tell.

"I was born in Luskan, to a tavern wench. I never knew a father, and when I was young, I once asked my mother what he looked like. She said it was hard to know, as there's little to see when your skirts are thrown over your head."

Faendra winced. "Your mother was ... forced?"

"Paid is more like it," Lark said bitterly. "From birth, I was indentured to the tavernmaster. My mother owed him for her keep, as she downed more drink than she served and never won free of her debt. Not that she tried. She was well content with the place and her life, and had grown fond of some of her regular customers."

"Indentured," Naoni murmured, understanding dawning.

"In my twelfth winter I was told to take up my mother's debt ...and her duties. I'd cleaned and worked in the kitchen, all along, and never minded the work, but this other ..."

Lark stared into her memories, then tossed her head and said briskly, "I had no choice in matters and couldn't flee; my arm was branded with the inn's mark."

"So you always wear a ribbon," Faendra murmured.

"Any guardsman of Luskan, any seacaptain anywhere, and every caravan master headed to Luskan could return me for a reward—that'd be added to my indenture. I was determined to earn my way free, but my mother's debt had grown large. She died birthing another twelve-fathered bastard, but lingered long enough to need a healer. I had no love for her, but *couldn't* let her die untended. By the time they found someone who'd venture those rough streets, she was past healing, and the babe as well. Then there were burial costs . . ."

Lark dismissed memories with an impatient wave. "By then the debt was more than I could hope to pay. No matter how hard I worked, I'd never be more than a slave."

Faendra winced, and Naoni squeezed Lark's hand in silent sympathy.

"One night a young lordling came to the tavern. A half-ogre was with him, a beast dreaded across Luskan—but when coins're on the table, most tavernmasters care little for servants' safety. The wealthy lord paid for his companion's food and entertainment, and watched while the monster dragged me to the stairs."

Tears glimmered in Faendra's eyes.

Naoni had gone pale. "You needn't say more."

"Nay, the story turns brighter: Chance brought a paladin from Waterdeep through the doors just then. He slew the beast, asked the tavernmaster my debt, and handed over coin on the spot. We left that very night for Waterdeep."

Lark smiled faintly. "At first I thought he'd bought me for his own pleasure on the road south, but he understood nothing of what my life had been. Doubtless he thought he was rescuing a virtuous maiden." She frowned, and added wonderingly, "or perhaps he knew what I was and cared not."

"Texter!" Faendra exclaimed. "He you sent a message to, at the Serpent's revel!"

"Yes. I tried to repay him, but he refused my coins. I'll be beholden to no man, not even a good one, and told him so. Seeing I was steadfast in this, he asked me, in lieu of coin, to send him word whenever I saw possible danger to Waterdeep or its people."

Naoni frowned. "How does Elaith Craulnober come into this?"

Lark stared at her pleadingly. "Try to see things as I do, Mistress. I've ... known wealthy men, titled men, even a High Captain of Luskan, once. Under their finery, they're little different than the roughest sailor. Like men everywhere, the masked Lords of Waterdeep are—no better than they *have* to be. Elaith Craulnober went straight to the hiding-place where Texter had told me to hide my message, so I thought ..."

"He was a Lord of Waterdeep." Faendra concluded.

"Yes. I wondered if I'd been mistaken when Jivin was killed, but then, if your father's right, 'twould be a small matter for a Lord to order a man's death. I know Elaith's interested in the New Day; he's asked me about it."

Naoni caught her breath sharply. "What did you tell him?"

"Forgive me: That Master Dyre and his friends, like many old men, said much but did little."

"Words lead to deeds," Naoni said grimly. "The riot in the City of the Dead began with those old mens' words."

Faendra regarded Lark shrewdly. "You're not so loyal to Waterdeep—nor half so stupid!—that you'd do what the *Serpent* demands, just because you think he might be a Lord of Waterdeep. He knew your past and threatened to tell the city, losing you your employment here—and everywhere respectable. *That's* why you took the charm from Lord Taeros: The Serpent demanded it."

"Yes," Lark whispered miserably.

"Did you give it to him?" Naoni asked.

Lark pulled up her kirtle, clawed open the small cloth bag sewn to her shift, and handed the charm to her mistress.

Closing her fingers around it, Naoni gave Lark a long, level look. "You told us Beldar took it from you."

"He did."

"You also said you didn't have it!"

"I said it wasn't in my *belt-bag*, words as true now as when they were spoken." Lark sighed. "I beg pardon, Mistress, for deceiving you with ... truth untold."

Naoni shrugged. "Well, at least you didn't give it to The Serpent."

"I couldn't, not knowing for certain what it was or why he wanted it, so I had Lord Roaringhorn take me to a mage and pay for her seeking-spells. She found no magic in it at all."

Faendra frowned. "But why would he—"

She snapped her fingers. "*Beldar* was the wealthy young man in Luskan!"

"I hated him ... but have since come to know he never knowingly pandered for that beast. Please, let's speak of this no more. I want nothing more in my life than an end to all this."

"Gods willing, you'll have it," Naoni said briskly. "When the elf asks about this, tell him Taeros no longer has it, nor do you."

"And if he persists?"

Naoni looked down at what she held. "Tell him," she said slowly, "that the charm was taken from you by a metal worker, who made something else of it."

"Mistress, his magic will test my words for truth."

There was steel in Naoni's sudden smile. "True they will be! Faen, fetch me my spindle!"

🏰   🏰   🏰   🏰   🏰

Beldar stood in silence, staring at the stone skull. He wasn't sure what the old witch could do for him, but where else could he turn?

One of the teeth shifted. "Are you alone this time?" the Dathran asked coldly.

He touched his eyepatch. "No man or monster stands with me or follows me, as far as I know, yet I can't in all honor claim I'm truly alone."

"More puzzles you bring Dathran? Very well, so long as you also bring gems and gold."

Beldar shook his bag of gems, and the skull grated open.

Climbing into the room, he was surprised to find the Dathran already at work, settling a large, shallow bronze bowl onto a spiked iron tripod, and pouring dark fluid into it.

She looked up and made the usual demand: "Blood."

The Roaringhorn drew his dagger and carefully cut his forearm. As blood dripped into the scrying bowl, its surface began to roil and seethe. When the surface calmed, the Dathran leaned over it to peer intently into its depths.

A gout of steam burst from the bowl, scalding the old woman into staggering retreat. The steam darkened to smoke, and with horrified speed thickened into—

A pair of long, black tentacles!

One lashed out, snapping around the Dathran's throat with vicious force. She clawed at it, her fingers passing through it to leave bloody furrows in her own skin, and tried in vain to gurgle out a spell.

Beldar flung down his dagger, drew his sword, and swung it high overhead. He brought it down with all his strength behind it—straight through the tentacle as if he'd been slicing empty air, to strike sparks from the stone floor.

The tentacle undulated unharmed, the Dathran gagging.

The imp streaked off a shelf to pounce, shrieking and clawing. Its claws and fangs *could* find and harm the tentacle, slicing long, bloodless rents in the dark flesh. The imp sprang from the second tentacle to the first, slashing and gnawing in frenzy as the dark suppleness choked the Dathran.

That sinuous limb never slowed, dragging the witch toward the scrying bowl.

The second tentacle stabbed down—not at Beldar, but to flick the imp away. It spun into a hard, wet meeting with a wall and slid to the floor, spasming, to crouch hissing like an angry cat.

That tentacle darted menacingly at Beldar. He sprang aside, hefting his sword, but it swooped aside to dash the bowl off the tripod.

Dark fluid splashed in all directions, and the smoky tentacles thinned to the girth of ropes. Beldar hacked at one, but it curled away from him as the other tentacle hauled at the Dathran, hard. Snatched off her feet, the feebly struggling witch was jerked forward.

Her body struck the three iron spikes with a thick, wet rending thud, and rode them downward.

The tentacles collapsed into smoke. Wisps curled almost tauntingly around the twitching woman . . . and were gone.

It had all happened so *fast*. Beldar stared at down at what was left of the Dathran. Blood drenched the floor below the tripod, and the witch's flesh seemed to be *melting* away from the barbed spikes thrusting wetly up through her body.

A delighted cackle arose from the imp. It flapped unsteadily up from the floor to hover in front of Beldar.

"You've freed me from her service, so I don't suppose we'll meet again," it hissed. Then it leered, pointed at its right eye, and added, "And then again, we just might!"

It disappeared in a puff of stinking smoke, departing much faster than its parting chuckle.

Retrieving his dagger, Beldar clambered hastily through the skull, half-fearing it might start to close, and staggered away. Waterdeep held men who might help him without magic. Everyone knew of the barbers who sewed and slashed flesh in dark Dock Ward rooms, aiding—if that was the right word—those who spurned priestly prayers and couldn't afford potions. Surely one of them would be willing to free him from this abomination in his head!

If he died, what of it? It was becoming increasingly clear to Beldar Roaringhorn that his life was no longer his own.

⛫ ⛫ ⛫ ⛫ ⛫

The second bell past dawn was striking as Elaith Craulnober strode through the smoking ruins of what had been a barber's hovel and kicked aside the blasted, twisted thing that had been its owner.

The dead man's patient looked little better. A magical backlash had thrown him across the room before the Watchful Order's firequench spell had taken effect, and greasy soot from the barber's badly burned corpse had settled thickly over him. His eyes—the right one markedly larger than the left—were closed, but his chest was rising and falling shallowly. He was larger and heavier than the elf, but Elaith lifted him onto one shoulder with seeming effortlessness and carried him out onto the street.

A few curious onlookers saw the grim face of The Serpent and scattered like a flock of startled birds.

Elaith tossed a small glass vial to the cobbles. From its bursting spilled a glimmering liquid that promptly spread into a perfectly round puddle, which in turn birthed a rising cylinder of glittering motes. The elf stepped into it with his head-lolling burden and promptly vanished, taking all traces of his portal magic with him.

Handy things, jumpgates. Elaith's boot came down on the forehall tiles of one of his quieter Waterdeep houses.

An elf matron stared at her master and his burden and promptly hurried to a sweeping sculpture on a plinth. As Elaith dropped the scorched noble to the floor, she did something to its rainbow teardrops that made it chime and shift its outlines, offering her seven vials. Snatching several, she hastened to Elaith's side.

The Serpent had already gone to one knee and started to pry open Beldar Roaringhorn's jaws.

"Stupid, stubborn human," he murmured, as his housekeeper carefully emptied a vial into the opening he'd forced.

She studied the result calmly, poured two more potions after the first, and announced, "He's not swallowing."

Elaith promptly punched the handy Roaringhorn gut. Air wheezed out of the noble, potion dribbling from the sides of his mouth, but there came a rattling intake of air, and Beldar sat up, coughing and sputtering.

"He's supposed to swallow them, not breathe them in," the housekeeper pointed out.

Her master shrugged, rising from his heels in one swift, fluid movement. "He's alive—more or less. Argue not with success."

Beldar Roaringhorn writhed and spasmed, helpless racking coughs roaring out of him. When his agonies finally faded, he found himself looking at a patiently extended hand. A long-fingered, graceful, somewhat familiar hand.

He stared at it for a moment and then accepted it. With casual strength Elaith Craulnober pulled Beldar to his feet.

"The . . . barber?"

"Dead as last summer's hopes," Elaith replied, watching Beldar's shoulders slump and bleakness creep into the noble's eyes. "Care to reconsider my offer?"

"I seem bereft of options," the young Lord Roaringhorn observed. "What d'you want of me?"

Elaith pointed at Beldar's right eye. "Take me to whoever did that. I'll do the rest."

Beldar nodded. "When?"

"Immediately. They have one of my . . . companions."

The human studied Elaith's face. "The half-dragon. You're truly concerned about your underling."

"They cut up a beholder like cooks gleaning morsels for exotic dishes; do you imagine a half-dragon can expect a long and pleasant life in their hands?"

Beldar frowned. "I'll take you, and fight beside you as best I can, but you must understand that I'm not in full control of my actions. I might be forced to betray you."

The elf shrugged. "As long as you don't expect a similar confession from me, we're agreed."

Beldar's lips twitched.

Elaith smiled back. "Is there anything else I should know about you?"

"Yes," the youngest Lord Roaringhorn said grimly. "I require your promise that you'll kill me if I become a threat to innocent folk."

Elven eyebrows rose. "For a moment," Elaith said dryly, "I feared you might ask me to do something unpleasant."

⚜ ⚜ ⚜ ⚜ ⚜

The ringing in Beldar's ears became deafening ... and then faded. He swam up out of darkness and pain to find himself staring into the mismatched eyes of Golskyn's son.

"He's awake," Mrelder announced flatly.

Golskyn of the Gods bustled over, wild-eyed. Tentacles emerged from beneath his robes, curled about Beldar's waist and arms, and yanked the noble upright.

"Stand, as befitting Piergeiron's heir," the old man thundered.

Beldar looked inquiringly at Mrelder, who seemed the saner of the two.

"You've been granted an improvement because Lord Unity desires to place a puppet of the Amalgamation on the First Lord's throne," Mrelder said flatly. "As you've guessed, you won't be able to speak of this to anyone. You've already seen what results from any attempt to have the magic traced or the eye removed."

"This one betrayal will be pardoned," Golskyn added, "but the next will not. You destiny will soon be upon you. The gods have shown me the best time and place: Midsummer night, at the Purple Silks revel." Tentacles reared menacingly. "Accept this destiny, here and now, or it will pass to another. Do you take my meaning?"

The noble managed a nod. The priest dismissed him with a wave of tentacles, and Beldar all but ran from the building.

🔱 🔱 🔱 🔱 🔱

This one betrayal, the mad priest had said. What had happened? Where was Elaith Craulnober? Had the Amalgamation managed to slay the justly feared Serpent?

Beldar frowned, dodging through the street crowds. The shop wasn't far ahead ...

He vaguely remembered Elaith casting a spell on him that hadn't seemed to do anything but dull his thinking. Had it hidden his recollection of their agreement? Was The Serpent lurking, watching the monster-lovers right now?

There'd been no battle, as far as he could recall, no grand

confrontation between Elaith and Golskyn—and no sign of the half-dragon . . . or his recycled limbs.

Beldar winced and shook his head. First Lord of Waterdeep? Never in all his grandest fancies had he envisioned such a future, yet this ghastly parody of his dreams wasn't even slightly tempting.

★ ★ ★ ★ ★

In a dark tunnel, Elaith wiped blood from his blade and rose, his inquiries complete. It had taken more time than he'd expected to cut the truth from the massive, six-armed man who'd fought Tincheron, but it was good news.

Tincheron hadn't fallen into the hands of the Amalgamation, but escaped into the sewers. Golskyn's cultists were searching for him, but so now were Elaith's agents; they should find the half-dragon first.

Which meant Beldar Roaringhorn's tormentors would outlive this day after all. Lord Unity's spells and servitors were astonishingly strong: It had taken most of Elaith's ready magic just to shield himself from the mad priest's wards and seeking-spells.

The Serpent grimaced as he sheathed his sword. No triumph, but a clean escape.

He shrugged. Now that Tincheron's safety was no longer an immediate concern, it would be wasteful to slay any potentially useful players just yet—especially when they had such interesting abilities and ambitions.

Elaith smiled. Coins and power were nice, but increasingly he preferred something else: entertainment.

And whatever befell, the Amalgamation couldn't fail to offer that.

★ ★ ★ ★ ★

There were only two customers in the Old Xoblob Shop. A pair of boys of about thirteen winters were sniggering over their anticipations of how a lass would shriek when fanged rat skulls sprouted from her Midsummer flowers. Beldar sent the lads a glare that sent them hastening out of the shop.

Dandalus gave Beldar a level look. "Scaring off paying customers?"

In reply, Beldar pointed at the stuffed and mounted beholder overhead. "How'd you kill Xoblob?"

Dandalus stroked his chin. "Well now, it's been years... haven't minstrels sung a song or two about it?"

"I need truth, not tavern-tales! Is there a way to destroy a single eye without slaying the creature?"

"Aye, but you know the saying: if you're going to sword a king, best kill him in one thrust. Beholders are much the same."

Beldar turned his head so as not to wound the shopkeeper and tore off his eyepatch.

Dandalus regarded him in silence for a long time ere replying, "Aye, there's a potion that might do what you're after. Be warned: It'll burn like black dragon venom, and there's no certainty the beholder will survive his blinding."

"Understood," Beldar said crisply. "How much?"

Dandalus reached under the counter and produced a small crimson vial. "No charge. You've been a good customer."

Beldar's smile was wry. Such an elegant farewell.

🔺 🔺 🔺 🔺 🔺

Elaith Craulnober watched Beldar depart then turned from his hiding place among the jars of monster bits and pickled curiosities lining the shelf and slipped back through the crevice in the wall behind. Mouse-size made it easy to enter and leave many a building.

In the adjacent alley his tiny form expanded, flowing like smoke into his normal size. He nodded to a pair of burly laborers loitering nearby, and they pushed away from the wall they'd been leaning on and ambled off, following Lord Roaringhorn until the next team took over. Folk Elaith had followed were seldom aware of their watchers.

Beldar Roaringhorn was growing steadily more interesting. At first he'd been no more than the easiest route to reclaiming the slipshields held by the Gemcloaks, but now ...

He *had* tried to kill a certain notorious Serpent, but then most men—to say nothing of many elves—would do the same if given half a chance. And he was strong enough in mind and body to fight off the mind-numbing spell Elaith had cast in hope of breaking Golskyn's hold, and to be seeking his own death right now, to win free of his Amalgamation servitude—another stupid but noble human gesture.

It might still prove necessary to eliminate him, but Elaith liked to take the measure of those who crossed his path. Beldar Roaringhorn would be, at the very least, an interesting diversion.

First he had to keep the young fool from killing himself.

"Lord Roaringhorn," he called.

Beldar turned slowly to face him, his uncovered eye burning with cold fire. "I've heard elves measure time differently than men do, but is it common to wait until *after* a battle is over to honor an alliance?"

Elaith let the insult pass. "Your right arm—how fares the wound you took in the tunnels?"

The Roaringhorn stared at him for a long moment before reaching into the ornamental slashing of his upper sleeve to explore a shallow cut. His expression suggested he was just now feeling the sting of that injury.

"When? How ...?"

"Let's start with 'who' and 'why,' shall we? I dealt that scratch with a blade poisoned to numb into immobility. You seemed determined to kill me at the time, so it seemed a prudent tactic. Remember you nothing of the fray?"

"I led you to the Amalgation," Beldar said slowly. "Through the tunnels, to take them by surprise."

"As we did, though they were not nearly as surprised as I'd have liked. The spell I cast on you wasn't equal to your will—"

"Which in turn, fell before Golskyn's magic," Beldar remembered bitterly. After a frowning moment, he asked, "How fares the half-dragon?"

"He's back among friends. How fares your eye? You seemed in considerable pain."

The Roaringhorn smile was grim. "A faint shadow of things to come."

"The potion," Elaith said flatly, drawing a gasp of surprise from the noble. "A brave notion, but somewhat premature. Better to uncover all the mad priest's designs and shatter them and him together."

The lordling's face emptied of expression. "I'll think on your words, and I thank you for your council." He turned away.

Elaith glided forward to smoothly the noble's sleeve, and said quietly, "If you require assistance, you need look no further."

Eye to eye, they studied each other for a long moment.

"Your word on it?" Beldar asked, just as quietly.

"I swear upon my honor as a Lord of Evermeet." Elaith grew a wry smile. "And, apparently, of Waterdeep as well!"

🏰   🏰   🏰   🏰   🏰

Every noble house employed errand-runners, but Korvaun Helmfast was surprised, to say the least, to see the steward of Helmfast Hall—a man of such years that he was white-haired to the tips of his downdagger mustache—come puffing up to proffer a small, neatly folded square of parchment. Gilt-edged, which meant the writer of the note was noble.

"What's this, Thamdros?"

"The Lord Roaringhorn impressed me with the urgency of his missive," the steward wheezed, "and *urged* me to deliver it myself."

"*Urged* you?"

"With a sapphire, Lord. The smallest such I've yet seen, but it must have been worth a good hundred dragons. I refused it of *course,* my Lord."

The steward's mustache fairly quivered with indignation. No honorable servant would accept such a gift from a noble not of his household, for doing so implied he wasn't adequately paid—or worse, that he was untrustworthy. Thamdros was clearly offended by this breach of etiquette, and Korvaun promptly committed another: he clasped the old man's shoulder as one close friend might reassure another.

"Lord Roaringhorn knows your measure as well as I do, and I promise you he meant no offense. He was counting on your integrity to relay something he dared not entrust to paper. He knew you'd report his behavior to me, letting me know without dire words that matters are not as they should be."

The steward's face cleared, and he bowed. "Thank you, Lord."

Korvaun broke Beldar's seal, unfolded the note, and read: *Meet me within two bells at Tamsrin's? Firm friendship always.* Beldar's rune was scrawled below. Shaky handwriting, obviously scribbled in haste.

What *now?* Tamsrin's Thirst was as bright and busy a wine-and-chat bower as North Ward offered—far too crowded for conspiracies or dirty work. Too noisy and too plagued by the preeningly self-important for Korvaun's taste, but like everyone who dwelt north of Waterdeep Way, he knew where it was.

"Trouble, Lord?" Thamdros dared to ask.

Korvaun held out the note. It might be wise to have someone know his whereabouts.

"An invitation to wine and idle *chat?*" The old steward was indignant.

Korvaun smiled. "That I don't believe for a moment. I'd best go see what's on Lord Roaringhorn's mind. Perhaps this most important matter is happy news rather than grave. He might even have fallen prey to a lady's charms at last."

"If so," Thamdros observed sourly, "you'd do better to hasten to the lady's door and attempt to bring her to her senses." He promptly purpled in shame, clearly regretting that the words had ever left his mouth.

His jaw dropped open when Korvaun gave him a wide grin.

"Better yet, I'll introduce her to Lord Jardeth's new ladylove. Perhaps the gods will smile on two otherwise doomed ladies and bring them to their collective senses."

The aged steward emitted a swift, hard wheezing that might have been laughter. Korvaun waited long enough to be sure Thamdros wasn't choking or plunging into a fit and then broke into a run, dashing to answer Beldar's summons.

He smiled wistfully. *Just as in our days of yore.*

Just as things should *be.* Korvaun knew his friends were now looking his way for leadership, but in his mind, that mantle and a certain red gemcloak would ever be one and the same.

⚓ ⚓ ⚓ ⚓ ⚓

Tamsrin's was as crowded as always, both with chattering revelers and with all manner of ferns and hanging floral vines, dappled with sunlight falling through glass roof-tiles. Amid all the delighted shrieks and tipsy laughter, two men could have bellowed treason back and forth at each other without being overheard.

Silent gestures summoned wine, whereupon Beldar and Korvaun sipped, clinked glasses in salute, and bent their heads together over the table, sliding the inevitable basket of hot onion bread out of the way.

Before Korvaun could speak, Beldar tilted his glass of foaming firemint, inspecting its contents as if he'd never before tasted one of his favorite wines. A dollop of foam fell to the table. He swiped it flat, and casually began to draw in it with a forefinger.

Korvaun's eyes narrowed.

Beldar smiled a little sadly. "No fell magic. I'm still the Roarer who's led us all into . . ."

"So much trouble," Korvaun finished dryly, as Beldar realized where his own words were going and let them trail off.

"Yes, but let's permit the, ah, unfortunate wagers of yester-times be forgotten, shall we? Those horses might not have won, but some of them made excellent glue!"

Beldar went on to another weak jest, but Korvaun barely heard it. He was watching a Roaringhorn forefinger wandering idly through the puddle—and realizing what it was doing.

Sometimes boyhood codes can come in useful. Beldar chuckled loudly at his own joke, and Korvaun joined in with a grin, lifting his gaze long enough to give Beldar the slightest of nods. Then he raised his glass again, to make anyone watching think he was saluting the jest, and glanced down once more.

"*New eye under patch. Controlling me.*" Beldar's hand waved idly across the foamy puddle, sweeping away his writing.

"Hah! *I've* got one for *you!*" Korvaun announced delightedly, and leaned even closer. Nose to nose with Beldar and very curious as to what was lurking under the eyepatch so close to him, he murmured, "Who?"

"I can't say," Beldar said with a wide, false grin, "and I mean that quite literally: I cannot shape the right words."

As he spoke, he drew their private runes for, "*They're seeking next Piergeiron.*"

Korvaun reached for his own tallglass, deliberately jostling it so that some spilled onto the table. "We're going to need more wine soon," he said loudly, quickly finger-writing, "*Piergeiron ALIVE. Healing well!*"

Beldar sat back, slapping the table as if Korvaun had said something uproariously funny. "So I've heard, but who knows what to believe these days?"

"You'll hear even better tales at the Purple Silks revel," Korvaun said, trying to impart some important information of his own. "Everyone'll be there, even—"

"No, no, no!" Beldar interrupted loudly and delightedly, waving his hands in a wild caricature of a gossiping housewife. "*Don't* tell me!"

Then he leaned closer, offering his ear in broad parody of that delighted gossip, and wrote, "*Say nothing. Being listened to.*"

"*WHO listen?*" Korvaun wrote as he whispered some meaningless scandal. "*Whence came eye? Wizard?*"

Beldar roared with laughter and wrote: "*No. Beholder.*"

Korvaun felt his face change. He forced the horror from his eyes and levity into his voice. "What news of Roaringhorn acquisitions?" It was a standing joke that Beldar's elder male kin almost daily bought horses or small city shops—or tried to buy beautiful women. Yet even as he spoke, Korvaun winced. "Roaringhorn acquisitions," indeed!

Beldar's smile went wry. "My esteemed cousin acquired three this morn, I'm told, each crossing the finish line first. Impressive, until one heeds the gossip of disgruntled fillies claiming the future Roaringhorn patriarch confuses racing grounds with bedchambers."

"Far be it from us to spread gossip," Korvaun responded archly, lifting his tallglass.

"Far indeed."

They clinked glasses in an ironic toast, not incidentally spilling more foam, and sipped again.

Suddenly Beldar touched his eyepatch, and his face cleared. "They're gone for the moment, gods be praised," he muttered. "Doubtless driven off in sheer disgust. Now heed: I may not have time to repeat this."

Korvaun leaned close. "Speak!"

"Come to the revel, Gemcloaks all, ready for trouble: Real weapons, not fancy show-blades. Expect to fight men with monster claws and tentacles and such, two score or more, led by a mad priest who wants to put his own thrall on Piergeiron's throne: Me—did I not say he was mad? His son's a sorcerer, and they can move the Walking Statues to do their bidding. *Through me.*"

"*Marvelous,*" Korvaun replied loudly, slapping the table and sitting back as a serving lass saw the state of their glasses and hastened up with fresh wine. "Simply splendid!"

When she was gone, he hissed, "Beldar, we should tell the Palace at once! Piergeiron plans to attend the revel!"

"Tell them *what?* That I'm hearing voices? I'm sure they'll drop everything to listen to an idle young blade so *stupid* he'd allow his own right eye to be cut out of his head and a beholder eye enspelled into its place! Something that's strictly illegal, according to magisters' case-law, by the way. Did I mention that?"

"No."

"I suppose I also failed to mention the halfling I killed last night, when the eye was controlling me."

Korvaun stared at his friend. "Surely a mage or priest could prove your words true—and break this hold over you."

Beldar shook his head. "I've tried. A onetime witch of Rashemen lies dead not far from here, as does a barber whose only fault was greed. I'll not be responsible for more deaths. This is my fate, and I must put it right."

"We'll stand beside you, of course! Yet twoscore monster-men! What can our four swords—five if you can stand with us—do against such foes?"

"Little, but perhaps we can offer our assistance to someone with more experience in such matters."

"Oh? Who's this great champion?"

Beldar stiffened and grew a wide, sickly smile at the same time. "You'd *never* believe me!" he chortled, slapping the table.

The unseen listeners must have returned. Korvaun could not quite force a smile onto his own face as he downed his wine, rose, and said quietly, "There's no man alive I'd trust more than you."

And with a merry wave he turned away, letting his friend's unseen tormentors make of that what they would.

CHAPTER TWENTY-FIVE

'Lord and Lady Manthar," the doorwarden of the Purple Silks announced grandly, as that impeccably garbed couple swept imperiously past.

He blinked at the next pair stepping up to the threshold, winced visibly at what the male half of the couple whispered into his ear, and declaimed: "Delvur Morrowlyn, proud vendor of garderobe seats, with his, ah, bedmate Lahaezyl, twenty dragons per night!"

Delvur and Lahaezyl grinned broadly, clasped arms, and sailed into the waiting tumult every bit as serenely as had the Manthars.

There were some titters from folk waiting on the steps—those who weren't looking darkly scandalized—and one of them belonged to Lord Taeros Hawkwinter.

"My, but our hosts have fine senses of humor," he remarked to Korvaun, who stood just ahead of him with Naoni Dyre, as everyone ascended a step and the doorwarden made ready to announce Elphoros the Fishmonger and his fourth wife, Burdyl. "'The city entire' evidently means just that! This should be a Midsummer Eve to remember!"

"And just what," Lark inquired in a low but icy purr at his shoulder, "do you mean by that, *Lord* Hawkwinter?"

Taeros grinned into her glare almost fondly and murmured, "Ladylark, you *almost* behave as rudely as a noble. I'm looking forward to an evening of being raked by your verbal claws, but could you not at least wait for due cause? 'Tis more sporting that way."

"*Lark*," Naoni Dyre said quietly, before the servant could make any reply.

"Mistress," Lark responded stiffly.

"Gods deliver me," Roldo Thongolir murmured, staring up into the sky from the step below Lark and Taeros, where he stood with Faendra Dyre on his arm. His wife had crisply informed him he could attend the revel with anyone he desired to, but if it was going to daggers drawn all night, Roldo knew he'd be seeking solace in emptied goblets—*lots* of them—rather than enjoying dances—lots of *them*—with Faendra.

"How *common*," sighed Starragar's date, from the next step down, as they all moved up again. Phandelopae Melshimber was a distant cousin of her Waterdhavian kin, but her years as one of the most frigidly voluptuous beauties in all Athkatla had stolen nothing from her arresting looks and tall, spectacular carriage. Her gown was of the deepest black shimmerweave, her curves magnificent, and she drifted up the steps with deft grace despite wearing almost her own weight in glittering falls of precious gems.

Taeros enjoyed verbal fencing, but in his opinion the Gemcloaks should have left their ladies behind this night. None of them were trained fighters. Naoni had insisted that if trouble came, her sorcery might be needed. Lark had made no secret of her misgivings but insisted that where her mistresses went, she followed. Faendra hadn't shared her thoughts on the matter.

He glanced back at the younger Dyre sister. Her strawberry blonde mane fell in shining curls down a gown of shimmering sky-blue gemweave. Her benefactor for that costly fabric was Roldo; Sarintha had given her blessing, so long as *she* wasn't required to rub shoulders with Waterdeep's great unwashed. Roldo and Faendra seemed to share an easy affection that left Taeros frowning inwardly. He begrudged his friend no warmth and solace, but what of Faendra? What could this glittering evening be for her, but the beginning of certain heartache?

Then the doorwarden was announcing: "Lord Roldo Thongolir and his business partner, Mistress Faendra Dyre, of Faendra's Fine Gowns."

A smile of admiring relief spread across the Hawkwinter's face. Faendra had come to this revel to declare herself her *own* mistress, not Roldo's or anyone else's!

"She sewed her fingers raw to finish that gown in time," Lark murmured. "Judging by the envious eyes of all the fine ladies she's outshining, she'll have enough orders in a tenday to pay Lord Thongolir back with interest."

The Purple Silks—the largest and most exclusive festhall in North Ward—had been closed for a month in preparations for this night, but it had been only this morn when the invitations had gone out, borne all over the city by no less than the City Guard in full uniform. Everyone who was anyone—and many wealthy and influential commoners, for once, too—had been personally invited to a freecloak revel to celebrate "the return to health of our beloved Open Lord of Waterdeep, Piergeiron the Peerless."

'Freecloaks' had until recently been the exclusive conceit of the oldest, grandest noble houses of Waterdeep. At such an occasion, guests arrived and promenaded in whatever finery they preferred. Thereafter, those who desired to retired to private chambers, to assume costumes and masks under the ministrations of skilled dressers and tailors, that were worn to the last bell-chime of midnight. After the unmasking, until dawn, the Silks would quite likely host the most wanton revelry Waterdeep would see this season.

Wherefore the street was full, an orderly line of couples stretching back out of sight, reputedly halfway to Dock Ward. Some were here for the food and fine drink, some to gawk and gossip, some to see if rumors of wanton orgies were true, and undoubtedly a few were here to make grimly certain beyond any doubt, by hard and direct questioning if need be, that whatever Open Lord got paraded before them really *was* Piergeiron himself and not some luckless dupe cloaked in spell-guise.

No sooner had they stepped into the high-vaulted forehall than a serving-lass stopped beside Lark to whisper, "Is this . . . ?"

Lark nodded, rolling her eyes, and towed Taeros firmly away.

"What was that about?" he demanded.

"You're gaining a following among the serving women of Waterdeep. Some of their mistresses, too, I'll warrant."

"Well, naturally. Ah, could you be more specific?"

"*The Queen of the Forest*—your tale of the great tree spared because a woodsman loved its dryad. It's become a great favorite—I liked it myself. The end surprises, and tells truth about the treachery of love."

Taeros's stomach plunged in the general direction of his boots. "A favorite? One of my stories? But how—?"

"Crumpled parchments," Lark replied matter-of-factly. "A Hawkwinter maid found some of your discards and smoothed them out—parchment should never be *wasted*, Lord. She liked what she read and has been collecting them since, piecing together tales and passing them around. You could make an honest living with your quill, were you so inclined."

"All gods forbid!" he said, jesting to cover his embarrassment. "That sounds far too much like work."

"Hmmph," Lark replied.

Then they were in the main hall, and she said no more.

The floors and walls were of glossy-polished marble, the former expansive and the latter towering and draped in rich purple draperies, falls of gathered and pleated luxury larger than the sails of many of the ships currently crowded into Waterdeep's harbor.

Judging by the din and elbow-close crowding, all Waterdeep was here, talking and drinking excitedly in finery that bid fair to outshine many a royal court.

As the Gemcloaks swept forward with their ladies on their arms, Faendra was pleased to note how many heads turned to measure them. A fanfare drew her eye to a raised stage. On it stood Piergeiron himself, pale of face but as erect and tall as ever, clad in dazzling half-armor that shone with gems and glow-spells and undoubtedly with protective magics, too. Beside him, lounging with one elbow resting on the rather dubious charms of a carved mermaid statue that was slightly larger than life, was Mirt the Moneylender, in crimson silks hung with gaudy golden medals larger than his hairy fists. In the shadows not far behind the stage, slender and dark and half-smilingly watchful, stood Elaith Craulnober.

"He's here," Taeros murmured. "Let's hope Beldar's trust is well placed."

From the gasps and murmurs arising from behind them, it seemed others were far more alarmed—and, yes, scandalized—by the sight of the notorious Serpent than the Hawkwinter.

"Well!" One matron's voice cut through the chatter like a falling axe. "So 'tis true: they're letting just *anyone* in here!"

"That how you got in, Sharpfangs?" someone else drawled, and there were chuckles and titters amid the outraged feminine roaring that followed.

"Guildmasters!" an elderly voice quavered with indignation, on its way past. "*Tradesmen!* Has proud Waterdeep sunk so low? They'll be opening the doors to *sailors* next!"

After an initial admiring glance at the slender maidservant, clad in a simple black gown and free of all ornamentation but a single emerald ribbon bound high about her left sleeve, Taeros Hawkwinter had refrained from glancing at the Lark on his arm more than briefly. But he couldn't help but notice now how she stiffened beside him at the sight of Elaith Craulnober and how her hand tightened, just for a moment.

"Easy, lass," he murmured, as gently as he might soothe one of his falcons. "He's only one elf, and standing on the far side of two men who could best him in battle, either one."

Lark gave him a unreadable glance, then turned to take the tallglass of Midsummer wine a servant was offering her.

"Aha!" Roldo exclaimed. "Proper drinks! Delopae, are you going to—?"

"Balance two tallglasses on my bitebolds? I think not, Lord Thongolir—just as you obviously *think not!*" Phandelopae snapped.

"Though considering some of our fellow guests, such a show might meet with approval."

Whereupon Lord Starragar Jardath turned with a flourish and pressed his lips against hers, kissing Phandelopae into startled silence. Their clinch continued—as Faendra and then Naoni stared in astonishment—until the tall Athkatlan moaned and moved ardently against Starragar.

"Ah, the dour act melts them every time," Beldar Roaringhorn purred, stepping out of the crowd to run a teasing finger up the exposed and sleekly muscled Melshimber back as if her gown had been designed to lay it bare just for him. "Fair shine the Midsummer Moon on our meeting, friends! I see the fair Lark conquers all, as usual!"

"Well met, old friend," Korvaun Helmfast said firmly and heartily, reaching out an arm to embrace Beldar, who grinned, bowed floridly to Naoni, then rose to clasp Korvaun warmly.

"Full battle-steel this night, I see! The martial look—a fine choice!"

"We are ever tasteful," Taeros purred, winking. Faendra giggled, and a faint smile rose to Lark's lips. Still wearing it, she gave Lord Roaringhorn a firm nod.

He smiled and nodded back. "I hope we shall all have a chance to—but hark! Eleven bells already? I must pay my respects to our hosts without delay!"

"About our hosts," Roldo said suddenly. "What if someone decides to put a dagger through Piergeiron in all this rub-elbows chatter? Or Mirt, for that matter?"

"No fear," Korvaun said quietly. "Not until swords are out openly, at least. Look you behind Piergeiron."

"In the shadows?"

"Aye; what see you?"

Roldo peered, as Taeros accepted drinks for them all, and deftly snared a platter of fancy-fish from a passing servant.

"Someone . . . no, two heads. Men, sitting down."

"Not mere men: Madeiron Sunderstone, the Lord's Champion, and the other is Tarthus, Piergeiron's pet guardian wizard. Near as deadly as the Lord Mage Khelben himself, they say."

It was at that moment that Naoni Dyre drove a clawlike hand into her sister's leg. Faendra squealed, gave her a glare and then froze at the sight of her pale face and horrified stare, and reluctantly followed it.

Across the cavernous but crowded hall, resplendent in gaudy flame-orange silks that would have looked better on him if they'd been cut to fit or he'd been a bit less, as ladies were wont to say, "ample of haunch," Jarago Whaelshod was proudly escorting a lush beauty the Dyres knew was a highcoin lady from the Lasheira's Low Lamps festhall, because she frequently needed Faendra to repair torn gowns.

The master carter had stopped to display his nicely gowned ornament to . . . someone else strolled out of the way, and Naoni and Faendra gasped in unison: Karrak Lhamphur, in a green swallowtail jackcoat of great lushness, that made him seem to be an officer of some unknown but far-behind-the-times navy. Lhamphur, too, had brought a beautiful female along, but at least he'd had enough measure of honor to have it be his wife.

The two New Day members were not much more damaging to watching eyes than dozens of the wincingly clad, overexcited, ill-at-ease tradesmen here in the Silks this night, but they could hardly fail to recognize the two daughters of Varandros Dyre . . . and worse: if they'd been invited and had seen fit to attend, so too probably had the Shark of Stonemasons himself!

"Father!" Naoni gasped. "He *must* be here, somewhere!"

"Gods, what if he sees us?" Faendra wailed.

"What of it?" Korvaun asked quietly. "You're both among the brightest flowers in all this hall, and do him proud. Moreover, you're conducting yourselves as ladies—though, Faendra, might I warn that ladies *don't* squeal?—and we shall treat you with all chaste honor, wherefore he should see nothing to cause him complaint."

"Indeed," Roldo put in helpfully. "Just act and speak as if your father's standing right behind you, henceforth, and you should be fine."

Lark and Phandelopae Melshimber snorted in unison at these words and then gave each other challenging glares.

"The Mistresses Dyre are *greatly* comforted by your helpful suggestion, I'm sure," Taeros Hawkwinter observed sarcastically.

Naoni and Faendra exchanged unhappy glances, but they'd have been far more upset if they'd turned in just the right direction at that moment to peer into the laughing, chatting crowd, and so behold a particular face that had gone from ruddy to white in an instant, upon commencing to stare at *them*.

Varandros Dyre was extraordinarily uncomfortable in his hired finery—Gods above, why did these collars have to *itch* so?—and too hot besides . . . and this din was *deafening*.

Yet the drinks were free and potent—*firewine*, by the Altar, the best that had ever raged down his gullet!—he'd never tasted smallmeats so fine, and Nalys was even more beautiful than he'd paid her to be. Quite the actress she was being, too, looking and sounding the part of a fine lady. None of the overloud haughtiness of the real noblewomen he'd observed here thus far. His daughters would doubtless be disapproving, but blast it, a man has to—

His gaze, roving across the noisy tumult filling the vast, crowded hall, fixed upon a distant face.

And froze with a gut-dropping lurch.

Naoni! His Naoni, looking as serenely noble and as beautiful as—as any *ten* women here, by all the Watching Gods! And there—aye, his little Faen was right beside her, standing in a little cluster of the Gemcloaks. Faendra might have been her mother, come back to life, and Varandros felt his throat tightening.

Oh, Ilyndeira, if only you'd lived to see this . . .

He could not stop looking at his daughters. In, yes, in awe. When had they turned so *beautiful?*

Someone stepped into the way of his stare, pointing. "Who's that yonder—the incontinent dragon?"

"Lord Tesper? No, couldn't be! *What* a costume!"

"I know the lady with him, I do, but can't quite . . . well, we'll know at the unmasking."

"Yes! How soon—?"

The floor beneath the chatterers trembled briefly, and someone let out a startled shriek. Dyre frowned. Well, at least the disturbance had shifted them out of the way, so he could look at Naoni and Faendra again, but . . . this was a *big* building; it would take a lot to make it shiver so. A spell?

There was another brief, heavy shuddering, soundless but strong enough to make someone drop a platter and evoke several screams.

"What by the Nine *Hells*—?" a shipwright snapped, nearby, as the chatter turned to voices rising in alarm and query.

Up on the stage, Piergeiron had stepped back, looking even more pale, and Madeiron and the mage were on their feet, peering around watchfully. Magic started to twinkle in the air all around them, and Elaith stepped quickly away from it.

Varandros Dyre didn't see what was happening on the stage and could have cared less. *His daughters* were over there, and something was very wrong, and—and Nalys was plucking at his arm and murmuring, "Varandros? This is—not right, is it?"

"No," Dyre snarled unnecessarily, as the tremors acquired sound—a ponderous, heavy thudding—and rhythm. Boom. *Boom.* Again, and again, for all the world as if Mount Waterdeep had decided to get up and start walking nearer . . . and nearer . . .

"They're trying to kill us all!" the shipwright shouted, before Dyre could. Folk were screaming all over the hall now, and running this way and that. Grandly garbed men were cursing and peering around wildly, more than one spectacularly gowned woman was swooning theatrically, and servants all over the hall were turning and peering at the stage.

Varandros started across the hall toward his daughters, towing Nalys in a grip so hard that she gasped in pain, but she hurried with him rather than protesting.

He found himself looking at Elaith Craulnober, who'd just sipped some wine and lowered his tallglass unconcernedly. As the rhythmic, growing thunderings got louder and tapestries and hanging lamps started to sway, the Serpent looked up and out across the crowd, smiled, then nodded, slowly and deliberately.

Right in front of Dyre, a servant cast aside his tray of tall-glasses with a spectacular crash, tugged at the gold shoulder-braids of his jackcoat ... and drew forth a wicked-looking shortsword. Bending to draw a matching dagger from his boot, the platter-jack straightened with sharp warsteel in both hands and strode across the room.

Other servants were doing the same, everywhere in the hall, hurrying purposefully through the frightened crowd with drawn swords, converging on ... an archway in the wall a little way along from the stage.

Nalys had worked here at the Silks! Shaking her as if she were a dusty mop rather than a regal-looking woman, Varandros snarled, "Where's *that* lead?"

The screaming and the thunderous shakings were almost deafening now, but Nalys put her mouth to his ear and gasped, "The winecellars—and below that, the sewers!"

Dyre snarled something incoherent and furious and started racing through the crowd again, towing her along helplessly in his wake. Dust was falling in great drifts, now, and small fragments of ceiling were clattering down here and there. Everywhere, people were running, running ...

Boom. *BOOM.*

With a sudden, shattering roar, chunks of curved stone—ceiling-vaultings!—plummeted down to shatter on the hall floor.

"No!" Dyre roared, snatching up Nalys and starting to really run, lurching and pelting along. "No! *Not my daughters!*"

Then all was darkness and a flood of tumbling stone, and Varandros Dyre was dashed to the floor, dead or senseless. Nalys tumbled helplessly across spilled wine and shattered glass, seeing a pleasure-lass she vaguely knew beheaded in an instant by more falling stone. The headless body toppled and was promptly half-buried ... and then, though the shakings went on, the ceiling-falls abruptly stopped.

Nalys suspected that if she could somehow sweep aside all this choking dust and look up, she'd be seeing the star-filled night sky now, but she couldn't manage to do much more than roll over and wipe her streaming eyes and look along the floor in the direction they'd been hurrying, before . . . before . . .

Bodies were lying crumpled everywhere on it, amid scattered shards of stone. Not much had really fallen, it seemed, but folk were fleeing wildly, everywhere, and shouting from the walls—from the doors!—that they couldn't get out.

There were Dyre's daughters, looking terrified but standing unharmed, with the Gemcloaks holding them firmly. As Nalys watched, the young nobles drew their swords in flashing unison.

Boom.

Boom.

BOOM. *BOOM.*

Every thunderous impact made the Gemcloaks and their ladies sway, now, and cracks were opening here and there in the formerly flawless marble underfoot.

Naoni Dyre clutched the dagger Korvaun had given her in the City of the Dead and went a little pale as she saw Taeros calmly draw two smaller knives from his boots and pass one hilt-first to Faendra, who clutched it so hard her knuckles went white, and the other to Lark, who hefted it thoughtfully.

"Delopae?" Starragar snapped. "Are you—?"

"I'm *fine*, Lord Jardeth," the tall Melshimber noblewoman replied briskly, momentarily lifting her gown to reveal a total lack of undergarments—and a high-thigh sheath from which she calmly drew a dagger of wicked length.

Letting her skirts fall again, she hefted it and added, "Just fine, and ready to take care of myself—or rather, of all the rats Waterdeep may choose to send against me!"

"Oh," Taeros chuckled, as he as Korvaun watched a distant Beldar Roaringhorn salute them with drawn sword and then race into the winecellars, "our fair City of Splendors seldom has a shortage of those!"

CHAPTER TWENTY-SIX

'Tarry," Korvaun told Taeros firmly. "Beldar and his allies will tend to business below. Our task is to hold the portal if the fight goes badly, and keep the foe from gaining the hall."

🏰 🏰 🏰 🏰 🏰

"The roof is falling! The *ROOF! Get out of the hall!*"

"How the *tluin* d'you expect me to do that? The *tluining* doors are jammed! Just *look* at those splinters!"

BOOM.

"Go 'tother way, you fool! Up through there, into the feasting hall! Haven't you ever *been* here before?"

"No, Lord Anteos, I've *not!* Unlike some, I try to remain faithful to my wife!"

BOOM.

"Oh? So who's this on your arm, then, Brokengulf? Your long-lost daughter? In *that* dress? Ah, nice brighthelms, by the way, lass!"

BOOM.

The highcoin-lass in question had never much liked the blustering Lord Anteos or his glowerings of open disdain as he bruisingly handled her or her fellow lasses on his frequent visits to the Silks, so she contented herself with replying, "Why, *thank* you, discerning Lord!" as she plucked his ornate codpiece aside and lifted her leg in a whole-hearted kick up into the region thus revealed.

BOOM.

As the Purple Silks shook and shuddered around them, Lord Anteos emitted a chirp that might have impressed a giant canary and crashed to the floor, eyes bulging.

"And for your information, Anteos," the highcoin-lass told the agonized noble, as she tucked her charms back into the dress, "Lord Brokengulf hired me to dance with him this night—*just* dance! The gown tore when the ceiling came down and he tried to shield me—which is *far* more than you'd have done!"

BOOM.

"Ah—hem—yes," Brokengulf ventured hesitantly. "*Shall* we go into the feasting hall? I don't much like the look of what's left of yon ceiling, and . . ."

His hired escort gave him a bright smile and her arm. "I'd be delighted to accompany you into the feasting hall, Lord Brokengulf. Though we may have to go elsewhere to dance, after all."

"I—ah—yes!" the old noble agreed awkwardly, hurrying her away through the roiling dust as fresh fragments fell.

BOOM.

Not far away, in the midst of the Gemcloaks as they hastened over against a wall, Faendra was gasping, her voice on the tremulous edge of tears, "Can we get out? What's *causing* that? We're going to die, aren't we?"

BOOM.

"We all die sooner or later," Phandelopae Melshimber snapped, "but I'll be able to do so in much greater ease if you'd still your tongue for a breath or two! Let the men think!"

"Why the men?" Lark asked, her voice as sharp as the knife in her hand.

"Because they've probably been here before, Sweetness, and if they're like *my* kin, they'll know a few back ways out, that's why!"

BOOM.

"That's being caused by something striking the ground." Korvaun Helmfast peered into the dust that was all but hiding the rest of the hall from them now. "Something very large and heavy. And I'm afraid I know what it is. Beldar was right, and there's—"

"There's light yonder!" Roldo shouted, pointing. "That's the feasting hall. Let's get there! *Now!*"

BOOM. BOOM.

"Oh, I like *that* not," Starragar muttered, as they started to move along the wall, rubble shifting underfoot. "Whatever's causing that, 'tis getting worse."

BOOM.

BOOM. BOOM.

"Or there's *more* of whatever's causing it," Roldo offered, kicking fallen stone aside. "Some sound very close and others farther off."

"Come *on*," Starragar snapped. "The rest of the ceiling in here could come down any time."

BOOM. BOOM.

There was a shrieking, splintering crash somewhere overhead, and stones rained down in a thunderous torrent that thankfully shattered the floor into bouncing shards in a far corner of the vast hall.

BOOM.

"Where'd all the armed servants run off to?" Phandelopae asked. "And Beldar—what's *he* doing?"

"He's down in the sewers right now," Korvaun told her, "with all of Elaith's agents—the servants—fighting off some men who're trying to turn themselves into monsters and replace Piergeiron with a puppet Open Lord of their own right here this night. They intend to take over the city."

"Blast," Phandelopae swore. "I would have left this useless gown at home and brought my blades, if I'd known we were going to be—"

Lark opened her mouth to say something really rude and then closed it again and said nothing.

BOOM.

Korvaun, who was in the lead with Taeros just a stride behind him, staggered over some loose rubble and through the arch into a sudden bright absence of dust.

It was like stepping through a curtain.

Into bedlam.

On one side was all dust, falling stone and slumped bodies, and on the other: a grand hall free of dust and roof-falls but filled with a wild revel in full riot under the brilliant illumination of huge hanging glowlamps.

They halted at the entrance, staring around in disbelief.

"Behold Waterdeep gone mad!" murmured Roldo.

"Mind-magic," Taeros muttered. "It *has* to be."

The continuing thudding shook this new and only slightly smaller chamber, but their thunders were muffled and almost lost entirely in the din of all the shrieking, shouting, and crashing.

The Gemcloaks and their ladies stared around at three—no, four!—tiers of open, sculpt-fronted galleries rising to a lofty ceiling, surrounding rows and rows of glittering tables set with food and adorned with bubbling fountains of drink. The bell-like chiming of thousands of rattling tallglasses arranged around the fountains alone was hard on the ears.

In all directions, red-faced nobles and wealthy merchants were furiously wrestling with each other, monocles a-steam and jowls quivering. Some were waving toylike ceremonial swords at foes, and others were furiously chasing folk with evident intent to slay—at least as much as the intent of someone huffing and puffing and bellowing incoherently could be discerned.

There was no sign of Elaith Craulnober, but through an archway at the far end of the hall they could see the golden glimmer of a strong ward-spell, with the shadowy figures of Piergeiron, Madeiron Sunderstone, the wizard Tarthus, and a stout and ruffled someone who was probably Mirt the Moneylender just visible within it. Three of those four were standing and watching the chaos, but Piergeiron seemed to be slumped over in Madeiron's arms, senseless or worse.

Among the tables piled high with food and the fountains bubbling with sparkling drink, every noble seemed to be thinking—and shouting—that their various personal foes were attacking. They bellowed to absent bodyguards to rally around. If any message-magics were carrying these commands to distant ears, no one had yet responded.

Not that there was any shortage of violence. Some snarling carters, greengrocers, and carpenters were gleefully slugging noble teeth out of noble jaws and settling old scores with each other, as others scooped and gobbled handfuls of food, weirdly oblivious to the mayhem.

As Naoni and Faendra exchanged incredulous glances, someone running along a gallery leaped over its rail with a despairing cry. A bright, pursuing swordblade jabbed the air just behind his running legs.

Wailing, he plunged down through a glowlamp, which burst apart, scattering its magical radiance like a great shower of sparks, to crash onto a high-piled platter of sliced meat, and slither floorward in a greasy slide of meat, jelly, limply senseless noble, and ornamental rings of diced fruit.

Someone else shrieked in pain from the next gallery up, and a sword—with a severed hand still clutching it—spun out of the gallery-shadows, whirling down to its own smaller but still violent landing somewhere in the feast-spread.

Women could be heard sobbing and shrieking from under tables, and others were fleeing wildly around the hall—pursued, in many cases, by determined men.

"Lord Brokengulf, and Lady," Korvaun politely greeted the nearest noble, an astonished-looking older man who was shaking his head as he peered about, clasping a needle-like ceremonial sword uncertainly in one hand and the waist of a statuesque lady in the other. "Have you any idea what's caused . . . all this?"

"None at all, m'boy," Brokengulf snapped through lips that were thin with disapproval. "Folk seem to have taken leave of their senses, hey?"

As the quiverings and tremblings of the hall grew more frequent and severe, setting the glowlamps to swaying wildly, more folk shrieked and ran. A few strides from the Gemcloaks, a pair of gray-haired nobles faced off against each other with belt daggers, waving steel and shouting, until someone wearing a large sword thrust right through his body came hurtling over the edge of the nearest gallery to land in a loose-limbed crash atop a cart-sized platter of roast darfeather fowl in gravy.

The resulting splash blinded both nobles with gravy-spatterings that reached as far as the overlarge bodices of their wives, who were cowering under different nearby tables, watching.

Here and there about the galleries and under the tables were servants who hadn't joined in the rush to the cellars—maids and jacks evidently not in Elaith's pay—and they were all watching bright-eyed and grinning or applauding as the madness unfolded.

A roaring guildmaster—Azoulin Wolfwind of the Stationers—bounded up onto a table and proclaimed himself more than willing to sword any man within the walls who dared to challenge him, the first bellow of a rant that ended abruptly when someone shoved a halfling-sized flowerpot off a gallery railing above.

Wolfwind's heavy-as-a-grainsack collapse took down the table he was standing on, too, causing it to split in half.

Korvaun said briskly, "I know not what fell magic is causing this, but form a ring of steel, Gemcloaks. No one eat or drink *anything*—this madness might be born of a drug or poison."

"Gods, that's my *father*," Taeros gasped suddenly. "What's he—oh, Sweet Harbor, they're *all* here! All our parents; they all got invitations, didn't they?"

"And were told attendance would be considered their demonstration of loyalty to the Lords of Waterdeep," Roldo said, "or so said the invitation the Thongolirs received."

"I wonder," Korvaun murmured, "just who sent those invitations."

⚜ ⚜ ⚜ ⚜ ⚜

"Of course the beast-madness won't last forever," Golskyn told his son with an unlovely smile. "The spell's starting to fade now ... which should just give us time to find our next Lord and let the lad save the day. Hurry, before those Watchful Order fools realize something's wrong inside their precious strong-ward and know the Paladinson no longer commands the Statues!"

Mrelder listed to this spate of nonsense in grim silence. Did his father think Piergeiron's guards credited the *First Lord* with this destruction? Had Golskyn forgotten Piergeiron no longer had the Gorget? Or was he utterly beyond clear thought?

The priest chuckled, strode a few restless paces, and then wheeled around to cry, "Move, boy! *Move!* Deepnight falls, Midsummer's here, and our day is come at last!"

Then Lord Unity threw back his head and laughed wildly. His mirth was loud, long . . . and utterly insane.

Mrelder kept his face expressionless, trying not to shiver.

♦ ♦ ♦ ♦ ♦

The hall shook under ever-louder impacts, sending more flowerpots toppling from the galleries in a deadly rain. Many revelers were cowering under tables now or lying dead or senseless.

"This avails nothing," Starragar snapped. "Let's go hunt beastmen—after we find a way out of the hall and get the ladies to safety."

"No!" Four angry women cried as one.

"We're in this with you," Naoni added, "until the end for us all, if that's what the gods grant."

"Naoni," Korvaun said gently, "I don't think—"

"*Precisely.* If you did, you'd not speak such foolishness. Why would I want to be anywhere in all the city but beside you right now?"

Unexpectedly, it was Starragar who laughed and replied, "Why, indeed?"

"We've got to do something," Taeros muttered. "The longer this goes on, the more of our kin will get hurt—or worse."

The thunderous shakings were heavy enough now to throw some of the guests in the hall off their feet, and one of the drinks-fountains toppled over with a mighty crash. Starragar winced.

"That's a lot of good gullet-fire wasted," he murmured. "Whoever these beastmen are, they—Watching Gods Above, what's *that?*"

From the gallery just above them came an approaching series of heavy crashes, as if something wooden and very large was bouncing down stairs, toward—

"Come *on!*" Delopae snapped, bursting between Korvaun and Taeros and racing to the nearest ascending stair. Ornate wrought-iron clawed at her gown as she whirled around its spiral, and she impatiently tore herself free and ran on, the others at her heels.

They burst up onto a gallery littered with bodies lying slumped in dark pools of blood just in time to see what was descending so ponderously toward them: a wardrobe the size and height of four armored men abreast, its corners already battered to splinters, that was rolling and crashing its way down an openwork stair from the floor above.

The shudderings of the impacts outside the Purple Silks were magnified up on the galleries—the floors flexed visibly, and pillars and walls swayed. The Gemcloaks exchanged worried looks, spreading apart to let the wardrobe crash past, and Roldo spun around to shout down into the hall below, "Get back! *Get out of the way!*"

The wardrobe gained the bottom of the metal-shod stairs and sprang down onto the gallery with a crash that drove it deep into buckling floorboards—and buried it there, its ornate doors shattering and springing open.

Out through the greatsword-sized splinters and wood-shards spilled two limp, senseless bodies. The noble lass in the fine gown who was on the top of that ardent embrace was whimpering softly—but the gore-drenched, half-collapsed head of the lad in servants' livery beneath her lolled loosely, broken and forever silenced.

Faendra retched and turned hastily away—to find herself in the path of a tall, lurching nobleman who was feeling his way along the shuddering gallery, sword drawn and patrician face pinched with anger and disapproval.

"Young Helmfast and Hawkwinter, I see," he snarled, as he came closer. "Can't you striding young codpieces put your doxies behind you for even *one* night? Must you bring them here, to so soil our salute to Lord Piergeiron?"

He pointed with his sword at Faendra, and then at Naoni and Lark beyond her.

Taeros Hawkwinter stepped in front of them, gently striking aside that ornamental rapier with his own blade. "Lord Dezlentyr," he said firmly, "you are as mistaken as you are rude. I must demand a full apology, upon this instant, or your honor is forfeit."

The eyes of the patriarch of House Dezlentyr flashed fire, and he growled in disbelief. "Why, you young *pup!* D'you know who I am?"

Another thunderous impact made the gallery shake deafeningly around them, as if in reminder that family pride was far from the most urgent matter at hand.

"I know," Taeros said coldly, "that you're a bloated pig-bladder of a man whom someone should have let the air out of years ago!"

The Hawkwinter sword darted out, sending the patriarch's rapier clanging out and down into the hall—and then its flat struck Dezlentyr's broad rump, sending him staggering with a roar of pain.

He fetched up on against the gallery rail not far from Delopae Melshimber, who gave him a sweet smile, knelt before him as he sneered uncertainly at her—and then caught hold of both his legs under his knees and thrust him up and over the rail.

Lord Dezlentyr's landing was marked by a satisfying crash of rending wood, as he demolished no less than three chairs ... and in its wake the Gemcloaks and their ladies became aware something had changed in the hall.

Thunderous impacts were still shaking the great chamber—more and more loudly, as boards and ceiling-tiles fell—but the fighting, shouts, and capering had died away, leaving bewildered faces everywhere. It was as if folk were awakening from a dream—or a mind-magic that had seized them all.

"W-what befell?" a graying merchant in rich emerald silks asked roughly, staring at the blood all over his hands. None of it was his own.

A noble lying under the sprawled bodies of two others asked weakly, "I—is it time for the unmasking yet?"

The Gemcloaks and their ladies traded frowning glances.

"Is it time for the unmasking yet?" the noble asked no one in particular again.

Someone burst into sobs as they discovered someone dear to them messily dead. Everywhere bewildered folk in bedraggled finery were emerging from under tables and behind tapestries, to mill around and stare at each other, asking what had happened.

"Is it time for the unmasking yet?" an unregarded voice demanded dazedly.

Beyond them, the golden radiance of the shielding-spell grew brighter. Piergeiron, the Open Lord of Waterdeep, was striding unsteadily into the room, leaning on the mighty strength of Madeiron Sunderstone. The dark-robed wizard Tarthus and the flopping-booted Mirt the Moneylender came in their wake.

"Nobles of Waterdeep!" Piergeiron called, his magnificent voice rolling out across the hall. "The city needs your valor and your blades! Great evil attacks Waterdeep from below!"

"Is it time for the unmasking yet?" the quavering voice asked no one again.

"*Yes!*" Piergeiron roared. "Arise, just as you are—fancy-costumes, finery and all—and go out through yon arch into the other hall and down into the winecellars! For your proud names and your forefathers, strike hard and strike true! Smite and slay those you know not, who seek to ascend into this hall and slaughter us all!"

The nobles stared at the Open Lord, as the pale-faced Paladinson drew his own sword. The shielding-spell made it flare golden as he swung it on high and cried, "For Waterdeep!"

All over the hall, monocles dangling on ribbons and faces flushed, old Lords of Waterdeep brandished their own blades, or belt-knives, or chair legs and roared back, "*For Waterdeep!*"

Lord Brokengulf was the first to start running, his hired lass sprinting along at his side with his dagger flashing ready in her hand . . . and then all the nobles were hurrying, men and women both, roaring wordlessly and awakening glow-spells on blades as they went, racing out into the other hall in a howling stream.

"How does he know foes of the city are attacking?" Naoni demanded with a frown. "You said Beldar didn't warn—"

"Mayhap someone else did," Korvaun replied. "Or perhaps no warning was needed. I doubt yon shielding stops Tarthus from hearing the spell-sent words of other Watchful Order wizards. They always work scrying magics when the Open Lord appears in public, and no doubt saw something sinister."

"Speaking of which ..." Delopae Melshimber said urgently, pointing across the hall at the gallery above theirs.

Flame had just blossomed there, spitting from a torch held high by a familiar figure leaning over its rail. The elf all Waterdeep called the Serpent pointed at the last of the disappearing nobles and then spread his hands and addressed those still in the hall, uncertainly hefting belt-knives and swords of their own. "The hall trembles ever-more-perilously around us! And behold: The fine Lords of Waterdeep all flee into the wine cellars, whilst we remain here. What do they know that we don't?"

There was a silken edge to the Serpent's voice that suggested magical persuasion was at work—powerful magic, judging from the chorus of angry and frightened yells that rose in response, and the general stampede after the nobles.

The wizard Tarthus glared up at Elaith Craulnober, but he merely smiled, stepped back into darkness, and vanished—as another thunderous crash shook the hall.

"The hall's coming down," Korvaun said in sudden understanding, "and the elf, bless his black heart, is getting the people out!"

A fierce grin engulfed Taeros's face. "Then it's the tunnels for us, after all."

They worked their way swiftly through the chaos. The stream of running tradesmen and crafters was melting to a trickle, leaving a handful of revelers whose avarice was more powerful than Elaith's compulsion. Greedy hands plucked swords and daggers and gems from those who'd never need them again.

Then Faendra Dyre stiffened and cried, *"Father!"*

The man who'd just come staggering out of the dust-filled archway into the other hall was dazed, his face covered with lines of dusty blood, and he did not seem to hear her. Yet under the stone-dust that made him almost entirely gray-white, it was Varandros Dyre clearly enough.

"Come *on*," she said, in a voice that was almost a sob, and flung herself at the stairs back down out of the gallery. The others exchanged dismayed glances and followed her.

"Dyre! What happened to you?" Jarago Whaelshod rose from snatching a dagger out of a sprawled noble's sheath and blinked at the stonemason.

Karrak Lhamphur was hastening down the hall with two swords in his hands to join them and the words, "Who's this?"

'This' was the highcoin-lass Nalys, a lit lantern in her hand and a worried frown on her face, stepping out of the dust to seek Varandros. He wheeled around, embraced her with a fierce grin, and growled, "Lead us, gel! The winecellars!"

She nodded, smiled, turned—and the three New Day stalwarts plunged into the swirling dust a pace ahead of Faendra's rush across the hall and shouts of, "Father! *Father!*"

A fresh booming swallowed her cries, and with an ear-splitting crash brought down the uppermost gallery onto the one below, all along one side of the feasting hall.

The wizard Tarthus shouted something to Madeiron. The Lord's Champion snatched up Piergeiron as if he was an infant rather than a tall and well-muscled man, and hurried back through the arch with Mirt and Tarthus close behind.

And the dust swallowed them.

🏰 🏰 🏰 🏰 🏰

The smiling weaponmaster stepped away from the sewer-wall he'd been leaning against.

"Here we stand, all mustered as the Master commanded! And may I add my pleasure at hearing of your safe recovery, Tincheron. The Master can call on powerful healing."

Golden eyes remained cold, and massive silver-scaled shoulders lifted in a shrug. "Indeed," the half-dragon said curtly. "You know your orders?"

"Hunt down and slay every monster-man we see. Otherwise, butcher older nobles and *all* guards wearing the livery of noble houses. No heirs, and no servants."

"Correct. As we're being so talkative, Lurlar, know that Lord Craulnober doesn't want the noble houses destroyed, only weakened. Younger nobles are far more . . . pliable."

"Corruptible," sneered one of the roughblades Lurlar had mustered.

"So we're not murdering nobles," Lurlar offered, "but ah, *pruning* them—gardener-like."

"Precisely. Come, efficient gardeners!"

⛫   ⛫   ⛫   ⛫   ⛫

Beldar Roaringhorn ducked around a pillar and drove his blade into the throat of a man who had horns like a bull thrusting straight forward from his temples.

With a bubbling roar of agony, the man spewed blood and went down. A torch guttered out nearby, plunging that part of the sewers into near-darkness. Everywhere men were running and stamping and grunting, and steel was skirling on warsteel. Off to the left, lamps bobbed wildly, and all around Beldar, men who were part monster were rushing and pouncing. As he watched, one stepped from pillar-shadows Beldar would have sworn were deserted and slapped a tentacle around a noble's neck, twisting with brutal force.

The old lord—Beldar didn't recognize him; probably a drone-uncle like Beldar himself might become, if he ever lived so long, not that the gods were likely to grant *that*—died in a red-faced, eye-bulging instant. Two monster-men swarmed the body for knives and coins almost before it hit the floor.

A blade thrust past Beldar's shoulder, so close that he heard the cloth of his tunic whisper as it was cut. Then something that looked like the maw of a lamprey spiraled at his face. . . and he was fighting for his life. Again.

Blood was everywhere underfoot, slick and slippery, and the bodies were—

Naoni tripped over huddled death for perhaps the twelfth time, stumbled, and fetched up bruisingly against a wall. Everywhere men were crossing swords in these tunnels, shrieking, shouting and dying, and there was no sign of Father or those who'd been with him, lost in the wild rush from the feasting hall down into these tunnels. Faendra was streaming silent tears but kept her lower lip firmly between her teeth to keep back her sobs —and held her dagger out and ready.

The dull, rolling boomings went on, slower and more ponderous, but showers of dust and grit fell at every echoing impact. Torches and lanterns flickered here and there in the gloom, and spell-glows of magical weapons flashed where stronger lights had failed.

They were in a warren of intersecting tunnels, the wine racks far behind. The Gemcloaks kept close together, fighting off nobles, frightened merchants, and what seemed like half the thieves in Dock Ward. The vicious half.

A man lunged out of a side way to topple a barrel, sending apples rolling underfoot. Korvaun and Taeros both flailed arms, cursed, and fell.

The man sprang forward, extending impossibly long arms. The fingers of his hands became long, slender biting snakes. One almost sank its fangs in Faendra's face but bit only hair as she shrieked and ducked away. Another struck at Lark's cheek, but Delopae's wicked dagger reached out of nowhere to slice away its tongue and part of its snout, trailing blood and venom, and the man roared in pain.

A moment later, Roldo and Starragar had ducked under those snake arms and buried their blades in the monster-man's ribs. He sagged to the unseen floor, sobbing and gurgling.

Naoni stumbled on rolling apples, went to her knees, and down the passage saw a cloak catch fire from a torch. It flared up brightly, casting light across a face she knew. "Baraezym!"

As he drove his belt-dagger deep into the burning man's throat, her father's surviving apprentice heard her and peered toward her in astonishment.

Two creatures who seemed more wolf than man, but with large crab-pincers instead of paws, promptly burst out of another passage and pounced on him.

"Get to Baraezym! *Save him!*" Naoni shouted, pointing, and Starragar ran past her, wincing as he crushed an apple underfoot and wrenched his ankle in the doing, and sprinted down the passage. Taeros scrambled up and after him, running hard.

"Faen?" Naoni gasped. "Are you—?"

Her words were lost in the sudden roaring charge of a man who came out of the darkness behind her, slashing at her with one long, furry arm that had the claws of a great bear.

Naoni and Faendra screamed as Korvaun slashed furiously from his knees, forcing the bear-man into a twisting sideways hop just as Lark sprang past, dagger flashing.

Throat laid open, the bear-man gurgled, staggered, raked the wall vainly with his claws . . . and died.

Fresh screams erupted down the tunnel, and someone far off shouted the name of a noble house like a battle-cry.

Then Korvaun roared in pain, steel clanged on steel very close by, and Naoni flung herself away and rolled in blood and apples, to come up facing—

Roldo Thongolir and Lark, furiously stabbing a man who looked like any back alley sneak-thief—except that rows of fanged mouths adorned both his bared forearms.

"All right back there?" Taeros called.

Lark turned with thief-blood all over her face, stepping back to let the dying man fall, and panted, "We'll live, Lord Hawkwinter. How fare you?"

"We've got Baraezym, but he's hurt. Starragar saw Karrak Lhamphur, alone and running *that* way."

"That" way was unknowable in the ill-lit gloom, of course, and Naoni found Faendra and clung to her as Korvaun and Taeros met and clasped hands, both breathing hard.

"All well?" Starragar inquired, half-carrying a stumbling Baraezym.

"Fighting is brisk," Phandelopae Melshimber replied almost proudly. "Any sign of Master Dyre? Or of any end to this foolishness?"

Her only answer was the approaching wail of a red-faced, portly noble, running for all he was worth. Four men in the dark breeches and jackcoats of Purple Silks servants were chasing him, long knives in their hands.

Another noble stumbled out of a side-passage with his own dark-coated pursuers close behind. The first lord burst right through the Gemcloaks, sobbing in despair—and Korvaun and Taeros closed together in his wake to meet the darkcoats with ready swords.

The next few breaths were frantic and bloody, with Taeros shouting in pain from sliced knuckles, a jackcoat sobbing as Korvaun ran him through, and steel striking against steel savagely enough to send sparks flying.

A jackcoat fell and rolled in under Taeros, seeking to topple him for easy stabbing. The Hawkwinter came down hard, but Lark jumped onto the thief's knife-wrist, and it was Taeros who struck first.

The man convulsed and sagged, dead or dying, and Roldo Thongolir bounded over him at the next jackcoat, whose blade was reaching for Taeros. The man struck aside Roldo's arm and blade with one hand and stabbed at Roldo's face with the other, slashing mainly hair and scalp as Roldo twisted desperately, knowing he was doomed to take the backslash.

Lark hurled herself feet-first into the jackcoat's chest, spinning him away. As she fell on Roldo, Taeros surged up to stand over them and drive back the *next* jackcoat.

Just behind them, Naoni screamed as a dagger slashed viciously through her sleeve. Her attacker had slipped around the fray, and was now stumbling helplessly forward as Faendra rolled hard into his shins. He grabbed Naoni's shoulder and dragged her down with him, hard, and then stabbed—

Nothing, as Delopae's knife caught his and held it, quavering, for just long enough as the noblewoman landed on him, for Lark to come scrambling over apples back to the man and sink her knife into his left eye.

Quite suddenly, jackcoats were fleeing into the gloom and there was no one left to fight. The Gemcloaks and their four revel-dates gasped and panted in the gloom, staring at each other.

"Well," Korvaun gasped, finding breath, "that was ... impressive. Lark, remind me never to stand against you in battle."

"Aye," Starragar agreed, "Well done, Lark and all of you. Quite the warriors ... we all are, coming to that. How many—"

"We can count the dead later," Faendra told him fiercely. "I want to find my father and get him safely out of all this. Is anyone hurt?"

"If someone'll bind my ready-cloth around my fingers," Taeros panted, "I'm good to go on."

Baraezym screamed suddenly. Roldo and Starragar cursed and flung themselves toward him—in time for Varandros Dyre's last apprentice to bounce limply at their feet and his slayers stalk forward over his body, advancing to attack.

There were two of them, misshapen nightmares of horns, jaws and great bone-hook talons, far more monsters than men. Roldo's sword broke in his first angry slash, and a talon tore open his tunic and sent him reeling. Both beasts reached for Starragar, and Taeros and Korvaun sprang hastily forward, swords flashing, only to fall in unison as a snakelike tail lashed across their ankles.

One beast sprang over them, pouncing on the lantern Naoni was trying to re-light, and as she screamed and talons lashed at her face, Lark Evenmoon leaped in to hack them aside.

The creature squalled in rage and pain, stabbing down with its great bone-hook at Lark's unprotected side.

A tall, dark-gowned figure flung herself out of the gloom to shield Lark, taking that fearsome thrust through her own flank with a groan.

Writhing in agony, Phandelopae Melshimber struck at her slayer with her dagger—wild slashes that sliced only air.

Two swords, thrust with all the snarling strength Korvaun and Taeros could put behind them, burst *through* the monster's shaggy breast and struck sparks when they clashed together. Lantern-oil that had spilled on Baraezym's body flared into dancing life and Roldo and Starragar could see to hack the other beast down.

Starragar let out a scream of his own as he saw the bloody bone-hook drawn out of Delopae and flung down his blade in wild and clawing haste to get to her. "I—are—"

Phandelopae Melshimber struggled to speak, her eyes fierce, but all that came out of her lips was blood. She lifted a hand, trying to clasp Starragar as he cradled her and sobbed, "I should never have asked you here this night! Delopae! I should never ..."

Quite suddenly, the light in her eyes went out and her wavering hand fell back.

Starragar Jardeth burst into tears—and horrified glances were exchanged above him as their black-clad friend sobbed over a corpse—by the light of another one, now burning in earnest.

⚜ ⚜ ⚜ ⚜ ⚜

Beldar Roaringhorn was tired of hearing death-screams and heartily sick of fighting down the urge that raged in him, telling him to run, to save himself for greater things.

He strode through the gloom, heading back up to the winecellars. Bodies were everywhere, fallen torches flickering among sprawled, silent men.

He had to end this. He had to stop the insane Golskyn and his beastmen, yet he dared not use his beholder eye—its whispering hold over him was growing stronger. Eyepatch firmly in place, he stalked on, his sword sharp, ready, and in his hand.

The world seemed to shift, just a little, and the voice he'd been struggling to ignore rose in strength. *This way. Just a few paces more. THIS way.*

Overhead, with thunderous tread, the Walking Statues of Waterdeep took a few more steps, rearranging themselves just so, at the bidding of ... of Golskyn, presumably, speaking through *him!*

"A man I really must find and slay," Beldar Roaringhorn whispered grimly, as he came up through puddles of wine and shattered glass into ever-brighter light.

Someone had been at work conjuring light in the shattered Purple Silks and banishing the dust, revealing a great webwork of cracks running from the huge hole in the ceiling to great gaps in the walls. Most of the tapestries had fallen, and the leaded panes of the windows behind them, too. As Beldar trudged across rubble to join the silently staring people in the feasting hall, he could see what they were staring at through those gaps.

Gigantic stone legs, blocking every way out of the trembling, crumbling festhall. Legs attached to stone bodies that towered over the shattered roof, like disapproving Watchmen standing above a fallen citizen.

The Walking Statues of Waterdeep had surrounded the Purple Silks and made of it a prison—a prison that with a few blows or kicks they could collapse into a tomb for all still inside.

CHAPTER TWENTY-SEVEN

Beldar's jaw clenched in fury. So Golskyn could control the Statues
through him, without his knowledge.

Well, he didn't want this power, but by all the gods, he'd not
let the mad priest use it!

Beldar growled aside the burning pain in his eye and hurled
his will into a silent command.

Overhead, the Statues took a single step back.

⛫　⛫　⛫　⛫　⛫

Mrelder looked up, hearing and feeling the Walking Statues
moving. That was it; this battle was lost. He put a firm hand on
his father's shoulder and steered the old priest firmly toward a
side tunnel and escape.

But Golskyn pulled away, giving his son a scornful glare. Once
it would have wounded Mrelder deeply, but he no longer desired
his father's approval or believed the insane plans of Lord Unity
could be made real.

"We can leave—or we can die," he said bluntly.

Golskyn raised hands that flickered with deadly magic, in
clear warning. "I go no farther without the successor! Use your
spells to bring us Beldar Roaringhorn!"

Mrelder wasn't sure that was still possible, but he nodded curtly
and began to weave the sorcery that would roar commands inside
the nobleman's head.

Terrible pain lanced through Beldar's skull. He tore off his eyepatch and sank to his knees, trembling. The beastman he'd been about to slay stopped his lurching retreat and trotted forward, spiked mace rising for an easy kill.

Beldar's beholder eye responded, forcing up the head that held it, to let it glare.

The noble watched a sore erupt on the beastman's face, oozing and spreading with incredible speed. It was rather like watching a wax party decoration tossed across a flame—if that wax figure melted, screaming, into greenish ooze and exposed bone.

The pain in Beldar's head ebbed, and he stared in revulsion at his dying foe. No one and nothing should die like this! He swung his blade across the beastman's throat and turned away as the gurgling scream faded.

Something stirred in his throbbing head: the faint echo of someone else's surprise.

So his watcher hadn't expected that mercy-slaying. Good. Then he knew that Beldar Roaringhorn was not yet a helpless puppet. His choices were still his own.

And by the gods, he would choose well!

▲ ▲ ▲ ▲ ▲

Taeros coughed smoke and staggered to his feet. The foulness was billowing from burning corpses. Nearby, Starragar clung to his dead love, still sobbing. Roldo's tunic hung in slashed rags, but he stood wincing as Faendra worked to staunch the blood running from the gashes across his chest. Naoni knelt over Korvaun, who lay sprawled on the floor. Lark stood guard between her mistresses, eyes alert and dagger ready. Her gaze touched his, and Taeros blinked at the realization that she stood ready to leap to his defense, too.

A soft murmur came from the floor, and Taeros looked again at Naoni and Korvaun.

A good pair of Helmfast breeches had been slit away, revealing a row of round, red welts on his thigh. Naoni was lying beside Korvaun now, her head on his chest and her face deathly pale. Korvaun held her with one arm, but his other twitched, often and sharply.

Fear swept through Taeros in an icy tide. "Up, man," he said gruffly. "We're far from done yet."

Korvaun's smile was faint. "True enough . . . for you."

Taeros glared at the welts. "Venom," he said grimly. "That snake thing that took us down must have been—oh, blast it all, it matters not!"

He drew his dagger and dropped to his knees beside Korvaun. "This'll hurt, but lacking magic or the right poison-quell . . . I'll have to cut open each of those and suck the venom out."

"Too late," Korvaun said. "Look at my arm: 'Tis in my blood." He smiled faintly. "If you were a flock of stirges you might drain me dry, but that'd hardly be an improvement."

They stared into each other's eyes until Taeros shook his head angrily and snapped, "Faen, Lark: help me! Let's get Korvaun into yonder cellar-end."

"And what?" Roldo demanded. "Just *leave* him there?"

"Lark can stand guard. We'll go get a healer, and return as fast as we can."

Roldo looked to Korvaun.

"Listen to Taeros, my friend," the youngest Lord Helmfast said, his eyelids drooping. "He knows what must be done."

His eyes drifted shut. "Advising sage," he murmured. "The role you seek . . . suits you well. Take it up again when you can. For now, you must lead."

Taeros found himself choking back tears, for he knew no healer could come in time. "I'll take it up in Torm's halls," he said roughly, "when again I find myself at Korvaun Helmfast's side."

Korvaun smiled faintly. "I'll keep your seat warm and your ale cool. Go now, and see this through!"

A man with serpents as long as spears sprouting from his forearms dodged out of a sewer-tunnel behind one of Elaith's hurrying jackcoats.

The man whirled, sword flashing, but by then three or four snakeheads had sunk their fangs into him, and a fifth made short and savage work of his face.

Taeros Hawkwinter crouched grimly watching, one hand raised in an imperious "all keep silent" signal, his sword ready in the other.

Roldo whispered, "Are we just going to *watch?* Why aren't we—"

The beastman left the writhing, foaming jackcoat to die and ran on, calling some sort of wordless signal. Side-passages erupted with streams of monster-men, running up into the winecellars of the Purple Silks.

"*That's* why," Taeros muttered, eyes fierce and face hard. "If we throw our lives away trying to be glorious heroes, Waterdeep won't get warned in time, and all of *those* will be out in the streets, lurking and awaiting every nightfall, to slay at will!"

A tunnel rang with a sudden clash of steel, and a beastman staggered out of it, body transfixed by the blades of half a dozen of Elaith's jackcoats. Groaning, the man-monster fell on his face. The jackcoats jerked forth bloody blades and ran on—back up into the winecellars.

"It seems the Purple Silks is filling up again," Taeros observed caustically. "Ready for more festivities, everyone?"

More jackcoats and a few beastmen darted out of various tunnels to ascend into the wine cellars. The sewers were growing quieter—and darker, too, with almost all the lanterns and torches gone out. Soon there'd be none left but the dead . . . and whatever might come along to feed on them.

"Everyone's ready," Roldo announced grimly.

The Hawkwinter nodded curtly. "You step out that way, facing down into the sewers, and I'll face *that* way, toward the cellars. Everyone else come out between us. We form a ring of steel and go up, everyone looking to the sides as we go. Roldo, keep watch behind, and shout the moment you see any movement, even if it's something very small coming at you."

Roldo stared at his hitherto easy-going friend. "You sound like a veteran warcaptain of Hawkwinter Hall!"

For once, Taeros wasted neither time nor wit on a sharp response. If he fell short of a warcaptain's wisdom this night, there were graves waiting for them all.

Lord Ulb Jardeth staggered wearily into the feasting hall, face blood-streaked and leaning on a notched and blunted sword. He blinked in surprise at all the bright light.

There was a little cry of relief, and a familiar, long-gowned woman burst through its archway and came running to him, arms spread.

"Allys," he growled, throwing his free arm around her as she embraced him fiercely, sobbing. "I'm—I'm all right. Steady, pet, steady. What by the Harbor Deep has befallen up here, while we were all killing each other down below?"

Lady Allys Jardeth pointed with the hand that held her little jeweled belt-dagger. "Men who look like *monsters* have been coming up—just a few of them—and when they saw us all looking, they went through those doors there, and there—and there!"

"The big bedchambers," Lord Jardeth said grimly, not caring if he was revealing his familiarity with the festhall to his wife. "Well, they can only get out of there through a stair up onto the galleries or a tunnel back down to the sewers ... or right back out yon doors to face us again, so they'll keep for now. Gods, lass, 'twas butchery down there—who else has come up?"

Allys Jardeth stiffened in her husband's arms. This time words failed her, so she contented herself with screaming.

Lord Jardeth swung them both around—in time to see an army of monster-men running across the shattered forehall toward him. "Oh, blast," he growled, "I'm getting too old for this! *Allys, get out of here!*"

Shoving his wife behind him, he hefted his sword and planted his feet to await the doom charging so swiftly down upon him.

♣ ♣ ♣ ♣ ♣

Screams burst from the watching women in the feasting hall as the beastmen raced toward them.

"For the Amalgamation!" a huge, caterpillarlike monster-man thundered, rearing up amid the running throng as tall as two men.

"For Waterdeep!" someone shouted from behind the running beastmen, as Lord Jardeth swung his sword and prepared to die.

Then a bolt of lightning crackled between two drawn blades, searing the hands of the astonished jackcoats who wielded them and dealing death to a score of beastmen caught between.

"We're under attack!" a stag-headed man snarled, whirling around, and the loping, wolflike creature who was about to pounce on Lord Jardeth turned as swiftly as most of his fellows.

Not much more than a dozen of Elaith's jackcoats had come up out of the cellar on their heels, but until that war-cry, they'd been stabbing, tripping, and slaying with swift and stealthy ease, leaving a trail of half-beast bodies.

Seeing their own losses, the monster-men of the Amalgamation turned their backs on the feasting hall in an instant to face their dark-clad foes.

The cavernous forehall became a furious battleground in the space of an angry breath, as beastmen howled, trumpeted, roared, and died. Jaws, claws, and tails, both scything and stinging, made short work of unarmored jackcoats, but many of Elaith's men fought with poisoned blades, and there was fearsome slaughter.

When all the jackcoats were dead, less than a dozen monster-men remained to turn and rend the lone old lord who stood in their path—which was when the Gemcloaks came racing up out of the cellar to plunge in among them, hacking and stabbing with neither war-cry nor hesitation.

With shouts and roars of rage and dismay, the monster-men

whirled around *again*—to find a foe already in their midst.

"*Die*," Taeros gasped furiously, as he chopped aside eyestalks and fangs, his hands as black with blood as his sword. "Stop being so bloody stubborn and just *die!*"

"*Starragar?*" old Lord Jardeth roared, catching sight of a face he knew in the fray. "Starragar? To me, boy! *For Jardeth and Waterdeep!*"

That war-cry was echoed from Ulb Jardeth's flank. He turned in astonishment as his wife, tangled hair flying around her, burst in among men with scales and horns and barbed arms. She stabbed with her dagger, grunting with effort. Tearing it free, she gasped, reeled, and struck again.

Other elderly nobles and merchants were advancing from the feasting hall now, unsteadily or uncertainly or both, with canes and belt-knives and table legs in their hands. "That's young Hawkwinter!" someone shouted. "And the Thongolir heir, by the Mountain!"

Lord Eremoes Hawkwinter shot to his feet from where he'd been bandaging and comforting the injured among the tables. He dragged out a wicked warsword, cast aside its jeweled scabbard, and bellowed, "A Hawkwinter? *Where?*"

His lumbering run brought him into the forehall in time to see Taeros Hawkwinter smash aside a lion-headed man's sword with his own, snarling as fiercely as if he himself had lion-fangs, and sink his dagger hilt-deep in a leonine throat.

"Blood and valor! *Taeros!*" Eremoes cried in pleased wonder. He pointed at his son with his sword and roared in a voice that echoed around the shattered hall, "Rally to Hawkwinter, men!"

🏰 🏰 🏰 🏰 🏰

"I *hate* this," Piergeiron raged. "To stand here doing naught, while brave folk of Waterdeep fight and die before my eyes! Friends, this is *killing* me!"

"Nay," Mirt growled, "any attempt on an over-foolish paladin's part to get out there will result in *me* killing *ye*. Take your brains out o' your sword-scabbard for once and *sit tight*. Your staying inside the shielding here is all that stops whoever's behind all these man-beasts from burying us all! If they can make the Statues Walk, they need no blasting-spells to bring the Silks down on our heads! Only knowing this magic is protecting *your* head stops them, as 'tis *your* head they want!"

"Mirt's right," Madeiron Sunderstone said quickly, seeing the lack of logic in the moneylender's words but praying the First Lord would not. Stones had bounced from the golden shield—hardly the actions of a foe who wished to take Piergeiron alive! "So sit down again and belt up. For once."

The wizard Tarthus was doing more than sitting down: he was lying down, face pale and sweat streaming from it. Holding up the shielding under a succession of swift, hard probing spells was exhausting. It was flickering on the verge of collapse. "We're . . . we're going to have to risk it," Tarthus gasped.

"Right," Mirt growled, lurching as far away from the others as he could get. Drawing a little carved gem from its own inner belt-pouch, he set it on the floor, joined it with a good deal of huffing and puffing, and touched it with his outstretched arm, muttering, "Fancylass, I need ye."

There was a flash, the shielding pulsed with a throbbing groan that made them all wince—and there was suddenly a fifth person standing under the golden dome.

She was female, of mature years, and wore a revealing ruffled nightgown and a startled, less-than-pleased expression.

Most mages of the Watchful Order were frankly scared of "Mother" Amaundra Lorgra. There was something forbidding about a woman who refused all rank but gave no polite word to anyone and whose glares and simple utterances could cow noble lords and senior Guard officers alike. Her bare feet were covered with corns, her thin legs a-crawl with blue veins, and her eyes were already beginning to flash in exasperation.

"Mirt, what by all the lusts of Sune have you and these idiot lads gotten themselves into *this* time? Can't a woman get some sleep in Waterdeep these nights? Must you little boys always be waving swords and *shouting* around the place?"

"Fancylass," Mirt growled back, not a whit abashed, "I'd not have disturbed ye had the present threat not been too great to deal with by lesser means. Consider yourself our sharpest blade, if ye will."

"How so?"

"Ye have the strength and the skill to join with Tarthus, here, and keep the shielding up. They've made the Statues walk and are trying to bring this festhall down on all our heads."

Amaundra shook her head, went to the floor with the fading remains of graceful agility, and clasped hands with Tarthus. "You can tell me who 'they' are later—and why young Piergeiron here can't just send the Statues back to their places. Right now, let me dispute something more immediate with you. Are 'they' sane? That is, do they intend to still have a city left to rule, once they've prevailed?"

Mirt shrugged. "I presume so. Why do it, else?"

"Well, then, if our foes are sane and have enough wits to know anything about magic—and they must do, to move the Statues—they won't want to bring this place down."

"Oh?"

"Don't act the wide-eyed innocent with me, Mirt—you do it poorly indeed. You *are* a Lord of Waterdeep, no matter how secret you little boys like to keep such things, so you know about Ahghairon's wards—and all the embroidery Khelben and others have added since."

Mirt nodded. "The phantom city walls, the dragon-wards, aye."

"Aye, indeed. Such castings have multiple anchors. One is a stone in this building's foundation. If this place falls and those stones get shattered or shifted, spell after spell will collapse in a rolling, ever-increasing chaos only Khelben or Laeral can fix—unless Azuth or Holy Mystra herself happen to be strolling by."

"Barring that, the collapse comes, and what then?"

Amaundra shrugged. "Nothing much, perhaps. Wards that won't work when we call on them, later, city walls that won't appear when the orcs come howling . . . that sort of thing. On the other hand, the breaking spells might shatter others nearby, in magical mayhem none can predict—mayhap awakening spells any of Waterdeep's defenders can use or causing old enchantments to fail here and there."

"Making buildings fall, and all that."

"And all that, indeed. The problem isn't so much the wards we know about. It's all the ancient, half-forgotten, lingering Ahghairon-cast-this magics everywhere."

"Oh, *tluin*," Mirt growled.

"Oh, *tluin*, indeed," the magist agreed tartly, "which is a fine word for a woman to be using while she's lying flat on her back wearing only a bit of rag with three lusty men about!"

Madeiron Sunderstone promptly stood up, unbuckled his ornate revel-cloak, and laid it gently over Amaundra. "I believe the appropriate phrase is: 'The things I do for Waterdeep.'"

"That, young sir," came the tart reply, "is the appropriate phrase for us all."

⚓ ⚓ ⚓ ⚓ ⚓

"I thought they were just young ne'er-do-wells, wasting our coins and their days wenching, mocking and breaking things," Ulb Jardeth growled. "For once, I was wrong, and I don't regret my error one whit."

"Likewise!" Eremoes Hawkwinter laughed. "Gods, but that was splendid! Our new young lions, fighting for Waterdeep!"

"And some older lionesses, too," Lord Jardeth added, looking down at his wife.

There was dried blood all over Allys Jardeth's hand and bodice and dagger, none of it her own, but she was nestled in the crook of his arm quite happily, with none of her usual fussing about how she looked or who was wearing a better gown.

She grinned up at him. "So is it all over?"

"You sound disappointed," her proud husband observed. Lord Eremoes Hawkwinter gave the handful of surviving monster-men a hard look—where they were spread out bound on the floor, with swords held to their throats—and shook his head, frowning.

"We're still prisoners in here," he said quietly, "with the Walking Statues blocking all ways out, and there's something wrong with Piergeiron, or he'd be commanding them elsewhere. Moreover, the Lord Mage of Waterdeep, who could do the same with a wave of his hand, seems nowhere to be found. I've been hearing rumors no one's seen him for days—including some powerful outlander mages who came a long way to climb the steps of Blackstaff Tower. I'd say we're far from out of the shadows yet."

CHAPTER TWENTY-EIGHT

Lark almost swallowed her tongue in startled fear when the quiet voice nigh her ear said her name.

Her mewing jump brought her around, dagger up—to face Elaith Craulnober. He held a sword and a roll of parchment, and there was a small band of warriors behind him, one of them a silver-crested, scaled man who looked to be half a dragon.

"Well met," Elaith said dryly. He slapped the parchment into her hand. "A sewer map. Use it. Round up as many of these idiot humans as you can and get them out."

Then he was gone, and all his blades with him, leaving her staring at empty darkness.

Shifting stones grated and rumbled overhead.

Then something burst into sudden brilliance at her feet. Lark jumped back again, hissing out a curse, and stared at the lit torch that hadn't been there a moment earlier.

Then she swallowed, looked up to find three halflings from the Warrens nodding gravely to her with swords ready in their hands, sighed—and unrolled the map.

"Come," she said to Naoni.

Her mistress shook her head. "Taeros said to stay here. He'll not know where to find us otherwise."

There were more stony rumblings from overhead, and a spray of dust and small stones showered down around them.

"Go!" Naoni commanded.

Lark looked to Faendra, who slipped an arm around her sister's waist. It was clear that nothing Lark could do was going to shift either of Varandros Dyre's stubborn daughters.

Lark bowed to them, spun around, and trotted off. One of the hin plucked up the torch and ran with her. There were more rumblings and then a shout. She looked for its source and saw two bloody, bedraggled merchants and an old noble.

"Follow me," she called, waving the map. "I know a way out!"

They fell into step without argument, as the rumblings overhead grew louder—and closer.

Lark turned a corner and found herself staring at their source: a tunnel-team of dwarves, hastening to toss stones into a side-tunnel and shore it up. Those stones lay in a huge flood of light that was, yes, moonlit!

A street above had collapsed, and they were looking at the surface! The merchants swarmed past her with glad shouts.

Lark helped the old nobleman clamber after them, up the shifting drift of cobbles and building-stones. Then she turned back into the darkness to seek others.

It was what Texter would expect of her—and what she'd now come to expect from herself.

🏰 🏰 🏰 🏰 🏰

The voice in Beldar's head was growing stronger. He groaned. His beholder eye was pounding, burning, and his actions were no longer wholly his own. Against his will, he was stumbling through the festhall. He had little doubt who awaited him.

"Our labors being not done," he gasped aloud, dredging up fragments of a warriors' ballad a stern Roaringhorn tutor had forced him to learn years ago. "We fared forth, our swords ready. For perils broad and deep continueth, and we are beset . . ."

The inexorable mind-voice grew firmer, stronger . . .

"And no strength shall deliver us but our own, for the gods but watch, and are amused, and reward those who best entertain by their strivings . . ."

Beldar's memory failed him, and the thunderous pain rolled in.

He was staggering along a ruined, deserted gallery with sword drawn, just one more lost, wounded noble in a feasting hall full of lost, wounded nobles.

A door presented itself to his right, and he hurled himself against it.

It held, bruisingly. With a snarl, clutching his eye now, Beldar staggered on.

A second door also held, and a third.

The fourth burst open, spilling Beldar into a cluttered chamber—a storeroom? It was crowded with wardrobes, heaps of cushions, and several man-tall oval mirrors with suggestively carved frames. Beldar stumbled past them and over a low, padded-top sideboard—*padded-top sideboard?* Oh, aye, *fest*hall, stonewits—into a little open area by a window.

Beldar Roaringhorn turned around to face the door, and took off his eyepatch.

It wasn't the battleground he might have chosen, but he would make the best final stand he could.

Cracks widened, and great drifts of dislodged stone tumbled down the walls to burst and shatter against the floor. More than once, the Purple Silks groaned—almost as if the festhall was a weary wounded Waterdhavian, knowing death was near—and that the slow slide into darkness had very much begun.

Folk were fleeing once more into the tunnels, following shouts that promised a way out had been found.

On their backs under a fading, flickering golden dome, Tarthus and Amaundra Lorgra of the Watchful Order trembled and sweated, exhausted beyond their endurance, but somehow holding on . . .

For now. Every breath a victory, every victory harder than the last. For now.

"Come *on,* then," Beldar Roaringhorn murmured, watching a crack crawling slowly up the wall, to where it could send stabbing fingers across the ceiling.

Golskyn and his son Mrelder were very near; the voice in his head was like the roaring of vast, inexorable surf. Skull pounding, Beldar went to his knees and groaned, long, low, and loud.

There was a great pile of tasseled cushions over yonder, behind the—

His feeble thoughts were shattered by the crash of the door being hurled wide. Smoke curled from it—gods, they'd used a *spell* to open an unlocked door!

Lord Unity of the Amalgamation swaggered into the room, the shimmerings of a protective spell singing around him. Beldar bent the power of his gaze on the man, but Golskyn merely sneered.

"He's in here, right enough, son," he announced. "I don't think your spells will even be needed. There's not much left of him."

Beldar staggered to his feet, used his sword to spear a cushion, and hurled it in Golskyn's face.

The protective spell flared, and the priest threw back his head and laughed.

He was still laughing when Beldar flung himself against a mirror. He twisted it as it toppled, riding it as its edge crashed through Golskyn's shield and into the arm of the man beyond. The mirror shattered as it bit down, glass shards sinking deep.

Golskyn screamed, and Mrelder came through the door fast, fingers a-crawl with magic.

Beldar ruined that spell with the same cushion, booted up from the floor into Mrelder's face, and followed it with the mightiest slash he'd ever swung.

Mrelder ducked away, but not quite far enough.

As warsteel bit into his shoulder, the sorcerer shrieked, and the voice in Beldar's head was silenced as if chopped off by a—sword.

Something slapped around Beldar's ankle and jerked. He crashed onto his rump and bounced. A thigh-thick tentacle had downed him; its wart-covered length curved back under the priest's robes.

Laughing, Golskyn tore off his eyepatch. A fiery beam leaped forth.

Beldar drove his blade into the tentacle and thrust it up in time to intercept the beam of light. There was a sickening hiss and a foul stench, and the tentacle writhed away as the priest cried out.

Beldar sprang from the floor and hurled himself at Mrelder.

The sorcerer jumped back, stumbled, and fell heavily. Beldar slammed into the floor beside him, sword reaching out to stab and hack, but Mrelder had rolled out of reach, heading for the door.

Fire seared Beldar from behind.

Roaring, Beldar spun around and glared back at Golskyn. What his eye sent forth could not be seen, but the priest's eye-fire wrestled something unseen in the air between them ... and was slowly forced back, quivering and spitting sparks.

Keeping his gaze on Golskyn, Beldar retreated toward the window. One of the tall swivel-mirrors was in his way.

In his way ...

Beldar ducked behind it, caught hold of it, and thrust it at Golskyn. Fire splashed off the mirror and rebounded, and the priest gasped and then snarled in pain and fury.

Beldar ducked away as the glass shattered, sparkling shards flying everywhere, and the fire-beam lanced forth again. It took but a moment to pluck up the mirror up by its wooden stand and thrust its jagged remnants into the priest's face.

Golskyn screamed in earnest in this time, a howl of agony that broke off into frantic flight when Beldar slashed with the mirror, again and again, glass tinkling down until he was holding a bare frame. By then, the room was empty of haughty priests and sorcerous sons alike.

Beldar snatched up his sword and some cushions and got himself over to the wall just beside the door. In another breath Mrelder would think of some clever spell. They needed him alive, unless they were abandoning use of the Walking Statues, so it would be something disabling, not deadly.

An icy cloud hissed past Beldar. He shrank down as most of

the room vanished under a frigid coating of glittering ice.

Flattened against the wall, cushion in one hand and sword in the other, Beldar waited as silently as he could manage. He tried to breathe gently, slowly ... so quietly.

"It'll take too long, Father," Mrelder said suddenly, from just outside the door. "If I'm still feeling around for the lordling's mind when some nobles get up here with their swords and their anger—with you like *that* ..."

Cautiously the sorcerer peered into the room, and Beldar swung the cushion as hard and fast as he could.

It caught Mrelder in the face, trailing feathers, and burst into flames as the sorcerer got it with some lightning-swift cantrip or other, but by then Beldar had swung his blade, slicing through fire and feathers into flesh.

Mrelder sobbed, and Beldar's blade came back wet with bright blood. He hacked again, hard, but this time his seeking steel bit only air, and he heard the moaning sorcerer stumbling away.

"Couldn't you even—" Golskyn began angrily, and Mrelder hissed something furious and pain-wracked ... then two pairs of stumbling footfalls receded hastily down the gallery.

Beldar Roaringhorn ran to the window with bloody sword in hand, his mind free of shouting voices, and glared at the stone legs.

Step away, he thought angrily. *Step AWAY.*

And with the sound of ponderous thunder, the wall of stone outside the window moved.

Beldar thought hard, seeking to thrust himself into that heaviness, the great stone weight he could now dimly perceive in his mind.

As a great foot came down and Beldar's room rocked, plaster falling in tumbling plumes, he became aware of movement. He was moving, or rather, the statue was moving and he was a part of it.

Buildings all around him, at knee and thigh level, bright lights in the night ...

He *was* the Walking Statue. Great power, slow but unstoppable, surging cold and dark and heavy, surging ...

Beldar beheld a garden wall across the shattered street from the Purple Silks. *Strike that down!*

A fist swung, and stones melted before it, spraying down across the street to shatter against the festhall walls. Blocks crumbled and fell, opening rents that gave Beldar a glimpse of the sagging feasting hall galleries inside as stone fell into dust and rubble, and tumbled into the festhall.

From his great height, Beldar looked down. There were holes in the street, great pits of collapsed cobbles, and behind him, pits that laid bare the sewer-tunnels where frightened men and women were scurrying, some looking up at him in pale-faced horror as they ran.

Around that terrified human flood, smaller folk were at work: dwarves, hammering and hefting in expert haste to shore up the walls and crumbling ceilings of the damaged tunnels. Beldar plucked up a great handful of stones from the rubble he'd caused, turned with infinite care, bent, and tilted his great hand into a chute, lowering it to just beside a dwarf.

That bearded stalwart squinted up at him for a moment—it must have been like gazing up at a mountain—and then leaped onto the great hand and tugged at the nearest stone, passing it down to others below. Beldar kept the Statue motionless as the dwarf worked, thrusting and tugging. A great iron bar was tossed up, and a second dwarf joined the first, huffing and shoving, tipping the stones one by one to the swarming dwarves below.

Gods above, he was *rebuilding* Waterdeep! Beldar grinned into the great cold darkness that engulfed ... and was still doing so (there was something about the Statues that made one's thoughts slow and heavy) when his hand was emptied of the last stone. One dwarf and the bar promptly disappeared over the edge of his finger. The last dwarf—the one who'd first been brave enough to leap onto his hand—looked up and gave Beldar a laconic nod of thanks ere leaping down out of sight.

Beldar made the Statue straighten slowly and carefully and then was struck by the whim to look back at himself in the window and see what wayward sons of Roaringhorn look like.

That was a mistake, because something roared and flashed in Beldar's head ... and he found himself sprawled over the padded sideboard, sword in hand, back in the shattered room full of cushions and mirrors. Back in the festhall, where Mrelder and Golskyn of the Amalgamation were lurking.

Beldar found his small crimson vial and unstoppered it. He was free for the moment, but who knew when the voice might return? Of one thing he was certain: they must not regain control of the Statues.

With one hand he held his eyelids firmly open—and with the other he emptied the vial into his beholder-eye.

White fire exploded in his head.

Agony like he'd never known ... the potion spilled down his face in corrosive tears, searing bubbling furrows.

Darkness swept in, the white light dwindling ... somehow Beldar pushed away oblivion and took a step.

The room tilted and swayed. He took another cautious step. Glass crunched underfoot as he felt his way to the doorway.

Tears were glimmering in his remaining eye, but he could—just—see. There was no waiting sorcerer or priest, just a deserted, sagging gallery.

A deep-voiced shout called for more stone. Beldar turned back to the window, wistfully eyeing the Statue. He'd been too quick to destroy the beholder eye—and with it, his connection to the Walking Statues. Another load of stone, just one, might make a vital difference.

To his astonishment, the great construct stooped, gathered up rubble, and lowered it to the waiting dwarves. The Statue still obeyed his unspoken commands!

Too numb and pain-wracked to ponder this mystery, Beldar hefted his sword and staggered out into what was left of the Purple Silks.

If he survived this, he'd have to ask Taeros why ballads never mentioned how *tired* heroes got or how their victory battles seemed to never end.

CHAPTER TWENTY-NINE

The winecellar seemed endless. Beldar picked his way over bodies and more bodies, seeking his foes.

Two halflings faced him, weapons drawn. Beyond them a lantern flickered on the floor, shining on glimmering blue cloth, and showing him two faces he knew: the Dyre sisters.

Blue gemweave . . .

"Korvaun!" Beldar shouted. Crossed swords barred his way.

"Let him through," ordered Naoni.

Beldar went to his knees beside his oldest friend. It took only a glance to know that Korvaun Helmfast was dying.

The blue eyes gazing up at him were serene and clear. Korvaun smiled. "You're free. Your own man again."

Beldar touched his ruined face. "Such as I am."

"You must lead," his friend said faintly, "and not just the Gem-cloaks." A spasm racked him, and he fell still.

Beldar looked helplessly at Naoni and Faendra Dyre. They gazed back, mute queries in their eyes. They were looking to *him* for guidance! Despite all he'd done and become . . .

Korvaun whispered abruptly, "I swore to carry this secret to my death. Lady Asper will not mind, perhaps, if I'm . . . somewhat previous."

His eyes moved to Naoni. She swiftly undid the fastenings of his tunic. Beneath was a metal vest—not chainmail, but a metal fabric as light and soft as silk. Faendra moved to help, and the sisters eased both garments off him.

Their gentle handling left Korvaun parchment-white, his face a mask of sweat. "Tell him," he whispered.

Naoni quickly told Beldar about the slipshield, what it could do, and how she'd spun it into a new, undetectable form.

"As long as you live," Korvaun added hoarsely, "those who gave you the eye will seek you, to slay or enslave. Hold this secret, and use it well."

Naoni held up the vest.

Beldar finally realized what his friend was asking of him.

Korvaun wanted Beldar to *take his place*, to take up the mantle of leadership once more.

"They'll think you dead," Naoni whispered tremulously, through tears, "and leave you in peace. It will be hard for you, and harder for your family, yet it's . . . needful."

Beldar's thoughts whirled. His monstrous eye might be ruined, but its other magic still held. He could—in secret—join the ranks of Waterdeep's protectors.

'Twasn't the glorious, sword-swinging heroism he'd dreamed of, but . . . needful, yes. More than that, it was what the Dathran had foretold. He'd be the hero who defied death. He would become Korvaun Helmfast, who would live on in him.

Because he could not do otherwise, Beldar inclined his head in agreement.

"One thing more," Korvaun gasped, his voice barely audible now. "I pledged that no shame would come to Naoni while I lived. She has my heart, my ring, and my promise. My dearest wish was to give her my name! If she bears my child . . ."

"He'll be raised a Helmfast," Beldar swore, "and in time will be told the truth about his father."

Korvaun managed a smile. "Naoni . . ."

"Hush now," she told him gently, kissing his forehead. "You've done all that's needful, and done it well. All you've said will come to pass. Beldar will keep his promises and carry your name with honor—or he'll deal with my sorcery, and Faendra's wrath."

Korvaun nodded and said with sudden firmness, "Do it. Now."

Beldar shrugged off his tunic and slid on the soft, shining vest. Korvaun changed instantly, his blond hair darkening to deep chestnut, his body becoming smaller and more slender.

Beldar ripped off the eyepatch and found he could see quite well with both eyes. The change wrought by the slipshield must go far deeper than mere likeness.

The awe on Faendra's face—and the tearful resignation on Naoni's—told him his transformation into Korvaun Helmfast was complete.

Beldar looked down at his dying friend and found himself gazing into his own face.

"They'll say of me," he said softly, "that my death was better than my life."

Korvaun struggled to speak, but through his last, ragged breath they heard him say: "Prove them wrong."

⛫ ⛫ ⛫ ⛫ ⛫

The whirlwind of magic that had seized Mrelder died abruptly, and the sorcerer found himself sprawled on the cold stones of a well-lit cell with his father beside him. Groans behind him told him that the spell had brought along others of the Amalgamation.

A tall, silver-haired elf stood over him, leaning on a drawn sword. At his shoulders stood a small army of jackcoats, swords and wands out and ready. "Elaith Craulnober and minions," he introduced himself pleasantly.

Mrelder tensed, and the elf waved a languid hand. "Don't trouble yourself to cast spells or wave weapons; this chamber's heavily warded, and my companions are more than equal to any challenge by monk, sorcerer, or ... whatever."

By that last word, Elaith meant the man he was glancing at: Golskyn of the Gods, who'd found his feet with the help of several monster-men. The old priest was staring in wonder at the silver-scaled warrior standing beside the Serpent.

"A half-dragon indeed," he breathed. "So many questions! Tell me, how did you come to be? From whence came your draconic blood? Was your mother ravaged, and did your dragon parent mate in elf, human, or draconic form? Did your mother bear you alive, or as an egg? Did she survive the birthing?"

He rubbed his hands thoughtfully. "If not, I'll need a number of elf-shes as hosts. And a dragon stud. A host of half-dragons! What warriors! Imagine the savings in coin for armor alone!"

Eyebrow crooked, Elaith turned to Tincheron. "Would you like to respond appropriately, or shall I?"

The silver-scaled warrior silently stalked forward and backhanded the old priest's head.

Golskyn fell like a sack of meal, senseless and silent.

The elf smiled at Mrelder. "I trust you'll prove more sensible?"

The sorcerer nodded cautiously. "You fought and defeated us. Are you offering swift death or ...?"

Elaith inspected his nails. "A strategic withdrawal."

"I—I thank you. May I ask why?"

"Waterdeep," the Serpent replied coolly, "is *my* city, off limits to such as you. That's not to say that we might not do business elsewhere to mutual advantage."

"And what price does your mercy carry?"

The elf smiled. "You're quick, sorcerer. In return for your lives, I require the Guardian's Gorget."

Mrelder sighed, surrendered to the inevitable, and told the elf what had become of the artifact.

A faint groan came from the floor, followed by mutterings about half-dragons.

The sorcerer glanced down at his father. "I rather wish your ... trusted companion had struck a little harder."

"Revenge is pleasant, but often wasteful." The Serpent let his gaze sweep slowly over the surviving beastmen. "Your father's mad-witted, but he's caused enough trouble to make his methods worthy of study." His gaze came to rest on Golskyn. "Even the oldest wagon has parts worth scavenging."

Mrelder's eyes flashed to his father's fallen but still-mighty form and narrowed in speculation. "Indeed," he murmured. "Are we free to go?"

Elaith Craulnober gracefully indicated a door. "That tunnel

leads to a shop kept by a man who knows that anyone emerging from it is to be helped to discreetly depart the city. Trust in him, for he answers to me."

Mrelder gave a slight bow, in the manner of equals parting in mutual respect.

Elaith smiled. So much for the gratitude of the conquered whose life has been spared. He watched the cultists go, mulling over a feeling that Mrelder had taken some meaning from his words that he hadn't intended.

He turned, nodded, and watched his own forces swiftly scatter into their war-bands and plunge into various tunnels that led under the Purple Silk. Only when he was alone did he open a concealed door to take a hidden way to the festhall only he knew.

Old habits died hard, and Elaith would no longer deny the duties of his heritage and nature. He *was* a lord, wherever he chose to live and whatever he chose to rule. By his lights, he'd done Waterdeep many services this night—warning the First Lord of danger, standing guard over Piergeiron lest an enemy use the still-missing slipshield to approach him in the unreadable guise of a friend, casting magic that sent many of the revelers safely away from death from stonefall, helping them find their way out of the tunnels, even culling some deadwood from noble family trees. He had one more service to give, though it irked him to yield such an advantage: the name and nature of he who would be Waterdeep's next Open Lord.

It occurred to him, suddenly, that perhaps Mirt and the rest knew their business better than he'd thought possible. Why else would they give such valuable magic as slipshields to a pack of noble pups?

Elaith hurried through the tunnel, a bemused smile on his face. Though he had lived long and seen much, this city never ceased to astonish and amuse him!

🏰　🏰　🏰　🏰　🏰

Suddenly, in silence and without any fuss at all, Amaundra fainted. Her eyes rolled up, her body quivered, and she stopped breathing.

"Wizard," Piergeiron snapped, springing up from where he'd been sitting, "you're *killing* her!

Tarthus, lying flat on his back trembling uncontrollably, didn't look as if he could kill a fly. He stared up at the Open Lord with eyes of forlorn pain.

"I can't accept this any longer!" Piergeiron snapped. "I must fight for Waterdeep! It's my duty, and I'm *needed!* Drop the shielding!"

The golden dome persisted. Piergeiron repeated his order, shouting this time.

"N-no," Tarthus gasped faintly.

Madeiron Sunderstone laid one great, restraining hand on Piergeiron's arm and bent over the wizard on the floor. "I remind you that your oaths require you to obey any direct order from the Open Lord of Waterdeep."

"A higher authority forbids," Tarthus gasped, eyes still closed.

"*What?* There *is* no—"

Mirt waved a reproving finger in Piergeiron's face to quell his outburst, then laid it to his own lips, and pointed down at Tarthus.

On cue, a very different voice came from the wizard's trembling lips. "Most of this last bell," it said in feminine tones all four men knew, "my strength has been holding the shield around you, Piergeiron. Tarthus has been obeying me—and in this matter, *I* am obeying Mystra herself."

"Laeral," Piergeiron breathed.

"Holy Mystra," Madeiron Sunderstone gasped, making a reverent gesture.

At that moment Mirt became aware that someone was standing just outside the shielding. A slender, handsome figure: Elaith Craulnober. Their eyes met.

Mirt lifted his eyebrows inquiringly. Elaith made a certain swift gesture. Mirt replied with another, and the elf confirmed the silent question with a nod.

They both made the chopping motion that signified agreement, and the moneylender shuffled forward, went down on one knee beside Tarthus, and firmly cuffed the wizard's head with one hairy fist.

That head lolled, the shielding went pale—and as Madeiron looked up and glared at the elf, clapping hand to hilt, Elaith calmly worked a spell.

Golden radiance fell away into dying sparks that flared into a sudden bright roaring that stabbed into every ear and eye and swept all Faerûn away . . .

🏰 🏰 🏰 🏰 🏰

The first thing that Mirt the Moneylender heard was Piergeiron the Paladin groaning, "What *happened?*"

There was a low rumble of bafflement from Madeiron Sunderstone.

Boom.

Oh. *That* sounded all too familiar.

BOOM.

Through a glimmering of tears Faerûn returned to him, and Mirt found himself groaning, rolling over, and peering at the bare feet of Amaundra Lorgra. The boots of Tarthus were right next to them, and above, the feasting-hall of the Purple Silks was still standing.

In a manner of speaking.

Boom-BOOM.

There was no sign of Elaith Craulnober. Nor were there Walking Statues at every window—though the ground trembled under the weight of their retreating footfalls, sending bits of the walls cascading down into dust at every blow.

BOOM.

"Hoy!" Mirt cried, causing Amaundra's head to jerk up. "We're free to flee this tomb-in-the-making! Get *up*, all of ye!"

Even barefooted Watchful Order magists of some seven decades of experience can move swiftly on their corns when they need to, it seemed—and in a few frantic, hurrying breaths of dodging falling stones, the five eminent Waterdhavians were outside and staring across the night-shrouded city.

The wall-lamps glimmered as always, and by their light the great stone guardians of Waterdeep could be seen resuming their usual places.

Piergeiron's eyes narrowed. "Who commands them? And just how by the Nine Hot Hells did whoever it was manage *that* trick?"

And then his gaze fell on the scrap of parchment Mirt held out to him, and the terse message written on it—the answers to his just-spoken questions.

"Where," he asked softly, "did that come from?"

The old moneylender stared at what he was holding with a strange, perplexed expression, and then said slowly, "I've no idea. *No* idea."

A memory came into Mirt's mind then, through a golden shimmering: the wry smile of a certain elf.

Well, now, perhaps he knew the answer after all.

CHAPTER THIRTY

The strangest and most painful day of Beldar Roaringhorn's life was the day he attended his own funeral.

He wore Korvaun Helmfast's form, of course, his fallen friend's blue cape around his shoulder and a pale but composed Naoni staunchly at his side.

It was ... odd, watching others mourn him. His family's grief was deep and genuine—and puzzling. How could they mourn someone they'd never really known? All his life he'd felt apart, ignored, even scorned, yet the senior Lord Roaringhorn spoke with tearful pride of his son's accomplishments, his swordsmanship, his riding, and his eloquent knowledge of law. The Roaringhorn heir confessed to feelings of envy—even inadequacy—that his fallen junior had been most fitted to inherit, to lead.

Nearly as hard to hear were the words of his friends—apologies for doubting him, praise for saving Korvaun Helmfast by giving him a potion that transferred his wounds to Beldar himself.

For that was the comfort every mourner held dear, and only three knew to be false: Beldar Roaringhorn had died that a friend might live.

Well, Beldar *lived* that his friend might live, and he stood in silent tears, iron-determined to leave a legacy that Korvaun would be proud of.

Only the Dyre sisters knew his secret, and Faendra had already cornered him alone, and told him in no uncertain terms that he would treat Naoni well or answer to her. Beldar needed no threat but rather admired the way she'd delivered it. The Dyre girls were superb—as fine as the magic that spilled from Naoni's clever fingers.

He looked at the woman at his side, noting her grace, her quiet strength. Small wonder Korvaun had lost his heart to Naoni Dyre. Beldar was already half in love with her himself. Perhaps, in time, she might . . .

"Korvaun, they're waiting for you to speak," Taeros murmured.

Korvaun had spoken at Malark's funeral, not so many days past. Those words had honored, comforted, and inspired. Now it was his turn to do the same for his friends and family.

He strode to the coffin wherein Korvaun had been laid to rest, wearing both Beldar's form and—as a shroud—the ruby gemweave cloak. Drawing a deep breath, he began.

"We are none of us quite what we seem. Beldar Roaringhorn had dreams of greatness and perhaps the seeds of it too. He found not lasting greatness but brief glory, when he gave his life in service to others."

He stared around slowly at tearful faces.

"That greatest of deeds leaves an obligation upon all who knew him, and upon me most of all. It will henceforth define for me what it truly means to hold power, position, and wealth. Rest well, Beldar Roaringhorn, knowing that we will never forget this."

It was a short speech, but he saw in all those faces that it had been enough.

He walked back to his friends, accepting their nods and handclasps as what they were: warriors raising swords to acknowledge their leader.

What he once had been, he was again. This time, he would honor his responsibilities by becoming the man he was truly intended to be.

The summons to the Palace came the morning after Beldar's funeral. Taeros wasn't surprised; after all, he'd yet to account for the slipshield entrusted to him.

He made all haste, but when the seventh set of guards showed him into the room, Taeros found that there was only one vacant chair left—his. Korvaun nodded to him, seated with an exalted trio: Lord Piergeiron, Mirt the Moneylender, and the archmage Khelben Arunsun, who looked somewhat the worse for wear.

The Open Lord inclined his head. "Well met, Lord Hawkwinter. I trust you know us all?"

Taeros cleared his throat. "One only by repute."

Khelben fixed him with a stern eye. "Reputations you've labored to enhance, young scribbler, as a seabird enhances a statue."

Taeros felt his face grow warm as he recalled some of his more biting ballads. "If—if I've offended, I most humbly beg pardon."

Piergeiron waved a dismissive hand. "Waterdeep has need of men such as you, who make us all laugh and think at the same time. Four out of five snore during sermons, but sharp humor keeps them awake long enough to listen. 'Tis far easier to rule men who listen, think, and laugh than those who do none of those things."

A smile came unbidden to Taeros's face. It would seem he *did* have a role in the governance of this city, however small.

"Fewer than a dozen people in Waterdeep know of slipshields," the Blackstaff said abruptly. "It's been decided we'll keep the number small, rather than finding another man who can keep track of his property."

Taeros stared at what Khelben Arunsun held out to him then: A tiny shield affixed to leather thongs.

"Is that . . ."

"Against my better judgment, it is. Important in safeguarding this city and its leaders. Secrecy's vital."

Taeros closed his fingers firmly around this second chance. "I gave my vow, and I'll give it again if you require it."

"No need," said Piergeiron. "You fought loyally when the Statues walked, but understand that carrying a slipshield binds you not only to secrecy, but to service."

Taeros found this notion deeply satisfying. "That's my desire as well as my duty. It's all I've wanted in my life."

The three elders of Waterdeep nodded. Mirt then turned to Korvaun.

"And what of ye, young Lord . . . Helmfast. What'll ye make of *your* secrets? Some lordlings are all too boastful and proud, the more so when in their cups or feeling slighted."

Korvaun met the old man's sharp gaze calmly. "Some young lords are all that, and worse. As for me, know this: I am determined to live up to the *name I bear.*"

His words rang across the chamber. After a moment, he added in a softer voice, "I've learned that some secrets are worth dying to protect."

Emboldened by his friend's fervor, Taeros said, "When I said my desire was to serve Waterdeep, I omitted something important to me: it's always been my desire to advise and stand with great men."

"We would be grateful for your advice," Piergeiron said gravely, with no hint of the patronizing tone Taeros thought he'd be more than justified in using.

"He's not speaking of *us*," Mirt growled. "He's talking about *him.*"

The moneylender waved at Korvaun, a faint smile curling the corner of his untrimmed, food-hoarding mustache. "And mayhap— just mayhap—he might blasted well be right."

⚓ ⚓ ⚓ ⚓ ⚓

The faintly giggling man on the slab beside Mrelder didn't seem to know where he was or who was with him.

Setting his jaw, the sorcerer looked from his father to the beastmen standing over him, and said, "Do it."

The two Amalgamation priests started chanting.

As one of them lifted a knife, Mrelder smiled. "Just don't make me lopsided."

The shining blade swept down.

Out of purple agony he swam up into ruby-red pain. Mouthless, he shrieked . . . eyeless, he wept . . . voiceless, he prayed—and shot into the light.

Flaming torches overhead, and pain, *pain, PAIN.*

Mrelder screamed.

A face swam above his, grim and somehow familiar, blotting out torchlight. Cruel fingers forced his jaws apart, pouring gurgling iciness that soothed . . . soothed . . .

He sank thankfully away from the pain and the light, sinking into shadows warm and welcome, that—

His head was struck into fresh fire. "Stop that! Rise, Mrelder of the Amalgamation!" The priest slapped him again, and Mrelder found himself blinking up at the torches. His throat was raw, his body ached and, yes, *itched* despite all the healing potions they'd poured into him . . . and he was still screaming.

Or, no, the shrieking wasn't his. It was coming from beside him, and weakening into gurgles.

Golskyn of the Gods writhed on his slab, one eye socket empty and weeping, and a raw stump where his nearest arm ought to be.

Mrelder's father was dying, literally drowning in his own blood as he thrashed feebly.

Mrelder looked back up at priests. "How well did it go?"

"Very well. If your grafts remain alive, you've gained your father's fiery eye and his best arm."

That was saying something, considering how many powerful appendages the man who'd called himself Lord Unity had sported. Mrelder glanced down at his new limb, strong-looking and promisingly ruddy. "Well, we'll know soon enough."

"We will indeed." The beastman's voice was flat.

Their eyes met. Both knew that if Mrelder's grafts started to fail, the priests would slay him without hesitation. There was an old saying: Those who smite kings had best slay at first strike . . .

Mrelder struggled to sit up. Raw fire surged through him, and the only thing that kept him from weeping and vomiting was his body's struggle to decide which to do first—and the awe and respect on the faces of the priests.

With a smile of satisfaction, Mrelder forced himself upright. "To come to Waterdeep was no mistake," he announced to the dozen surviving Amalgamation faithful. He discovered that he was drooling blood but went on anyway. "Even so, Golskyn's deeds have made this city a trap for us now. We'll return here in time, but not before we are ready to triumph. Make ready for the journey back to the temple-cellar in Scornubel."

"And this?" One of the beastmen pointed at the mutilated and dying Golskyn.

Mrelder looked down at the weakly mewing man who'd filled his entire life with terror and pain. "He no longer matters. It's past time to leave him behind."

♦ ♦ ♦ ♦ ♦

Mrelder hugged himself against gnawing pain as the lurching wagon creaked and groaned.

He lived, and the spell he'd so carefully prepared burned in his mind like an overwhelming lust.

"Stop the wagons," he ordered, thrusting aside the wagon-flap with his new arm. "This is far enough."

He clambered out and down and walked a little way along the ridge to look back at the distant walls and towers of Waterdeep.

"The City of Splendors," Mrelder murmured, and cast his spell with slow, deliberate care.

"There will come a day when this City of Splendors is mine . . . and that day will come sooner than any think."

The monstrous priest bowed his head. "Lord," was all he said, but his voice was husky with reverence.

♦ ♦ ♦ ♦ ♦

The beast-madness is a powerful spell, and during his time in Waterdeep, Mrelder of the Amalgamation had managed to touch or wound no less than six magists of the Watchful Order.

One of them erupted from quiet spell-study when the sorcerer's words crashed into his mind. He raced out and over a handy parapet, to a wet and bone-shattering death below.

Another whimpered, stopped in mid-stride on a busy street, and then burst into roaring, capering madness. Merchants recoiled from the wild-eyed, foam-mouthed wizard, and when he clawed at a shopkeeper's face, the frightened man snatched out his belt-knife and slashed the wizard's throat.

The other four erupted into madness inside Watchful Order moots and spell-chambers, where alarmed colleagues kept maddened magists from harm. All of those four survived, lapsing into calm, forgetting-all-that-had-befallen normalcy after announcing softly: "There will come a day when this City of Splendors is mine . . . and that day will come sooner than any think."

For the next tenday or three, there was much debate in the Order over those words, and the fell magic that had brought them—but Waterdeep is a busy, bustling city, and the wonder of today is the old news of the morrow. That calm promise, like the Night the Statues Walked, seemed likely to join the fading memories only bards and sages recalled.

But then again . . .

⛫　⛫　⛫　⛫　⛫

Winter was coming. So promised the brisk morning wind tugging Taeros Hawkwinter's cloak into a writhing amber semblance of flame as he reached the newest shop on Redcloak Lane.

It was smaller than the predecessor destroyed by sahuagin, fire, and playful nobles, but it was sturdily built of dressed stone. Its newly carved overdoor sign announced that *Larksong Stories* was open for business.

Taeros stepped inside and looked around with his usual pleasure. Bright new books lined the polished shelves. Comfortable chairs and heaps of cushions welcomed those who stopped by after tools-down to hear hired taletellers spin stories of Waterdeep.

This was a home as well as a business. Through a window he

could see the neat herb-garden, and beside it a small kitchen flanking the old well house. Above the window, a staircase curved up to two rooms above; all the abode an independent tradeswoman needed.

Lark came out of the small back room to greet him. Respectability sat well on her shoulders. She was dressed as simply as the small brown bird she resembled, but there was pride in the lift of her chin, and some of the wariness had faded from her bright brown eyes.

"The 'Queen of the Forest' chapbook did as well as I thought it would," she said, without preamble. "But where, pray tell, is 'The Guild's War?'"

"And a fair morning to you, Taskmistress!" Taeros replied with a grin. "Long finished, and yestereve Roldo promised me two hundred copies would be delivered here within a tenday. Lady Thongolir's so pleased by the success of your venture that she nearly smiled." Taeros shuddered a little at the memory.

"I'm happy for Lord Thongolir," Lark said briskly. "When next you see him, tell him I'll need four hundred. Nigh every tutor in the city has been in here asking for it. A 'cautionary tale,' they're calling it. 'Tis high time people paid attention to stories of their past. Mayhap they'll be slower to start New Days if they know how the old ones ended!"

Her words echoed Taeros's private thoughts rather too closely for comfort. Instead of saying so, he asked, "There're *four hundred* tutors in Waterdeep? Ye gods, no wonder we drove the sahuagin back into the sea! I'd retreat at the sight of that many sour-faced men with foul breath and sharp-edged ferules!"

"Not just tutors have been asking; many are interested in tales of the common folk," Lark replied, adding a sly smile. "Don't take that as an excuse to ignore *Deep Waters*."

"You know about that, too? Is *nothing* sacred?"

"Business is, and judging by the success of your hero-tales, I can sell several hundred copies. Lady Thongolir is complaining about parchment costs and the wisdom of investing in a Dock Ward shop, but I'll have my own rag-paper soon. A deal with the

Dungsweepers, another with a woman from Amn who knows the craft, and I know a suitable warehouse for hire in South Ward. By mid-spring we could—"

She broke off abruptly as Taeros lifted one of her hands to his lips. She tugged it hastily free. "What was *that* about?"

"Better become accustomed to it. With your wits and drive, you'll soon be ruling us all."

Lark's scowl became a sly smile. "Just why are you so certain, Lord Hawkwinter, that I'm not?"

They laughed together, and when he kissed her hand a second time, Lark stood proudly, not pulling away in the slightest.

🏰 🏰 🏰 🏰 🏰

The fall wind was growing stronger, and Taeros put his head down and hastened. He'd promised to meet Korvaun at the Dyres' house for the highsunfeast.

It was a hectic place these days, what with Naoni preparing for her wedding and training a new housekeeper, and Faendra busily creating a wardrobe worthy of her sister's new station. It hadn't escaped his notice that she was making tiny garments, too.

So Korvaun was soon to be a father. Strange, to someone who'd known him since boyhood, but no doubt the surprising Helmfast would rise to this challenge as well as all others he embraced.

Since Beldar's death, Korvaun had devoted himself to studying Waterdeep's laws and history, and to the amazement of his family, their formerly reluctant student was now the shining pride of sages, not just tutors. Korvaun now spent most of his days attending magisterial courts or working at the Palace, learning the daily business of governance.

Well enough. Taeros hoped Lord Piergeiron would live long and rule well, but the day would come when other men and women would have to rule, masked or openly, and they'd need a counselor they could trust.

Until then, Taeros had his own work to do and—for the first time in his life—he was quite content. He could leave the governance of Waterdeep to its masked Lords. As Korvaun often said these days, some stories were great only if they remained untold.

Taeros wondered if this was Korvaun's kind caution to a tale-writing friend, his commentary on the system of secret Lords, or something deeper and more personal. Secrets rode his friend's shoulders, and sometimes Taeros sensed odd, unsaid meanings in Korvaun's simplest utterances.

Of one thing he was certain: The value of untold stories was *not* a sentiment one Taeros Hawkwinter would repeat in Lark's hearing!